Diluted Reality

Jessica Spinelli

ISBN: 1494926814
ISBN 13: 9781494926816
Library of Congress Control Number: 2014900412
CreateSpace Independent Publishing Platform
North Charleston, South Carolina

one

"WHEREFORE TAKE UNTO YOU THE WHOLE ARMOR OF GOD, THAT YE MAY BE ABLE TO WITHSTAND IN THE EVIL DAY, AND HAVING DONE ALL, TO STAND."

Ephesians 6:13

She kissed me gently on the forehead, her chapped lips scratching my soft skin, her ratty hair brushing against my face, and she then quickly turned and walked away. I was left alone, standing silently on the doorstep. As she got in the car, I noticed her wipe away the evidence of a single tear from the corner of her eye. She blew me one last kiss and then drove away, not looking back for even a moment. That was the last and only significant memory I have of my mother.

The shouting from the kitchen echoed through the hallway, vibrating throughout my entire body. My aunt and grandmother didn't stop arguing for hours. Though I was only five, I was completely aware of what was going on. The argument ricocheted back and forth. "He's not my fucking kid, not my responsibility. You're his grandmother, for fuck's sake!" I sat on the bottom of the staircase next to the living room, my tiny feet sinking into the musty, red shag carpet. I had only been in that house a few times before, and every time I passed through that old iron door I would shudder. But this time everything seemed even more terrifying.

The yellow walls were filled with framed pictures of Catholic heroes, as well as shelves holding a grandiose display of religious icons. I would've sworn that every set of eyes was staring straight at me. At the bottom of the steps, right above my head, was a tremendous, eerily lifelike painting of a tortured Jesus, his blood-framed eyes searing right through my flesh. I looked down at Blue Boy, squeezing him with all my might. He was the only toy I remember my mother ever giving me—a big stuffed blue dog with floppy ears and oversized feet. His fur was stained and torn, and only one eye remained, holding on for dear life by a flimsy string. That droopy eye seemed filled with sorrow, accentuated by a tiny tear stitched into his fur. When my mother gave him to me, she told me that whenever I felt sad, to squeeze him tight and remember that I am not the only one. That was exactly what I did those many nights when I was left alone and hungry, staring at the door, waiting for her to come home. I would still be squeezing him tightly after the sun had risen and she would finally come stumbling in, tripping over my frail body on her way to bed. But that day, as I sat on the steps of that strange, unwelcoming house, squeezing Blue Boy with all my might, his misery offered me little comfort.

"I've raised my children. I'm too old to go through this again. Besides, with that boy, there's no way I could do it now." My grandmother looked towards the ceiling, tears in her eyes. "What now, Lord?" she cried out. "What did I do now to deserve THIS?!" The porcelain St. Anthony statue on the mantle seemed to be vibrating from her screams.

"Well maybe if you raised your daughter better..." Finally I retreated to that place in my head in which the rest of the world disappeared, a wonderful benefit of childhood.

I was finally retrieved from my imaginary escape by my grandmother's shrill voice. "It looks like we're stuck with each other, kid. You can take your no-good mother's room. It's up the steps and at the end of the hall, the last door on your right." I solemnly grabbed my Charlie Brown book bag containing a few articles of clothing and a coloring book, and climbed up the creaky wooden staircase, dragging Blue Boy along by his big front paw. I froze at the top of the stairs from the complete darkness and stale smell. "The light is on the right side above the railing!" she called from down below. I clicked it on and slowly made my way down the hall.

Along the walls was a clutter of pictures, mostly of the Virgin Mary, and others of a young, ugly woman that must've been my grandmother in better days. I glanced quickly at the photos, noticing that she was not smiling in a single one. I stopped, entranced by a red glowing light leaking from beneath one of the doors. My boyhood curiosity took control of me and I went to look inside. Just as I began to turn the old brass knob, I felt a tug at my ear. "I told you, your room is at the end of the hall," my grandmother squeaked. "Don't you understand English? This room is off limits! If I catch you trying to sneak into my room, I'll chop your mischievous little hands off! Now get to your room!" I lowered my head and silently obeyed, continuing my walk down the long hallway.

My mother's old room was the cheeriest room in that dungeon of a house, with bright purple walls and a light grey carpet. The walls were bare except for a giant framed poster of a magnificent, sparkling white unicorn that hung above the headboard. I threw my stuff on the bed on top of the nearly unraveling purple, blue, and pink quilt. After taking a minute to absorb my new surroundings, I opened the wooden drawers in search of any remains of my mother. They were dusty and empty, with the exception of a few articles of clothing that once belonged to a young girl. The closet door was made of wood panels, with a few missing and many others cracked.

As I opened it, I was hit with the strong smell of moth balls. I held my nose and examined the closet. There was more clothing hanging in there, covered in dust and eaten by moths. There were a few books and shoeboxes on the top shelf, way too high for me to reach. I wanted desperately to know what was in those boxes, so I scanned the room for something for me to step on. My search was a failure, but I did notice a small silver jewelry box on the tiny, white paint-chipped nightstand. I walked over and opened it, revealing a crystal unicorn pin, its facets sparkling marvelously in the light. My mother's. I stuck the pin onto Blue Boy and gripped him tight as I crawled beneath the quilt and attempted to sleep.

My grandmother was a bitter ancient woman, imprisoned by her own radical Christian views. In the beginning, the mere sight of her made me wanna run and hide under the bed. Her skin was like scales that hung from her bones, causing her pale blue eyes to form two black holes that tried to suck me in if I stared at them for too long. Everyday she wrapped her head with a worn out black silk scarf, the only evidence of her ever-depleting, white straw hair falling out messily above her brow. I always wondered why she wore that raggedy old scarf day in and day out, figuring she was either completely bald beneath it, or hiding a deformed skull that would prove she in fact was not human. She was hunched over, and would drag her feet as she walked; a walk that I amusingly mocked as the shuffle of sorrow. Once familiar with that sound, I could hear her coming from a mile away. She had this rank aroma of decaying flesh that would linger in a room minutes after she had left, causing anyone unfamiliar with the stench to gag and tear. I could automatically tell when she didn't shower because the stench would penetrate into my pores and follow me wherever I went, never vanishing until I myself washed it away.

That old witch hated me with every decrepit bone in her body. According to her, I was the "spawn of Satan." She always believed my deviant mother was her punishment for her sins of premarital sex. My mother was a loose canon, always living moment to moment, never thinking about consequences. For a young kid, having that type of mother definitely had its moments. But they were outweighed by the numerous times having been left alone for countless hours cooped up in a dirty studio apartment. Or the other times when I was stuck playing silently alone in a corner of our apartment as my mother entertained a variety of guests high off of one thing or another.

According to my grandmother, my father was an even more despicable human being. Fortunately, I never really got to know him. He was too busy getting doped out to spend time with his son. My father and mother were together on and off for years, just like she was with her drug addiction. He finally asked her to make a choice, or so the story goes—either him and his lifestyle, or me. So she ran off to Vegas to get hitched and embark on their new drug-induced life together.

My Aunt May was older than my mother, and the complete opposite. She was very organized, never spontaneous, and carried a chip on her shoulder the size of Texas. Since they were young girls, Aunt May was hatefully envious of my mother. My mother was extremely attractive, while Aunt May was homely and overweight. My mother was always the center of attention wherever they went, while Aunt May was shy and insecure. My mother got higher grades in school, though she rarely studied, while my aunt would study all night and do mediocre. And as soon as my mother hit puberty, she would go after every boy my aunt had any interest in, even if she had no real interest in them herself. She stole boyfriend after boyfriend, leaving them high and dry once she had successfully pulled them. So it filled my aunt with great joy to watch my mother lose herself to addiction. She laughed even harder when my mother got pregnant out of wedlock at the age of seventeen.

My uncle, who moved back in with my grandmother a few weeks after I did when his wife of eleven months tossed him out, was the youngest of the three. If he bothered to take care of himself, he would've been a decent looking guy, with the exception of a disgustingly large mole on his bottom right cheek that seemed to pulsate when you looked at it. His hairline started to recede at an unusually young age and he had dark circles under his eyes, both of which gave the impression that he was about ten years older than he actually was. He too possessed a great bitterness toward my mother. She would flirt heavily with his friends, and Aunt May claimed he hated that his friends would want to come over just to see my mother. And when news spread of her promiscuous ways, the neighborhood kids would constantly tease him about his slutty older sister. As an adult, he was always in a bad mood, pissed off at the world for anything and everything. I don't know exactly what the cause was, but he must have endured something horrifying, for the rage that lived inside him was a creature all its own. Maybe just having that woman as a mother was enough.

My grandfather had committed suicide before I was born, my mother being the catalyst, or at least that is what the family concluded. His children rarely mentioned him, but everyday my grandmother would call to him, asking why he didn't take her with him. Sometimes I'd see her kneeling in the living room in front of his picture, which was placed on a wooden push cart surrounded by white candles and Mary statues. She would sob loudly, cursing him for his abandonment, burying her head in her hands and begging her god for salvation.

And then there was me, a stranger to my own family. Since my mother was gone, they needed someone to focus their hatred on. "You worthless little shit, you're gonna be a drug addict just like that wretched whore of a mother of yours. I can see it now." Those were my grandmother's daily words of encouragement. I admit I was no angel, but when someone is always going to expect the worst from you, no matter what, what's the point of trying to be good? In the beginning while in the house, I was an extremely quiet boy, speaking only when spoken to. I always felt as if I had nothing of importance to say. That formed from years of having no one to talk to. My mother had lived in a bad neighborhood and told me never to leave the house. She had no friends with children for me to play with and she was usually too busy with one thing or another to talk to me.

I tried to stay out of my grandmother's house as much as possible, roaming the streets of Raistland—a little shit town in California not too far from the San Joaquin Valley—getting into mischief with the other neighborhood kids. I hardly spoke when I was around them either, just participated in whatever childhood games they were up to. When I would return to the house I would retreat to my mother's old room, which never felt like my own. At first I didn't want to change a thing in there, because it reminded me of my mother. But that reminder never felt comforting; it only hurt. I'd lie in bed, squeezing Blue Boy, trying to figure out exactly what I had done to my mother that finally caused her to leave. I wondered if I was really that horrible, that worthless, for her to just give up on me. For her to leave me with those people. For her to never look back.

As I got a little older, my grandmother would force me to read excerpts and documents from all these Christian sources, and then quiz me on what I learned, withholding dessert, sometimes even food altogether, if I had not done my reading. So out of hunger I read what she gave me, never actually believing in it, just recording it into memory. She didn't care if I understood it; as long as I could recite it word for word, that's all that would matter. She would print and cut out these "inspirational" quotes that she found from one place or another, and slide them underneath my door every morning. Maybe she felt by that doing that, she was doing her good deed for the day and therefore could say whatever the hell she wanted to me for the rest of it. Some of them were quite dark, and I don't think she even understood most of them, probably just liked the way they sounded. Or maybe she just found them placed in some sort of religious context, which therefore made them important.

I never truly believed in any of her "teachings." Anything coming from her just seemed so false. And I had spent my earlier life listening to my mother mock religion, saying it was just a "stupid crutch." One of the few things my mother would repeatedly try and teach me was to never believe in anything I could not see, touch, taste, hear, or smell. So that slaughtered a lot of my childhood fantasies.

I spent a lot of time being locked in the cellar by my grandmother for my "evil doings." The light was broken, and purposely left that way so that I would be stuck there in complete and utter darkness. I would stand at the top of the thin cellar staircase, never daring to go down, partly due to fear that the termite-stricken stairs would collapse beneath my feet, the other part due to fear of what awaited me below. It smelt of mold and often the dead carcass of some kind of animal. If I leaned against the wall, whatever part of me that was touching it would become covered in black soot, origins unknown. It was cold and damp, and while in there I'd often find myself shivering and sweating at the same time. She would usually shout Bible verses from the other side of the door, as if she was conducting some sort of exorcism.

I could handle the imprisonments with flying colors; it was the beatings that broke me down the most. The ones that really counted were from Uncle Peter. They started off being punishment for mouthing off to my grandmother, getting in trouble in school, to eating the last of the leftovers, coughing too loudly during a football game, then, finally, for merely existing. His hands were huge, my build was so small; if I tried fight back he would just find it amusing and pound me harder. He made me refer to him as "Sir," and if I didn't, I would face a sharp smack on the back of my head. I tried to stay clear of him, often creeping along the walls, peering out from corners, trying to sneak quietly upstairs without him noticing me. I would sometimes make a game out of it in an attempt to entertain myself, playing the *Inspector Gadget* theme song over and over in my head as I stealthily made my way passed the enemy and onto "safe" grounds.

Since my first encounter with her room, my grandmother would always lock her door, even when she was at home. As a child, I believed she was hiding some magnificent secret of the universe. That eerie red light was always creeping out from beneath the door, projecting dancing shadows on the wall across the hall. I would envision some sort of creature from outer space whose radiation would emit that piercing glow. I desperately yearned to learn what lied beyond the yellow door, often lying flat on the ground trying my best to get a peek.

One night I caught my uncle using a knife to pick the lock. I wanted to jet in after him, but fear of his reaction held me back. He ran out with a suspicious look on his face, clutching something in his hand that I could not make out. It upset me that everyone else in the house knew this grand secret, except for me. So one day, when no one was home, I grabbed a knife and tried to mimic Uncle Peter's actions. Just as I figured out how to jam it open, I felt a large hand grab me by my hair. "You little fuck, you trying to steal from my mother?" His deep raspy voice pierced my eardrum. I tried desperately to shake my head no, but his grip did not allow me to do so. He banged my head against the wall and yelled, "Huh, are ya?"

"No!" I screamed with all my might.

"No what?"

"No, Sir!"

"Are you lying to me? Huh? Are ya?" He banged my head again.

"No, Sir!"

As I trembled, he hooked one of his monster paws tightly around my skinny pale throat, his unkempt nails digging into my flesh. "Then why the fuck were you breaking into her room? Huh?"

"I was curious, Sir!"

He smacked me across the face, causing stars to dance above my head. "Curious about what?"

"About what was in the room. I saw you use the knife to get in there the other day, so I decided to try it. Sir." He loosened his grip around my neck, but my body was still shaking.

"Did you tell anyone you saw me go in there?" His tone was calmer, slightly nervous.

"No, Sir."

His grip tightened again. "Let's keep it that way. I'll keep this a secret and you'll do the same. Got me?" I meant to answer yes, but he was squeezing so tightly, the words would not come out. He slapped me again, so hard that it caused my head to jerk around and smack against the wall. "Got me?!"

I forced out the words through limited breath, "Yes."

He stuck his face right up to mine, eye to eye, and whispered sternly, his hot breath burning my skin. "Yes what?"

"Yes, Sir." A single tear ran down my cheek. He wiped the tear with his thumb, and removed his great paw. He smacked me harshly on the back of my head as I scurried down the stairs holding my sore and scraped throat, heading straight for the iron door.

My aunt would join in her fair share of abuse when she came to visit. After a failed date she'd come take her anger of the male race out on me, telling me what a poor excuse of a man I was going to be. "You'll probably have five kids from five different women by the time you're twenty one. Then, while they're home starving, you'll be out blowing your money on alcohol and poker. You're all good for nothing," she'd tell me.

Often she would just vent about how much her life sucked. "You men, all you want is this, then you're gone," she'd say, grabbing her crotch. "Why can't I find a good man to take care of me?" She'd yell furiously at me, as if I had the answer and was hiding it from her. I'd usually sit quietly, picking at my nails while she'd rant and rave, hoping she would be finished soon. If she noticed I wasn't paying attention to her sob stories, she'd smack me on the side of my head or grab my ear, ordering me to listen. So I'd attentively look her in the face, clenching my fists – often so tightly that my fingers would be sore for the rest of the day—occasionally nodding in agreement as she'd tell me how worthless I was going to be.

Once, when I was eight, while alone in my room with Blue Boy daydreaming about my mother, I decided that I absolutely needed to know what was in those shoeboxes on the top shelf of the closet. I tore through the house in search of something I could step on to help me reach them. I discovered a rusty step stool in the linen closet down the hall. I had to tug hard to free it from the grips of the surrounding linens and towels. I pulled with all my might, falling backward with the stool landing on top of me, bruising my stomach. I had become so used to such bumps and bangs that I hardly felt a thing. Much of the closet's other contents had fallen out with it, but I ignored that, overwhelmed with excitement of what I was about to discover. Maybe she had some hidden treasures. Maybe she had some photographs to help remind me of how beautiful she was. Maybe there was a special message she had hidden up there for me, and that was why she had left me there. My imagination went wild with anticipation.

I climbed up the stool and was able to reach just high enough. Dust flew into my face as I pulled out the first box, causing me to cough violently, clutching the box with all my might and hugging it tighter with every cough. I finally forced it all out and slowly placed the black cardboard box on the floor. I was extremely gentle because I was unsure if it contained any breakables. The next box was big and brown, and was a great deal heavier, nearly causing me to lose my balance. I had to drop that box quickly as to prevent myself from tumbling over onto my back.

I climbed off the stool and started to search through them, starting with the black box. I took everything out and lined the contents up along the carpet. There was an old fuzzy teddy bear with a yellow bow around its neck, a pair of cheap plastic pink earrings, a beaded bracelet, and a sketchbook with a Lisa Frank drawing on the cover. I flipped through the pages and saw various penciled drawings, mostly of unicorns, some of birds, cats, dogs, and rabbits. They were well done. There was one magnificent drawing, complete with vibrant coloring, of a pink unicorn, with purple sky complete with a moon and stars. Looking at that piece of artwork, I felt warm inside from the thought that my mother had created something so beautiful.

I kept the sketchbook aside, and started searching through the other box. There were mostly books inside, some of fairytales, some of riddles and poems, and a few short stories. I picked up one with an interesting cover. As I opened the book, five Polaroid photographs fell out into my lap. I threw down the book to further examine the photos. They were of a young girl, about 14 or 15. She was wearing purple lacy underwear and matching bra in three of the pictures, while completely nude in the rest. She was very pretty, and never having seen a naked girl, I stared on in wonder and amazement. I felt a tingling sensation as I examined her every curve, running my fingers across the smooth surface. When I finally shifted focus to her smirking face, I noticed a certain familiarity about her. At the very moment I realized the lovely creature was my mother, my grandmother pushed open the door, barking, "Why in heaven's name is there such a mess in the..." She stopped suddenly and just stared at me sitting Indian style on the carpet, surrounded by my mother's old possessions. "What are you up to?"

"Nothing," I put by hands behind my back in a flagrant attempt to hide the photos.

"What are you doing going through these things? What's behind your back?"

"Nothing." My heart was racing.

She stuck out her hand. "Let me see."

I shook my head nervously. She grabbed my arm and pinched it with all her might. She didn't stop until I pulled around my arm and handed her the photos. Her eyes widened as she flipped through them. She looked at me with eyes full of fire. "You disgusting little pervert!" she howled, "Looking at dirty pictures of your mother! You filthy, no-good, delinquent, I'm ashamed to be related to you!"

"I...I...I..." I couldn't stop stuttering. She grabbed me by my ear and pulled me to my feet. I screeched in pain as she continued to drag me down the hallway.

"I'll teach you to be a pervert, you nasty little vermin." I figured she was taking me to the cellar, and desperately did not want to go. When she noticed resistance, she pulled harder, and I thought my ear was going to just rip right off. By the time we got to the bathroom, tears were inching down my cheek. "Stop crying," she yelled. She sat me on the toilet while she poured some water into her hands, then rubbed the flower scented soap, creating a thick liquid lather. The tears kept falling and my heart pounded as I looked at her in confusion. Before I had a chance to figure out her next move, she splashed the lather into my teary eyes. I squealed in pain, trying to rub my eyes, but she quickly pinned my arms back. "How does that feel, you filthy pervert?!"

"It burns!" I cried, still struggling to free my hands. It felt as if the soap was acid, eating through my eyeballs. I tried to dash toward the sink. She grabbed me by the hair and pulled me back. She always seemed to keep my hair long enough for her to get a perfect grip on.

"If you think that burns, just imagine what your soul will feel like in Hell, because that's where all perverts are sent. Do you want to go to Hell?"

"No!" I cried. She kept me like that for what felt like an eternity, the pain increasing with each passing second. Finally she allowed me to rinse out my eyes. I stuck my head under the faucet and let the cold water flush out the pain. Even after the soap was all out, the stinging remained. My sight was blurry and my body was shaking. I felt a great sense of relief, but feared that I would never be able to see correctly again.

"Now go to your room and pray for your redemption." I walked slowly to the room, head facing to the floor, running my fingers along the wall as I tried to feel my way back. I sat on the bed and rubbed my eyes, which only made it worse. I wanted to cry but was afraid it would hurt too much. I closed my eyes, but was plagued by visions of that place she called Hell. I saw fire and monsters, and people being tortured. My heart pounded. I didn't wanna go there. My mother always said that there was no Heaven and Hell, but when I brought this up to my grandmother, she claimed that she just said that because she was brainwashed by evil. Was that where I belonged? I thought about how I felt when I was looking at those photographs. I had liked what I was feeling. Maybe I was a pervert.

In sixth grade I got into a fight at school that led to my expulsion. There was one redheaded, freckled boy in the class who got his kicks at everyone else's expense. He loved to prey on me because I would quietly take the shots he threw at me, trying to convince myself that he didn't exist. One day the teacher had left our class alone for a little while to speak to another teacher. The second the coast was clear, that boy kept egging me on, saying that he had heard my mother was a drug addict and a diseased prostitute. I threw a book at him, and he told the teacher on me, saying he had done nothing to provoke me. The rest of the class played stupid, in fear that whoever ratted would become his next victim. When asked why, I would not reply, so she sat me in a desk facing the corner for the rest of the day.

The next day that same boy was passing a note around the class, and everyone who received it would bust out laughing, peeking over at me. I tried to ignore what was going on because the teacher was in the room and I did not want to get in trouble again. So I just kept doodling pictures in my notebook, which was what I usually did during class time, blocking out my surroundings. Suddenly I felt a crumpled piece of paper hit my head. I opened it up to reveal a poorly drawn picture of a hideous woman with excessive cleavage pouring out of her bra, wearing a miniskirt and boots, with an oversized needle, bigger than her, sticking into her arm. Above it in big bold letters read: "XAVIER'S MOM."

I snapped. I instinctively jumped up from my seat, disregarding the teacher's presence, and ran up behind the still chuckling boy, using all my strength to smash his head into the desk. Sobbing, he lifted his bloody freckled face only to have it met by my fist, and the teacher and my fellow classmates stared on in shock as he flew out of his chair from the impact. Just as I begin to kick him in the ribs, the teacher rushed toward me, wrapping her arms around my body in an attempt to pull me away. My legs kept going, and she screamed for help. A male teacher rushed in to find the entire class gawking with their mouths dropped, some of the girls crying, and a hysterical teacher on her knees gripping an enraged boy as my legs whaled about uncontrollably. As he got closer, he noticed a redheaded child curled up in a ball on the cold linoleum floor, covered in blood, afraid to look up. The male teacher immediately grabbed me, picking me up high in the air, squishing my bones as he carried me out of the room, my legs still going. They sat me in the principle's office, that male teacher standing behind me keeping one hand on my shoulder, as they called my grandmother. The entire faculty looked at me in horror as I sat with a smirk on my face, speckled with the boy's blood. Though I knew there was going to be hell to pay, I felt a tremendous sense of relief. That was the first time I had stood up for myself, and it felt terrific.

That soon faded when I passed through that iron door. The school had expelled me, and my family was beyond furious. They were all there when I got home, as to make sure that no one missed out on reprimanding me. My uncle held me tight as my grandmother beat me with a broomstick. She ended up breaking it over my head, but my aunt quickly filled in, grabbing a wooden spoon before I had a chance to recover. My uncle was squeezing my arms so tightly that they bruised, and he laughed as each wooden object made contact with my aching body. Nobody bothered to ask why I had beat that boy up; nobody cared. I had made them look like bad guardians.

And furthermore, they'd have to go to the trouble of lying and saying that I was living with my aunt in the next town so that I could attend school over there. They were too embarrassed to send me to another school in Raistland. That was the best news I had heard in a long time. I liked the idea of going to a place where nobody knew who I or my mother was. When I showed my enthusiasm over the idea, it just infuriated them more, and gave my uncle good reason to join in on the physical punishment with a few body slams into the walls, actually cracking one in the process. "Look what you did!" he yelled, pointing at the damaged stucco. They ordered me to my room, where I sat holding Blue Boy, rubbing the crystal pin.

I did make attempts to establish some sort of relationship with the others in that house. I'd propose that perhaps we could go out to dinner somewhere, but everyone was always too broke for that. We never ate dinner together; everyone would fend for themselves. If my grandmother did cook, I'd have to be there the moment she was done to ensure that I would get a plate. If I wasn't home, they would never save any for me. I mostly survived off of anything microwavable. I didn't mind; it usually tasted better than my grandmother's cooking.

I ate upstairs because I hated sitting in that kitchen. The walls were painted a pale orange with tacky borders containing farm scenes, with expressionless children pushing wheelbarrows while their parents stood watching with their hands on their hips. Smug bastards. Even the horses and pigs stood motionless while the kids worked their childhood away. The curtains were once white, but were stained from years of my grandfather's and uncle's smoking habits, and were never once cleaned. The gold trimming on the curtains was unraveling and loose strings had become part of the pattern. In the center of the room was an old wooden table with chipped green legs, and it seemed as if it was going to crumble at any minute. The chairs matched, and every single one of them wobbled. The placemats matched the tackiness of the wallpaper, and none of the silver or dinnerware formed a complete set. I don't think my grandmother ever changed a single thing in that house in the centuries she had been living there.

The family's idea of quality family time was sitting in front of the television. My grandmother sat on the couch staring at the large screen centered in the wooden hut, stuffing her face with sunflower seeds. Uncle Peter laid back in the old brown leather recliner, which was always covered with a stained yellow, red, and orange quilt. He'd drink his beer and eat his greasy chips, the crumbs forming patterns on his chin and lap. Neither of them ever chewed with their mouths closed, and their munching always seemed to flow in unison. I was never one for TV, except for select cartoons. I remember being afraid, feeling like the TV was sucking my mind dry so that it could replace it with whatever thoughts it wanted me to have. For my grandmother, the TV was the source of all worldly information and knowledge. She was constantly spitting out some crap she heard on TV. I'd always ask, "But how do you know the TV is telling the truth?"

"The TV doesn't lie," she'd reply, totally supporting my paranoia.

One day, when the fridge was empty and my grandmother was refusing to cook me anything because she was busy watching her "television programs," I turned to her and spat out, "You know, Grandma, I thought 'TV can be harmful by propagating degrading values and models of behavior by broadcasting porno and graphic depictions of brutal violence,' as well as 'carrying exploitative advertising that appeals to basic instincts and glorifying false visions of life that obstruct the realization of mutual respect.'"

She looked at me utterly dumbfounded. "Where in heaven's name did you hear all that crap from?" she questioned angrily.

"You. It was in a reading you gave me last week. Pope John Paul II said it."

Of course there was no praise for my studies. "Get the heck out of my face, you little smart aleck," she huffed, and marched away. I stood there confused, soaking in the notion that she was upset with me for actually paying attention.

There was one person in the family whom I had actually established a real relationship with: my Dad's sister, Dani. I saw her very rarely. She would only come to the house when no one else was home, just to check up on me. I met her three times when I still lived with my mother, and she made a reappearance into my life once she heard my father and mother had skipped town. She was the first female I was ever attracted to. She was so beautiful; long wavy red hair that shined in the sun, accepting hazel eyes, and a genuine smile. Her touch had such a warmth to it, something so unfamiliar to me. Whenever I was with her I felt like a different person; I was comfortable, and I always had something to say.

She'd take me for walks in the park, and name each species of flower and tree as we passed by. She seemed to know everything. She'd make sure I would stop to smell the ones with enticing aromas, and ask me to try to explain each distinct scent in detail. "It's important to be able to articulate yourself," she would constantly remind me. "If you can't explain what you're thinking and feeling, how is anyone else supposed to understand you?" Everything seemed so much more intense when I was with her. I'd hold her hand and be in awe of how soft her skin felt. When I was with her the sun shined brighter, the air smelled sweeter, the birds sang louder. Every bright sunny day that we were together she would look up at the sky and thank the sun for its glorious rays.

She tried to get together with me on nights there was a full moon, bringing a blanket for us to sit on and gaze at the stars. "You are at your most powerful when the moon is full," she'd tell me. She studied astrology and knew every single constellation, and always bestowed her knowledge upon me. I asked her questions about that place my grandmother called hell, and whether or not she believed that I was going to be sent there. She would reassure me that such a place did not exist and was only used to instill fear in me. “So where do bad people go?” I asked.

“To a place where there is no love and no sense of completeness. Sometimes they get another chance to redeem themselves.” I did not really understand what she meant by that, but accepted it anyway. If she said it, I believed it.

She would take me to movies, letting me pick which movie to see. If she felt it was inappropriate for me, she would find a way to make another movie playing sound so much more interesting. I loved watching comedies with her; she had the craziest, most contagious laugh. After the movie, we’d go out to eat, and discuss the film. Never fast food, though. She taught me to appreciate foods from different cultures, Indian being both our favorites. The first time she took me to an Indian restaurant I cringed from the overwhelming smell of curry that flooded my nostrils. When I tugged on her sleeve, asking to leave, she replied, “It’s important to have an open mind and be willing to try new things, even if they seem odd at first. If you try it and don’t like it, that’s fine.” I took one bite and was hooked. Wherever we were, whatever we were doing, Dani was always trying to show me the beauty in the world, reminding me that the terrible place I lived in wasn’t all there was.

I was only slightly nervous my first day at the new school. The incident at my other school had occurred a week before summer break, so I was not held back. I had spent a lot of time with Dani that summer, and she made me feel that I had nothing to worry about. She reassured me that the change would be a positive one, as long as I stayed focused. I had always received average grades in school, never really caring much, just simply going through the motions and doing as little as possible needed to get by. But we had gotten close over that summer and I wanted so desperately to make her proud, so I promised myself I would study as hard as I could.

The school was a lot bigger than the previous one I attended. I kept my eyes focused straight as I walked through the halls, hearing some of the kids whispering, "That's the new kid." I could feel their eyes examining me from top to bottom, but I just kept looking straight, trying to find my way. In the first period, as the teacher introduced and welcomed me, I just stared quietly at my fingers, which were gripping tightly to my pen. I cringed when she said my last name, but quickly reminded myself that I was an unknown there. For the most part, the other kids were friendly to me, especially the girls. They cheerfully introduced themselves, then started asking which school I transferred from and why. I gave them limited responses, which did nothing to quench their curiosity. The more they pushed, the more I withdrew, until they eventually gave up.

As time passed, I came to the conclusion that the teachers neither liked nor disliked me, and I was fine with that. As long as I did my work, they were happy. There were a few kids I would chit chat with, but I mostly kept to myself. At recess I would usually be off on my own, doodling in my notebooks, totally oblivious to the world around me. A lot of the girls would try to hang on me in an attempt to get me to play with them. But their games always seemed stupid and boring. When I'd shrug them off, they would stomp off pouting, telling the others about what a jerk I was. The guys would ask me to participate in their basketball, baseball or touch football games, but I never cared much for sports. I was never any good at them, and I found that frustrating. But I could run fast. Really fast. So sometimes I'd challenge the other boys to races, the loser having to buy the winner ice cream. I ate a lot of ice cream.

My grandmother finally found out about me and Dani's little excursions, after Uncle Peter had been driving and pulled up next to us at a red light. She called Dani up screaming like a maniac, forbidding her to see me. She claimed that Dani was into witchcraft and "all that mother nature shit" she was teaching me was an attempt to brainwash me into joining her cult. Uncle Peter laughed as he listened to my grandmother go on and on. “She is one fine piece of ass, though,” he added. It disgusted me to hear him say such things about her, so I picked up a plastic cup and flung it at him. It knocked him in the chin and the soda splashed all over him and my grandmother. They were both in shock. Uncle Peter got up and closed-fisted me in the chest. It knocked the wind right out of me and I fell backward into the kitchen table. “Put him in the cellar!” she cried as he dragged me by my hair.

“Don’t...(gasp)...ever...talk...” I tried desperately to get the words out.

He tugged harder on my hair. “I dunno where these set of balls came from, you little fuck, but send ‘em back where you found ‘em.” He tossed me through the cellar door by my hair, locking it behind me.

But Dani didn’t give up on me; she just went out of her way to keep our meetings undetectable. Sometimes she’d drop a letter off for me at school, telling me she was going to pick me up. I’d call home and tell the old hag I was going over a friend’s house. My grandmother always welcomed such news because she hated that I could no longer take the bus home and she had to leave her precious sanctuary to come pick me up (she hated driving and was terrible at it; every ride home was a terrifying rollercoaster.) Me and Dani would usually plan our next excursion before we parted, assigning a certain time and place to meet.

She would tell me all sorts of good things about my father, about the man he was before he got hooked. I don’t know if the stories were true, or just something she said to make me feel better about who I was. But she must have loved him very much to want to be a part of my life. I’m sure it was also partly because she couldn’t have children of her own. And just the fact that she loved him made me believe that he couldn’t have been as bad as he had been depicted to be. I wanted to believe her so badly, that I even pushed aside what little memories I had of him myself, high as a kite, sloppy and vulgar, always cursing out my mother. He never talked directly to me, but rather referred to me as he was yelling at her, often forgetting my name in the process. I tried to convince myself that such memories were false, that no one like that could’ve been related to Dani. Her love was the only real love I knew as a child, and it was of the purest, most beautiful form.

I asked her once if I could live with her, if she could "save me." Tears filled her eyes as she said she would've loved to take me away from everything, but could barely afford to take care of herself, never mind a child. But sometimes I would daydream of what life would be like with her, a place where hate was a forbidden word and pain a forgotten memory. But then another screeching growl would come from down the hall and break my illusion.

The school sent home a progress report, and my grandmother never even bothered to open it. It was lying on the kitchen counter by the phone, with the rest of the other junk mail. I opened it to find that my grades had improved immensely. I was so excited, I needed to tell Dani. I rummaged through the house to find change, and walked to the nearest payphone. I couldn't call from the house because my grandmother would always check the phone bill, monitoring every call made. Dani was so proud of me, and made me feel so proud about myself.

Next time we saw each other she had a gift for me. It was wrapped in paper from the pages of the Sunday comics with a thick green bow wrapped around it. It looked so cool, I didn't wanna even tear at it. But she insisted, so I complied, revealing a beautiful sterling silver, oval picture frame with unique designs etched in all around it. In the center was a photograph of us that we had someone take in the park. The sunlight reflected off the silver, nearly blinding me as I squinted to further examine the photo. She looked so beautiful, hair blowing in the wind, dressed all in white with a smile from ear to ear. And I looked so happy, as if I was holding back laughter. I smiled as she remarked, "You're very photogenic, you know. When you get a little older I think I'll take you to get some headshots."

"Isn't that what people do when they are trying to become a model or actor, or something?"

"Yup."

"Oh, I couldn't do that."

"Honey, with a face like that, all the modeling agencies would be banging down your door."

"You really think so?"

"Definitely. With those beautiful green eyes! That perfect smile! You're going to be quite the ladies' man when you get older." My skin got redder by the millisecond. But it felt good to be complimented.

When I got home I ran straight to my room. I stared happily at the picture, running my fingers along the shiny edges of the frame. I kissed the protective glass, and placed it under my pillow upside down so as not to crack it. I lied in my bed for a little while, just relishing in the thought that I now had her with me at all times.

I'll never forget the day I heard the news. I was almost thirteen. My grandmother screamed for me to come to the kitchen. I figured she had noticed the twenty dollars missing from her wallet, and started planning my escape. But instead, without any type of warning, "Your Aunt Dani died in a car crash two nights ago. The wake is tomorrow. If you want, you can go, but I'm not taking you." And with that she walked out of the kitchen. I just stood there, motionless, for I don't even know how long. I had become so numb to physical pain and verbal abuse that it had become impossible for me to cry anymore. But that pain was unbearable and the tears were unleashed. I did not attend the wake; I did not want to see her lifeless body. My grandmother had surprisingly allowed me to miss a couple of days of school to mourn. I stayed home locked in my room, head buried in my pillow. I slept holding the picture she had given me.

I felt as if my stomach had been ripped out of me, leaving me with a big gaping hole. Three days passed and I figured enough was enough. I put the picture at the bottom of the closet and told myself that's where it would stay. No matter how fucked up things had seemed, I was always able to get by because of the gift Dani had given me – hope. Hope that there was more out there, hope that I had the ability to give and receive love, hope that I was really worth something. But right then and there, all hope I had was destroyed, and that little bit of light inside of me died. From that point on, things would never be the same.

Living in a house saturated with anger, I somehow had managed to stay mostly free of it. But not anymore. I became just like them, bitter and pissed off. Getting through a day there became even harder. If my uncle hit me, I'd hit back full force, then, of course, get pummeled to the ground. One time I had to briefly use crutches from injuries obtained from him throwing me down the stairs for using his towel. It was just a sprain, so he made sure I was aware of how lucky I was. I would lock myself in my room with nothing but a pen and some paper. Retreating to that place inside my mind was no longer safe, for that place too had become a dark dungeon. So drawing became my means of escape. I never really mapped out what it was I was going to draw, but rather just put the pen to the paper and allowed the ink to take its course. The results were usually pictures that would normally only be seen in horror movies or nightmares. I had covered the hideous purple walls from top to bottom with posters of my favorite bands, movies, and artists. I filled the smaller spaces with cutouts from magazines. I'd often buy comic books just for the artwork, cut out anything I found interesting, and stick it on the wall. There was of course your occasional hottie. And anything I drew that I was particularly proud of went up there as well. It all came together and seemed to form a wallpaper. Just staring at the various eye candy would keep me busy.

One day while I was hanging out at a diner with some kids from school, I saw a redheaded boy walk in with two other boys, both older than he was, one being extremely tall and thick in build. Me and the redhead caught eye contact, and I realized that he was the boy I had beat up in my other school. His face filled with fright as he turned to the other boys and began to whisper, and then they all turned and looked in my direction. The kids I was with took no notice and kept blabbing on about some new comic book.

I kept my eyes fixed on the new patrons, blocking out surrounding conversations. I was unsure if a retaliation was about to take place, so I kept my guard up. I hadn't had a fist fight with anyone but my uncle since that incident, but remembered how good it felt to finally release like that. About a half hour passed and my group was ready to leave. As we walked through the door, I stared at their table. It was like something inside me was begging for something to happen. For some kind of excitement. Suddenly the big guy came outside and called my name. He was not the one I was hoping for, but I was ready nonetheless. "You beat up my cousin," he stated, looking me straight in the eye.

"He deserved it."

"Why, cause he called your mother a whore?" I clenched my fists and he detected the anger in my eyes. I said nothing, just kept his gaze. "You know, she *was* a whore. She slept with my friend's father, caused his parents to get a divorce. I heard she had a thing for married men. She was a damn home wrecker."

"You're lying!" I wanted so badly to hit him but something held me back. Maybe it was his size, maybe I wanted to hear what he had to say.

"Believe what you want. She slept with half the town. You could be anybody in this town's illegitimate child and you wouldn't even know it." By this time his cousin and their friend had come outside and were standing beside him. The people I was with had started to walk away, but quickly returned when they took notice to what was going down. The big boy laughed, amused by his wit. "Would you care if she was a whore? She didn't give a fuck about you, now did she?" His entourage joined in his cackling. Their laughter echoed through my head, eventually finding that precise button to push.

I lunged at the mouthy one, hitting him dead in the stomach, and as he hunched over, I hit him with a swift right uppercut to the jaw. He stumbled back and as I went to hit him with a left, I felt a sharp conk to the side of my temple. Everything turned black for a second when suddenly a fist made contact with my cheek. His friend had jumped to his defense as his redheaded cousin simply stood back on the side.

I elbowed the other kid in the chest and we exchanged a couple of shots to the face. I was running on pure adrenaline, each hit I endured seemed to make me stronger. The big one had recovered and now tried to tackle me, but I quickly kicked him in the groin and he fell to the ground. His friend wrapped his arms around me, squeezing me as hard as he could as I squirmed to break free. I head butted him with the back of my head, and blood squirted everywhere. I made eye contact with the redheaded instigator, and he shuttered with fear as I flashed a devilish smile through my bloodied lip.

The diner's manager came out screaming, threatening to call the cops. Everyone made a dash for it, except for the kid with the bloody nose, who was leaning on the redhead, trying to hobble away. I heard the big kid's voice, and turned to see that he was running full speed after me, grunting, fury in his eyes. But there was no way he'd catch me. I was too fast. When I got home, my grandmother took one look at my bruised face and rolled her eyes, calling to her god. "Did that happen at school?"

"No," I said, panting.

Not wanting to deal with me, "Go to your room. No supper for you tonight, you trouble-maker."

"I ate already," I said snidely. She flashed me disapproving eyes, contemplating where I had gotten the money to pay for a meal since she had withheld my allowance that week for some reason or another. I walked toward the kitchen but she stood in front of me blocking the entrance. "Can I at least get some ice for the swelling?"

"No. You want to be a tough guy, pay the consequences." I rolled my eyes, clicked my tongue, and ran upstairs. Before I reached the top, I turned to my grandmother and asked, "Was my mother a home wrecker?"

She laughed loudly. "Yes, she most certainly was. And she managed to wreck this home twice, by leaving you here." I walked slowly the rest of the way to the room. I took Blue Boy out from under the bed. I rubbed the unicorn pin as I said out loud, as if my mother could hear me, "Why do I always defend you? Did you ever defend me?" I could feel my pounding heart in the bruise of my lip. "Now I'm left paying for your mistakes." At first a deep sadness came over me, but, as the throbbing from my injuries increased, it turned into anger. "Fuck you!" I yelled aloud, "You *were* just a drug addicted whore! So what the fuck does that make me?" I ripped the crystal pin off the stuffed dog, threw it on the floor and stomped on it, crushing it into tiny pieces. I pulled out all her clothes, her sketchbook which I had put in my nightstand, and threw them all in a box, tossing Blue Boy in as well. When everyone was fast asleep, I snuck into the garage and threw them into an empty garbage bin, struck a match, and watched the memories burn.

The fights with my grandmother had begun to escalate to a whole new level. In the past when she'd throw one of her pointless fits, I would just mumble something under my breath, roll my eyes, or flat-out ignore her. But things changed, and I was just so tired of it all. I had started to curse harshly at her, even spat in her face. Then one time when she attempted that cellar shit, I overpowered her, pushed her past the door, slammed it shut and quickly pushed the deadbolt. I left her locked in there for a few hours, listening gleefully as she sobbed and prayed to her beloved god. I found her pointless pleas extremely entertaining. I finally freed her just in time before I knew my uncle would be home. Her face was pale and host to the remains of dried tears. She would not look me in the face, and just walked solemnly to her room, head hanging low. She told no one. Needless to say, she never tried that again.

When I got to high school, I had reached a point in which I was totally fed up with school, cutting every opportunity I could. All the rules started to annoy me, and I didn't feel like concentrating on the work. I would spend my time drawing or sleeping, so it was really pointless to be there. There was no one to be proud of me if I did well anyway. The high school was back in Raistland, where people knew who my mother was and about my situation. But I didn't care what they said about her anymore. I would usually agree, even sometimes be the one to initially bring up her lovely attributes. People found it hysterical when I'd say such things as, "that crackwhore mother of mine..." but I was never laughing. I spent countless hours with other neighborhood kids from broken homes, doing whatever would give us any sort of entertainment. That usually involved vandalism, breaking and entering, drinking, smoking pot. We even got so pathetic as to throw rocks at passing cars. It would give us a good laugh to watch them frantically swerve all over the road. One day my uncle exited a bar to find his precious white firebird covered in spray paint. In his drunken stupor, he punched the car window, shattering glass everywhere and slashing up his hand and arm. When I saw his injury I figured precisely what had happened. He had no proof that I had anything to do with it. Well, except for my uncontrollable laughter.

One afternoon after a horrendous argument with my grandmother over money that I did not steal, she denied me dinner, and told me I would receive no allowance for two weeks. As I walked quietly to my room, she once again reminded me of how no good I was. I sat in my room trying to calm myself, just staring at my walls. But they could not keep my mind busy. My thoughts were running dark and they were torturing me. Thoughts that I would never be free from that wretched place. Thoughts that Dani was wrong about everything; that I really was worthless; that hell really did exist, and I was already in it. I grabbed my head and applied pressure to the temples trying to make all the pain cease. I cried aloud, begging it to stop. But it wouldn't. Something kept telling me to end it all, to just slice my wrists and let the humanity flow out of my veins like crimson freedom.

I went into the drawer and pulled out the silver butterfly knife that I had stolen from an asshole kid who lived down the block. I flipped it open, weaving it in and out of my fingers, successfully executing the tricks I had been taught. I looked at the curvy blade. It was shaped like a curved zigzag. I put it up to my wrists. Just one quick slice to each wrist and it would all be over. I would be free. And I could handle the pain. But as much as I didn't want to be there, my grandmother had instilled a fear of damnation. What if I'd end up in a place worse than where I was? I hardly believed that was likely, but the fear was real nonetheless. But I needed to stop the pain. I put a palm to my forehead and yelled out in frustration, "Why? Why did you leave me here, you stupid bitch!?"

I suddenly, without even a thought to it, ran the sharp blade quickly and deeply across my arm three times in a row, and then dropped the blade. I did not seem to feel a thing as I stared at the blood emerge from my flesh. All my focus was on the red stream trickling down to my elbow, and the pain slowly crept up with a sudden sting. After just watching it trickle in transfixed amazement, I finally got up, grabbed a tee-shirt and applied pressure to stop the bleeding. The stinging had grown more powerful, but I did not mind. The pain in my head had ceased. I had found a new form of release.

My family knew I wasn't going to school, but didn't really give a shit as long as I wasn't getting in their way. As long as I didn't wake anyone up when I came home, they didn't care what time I came home on school nights, nor where I was or what I was doing. Eventually the school sent child services to the house when I had missed an obscene amount of consecutive days. My grandmother denied all knowledge of me not attending school, though I was aware she knew. She had just become too scared to say anything to me. They quizzed her and my uncle, who put on their best face, saying they did all they could to control me but I was just too wild. After their Oscar winning performance, the middle-aged, sun-bleached, chain smoking woman from child services interviewed me. Based on my callous attitude and the self-induced slash marks covering my arms, she thought it was in my best interest that I be sent off to the crazy bin.

two

"..NOT ALL THE CONSCIOUSLY IMMORAL ACTS OF A PARTIALLY INSANE PERSON ARE UNFREE...THESE ACTS CANNOT BE PRESUMED TO BE FREE ON THE SIMPLE GROUND THAT THE PATIENT IS AWARE OF THEIR IMMORALITY."

Christian Encyclopedia

I can't say that I minded being put there. I saw it as a sort of vacation. Three good meals a day, no bitching relatives, and free drugs. It was the discussion bits that I wasn't too keen on. Sharing my life with strangers was not something in my character. And all of those "why" questions. I never discussed my emotions with anyone, let alone some old fuck thinking he's god because he had a degree. Besides, I didn't even know the "why's" myself. At times I didn't really even know if I had emotions. So mostly during group discussions, I'd sit silently or doze off. With the one-on-one sessions, I'd stare blankly at the doctor, with his white toupee and glasses that seemed entirely too small for his face, and not say a word, no matter how hard he'd try to get me to speak. After a week of that, they became immensely frustrated, and moved me. That's when the reality of the situation hit.

I had originally been placed in the psychiatric ward of a local hospital. But after my silent treatment, they thought it would be best to put me in an institution, one which resembled a prison system. All the walls were white and the flooring was pale blue. The entire place smelled like a mix of bleach and vomit. The orderlies were assholes and treated the patients as if they were freaks of nature, which I can't deny that some of them were. And if you would voice your opinion too loudly, the staff didn't hesitate to use forceful repercussions. I myself had never fallen victim to their abuse, but I witnessed several occasions where they forcefully and physically reprimanded helpless crazies just trying to make sense of their situation.

Every night they fed me a pill of some sort, while some of the others were pumped chock full of various prescription drugs all throughout the day. I had no clue what it was, nor did I care. It made me feel mellow and made the nights more bearable.

There was one patient, an older Hispanic woman, who would constantly pace from one end of the floor to the other, scratching her head and mumbling to herself, never changing out of her hospital gown. This one guy, who strongly resembled Sammy Davis Jr., would sit in the corner and laugh out loud as he tapped his foot. There was a large array of other circus acts as well.

It was often difficult to sleep at night through all the screaming that echoed throughout the halls, even with the pills. One patient would start up, which would incite another, then another, creating a complete chain reaction of loonies bellowing out to uncaring ears. I would shove the pillow over my head, but I could still hear my roommate, an abnormally short, mousy haired middle aged man, sobbing to himself in his bed. There were a couple of other kids there around my age, mostly schizos and manic depressives, many with failed suicide attempts under their belt. It was a common occurrence to catch people arguing with themselves, carrying on a full-out heated debate with no opponent. There were people there who accepted their diagnoses, while others were in full denial that they were missing any screws. And maybe they weren't.

I still wasn't cooperating much in therapy. Whenever it was my turn to talk, I'd sit silently or make remarks about how ridiculous their methods were. The more I would make such comments, I would notice small changes in attitudes towards me. It was as if the doctors told the orderlies to be even ruder toward me, and do little things like be stingy with my food. When I mentioned this to the doctors, they would say that such thoughts were just examples of paranoid delusions. Fucking shrinks.

Amidst all those mentally "handicapped" individuals, I would find the one who would become my first and truest friend. I did have "friends" on the outside, but no substantial relationships, just people who accompanied me in deviant activities. If anyone of them had died, I wouldn't have shed a tear.

I was in my room scribbling on paper, as usual, when I heard this ear-piercing laughter coming from down the hall. I peeked out to discover a character unlike any other I had ever seen at the institution thus far. He was a little older than me, and seemed to be acquainted with some of the orderlies and other patients. He had a pink and blue mohawk, accentuating the large size of his head, which balanced on top of a tall lanky body covered in random tattoos. He had a crooked smile with crooked teeth which went with his crooked nose. He laughed hysterically as he was led to his room.

A few days passed. I analyzed the new kid from afar, but never exchanged words with him. He was loud and obnoxiously funny, constantly fucking with everyone around him, but never me. The others would roll their eyes at his behavior, but I found him rather amusing. Maybe that was why he never messed with me; I became his audience. One afternoon I was sitting by the window in the hall with my sketchbook, drawing some personally created fantasy creature. "Kick ass drawing," a voice startled me from behind. I turned to find that kid leaning over and staring at my creation.

"Thanks."

"You mind if I look at the rest of your shit?" I had never shown anyone my book before. It was filled with sketches and inscribed with random quotes, thoughts, and personal poetry. Basically my soul on paper. But for some reason I nodded, and handed him the book. "Thanks," he replied and disappeared into his room. I didn't expect him to run off with the damn thing, but I didn't try to stop him. Much time passed and there was no sign of him. Normally I didn't give a fuck what people thought about me. But this was different. Someone thinking I was an asshole or a weirdo, whatever, that I could handle. But this was my art and writing. Even though I didn't write or draw for anyone else, if someone thought it sucked....

He finally came out at dinner and sat next to me. "Yo, killer, the shit in that book is fucking amazing, man. You're one talented nut job."

"Thanks," I laughed.

He introduced himself. "I'm Avry."

"Xavier."

"What you in for?"

"I'm not even sure what they diagnosed me as. Bipolar something or other. Which actually makes no sense, considering bipolars have highs and lows, while I just linger somewhere in the middle. Also some crap about self destructive tendencies, blah, blah. These quacks don't know what they're doing. How about you?"

"I guess you could say for violent tendencies, rage, some shit. This is my fourth time here. Sometimes I just snap and," he laughed, "cause a little bit of chaos and destruction. I go through these episodes where I black out, and when I come to, someone is hurt or something is destroyed. Been going on since I was twelve. I'm sixteen now. I really thought I had it under control this time. It's alcohol, man. When I drink, self control just drifts away. How old are you?"

"I'll be fifteen next month."

"Shit, X, probably gonna spend your b-day here. That sucks."

"Hopefully not, but if I do, hey, at least I get free drugs."

"Yes, very true," he laughed. "See, what they don't realize is that keeping me in here is keeping me away from weed, which is one of the few things, if not the only thing, that keeps me calm. Don't really fuck with anything else. Get bad reactions. I dropped a hit of acid once, the whole world changed before my eyes. I swore it was Armageddon. I ended up attacking this kid and nearly killed him. Thought he was a demon trying to drag me to hell. Broke a few car and store windows. That was actually an event that led to my second time here."

I had never tried acid. I wasn't sure if I would be able to handle it myself. It was said to bring out things buried inside a person, and there were things inside of me that I just didn't wanna see. Also, I had always heard that it was important to do it around people you trusted, and I trusted no one.

"You know, I read a lot of books on psychology," Avry continued. "Been in here enough, wanted to see if there's anything to this shit. My synopsis: it's all bullshit. Doctors create these fictitious illnesses to compensate for human weaknesses. Everybody's got problems. In the words of the Cheshire Cat, "we're all mad here."

Days passed. Me and Avry were together twenty-four seven. I never knew anyone who I could speak to so freely. It was inspiring. I would say any thought that floated through my mind, and it seemed as if it resembled a thought that at one time or another floated through his. Nothing was too strange or out there. Plus, he was like constant entertainment. He found humor in anything. Before I had met him, I had never had one of those episodes where you laugh so hard you can't breathe. When hanging with him, that was a constant occurrence. The orderlies really thought we were totally out of our minds because we were always laughing, even at what seemed to be a moment of the utmost seriousness. So they would constantly scream at us to shut up. God forbid anyone was having fun.

"So, X, you got a girlie waiting for you on the outside?"

"Nope."

"Really, a good looking kid like yourself?"

"Never had a girlfriend, actually."

"Never?" he said in shock. I shook my head. "So you've never gotten laid before?"

"Nope. A couple of blow jobs, though. Girls don't wanna come off like sluts for fucking so young, but they won't hesitate to suck someone off."

"You just said you never had a girlfriend, though."

"I never did. Just because a girl gives me head, doesn't make her my girlfriend." I had messed with a couple of girls from my school at parties. Crept into the bathroom. They seemed to want to, and it just seemed like something to do. I didn't really care about girls at that point of my life. I was attracted to them, got horny, but never cared enough to try to form any kind of relationship with one. There were a lot of girls I met that seemed to want to get to know me, but the feeling wasn't mutual. Most of them weren't into the shit I was into. They always worried about getting in trouble. If a girl would be hanging out with me and some guys while we were doing our normal activities, they'd always be preaching and bitching, and would just get on my nerves. But all in all, I had never found anyone, girl or guy, interesting enough to form a solid relationship with. "You got a girl?" I asked.

"Me? Nah, girls don't like me."

"So you've never gotten laid either?"

"Slow down, killer, I didn't say that. I've fucked a couple of girls, but no prizes. Hormones take over and you take what you can get. Unlike you, pretty boy, I haven't been blessed in the physical aspect of things. And I'm very blunt, which tends to scare girls away. I'd really like to have a girlfriend, though. I wouldn't even care if she was pretty or not, as long as she was cool. Looks would definitely be a bonus, though. I'd love to be with a real pretty girl, but they seem to be nothing but trouble. This one girl, Maggie, god, I was obsessed with her. She was beautiful and popular; never gave me the time of day. When she finally did talk to me, her words were 'Leave me alone, you shithead!' Broke my heart. So one day I filled up a bag with shit, hid in a bush by her house, and chucked it at her head, shouting, 'Who's the shithead now!?!' Made me feel a lot better, until her pops came to my house and told my mom. Not like he could've made the circumstances there worse, anyway." I wanted to inquire about that last remark, but I figured then I would probably be asked about my own family, and that was a place I didn't want to dip into just yet.

Another day. It was dark and rainy outside. I sat by the window drawing in a new book, since I had completely filled up the other one. Avry paced around me, seeming especially high strung that day. He stopped, turned to me and said, "You know what I could go for now, more than anything?" Before awaiting a response, "My bass."

"Yeah? How long have you been playing for?"

"Two years. I love it, it soothes me. You play any instruments?"

"Years ago my grandmother got me a guitar for my birthday. I fucked around with it for a bit, but nothing too serious. I was getting the hang of it. But then I got caught vandalizing this fat fuck's car. Bastard kept fucking with this dude's little sister. He was real overprotective, so we got the dude's brand new Audi real good. Spray-painted the word "pedophile" across it in big green letters. Couldn't prove I had anything to do with it, but everyone knew anyways. So my grandmother took the guitar back. Pretty sure she sold it." Go figure, the only thing she ever really gave me, she took away.

"When you get out of here you should save up and buy yourself another one. It's a worthwhile investment. Being able to play and create music, that's the ultimate high right there. You're obviously creative, you'd probably be an awesome musician." It was quite a change hearing positive remarks being made about me. I hadn't heard anything like that since before Dani died. It felt good, having someone actually have some sort of faith in me. I thought of her and smiled.

"Yeah. Yeah, I think I'll do that."

Under Avry's advice, I started to open up more in therapy. Nothing too deep, but at least I was speaking. Avry told me that if I ever wanted to get out of there, I just had to feed them what they wanted to hear. Tell about my family travesties and inner wounds. But that wasn't me. I basically would just talk bullshit during my sessions. They were happy to hear me say anything at all. But honestly, I wasn't in the greatest rush to leave.

"So why do you cut yourself?" Avry questioned, staring at the scars on my arms. To anyone else the answer would be "because I feel like it" but he deserved a better explanation.

"It's just something I started doing. I know this may sound stupid, but it started off as a way to keep myself sane. But then the reasons changed. I'd be just sitting in my room, feeling empty, numb. I'd cut myself and I'd feel something. And honestly, most of them didn't even hurt. I'd end up having to go deeper, finally getting an adrenaline rush. But those get so messy, blood everywhere, obvious scars."

"Piercing."

"Huh?"

"You should pierce yourself instead. That's what I do. This place makes me take 'em out. For me, sometimes I get so angry, I need to inflict pain, if it's not on myself then it's gonna be on someone else. So I take a needle and shove it through somewhere. I've pierced my ears, eyebrows, labret, nose, nipple, even pierced my own dick, three times actually."

"Shit, I don't think I'd be down for that."

"Trust me, piercing is a rush. And they look good, and you don't have to worry about people seeing your scars and sticking you in here. I'm telling you, next time you get that urge, try it."

"How about those, what do they feel like to get done?" I was pointing to one of his tattoos. He had several visible ones: "FUCK" written across one of his hands, "YOU" written on the other, a fat frog one arm, a howling wolf on the other, a spider web on one of his elbows, and a shish kebab of eyeballs and severed fingers on his calf.

"They're nothing, kind of a soothing, burning sensation. I almost fell asleep with this one," revealing a cartoon devil face on his chest.

"Dontcha gotta be 18?"

"Not if you know the right people. Most of these were done at people's houses, for free actually. They wanted the practice, I wanted the ink. This one I did myself." He showed me a small one on his hip. "It's the symbol for Scorpio. Did it with a needle and some ink." Though it was sloppy, it was my favorite one, since he had put it there himself. At that moment the idea of getting a tattoo gun and drawing all over myself seemed brilliant.

Avry came charging out of one-on-one therapy into the TV room, all in a huff, yanking on his multicolored locks, mumbling, "Stupid bastards." I found his display amusing.

"What happened?" I cackled.

"These idiotic doctors, they think they know everything. They don't know their ass from their elbows."

"I could've told you that ages ago. What brought you to this brilliant conclusion?"

"They keep trying to convince me that I'm crazy. I'm not crazy!"

"I beg to differ," I remarked.

He playfully hit me in the arm. "For real, dick. I know I'm not crazy. I mean, I act up now and again, but that doesn't make me a psycho. They said that overall, my behavior is abnormal. That my perception of reality is distorted. What the fuck?"

"That means that your behavior deviates from the normal standards of society."

"I know what it means, dick. You know what I have to say to that: fuck society."

"Don't pay them any mind. They said similar shit to me. I think we all create our own perception of reality anyway. I mean, if I see something as real, who's to say it's not? What makes their perception correct and ours all wrong, or 'abnormal?'"

He pondered over my remark. "So you're saying, you think that there is nothing that is actually real? This chair, that TV, they aren't real?" My words confused him, and in return he confused me.

"Maybe nothing here is real, maybe none of us actually exist," interjected a thirty-something-year-old Asian woman, who was sitting in front of us, hunched over, hugging her knees. "You ever think about that? Or what if we are all just characters in somebody else's dream?" Me and Avry looked at each other, raising our brows.

An elderly man sitting next to the woman added his two cents. "Y'all know what they used to do in the olden days to people they thought was crazy?" We shook our heads. He continued on in his squeaky voice, complete with southern accent and an intense lisp. "Well, they thought people who acted crazy-like was possessed by evil spirits. Sometimes they'd drill a hole in someone's skull to release them spirits. Don't think most of them survived, though." We looked at each other and simultaneously grabbed our heads.

Another visiting day came. Of course I had no visitors. No one had come to see me since I had been in there. I didn't expect them to come, nor did I want them to. The old lady called a few times, trying to pretend she cared. Our conversations barely lasted a minute. That day Avry had a visitor though, and when I tried to talk to him afterward, he blew me off and retreated to his room, not even emerging for dinner. I let him be for the night, figuring his visit didn't go so well. When he didn't come out for breakfast the next day, I took it upon myself to see what was going on. I went to his room to find him just lying in his bed staring at the ceiling. I walked over and perched on the windowsill. "You all right?" I asked, knowing very well that he wasn't. He still just lay there frozen, eyes fixated on the ceiling. "Must be something interesting going down on that ceiling." Still no response. I waited a few more seconds and started to walk out.

"I just don't understand," he said. I turned around.

"What's that?"

His eyes remained straight upward. "I've done so much for that woman. I know I get into a lot of trouble, but I've always done everything I could for her."

I walked back to the windowsill. "Who?"

"My mother." His voice sounded so different, so weak, so full of pain. He started to talk, tell me about his life on the outside.

"When my father did that to me, I came to her crying, again and again. She wouldn't believe me. I was just a little boy, why the fuck would I lie about something like that. It doesn't make any sense."

"What did he do to you?" Part of me didn't wanna know, the other ached for the answer.

"Fucked me, my father fucked me!" he screamed out. The words hit me like a brick. A lump the size of a boulder formed in my throat. He continued, "And she wouldn't believe me, so she let it happen for years, till I was seven. Then she caught the bastard in the act. Came home early from work one day to find her beloved husband, pants down, burying their son's head into the pillow. She finally took me and split. But she always resented me for it, like it was my fault. Like I drove him to it." I felt sick to my stomach. I had put up with a lot of shit, but if it ever turned into anything like that, I always swore to myself I'd kill the fucker.

"Then," he continued, "she goes and marries this stupid bastard, who beats the living shit out of me. I may have took it when I was young, but not now, hell no. I got his ass good on several occasions. She always, of course, takes his side. Then she has the nerve to come in here crying, saying how she hates to see me in here. Then I tell her that I probably wouldn't be losing my mind so much if I didn't have to deal with her piece of shit husband. In my own home! That bitch starts screaming at me, telling me that I just have an ego problem and can't handle having another man in the house. That mother fucker is no man. No man beats the hell out of little boys. I swear, I'm gone once I get out of this shithole."

"Where you gonna go?" was all I could think to say.

"Anywhere, everywhere. There's a whole world out there to explore." We remained in silence for a while. Suddenly it was broken. "Shit dude, I'm sorry. Didn't mean to lay my life shit on you like that. On a higher note..." and with that he changed the subject. As if talking about it allowed him to push those thoughts aside. He became his normal self in an instant, sarcastic and energetic. It was rather eerie how he just switched. I pretended like what he had just told me didn't have an effect on me. I figured that's what he would've rather me have done. Inside it was eating away at me, but at the same time it made me happy. It felt good just to know I wasn't alone. I wasn't the only one who had gone through hell. And it was a lot more comforting coming from him than from a stupid stuffed blue dog.

I didn't sleep that night, just lied in bed thinking. I thought about things that I had been pushing aside for some time. I thought about my mother leaving, the father I never really knew, my uncle's beatings, and my grandmother's imprisonments. I even thought about those damn papers and books she would make me read, if they actually held any merit. All those thoughts replayed in my head over and over again until I wanted to scream. The most torturous thoughts were the ones of Dani. I had pushed thoughts of her as far away as possible for so long. Part of me wanted to hate her. For giving me a taste of what life could be like, of what love and happiness were, then just ripping it away from me. Like a damn tease. I felt cheated, almost raped in a sense. I believed I would've been better off never knowing. But deep in my soul, beneath all the anger and self pity, I knew she deserved better than that. The morning came and I felt completely mentally drained. I didn't eat and went and sat in the corner of the TV room staring at the wall. My brain wouldn't stop and it was driving me insane. Across the room, Sammy Davis Jr. chuckled merrily to himself.

Avry walked in. "Hey what's up, killer. Not hungry?" I looked at him and broke into tears. I hadn't cried since my aunt died. I hated crying, I felt so pathetic. But I couldn't stop. "Please help," I babbled out amidst my sobs.

"What do you want me to do?" He was in shock.

"Just listen." I somewhat gained composure.

"Yeah, no doubt, but let's get away from these crazies." We walked to my room, but my roommate was there, staring out the window twirling his hair. So we went to Avry's room, which was empty. As soon as we got inside, I let it all out. Everything, even the shit before my mother left. Things I never spoke about to another living soul. Once I began talking, I didn't stop. Finally, when I had nothing left to say, Avry put his hand on my shoulder, smiled and said, "Looks like we're both pretty fucked." That was just the response I needed. I wasn't looking for answers or sympathy. When I asked for help, I didn't know what I was looking for. But at that moment it was clear, I needed someone who could understand me. Someone who knew what I was about and still was glad that I was alive. And I knew I found that in Avry. He became my best friend, my family.

We sat in the TV room messing with everyone for entertainment. We were throwing crumpled up pieces of paper at this heavyset woman. She thought it was this other kid and kept yelling at him as he stared at her in confusion. When that lost its amusement, Avry turned to me and said, "You know what this country needs?"

"What?"

"A revolution, like an old school revolution."

"You definitely have too much time on your hands."

"No, I'm serious. People don't know how to think for themselves. They live in their little bubble believing everything they hear on TV. It's time someone burst that bubble and they had no choice but to fight."

"People like being ignorant. Keeps 'em safe."

"I don't get how people could be so blind. If people only knew the shit that goes on out there. You know, I had a friend from El Salvador. He told me that our country helped start some kind upheaval down there, supplied the firepower. Shit like that. We never hear about that shit. We have no fucking clue....Maybe I'll start one when I get out."

"What, a revolution?" I cracked up. "And how do you plan on doing that?"

"Haven't figured that part out yet. A lot of people try through artistic methods; music, writing. Before a real revolution can start there has to be a revolution in the way people think."

"Sounds like it will take way too much effort."

"Not really. If you can get people to listen, really listen, then you can get them to see."

"They'd probably just end up in places like this. People rather just go about their business, watch their television."

"Yeah, I guess the revolution idea is a bit too idealistic."

"Yup."

"You never know, maybe one day people will see. I don't think I'm gonna be the one to show it to them, though. Shit, but in a way, that makes me just like them, even worse. I see it all and still sit on my ass."

"What exactly is it that you want them to see?"

"The truth."

"Which is?"

He sat in silence for a moment, looking up into nothing, hoping for some sort of revelation. Finally, "Damned if I know. Oh well, I never said I was anything special."

Time passed. My birthday came and went. Avry had convinced this new female patient into giving me a b-day blowjob. He kept watch while she did the deed. She wasn't all that cute, plain looking, and I think she was definitely missing a few screws. But I was young and horny and didn't really care. I started to open up a little more in therapy, just enough to impress the doctors. I had been there a total of five months and according to the doctor, I had a significant change in attitude. That I owed to Avry. Our friendship made life a little worthwhile. Finally they set a date for my departure. Part of me was happy to go. I felt like I had a new perspective on life and could enjoy it more. But the realistic part of me remembered what waited on the other side, knowing what I had to return to. And Avry wasn't getting out any time soon. He had a couple of episodes during sessions that were gonna keep him there. The night before I was supposed to leave, Avry called me aside and showed me a little needle he had somehow acquired. "Where did you get that from?" I asked, surprised.

"That, my friend, is of no importance. So where do you want it?"

I looked at him, puzzled. "Want what?"

"Your tat, dick."

"Oh." I said, surprised. "I guess on my ankle." He pulled out this cup containing ink he had gotten from the destruction of many pens, and proceeded to ink me. He dipped the tip of the needle into the ink and poked it into my skin just beneath the surface. At first I twitched a bit, but soon eased into it.

"Alright, I'm done," a half hour later. I looked down to see some scribble of a symbol. "It's the Chinese character for strength." Though tiny and barely legible, I admired my first addition. "Well, killer, you better get some rest, you gotta big day ahead of you."

Morning came. I had hardly slept a wink; my nerves were too on edge. I didn't know whether to be happy or sad, relieved or afraid. My heart was pounding a mile a minute. My stomach was so in knots that I couldn't even get down my breakfast. Finally, the time had arrived. My bag was packed and I was ready to go. "So this is it, man. You're free," Avry said with a half smile. It hadn't really hit me that we would be parting. After spending every day with someone for months, it would be like losing a part of myself. He was the only person after my aunt that I ever cared about, whose company I'd ever really enjoyed. But that was over. I was going back to that cold loneliness. "C'mon, X, don't get all mushy on me, bitch." I knew he was serious about splitting when he got out, and I figured I'd probably never see him again. I wanted to tell him to find me and take me with him, but I didn't. We hugged, he punched me in my arm, hard. "Good luck, killer." With that we parted, and it was as if I was leaving a part of myself behind. I felt as if I was about to jump out of my skin. I exited those doors to find my grandmother on the other side. A reality check in the form of an old shriveled face.

three

"THERE IS NOTHING THE BODY SUFFERS,
THAT THE SOUL MAY NOT PROFIT BY."
George Meredith

Most of the car ride home was spent in silence, with the exception of my grandmother's apologies about how she could never make it to visit. She made excuses for my aunt and uncle, as if it mattered. I just stared out the window at the passing world I hadn't missed.

Stepping back through that iron door, I felt just like I did when I was six. Scared and alone. But this time I knew exactly what to expect. Upon my entrance, I made a promise to myself that things were gonna change. No more wars. I didn't wanna live like that.

My grandmother went into the kitchen and started making me food. She must've been feeling really guilty at the sight of me, whether it was for not coming to see me or missing my birthday; whatever it was, I wasn't complaining. It was forcing her to be nice. I decided to take advantage of the situation. "Hey, you still have that guitar you bought me?"

"Oh, no, I sold that a while back." Not surprising. "Why?"

"I think I'd like to take that up again."

"Well, how about this: I'll get you another one. Consider it a belated birthday slash welcome home gift."

She amazingly followed through with her promise, and within a few days I had a new acoustic Yamaha guitar. It was beautiful; shiny, light brown, and would soon become covered in stickers. I took it on full force, playing for hours everyday. I spent most of my free time in my room playing that guitar. I also discovered that I could sing quite well. I always knew I had a decent voice, but it was then that I realized its true great potential, playing around with different tones and various levels. And since my time was consumed, there was less time for arguing with the family. Things were running smoothly. My grandmother didn't worry about what was going on in my head; she just didn't want me getting into trouble. So she was satisfied. My uncle had a girlfriend, so that kept him busy and in a good mood. The basically relaxed atmosphere in the house provided me with an unexpected comfort there.

News traveled rapidly in that town. Everyone knew where I had been. I was ready for kids to start dishing out abuse for their own entertainment. But I decided it was time to switch roles: become the abuser. That didn't necessarily mean that I was going to start fights with people for no reason. I always viewed people who did such things as plagued by a pathetic desire to prove their self worth by preying on someone they believed to be weaker. But it did mean I wasn't going to let anyone step on me anymore. Avry once told me, "A lotta guys try to live off of intimidation. They act all big and bad to scare you, and that's how they get the upper hand. You gotta throw them off, give 'em a taste of their own medicine. In life it often comes down to this: you're either the victim or the predator."

I got in a fight my second week out. I was sitting in the park sketching in my book, when Rich, one of the popular jocks from my school, walked by, with another guy from the football team, and three girls. Rich snidely remarked, in a voice loud enough for me to hear, "Hey isn't that the psycho kid, fresh out the loony bin?" The others laughed and his male friend patted him on the back. Without hesitation, I put down my book, leapt to my feet and walked right up to his face. "You got a problem?" My tone was totally calm. They were all completely thrown back by my reaction, which added fuel to my fire.

"And, w...what if I do?" he said, stuttering over his words.

"You should be careful, messing with psychos could be detrimental to your health."

He tried to laugh it off, his nerves showing through. He looked back at his friends, and they nodded as if pushing him to keep going. He turned back to me and chuckled, "Whatever, bitchass." And with that I swung a sharp right at his temple, hitting him so hard that he fell right on his ass. The spectators looked on in awe. I wanted badly to kick him in the face, but restrained myself.

"Are you gonna get up, or do you need a hand?" I said, still totally calm. I waited as he got to his feet and brushed himself off. The other guy was cheering him on, begging him to kick my ass. After he collected himself, he swung at my face. I ducked and caught him in the opposite temple. He desperately tried to hold onto his balance. Weary, he swung again and missed. I kicked him in his stomach, but before he could topple over again, one of the girls, who was nearly in tears, ran and caught him. I figured that was enough; I made my point. I walked back to the bench and grabbed my sketchbook. "Later, bitchass," I snickered, as they all watched me leave in silence, except for Rich, who was holding his knees, whimpering.

I had to repeat tenth grade since I had missed so much school. Just as I expected, almost everyone in school had heard about the fight. I thought that the entire football team was going to jump me in retaliation. But instead, they seemed to respect me more. Or fear me. Either was fine with me. I figured they were happy I gave Rich a beatdown, probably would have liked to have done it themselves. He was an asshole. It's funny how things work in popular circles. Often many people involved don't even like each other, but pretend to in order to save face. It's all about image. My social status had taken a completely different turn. I was by no means "popular," more like infamous. Some of the other boys that I had never really talked to before I was institutionalized suddenly wanted to befriend me. Like it was cool to know the psycho kid, have him on their side. As for the girls, they went to two extremes. Some were completely weirded out by me, while others suddenly became really interested. Mini psychologists who wanted to figure me out. Mother Teresa complex. And since I started playing the guitar, I became the tragic musician in their eyes, and they found that so appealing.

I finally lost my virginity at a junior's party. She was a cute blonde from the track team. Grabbed me by the hand and led me to the empty guest room. I was wasted and the whole thing was kind of a blur, but I was happy to have finally done the deed. And for once, the actual ejaculation was more intense than the one I could bring about by my own hand. After that, my hormones grew to truly appreciate the female anatomy and I started fucking around with quite a lot of girls. One of them even became my first girlfriend. I didn't mind her much, but her presence was definitely not a vital part of my existence. She dumped me after only one week, complaining that I was too self-absorbed.

I found it incredibly ironic, though, the less I gave a shit, the more other people did. I'd go to a party with no intention of meeting a chick or making friends, just to go get shit-faced for free. Then somehow I'd find myself surrounded by people who were so interested in me, and girls dying to get in my pants. My relationship with Avry had enabled me to become more outgoing and speak my mind. Pre-Avry I used to keep to myself, thinking no one would understand what I had to say, nor care to listen. But afterward I just said whatever I wanted, not regarding how other people would take it, and people would just eat it up. I think they were just fascinated by the fact that there were people in the world different from the clones they were used to.

I continued to climb up the social ladder. I still wouldn't say I became really popular, at least not with the guys. But I wasn't an outsider anymore, I was an ally. The thing was, though I had acquired a great many acquaintances, I still didn't really have any friends. They were just people I bullshitted with in the hallways and at parties with. But never really with a one on one basis. Even at lunch I floated around, never hanging with a regular group of guys. They didn't truly know me, and I didn't truly know them, nor did I even really want to. My situation with the girls was different. I was "it." But it was like this big scandalous secret. They wouldn't want anyone to know about their dabble with the "dark side." It actually worked to my benefit. I could hook up with more girls, and they wouldn't know that I had already hooked up with most of their friends. But the only purpose females served was to quench my raging teenage hormones. I think the fact that the girls were so into me played a big role in why the guys wanted me around.

The first thing I pierced was my septum—the middle part of the nose. I didn't even do it to replace the urge to cut. I wasn't having such urges. I just did it to see what Avry was talking about. I doused one of my grandmother's sewing needles in rubbing alcohol and just stood in front of the mirror, my heart beating a mile a minute. I held the needle to my nose for a few minutes, completely frozen. Finally I took a deep breath and gave it a hard shove, keeping my eyes open the entire time. After an intense pinch and slight snapping noise, it was through. It definitely was a serious rush. The impact caused water to run viciously from my eyes. I just stared at the needle situated in between my nose for at least twenty minutes, with a huge smile spread across my face. After admiring my work, I headed to the piercing shop and bought a hoop with my allowance. My grandmother almost went ballistic when she saw it, but bit her tongue and walked away, as not to shatter the newly found peace between us.

With that initial piercing, I was addicted. In a few months I had eleven in my ears, one on each side of my lip, and, of course, the septum. It caused definite tension between me and the family. But I had recently started working at a local music shop and since I was working, it balanced out. I had to adjust to the people of the outside world's opinion of such a look, with the occasional smartass comment like "look, the circus is in town." Unless I felt threatened, I ignored it. And everyone at school seemed to expect it of me. Some thought it was cool, some a bit disgusted. But I kind of got off on those kind of reactions. I liked stirring things up a bit. There were even some copycats. But they mostly pierced their tongues; it's easier to hide. But what's the point of a piercing if you're just gonna hide it? It's like spending a lot of money on a necklace that you're just going to tuck under your shirt.

It felt good to finally be making my own money. Taking that power away from my grandmother. And it was a lot of fun working at the music store. I got to learn a lot about so many different types of music and instruments, as well as the opportunity to meet so many different kinds of people. Some were established musicians, some just starting out, and then there were the occasional music buffs who just wanted to get a look at the instruments used to create their favorite sounds. The manager, Jimmy, was in his late forties but didn't seem to want to embrace his true age. He had long hair and a scruffy goatee, and wore prescription shades. He loved jazz and old school heavy metal and was a definite stoner. He always talked and moved in slow motion, and the aroma of sweet cheeba seemed to constantly hover around him. But he never spoke of his habit, as to keep him from being perceived as a slacker. He knew everything about music and could play just about every damn instrument in existence.

It was a small shop, so there were usually no more than three or four of us there at time. I shared the same schedule with Ellen and Mark. Ellen was in her late thirties and was a very flamboyant lesbian. She was the first gay person I had ever known. She was constantly preaching about government corruption, which often got annoying, but she had some valid points. She was an expert on the drums and could play a large array of styles, but mostly stuck to punk rock, being a fan of the old school stuff. She was a stoner too, and we'd often smoke up on our breaks as she would tell me tales of the good old days, when she'd participate in protests, or when she lived in a squat with her first girlfriend.

One day, after listening to her babble on and on about some feminism nonsense, I came right out and asked, "So how do two girls fuck?" She froze in silence, and for a second I thought she was going to hit me. I don't know why I asked, it was part curiosity, part wanting to see how she'd react. She took a deep breath and smiled. "Bend over, bitch, and I'll show ya," she said as she playfully pushed my head down and pretending to ram me from behind, while shouting, "I bet I gotta bigger dick than you do!" The humorous charade was brought to an end when Jimmy came out ordering us to get back to work.

Then there was Mark, a seventeen-year-old nerd who swore he knew everything about music, but was mostly into Motown and R&B. He could play the bass, barely, though he had supposedly been playing since he was nine. If that was the case, he should have given it up long ago. I thought he was just a pathological liar, so I took everything that came out of his mouth as false. He always had some outrageous story of some great escapade he went on the night before with some beautiful slut. But he was horribly unattractive and incredibly dorky, and it all sounded like bullshit to me. He sensed my dislike of him, and eventually stayed out of my way. That was a smart idea on his part, because I was desperately seeking some excuse to hit him.

When no customers were around, we were allowed to play with the instrument of our choice. Jimmy was an awesome guitarist, and had no problem showing me chords and teaching me songs. "You got natural talent, kid," he'd tell me. I was a fast learner, and was pretty much able to pick up songs by just listening to them. Ellen taught me how to work the drums, which I found to be an excellent forum for releasing aggression. I even starting messing around with the bass, which is pretty easy to pick up if you already know guitar. But the guitar was my true passion. With the discount I got at the shop, I saved enough for my own electric guitar and amp. That's when the real problems on the home front started up again.

My grandmother couldn't stand the sound of the electric, always bitching about the volume. I had become used to not dealing with her shit, so that when it returned I would snap back much quicker, which instilled fear in her. I never threatened her in any way, just would basically tell her to fuck off. The calm atmosphere quickly began to fade. At least I didn't have to deal with any bullshit from my uncle. I made sure I only played when he wasn't home, which was often.

I got my first tattoo from an acquaintance of mine who had recently purchased a tattoo gun. He offered to do it for free for the practice. I told him yes, on the account that I could use his gun to do one on myself. He agreed. I chose the picture of the creature that Avry had first took notice of me drawing, and had him put it on my chest. It hurt, but the pain was bearable, like a burning sensation, just like Av said. It came out pretty damn good, considering. I was pleased. Before I attempted to tat myself, I practiced a great deal on pig skin he had given me. Then when I felt comfortable enough, I took the gun and drew flames on the bottom part of a leg. They came out pretty damn good, too. It wasn't an intense pain at all, but it was hard to concentrate while it was occurring. I could only do a portion of the flames myself, so the other kid finished it up. I was proud of the outcome, having discovered yet another new addiction.

That acquaintance of mine had a sister by the name of Dawn. She was the cutest little punk rocker chick. First girl I ever really liked having around, and noticed when she wasn't. We started hooking up, then things got fairly serious. She played the bass, and we'd often jam together. She was an atheist and an anarchist, and taught me all about those ideologies. I liked having people reassure me I wasn't going to hell. She wouldn't let me have sex with her, which I found to be an incredible turn-on. Gave me more reason to want to see her, hoping that day would be the day she'd give it up. At the time I toyed with the idea that it might've been love, but looking back I realized it was just the sensation of actually being interested in someone.

Our relationship was short-lived, though. We were supposed to go to a local punk show together, but I didn't think I would have the money, so I told her I wouldn't be able to make it. But that night I convinced a kid I knew to go with me and pay my way so I could surprise Dawn. I excitedly ran through the darkness to find her whereabouts. I finally did find her, leaning up against the back wall, kissing the lead singer of the band, one leg wrapped around his waist. The pain that I felt was completely foreign to me, and it totally freaked me out. I grabbed him by his bleached hair, mid-kiss, and bashed his head against the wall. As he stood their holding his head with blood dripping from his eyebrow ring, trying to figure out what had just happened, she froze with her eyes fixated on me, jaw dropped. Then she tried to grab my arm, but I shoved her off and just looked into her eyes, feeling sick to my stomach. I wanted badly to hit her, bust open those pretty little promiscuous lips, but I refrained. I left the venue, finally getting hit with the knowledge of love's everlasting attachment to pain.

After that, my music started to become more violent and angry. All the fury buried inside of me was released through music. My grandmother preached that it was the devil's music, and her prediction that I was the Anti-Christ once again began to plague her mind. And with that our arguments started to escalate.

As I walked through the iron door one afternoon after school, I was met by a seething old woman, who had been standing there impatiently awaiting my arrival. "You little thief!" she yelled. "How dare you take an old woman's money?" I had no idea what she was talking about. I tried to ignore her and go upstairs, but she stood in my way. "I want my money!"

I had no idea what she was talking about. "I didn't take your money."

"Liar! A liar and a thief, that's what you are! No good liar and thief!"

I was getting heated but remained calm. "Why don't you ask that son of yours? He's got some sticky fingers himself."

"How dare you accuse my son! He would never steal from me!" I laughed at that remark, having had personally witnessed that man robbing her on numerous occasions. Aggravated, I finally pushed past her and went upstairs, but she followed me up, continuously screaming "liar" and "thief." She then went on, "And I'm going to tell Peter you said that, and I bet he'll give you a good whooping." I was not afraid. My uncle had become too occupied with his piece of ass to care about me. I went in my room and closed the door, and she kept bellowing from the other side, "Straight to Hell! That's where liars and thieves go! They burn in Hell!" until she eventually got tired and retired to her room. An ominous feeling flooded my body as I shoved another needle through my ear.

Still groggy from a nightmare-plagued sleep, I went downstairs for breakfast one morning, forgetting to put on a shirt, exposing the demon-like creature on my chest. My grandmother lost her mind when she saw it. She started crying, reciting Bible scriptures. It made me ill. She had treated me in every way that her beloved god told her not to act toward another human being, yet would have the nerve to curse at me about my choice of art. I started screaming, calling her every foul name I could think of. She fell to her knees and cried, "You are my curse! You are pure evil! It's no wonder why even that wretched mother of yours didn't want you!"

At that comment I lost all sense of reason, becoming completely enraged. I starting running throughout the house destroying every piece of religious items my grandmother had, which was a shit load. The whole time I was quoting Bible passages and excerpts from that damn Christian Encyclopedia, screaming at the top of my lungs, as I broke portraits across my knee and hurled statues across the rooms. She curled up into a ball on the floor, sobbing. After everything was destroyed, I stepped back and looked at what I had just done. It looked like heaven had just thrown up. I ran out of the house and walked aimlessly for hours before returning.

When I finally did return, my aunt was there, waiting with her arms crossed and her signature sour puss. She looked at me coldly and said, "Pack your shit, you're moving in with me." My grandmother had threatened to take her out of the will if she didn't take me in, so she complied. I quickly gathered my belongings, and walked out without exchanging a single word with the old lady.

My aunt's house was a lot smaller than my grandmother's, with each room seeming to be only slightly bigger than a cubicle. Everything seemed to be decorated in different shades of beige and brown. On the bottom floor there was the living room, equipped with a hideous brown and beige-speckled rug, the tackiest of couches, an oval wooden coffee table, and a 27" TV that always had fuzzy reception. The room was separated from the kitchen by a counter that was used as the dining table, so as to make sure one could see the TV while one ate. To the right was the only bathroom, which was always cluttered with my aunt's hair and makeup products, and across from the bathroom was the master bedroom, which she kept locked.

The staircase was about as wide as I was, with the surrounding walls covered with paneling that gave the illusion of wood. It led to two rooms. On one side was the den, furnished with a computer desk and outdated computer, and a giant mess of books, spilling off the shelves onto the floor. On the other side was the guest bedroom, which was just big enough for the twin bed and wooden dresser. The air in the room was stale and I could tell that the bed had never been slept in. There weren't any blinds on the window, so I had to hang a dark sheet to block out the light. I stationed my amp, put my clothes and artwork away, and placed Dani's picture face down in one of the drawers. Despite the house's many downfalls, I liked it better there. There was no sign of religion; no beady little eyes judging my every move. And an average wooden front door.

Since my aunt lived the next town over, I could no longer walk to school. So every morning my aunt got up earlier than she had been used to—which caused intense bitterness—and drove me to school. Usually the drives were silent, unless she had something to bitch about. She had no interest in what was going on with me, nor did I have any urge to tell her. I soon bought a walkman, which made the ride a lot more bearable. There was a public bus that I could take back to her house from school or work. It was a long trip, but I preferred the extended bumpy ride to sitting in the car for a short period of time with my aunt.

Upon first entering the house, my aunt's words were, "Look, don't fuck with me. You stay outta my way, I'll stay outta yours." Seemed fair enough. "You can eat whatever extra food there is, but just don't be a greedy pig. Come and go as you please. Just respect my shit, and pay your own phone charges." Didn't appear to be a bad deal at all. "And keep that guitar volume to a minimum." Of course there had to be a catch. But at least I didn't have to ever see that old hag. The only real problem was my aunt's new boyfriend.

He'd spend a lot of time there even when my aunt wasn't. He seemed to hate me from first glance. Constantly had some rude comment to make. "You know, they use that ring for cows' noses," was always a favorite. "How do you get through metal detectors?" was another. Nothing I hadn't heard before. But soon his remarks started to transform into commands. "You need to cut that messy hair, you look like a bum." "You better change those clothes, you can't go in public like that." "Take that shit out your face, you look like a pincushion." For the most part I ignored him. I liked the set up. I knew if I flipped on my aunt's man, that would all change. So I bit my tongue. I could handle his words; I had heard worse. And it bothered him that he couldn't get to me. I actually found it amusing at times. Watching him seethe, knowing he couldn't do anything about it.

Eventually, he completely moved in, but didn't work, just stayed in the house all day parked in front of the TV, rubbing his fat belly which poked out from beneath his stained wife-beater, nursing a bottle of scotch. I especially tried to stay clear of him during his drunken states. Once he'd pass out, I'd steal some of his liquor, and he was always too drunk to notice. I never quite understood why my aunt stayed with him. There wasn't a single appealing quality about him. I figured maybe he was good in bed, but then I'd hear her complain that he was always too drunk to perform. I think she was just happy to find a man who was actually willing to sleep with her.

At that point in time, I was rocking bondage pants quite often. When he first saw me wearing them he looked rather shocked. "Those look mighty tight, boy," he said, just staring at my legs. "A bit on the fruity side, don't you think?" his eyes still fixated on my legs, voice in a strange tone. A wave of discomfort swept through me and I left without a word. Whenever I would wear them after that, he would say something like,

"Oh, those pants again?" His tone was always the same and the feeling of discomfort was always present.

I ran into a couple of guys from my aunt's town that I had known from junior high. There were a few who had went the route I had, and decorated themselves with piercings and tattoos. We shared and compared, and they introduced me to their clique. This acquainted me with a new group of kids to hang with, and girls to mess with. People I found easier to relate to, and weren't just hanging with me because they were scared of me or girls they wanted liked me. There were some crazy dudes in that group, and a lot who had been in and out of juvenile detention centers. There were even a couple who had been institutionalized like me. There was one kid, Jack, who was an amazing artist and pretty decent guitarist. When he was young he was institutionalized for depression and suicidal tendencies. I started spending a lot of my time with him, in which I learned a great deal.

He was into the goth scene, always dressing in black from head to toe, with long dyed black hair, a nose and eyebrow ring, black painted nails, and often wore eye makeup. He almost always had on his long black trench coat, no matter how hot it was, which would cause him to constantly give off a slight stench of body odor whenever he removed his coat. He was skinny and frail, and could be mistaken for a female at a quick glance. He was a bit of a pussy and way too overdramatic, but I liked hanging with him because he inspired me creatively. We'd usually get together and draw or jam out. He taught me how to paint and use charcoal, even how to sew, which enabled me to spice up some of my clothing. He also gave me a taste for horror movies, and often we'd verbally collaborate on a quick horror script. His ideas always went the dark romantic route, while mine were all violent and gory.

He was very introverted and liked to dwell on his depression, which I didn't mind for the fact that it cut out useless babble when we were together. He was agnostic, which was an ideology I came to adopt, though I viewed it as sort of a copout. His parents died in a car crash when he was really young, so he thought he could relate to me on a deep depressing level. But there was one major thing that made all the difference: he loved and missed his parents. And whenever he returned home, there were people there who were happy to see him. I witnessed it myself. His grandmother would scurry to the door and lay a kiss on his cheek, smile at me, then run and whip us up something to eat. When I first experienced this, it made me wanna beat his ass. Not out of envy, but for the fact that he had the nerve to be so engulfed in self-pity. Who was he to feel sorry for himself? He grew up with loving grandparents in a loving environment. That's more than a lot of people have. It was more than I had. Maybe I was envious.

One night after some goth chick's party, Jack had forgotten to take his keys and was locked out of his house, so he asked if he could crash on my floor. My aunt's boyfriend was awake when we got home, watching the tube. He looked Jack up and down, examining his feminine look, complete with dark eye makeup. He stared at us as we walked up to my room and gave me this look, as if he had just discovered a deep dark secret of mine. I knew what he was thinking, but I was too stoned to give a fuck.

The next afternoon when I woke up, Jack had already left. I went to the kitchen to toast a waffle. As I searched for the syrup, my aunt's bestial boyfriend turned to me and asked "So where's your friend?"

"He left early, I guess." He just gave me this peculiar look. I found his suspicions hysterical, figuring his macho persona was being overrun with disgust.

"Have fun?" he added sarcastically.

Playfully, I answered, "Definitely." Having had no luck finding syrup, I shoved the entire piece of dry waffle in my mouth. Looking straight at him, I chewed it with a smile and went back to my room to play guitar. After about five minutes, I heard a knock on the bedroom door.

"Hey." My aunt's boyfriend smiled and entered the room without my permission. He had never been up to that room before. "Whatcha playing?" he questioned, with a sudden, unwelcome interest.

"Music," I answered suspiciously.

"Can I hear?" Weirded out by the new situation, I decided to use it for amusement. I started playing the hardest, darkest shit I could think of, screaming "Satan" and "Father" over the notes. He gave me this piercing look and walked out mumbling, "You twisted little fuck." I cracked into hysterics.

That wouldn't be the last of his visits to my room. A few days later he knocked and immediately entered. I was on the bed drawing, hands covered in charcoal. I was stoned out of my mind, and my bloodshot eyes revealed my state. He sat on the bed next to me. I just stared at him as he examined my artwork. "Shit, you can really draw," he commented, seeming rather surprised. I thanked him and stared at him intensely, hoping he'd get the hint that his presence was not wanted. "You know, with that talent, you could really go somewhere" He put his hand on my shoulder and began to lightly massage it. I grabbed it and flung it off, leaving black residue all over his hand and arm. He looked greatly offended. "Look, I'm just trying to establish a fatherly relationship with you."

"Why? You're not my father. I never had one before, and I don't need one now."

"Fine," he said harshly and proceeded to exit the room, but before he left, "Your eyes are rather red there. Smoking a little too much weed? You know, your aunt wouldn't tolerate drugs in her house. If she found any weed here she would flip."

"Yeah, well luckily I'm smart enough not to keep any in the house."

"I never said you did." And with that he walked out. It took me a few minutes to realize what he meant: he could frame me. And she'd believe him. He seemed to be bribing me, but I didn't know exactly for what. His sudden interest in getting to know me had to have an ulterior motive. I was praying it wasn't the one I was thinking of.

I tried to stay clear of him, but it was somewhat difficult. I didn't like being out all the time, I'd rather be playing my guitar. So I'd spend as much time as I could tolerate at Jack's, because at least I could play as much as I wanted there. He had a basement and his grandparents had set it up as his music and art room. But I liked to play everyday, and I couldn't possibly take that much of Jack and his woe-is-me routine. So that gave me no choice but to be in my aunt's house with that man. And his ass was always stationed on the sofa in the living room in front of the damn TV. Since it was right by the front door, there was no sneaking by him if he was awake. Whenever he'd notice me, he'd tell me to take a seat and watch "the game." I always declined. Then I started to notice things were being disturbed in my room, so I bought a lock for my door. The idea of anyone touching my personal belongings infuriated me. I knew if I confronted the bastard he'd deny it. I hinted about it to my aunt and she went nuts, telling me to, "Save the bullshit." Still trying to keep peace, I once again painfully bit my tongue.

The lock also prevented those visits. He'd still try to enter. "Busy," I'd call out. He'd stand by the door for a bit, as if waiting for me to possibly change my mind. After he saw he was getting nowhere, the attempts finally stopped altogether.

"Do you ever contemplate murder?" Jack asked one sunny Saturday afternoon. He was lying on the floor, hands folded behind his head, staring at the ceiling, as I was attempting to strum out a new melody.

"Yeah, I wanna murder your ass if you don't stop asking me these stupid questions while I'm trying to concentrate."

"No really, Xavier," he sat up, "do you ever really think about killing somebody? And I don't mean like, 'Oh god I hate that kid, I wish I could kill him.' I mean like really think about the act of murder, what it would be like."

I stopped strumming. "No, Jack, I can't say I have," I replied in a sarcastic overtone. "Why, you got some murders planned on your agenda?"

"No. It's just sometimes I think about what it would be like to take a life. How I would feel afterward. Like if someone was a real bastard, I wonder if I'd feel guilty. Do you think you would?"

I pondered over his question. "I don't think I would. I mean, I don't remember ever feeling guilty for something I did. Why would murder be any different?"

He looked at me wide-eyed, excited that I was entertaining his babble. "Well murder isn't the same as stealing some money from your grandmother. It's like ending someone's life."

"Yeah, jackass, I know the technicalities. I'm just saying, if someone is a real bastard and does something that results in me having to end his useless life, then fuck it. I wouldn't go around shooting guys I thought were dickheads, but if I was provoked and it ended like that, better them than me. No reason to dwell on it."

"I think eventually I'd feel guilty. But I think at first I'd be turned on by it, like erection and all."

I looked at him crooked and returned to my guitar muttering, "You're a strange, sick kid."

I arrived at my aunt's house one Saturday evening, covered in paint from an art session at Jack's. "What the hell were you up to?" asked my aunt. When I told her I had been painting, her face lit up. She showed a sudden interest in me and my talents. "Please, please paint me a couple of paintings. Simple stuff, like flowers, scenery, stuff like that. Please! It would mean the world to me!" Totally taken back by her request, I agreed. I had thought she was planning to put them up in the house, which made me smile.

I went back to Jack's the next day and began working on them. I painted everyday until I had three 18x20 paintings completed. I even took off of work two days so I could work on them. One was taken from a photo Jack found on the Net of the Greek Isles, one was of a garden with a swan fountain, and the other of waterfalls. They were not anything I would have voluntarily painted, but I figured she'd like them. And that's all that mattered. When I excitedly and proudly gave them to her, she was ecstatic. "Oh thank you so much. Mary's garage sale is next week and I told her that I'd definitely have some stuff to give her, but I didn't feel like going through storage. It's way too packed." And she scurried off to the phone. My heart sank. The feeling of disappointment was soon overcome with anger for allowing myself to get my hopes up that someone in my family actually appreciated me.

This senior from school was having a huge party. She was incredibly rich and lived in a tremendous house. Her parents were gone till the next day, so we had all night to party. Just about the entire school was invited. I showed up with an entourage of freaks that I had collected from my aunt's town. The sight of all of us shook people up a bit. A scary looking bunch of mother fuckers. There were the outrageous looking ones with dyed hair and facial jewelry, as well as your tough bad-ass kids who just didn't give a fuck. Even the biggest jocks were shaking in their Nike sneakers. Since everyone knew me, they labeled me as the ring leader.

That was one crazy party. I made out with two girls at once, one who later gave me head in the bathroom. I loved when girls would try to compete with one another; the slut in them would shine. Even better was the looks on the jocks' and preppies' faces when they would catch sight of me with one of "their" type chicks. "How the hell did he score with her?" was a repeated comment. Despite my promiscuous tendencies, I never treated females with outright disrespect. I was always upfront. That converted me into a challenge to them, to see who could conquer me. At the party, a fight was getting ready to break out. It, of course, was between one of the kids I brought and a jock. Both got thrown out. The guy I brought somehow sneaked back in. He proudly boasted to me and the others about how he beat the shit out of that jock when they got outside. I was not surprised.

It was around two-thirty in the morning and the festivities were still continuing. Some dude I'd often associate with at school offered me some coke. We retreated to the bathroom, where he showed me the obscene amount he had. I had never seen so much coke before. God knows how long we stayed in the marble covered bathroom, blowing lines after lines, taking tweaked-out conversation intermissions, then blowing some more lines. There were enough bathrooms in that house to accommodate, and people stopped knocking after a few minutes, figuring someone was getting it on. We were both flying when he suddenly started on a personal tip that I wasn't expecting. "You know, we need to hang out more." Drug ramblings. I didn't know how to respond. He was a pretty decent kid but not someone I could stand to be around a lot. But I was high outta my mind as well.

"Yeah, yeah sure."

"I could see us becoming best friends." That one kinda hit me as strange. Jack had said that to me once before, and I looked at him like he had twelve heads. I had a best friend, Avry. Regardless whether or not we saw each other again, he'd always be my best friend. But that was not something I thought about regularly. Everyone was always so obsessed with making friends, establishing bonds, but that was something I just didn't care about. Friendship requires a distribution of trust, and that I could not give easily. And I also found it hard to tolerate most people for an extended time period. My version of friendship was associating with people who I felt I was getting something out of, whether it be inspiration or entertainment.

I tried to nod off that kid's remark. Then he got really close to me, all up in my face, breathing his beer-tainted breath on my skin. I don't even know how it started, but suddenly he was kissing me. And I was kissing him back. It didn't feel any different from kissing a girl, and for a bit it didn't even register that I was making out with a guy. There was definitely a lot of alcohol, weed, and coke involved. I was getting rather into it, until I felt something stab my leg. When I realized it was a dick, I freaked. I threw him off of me, slamming him into the wall. I grabbed my head; everything was spinning. He looked at me and said, "It's okay, your secret is safe with me."

"What secret?"

"There's nothing wrong with being gay." He tried to caress my face, but I dodged his effort.

"Fuck you, I'm not gay, asshole!"

He burst into laughter. "Oh yeah, then what was that?"

"Look, I'm really fucked up. There's nothing wrong with it, it's just not me."

"You're gonna try and tell me that you weren't enjoying that?" Truth of the matter, I was enjoying it, until I realized what was going on.

"Let's just forget the whole thing," I concluded.

"Xavier, don't fight it." He leaned over and tried to kiss me again. This time I slammed him even harder against wall and he took it the wrong way. "Oooh, I like it rough." So infuriated at his blind misinterpretation, I lost self control and punched him dead in the face. I didn't want it to come to that, but I couldn't help it. He fell to the floor and started sobbing, and I was suddenly hit with pity.

"I'm sorry, man, I didn't mean to do that to you, but you just weren't listening." He was trembling in fear. I kept trying to apologize, but he still wouldn't listen.

"Here just take this and get out," he said as he handed me the rest of the coke.

"No, you don't have to do that."

"Just take it and go!" I shut my mouth, grabbed the coke, and returned to the party. It was late, so I rounded up the troops and started to head out. As we started to walk out toward the street, we took notice of a huge group of guys loitering down the block. They were the defeated jock's friends, and they were waiting for us. Fully aware of what was about to go down, I scurried to the side of the house and polished off the rest of the coke. It was the largest amount I had ever done at one time. When I came back around, I was ready to take on an army.

The people I was with were always down for a fight, no matter how many opponents there were, especially in their fucked-up state, and we jumped right into the inevitable. We threw the first punches, and a brawl broke out. I was aware that I was being hit, but I felt absolutely no pain. Nothing could slow me down. I got one kid down, and I was sure I caused others damage. When sirens were heard, everyone, besides those too injured to move, took off. It was every man for himself. And at that moment I could run at the speed of light. I lived about a forty-five minute walk away, but I made it there in twenty minutes. When I got to my aunt's, I collapsed on the lawn, completely drained of breath and energy. I lied on the grass, staring at the star-filled sky, until I finally regained the strength to get to my feet, and stumbled inside.

Dumbass was awake and drunk on the couch. My aunt was working the night shift. "What happened to you?" he said upon noticing the scratches on my face, a bit of blood hanging from my septum ring, and the rips and bloodstains on my torn clothes. Still not breathing fully, I just waved my hands about and shrugged. "You look like you need a drink," he said, waving a bottle of scotch in the air. Overloaded by the events of the night, still tweaking on coke, I decided to take him up on the offer. My body was sore and it would've been impossible to sleep, so I figured a little alcohol couldn't hurt.

A few drinks later we were actually conversing and joking around. The coke made me talkative like a mother fucker. I couldn't shut up. "That thing doesn't look too good," he said pointing to one of my lip rings. I got up and looked in the mirror. It had been slightly torn. I went into the hallway closet and pulled out the pliers from the toolbox, and took out the ring. There was a tiny hole encrusted with blood. I shrugged it off and went back to the couch and had another swig. He suddenly slid up next to me and moved his hand as if to touch my face. I jerked my head away. "Relax," he said, "you just got a little blood." I wiped my mouth. "That's probably gonna scar, huh?" he said, staring at my lips. I nodded, starting to feel uneasy. "Well, you're good lookin' enough for it not to matter." He then placed his hand on my leg, "It's good to finally talk to you like this." He then started rubbing my thigh. I froze up. I was so incredibly fucked up and didn't want to believe what was actually occurring. I finally grabbed his hand and threw it off.

I got up. "Sleep it off, bro. Goodnight." But he grabbed my arm.

"Don't go yet," he pleaded as he pulled me back down to the couch. He pushed me down and tried to kiss me. I grabbed his face and flung him off, screaming, "Get the fuck off of me, you fucking perv! What the fuck is going on tonight?!" His attitude shifted in an instant. He became completely enraged. As I tried to scramble up, he grabbed my hair and slammed my head into the hard arm of the couch.

"Oh, no you don't. You little shit, you think you could do that to me?" He dug his knee into my back as he smothered my face into the couch cushion.

"Do what?" I yelled, my voice being muffled by the couch.

"You got some fucking nerve! Tease me like that and then try to leave me hanging!" I tried to get up but I was completely overpowered.

"Tease you? You're sick in the head, bro. Let me go, you fucking asshole!"

"Don't you know I could see past your little games? Strutting around in those tight-ass pants, flashing me looks. Then tonight you start flirting and getting me all worked up, then just expect to bail? Fuck that! You finish what you started."

"You're fucking insane!" I managed to elbow him in the ribs and jump off the couch. I tried to run to the door when I felt a big slam on the back of my head. Everything became fuzzy and I fell dizzily to the floor. I had been hit several times in the head that night and that last one almost knocked me out. As I tried to regain total consciousness, he managed to pull my pants down. He straddled me from behind and I was powerless to move. My vision was still blurred, but my other senses were fully intact. My body cringed as I heard him unbuckle his pants.

"Now you're gonna get it." He reached around and grabbed my dick, rubbing his bare self on my backside. I was weak, so drained. But the second I felt his bare dick touch me, life flooded back into me. That faithful friend returned: rage. Running on pure hatred, I reached around, grabbed and twisted his balls. He screamed in agony and toppled over to the floor. I held on until he was on his back and I was on my knees. Then I proceeded to punch him repeatedly. First in the face, then in the groin, then anywhere my fists would hit. I just kept punching and punching. I heard things cracking, but it didn't stop me.

When my arms got tired, I got to my feet and began to stomp him over and over again. I reached over and grabbed a nearby lamp and smashed it over his already bloody face. The loud crash snapped me out of my rampage. After I pulled up my pants, I fell onto the recliner and started to reflect on what had just happened. I looked over at him lying motionless on the floor. He didn't even appear to be breathing and I didn't know if he was still alive. I didn't want to know. But one thing I did know, my time in that house had just expired. I wasn't worrying about whether my aunt would believe me, I just knew I had to get the fuck outta there.

I went to my room and packed up as much shit as I could, washed off my bloodied and dirty face and changed my destroyed clothes. Then I went around the house and snatched as many valuables and loose money as I could find. It turned out my aunt had a pretty nice collection of expensive jewelry, though I couldn't recall her ever wearing most of it. Then I snatched the contents in the wallet of the possibly deceased man lying on the living room floor. I finally grabbed my bag and acoustic guitar, and momentarily and painfully acknowledged the fact that I would be parting with my electric. I ran down the stairs, but quickly turned back around to the room. I went into the drawer and grabbed Dani's picture. I ran out the door, stepping over the body, never to return, destination unknown.

four

"SECURITY IS MOSTLY A SUPERSTITION. IT DOES NOT EXIST IN NATURE, NOR DO THE CHILDREN OF MEN AS A WHOLE EXPERIENCE IT. AVOIDING DANGER IS NO SAFER IN THE LONG RUN THAN OUTRIGHT EXPOSURE. LIFE IS EITHER A DARING ADVENTURE, OR IT IS NOTHING."

Helen Keller

I stared at the various choices on the board in the train station, finally making my decision. The first stop of my new life would be San Francisco. I was barely seventeen, and all alone. Not much different from how it had always been. I had actually scraped together a fairly large amount of money at the house, including the money I acquired from pawning jewelry and CD's.

As I sat on the train staring at the window, I wondered if I had actually killed that man. I wondered how my aunt would react when she got home. I pictured her walking through the door to find her horny slob of a boyfriend lying on the floor covered in blood, and her precious sapphire collection missing. I wondered which she would be more upset over. As those thoughts swirled around in my head, the notion that I had finally proven my grandmother right entered the circulation. Annoyed by such a thought, I promised myself never to think about that poor excuse of a man again. I remembered the conversation I had with Jack. That bastard deserved what I had done to him. I told myself that when I would step off that train, it would be a new beginning and I would lock my past away. What was done was just that: done. I saw myself as finally free. Free to show the world that I was worth something.

San Francisco is an awesome city, with a laid back mentality, basically secluded from neighboring cities. Full of potheads. I knew the money I had wouldn't last forever, so I raised more panhandling and playing my guitar in the streets. The first couple of nights I rented out a room in a cheap motel, but that was costly, so I figured I was better off crashing on a bench or not sleeping at all. In a few days I became acquainted with some local young squatters while playing my guitar. They dug my sound and let me share their squat.

It was in an abandoned, uncompleted building, and you had to climb in the dark over pieces of crumbled cement, wood and other rubble, up an unsteady ladder, which led to a big open floor. There were three fairly large holes where the windows should have been, letting the sun in. When it rained, one of us would tape up garbage bags to block the water. At night the lighting was supplied by a sea of candles, leaving colorful blobs of wax everywhere. Wall beams were visible throughout the place, and the floor was connected in several spots by big wooden boards. There were old and dirty mattresses and blankets scattered throughout. I bought my own sleeping bag, which I rolled up and hid when I wasn't around.

The entire place was covered with graffiti, some mindless scribble, some true art, some words meant to live by, all of which gave it life. The anarchy symbol was spray painted all over the place in various sizes. The walls would soon serve as a giant canvas for me to play on. Everyone was pretty neat with their trash; I guess they figured the place was dirty enough. So many people were in and out of there; there was no way to keep up with names. They were mostly teenagers, some even as young as thirteen. But their faces bore the burden of pain beyond their years. Some left their families, some ran from group homes. They all had their own sob story.

It was very rare that a person was asked to leave the squat, and that only really occurred if the person stole from someone or was a complete crackhead or junkie. And that decision was made by the ones who had been there the longest. The cops didn't know we were there, or if they did, they never bothered us. Everyone there was in the same boat, just looking for somewhere to belong. But I knew I was different. The old Xavier was dead. I was a new person, as if I had been reborn. I needed no one and nothing but myself. I felt invincible; I even got the word tattooed across my stomach. For me it was only the beginning.

I mastered the art of networking, getting well acquainted with different people throughout the city who I knew would be of use to me. I kept everyone at a certain distance, though. It was safer that way. During my time there, I was exposed to way more drugs there than I had been in the other towns. They were everywhere and with great variety. I sampled crystal meth, various prescription meds, ketamine, whip-its, but never went overboard with anything. I did crack once, but found it utterly retarded because the high was so short, and I just felt disgusted with myself afterwards. But one thing I did go overboard with was sex. My appetite for sex grew insanely, transforming into an addiction. I don't know how it happened, but one day I woke up and realized it had become a need.

I still wasn't into the whole relationship idea, so sex was the best way to interact with a person without having to really deal with them. It was as intimate as you could get with a person without real intimacy. Fucking was the only way I knew how to fill the hole inside me. I became the poster child for one-night stands. I made sure that any girl I slept with was fully aware of my intentions. But it seemed the more I would explain that, the more they would take it as an incentive to try harder to make it into something more. But after my initial relationship experience, I wanted nothing to do with them. It just led to unnecessary pain.

Living in San Fran, I discovered something new about myself. Since I was extremely horny, I started not to care what gender would satisfy the cravings. I wasn't attracted to men at all. But I was spending a lot of time with gay guys and they seemed to take a liking to me. Mix in some alcohol and drugs, and a blow job is a blow job. But that's all it went to. Kind of ironic considering what had went down that night before I had left "home," but that was a different person. And I learned that the guys were more down for one-night stands than the girls. Some girls wouldn't understand what was absolutely obvious, even stated. So I'd have to be as blunt as possible and tell them to simply fuck off, which usually didn't go over too well, always causing drama.

There was this one hippie girl I spent some time with. Her eyes were empty, like her thoughts, but the sex was good. She lived with her mother, who was a hippie chick as well. She must've had her daughter at around sixteen, if not younger, because she looked incredibly young and was quite attractive. One night I went by their house looking for the daughter, but she wasn't there like she said she would be. He mother invited me in to wait. She offered me a beer, and we sat in the living room and started bullshitting.

A few beers later, we got on the topic of music and discovered we both played guitar. She went and got hers, and she started playing and singing some folk music. She wasn't half bad. Then it was my turn. I played a request, singing along. She made me play quite a few more until the drunkenness forced me to stop. She was impressed and started flirting as we drank some more beer. "You know, my daughter probably isn't going to be back for a long while." And that started it. We went at it, right there on the couch. She pulled up her skirt, pulled down my pants, and jumped on top of me. We finished ten minutes before her daughter got home. She greeted me with an excited hug and kiss, and as I peered over her shoulder, I saw her mother smirking. We went into the daughter's room, where she showed me how her yoga classes had paid off.

I ended up crashing at that girl's place a couple of times, sneaking into her welcoming mother's bed when her daughter was sleeping. Her mother was a way better fuck. But then one night the daughter's cousin was staying over and caught me sneaking into the mother's room. Curiosity caused the nine-year-old boy to peek into the bedroom and see what was going on, without us even noticing. The next day, once I was gone, he told the daughter what he had seen, and she came to the squat in utter hysterics. I never knew a hippie could be so violent. She started wailing her hands at me, screaming like a banshee. I grabbed her arms, and then she started kicking. One of the other squatters was witnessing the whole fiasco. He ran up behind her and grabbed her by the hair and yanked her away. She finally ceased her attack. He smacked her dead in the face and screamed, "Get the fuck out of here, you crazy bitch." And with that she ran off.

"You didn't have to do that," I said, feeling a bit of pity for the girl.

"Fuck that bitch, she was acting crazy. What did you do to her anyway?"

"Fucked her mother."

"Shit, dude, that's fucked."

I shrugged and he couldn't help but laugh.

After five months had passed, a group of us who occupied the squat migrated northward to Sacramento. One of the guys had connections with a huge pot dealer up there. There were about six of us: four guys and two girls. The guys were rowdy anarchist punks, and the girls were just some runaway chicks they met somewhere along the way. Us guys passed them around, and orgies were a common thing. The girls didn't seem to mind. They didn't speak much, just kind of observed and laughed when it seemed appropriate.

We crashed at the dealer's place, which was a huge flop house, and helped him sell, being big customers as well. He was happy with the new girls to fuck, so he never minded us being there. I hit the streets, making my introductions. Living a life like that was a lot easier when you knew the right people in the right places. The other guys had different methods of doing business than me. They were sloppy in their ways, drunk more than half the time when they were hustling the streets. Just about every day they had a new story about running from the cops. I always covered my tracks, always looked over my shoulder. And if I was dealing, I was sober so I could be on point. There was no way I was going to end up in a cage.

After about a month there, I started to get nervous. I often felt like I was being followed. I told the others and they decided that it was best that we move on, just to be on the safe side. They, plus a couple of other stragglers they had met, decided they wanted to move back south along the coast. Though I didn't mind the time spent with them; they were always good fun to get drunk with, but I didn't want to be a member of their traveling circus. I wouldn't be able to tolerate them for that much longer. I wanted to travel the country on my own, discovering new worlds everywhere I went. So, without informing them, I split and headed to Lake Tahoe.

I had remembered Dani mentioning Lake Tahoe, about how she used to take vacations there. It was full of casinos and hotels. I wasn't technically allowed into the casinos because of my age, but that was easy to get around. But I didn't really care for those places. Gambling intimidated me because I would see people who would just sit there and bet their lives away, holding on to that hope that they were going to hit it big. Each new day was going to be their lucky day. But for the most part, that day never really came.

I used go to the top of this one casino and draw, inspired by the panoramic view of the lake. It was so serene up there, I could just sit there for hours and let time pass me by. I'd pretend that nothing else existed but me and my music, and for those moments, I'd feel peace. I also discovered this other sweet spot with an awesome view of the Sierra Nevada Mountains. It was at that spot where I met the next girl in my life who would spark an actual interest: Veronica. She had the same idea as me, and was painting the view. I watched her as she gently laid each stroke on the canvas, her long wavy brown hair and flowing white skirt blowing in the wind. She looked like a painting herself. After watching her for some time, I walked up to her and took a peek at her work. I was greatly impressed, gave my compliments, and we just started talking. She was older than me, having just turned 21. She worked as a waitress and shacked up in a pretty decent-sized studio apartment. She wanted to be a famous artist and really believed it was going to happen. I grew to believe too.

She shared my views on relationships, so casual sex was never a controversial issue. We both claimed we didn't want anything resembling a relationship, but what I had with her was probably the realist relationship I had ever had at that point. She was the first girl I ever found myself able to comfortably talk to about personal things. She too was a nomad, and planned on moving to Florida soon to stay with her sister. Her dad split when she was a baby, and her mother died of cancer when she was fifteen. Her sister had raised her until Veronica left to live on her own at eighteen.

I admired her, the way I had admired Dani. She was strong, independent, and knew what she wanted from life. She was always positive, no matter what life threw at her. I envied her in that respect. I thought about going with her to Florida, but never mentioned it aloud. I was afraid even the mention of it would ruin what we had. She was one of the three people I had ever met who could challenge my mind. She always had a billion questions, like a child who always wanted to know "why." One night while lying in bed after a bit of a marathon, she turned to me and asked in her sexy mellow voice, "Xavier, what are you gonna do with yourself?"

I paused before answering. "I don't know, just take it day by day. See where each day takes me."

"Never settling?"

"Well, I just planned on searching around until I find a place that feels like, I don't know, home, I guess."

"But once you find that place, what do you plan to do?"

"I don't really know, haven't really thought about it."

"Do you plan on living like this your whole life?"

"Why not?"

"Doesn't it ever get scary, not even knowing if you'll have enough to eat for the day?"

"I manage."

"But is managing enough? I mean, I've met so many kids who leave home without any plan, expecting some great freedom, and end up having nothing and being miserable. It was different when I left. I had a plan. Without that sense of security, I think I'd fall apart."

"I've never felt a sense of security, so I guess I don't know what I'm missing."

She ran her fingers along the inside of my arm, not looking at me as she asked, "Would you say your choices have made you happy? I'm sure whatever miseries that caused you to believe that you would be better off on your own seemed worth the chance. But can you honestly say you're happier now?" I had honestly never known real happiness. There was always something standing in the way of it. But I definitely liked where I was at that moment better than where I was before. "My life's better now."

"Don't you ever get lonely?"

"Me and loneliness go way back, I grew accustomed to it. I mean, when I was younger I felt lonely, but then it transformed into simply feeling alone, and that's all I know." The only times I had never felt alone was when I was with Dani on our excursions, or with Avry in the institution. But I forced myself not to dwell on past memories. Letting things that can't be changed get to you is just adding on unnecessary baggage. "I don't know why people feel the need to seek comfort in other people. If you don't feel comfortable in your own skin, no one can help you. People obsess over trying to form bonds with others, finding love, just so that they can feel better about themselves."

After taking a moment to digest she continued her questioning, "What are your passions?"

"My art... sex." I tickled her. "And most of all, my music."

"Ever think about trying to make it as a musician?"

"No. I don't play music for other people, I play for myself. I do like sharing it with some people and totally get off when they appreciate it. I wouldn't mind playing gigs at some cozy little places. But I have no urge to try to 'make it.' I feel like I'd be exploiting myself."

She paused. "That's something I've never heard a musician say. Fair enough, I don't agree, but I guess I understand. Well, when you're all alone in the dark, what do you dream about? What do you hope for?" Hope. That was a word that hadn't been a part of my vocabulary since Dani died. I could never figure out what there was to be hopeful for anyway.

"Like I said, I live my life day by day. You never know what each day will bring. I try not to have expectations, just kind of take what's given. I don't really hope for anything."

"Damn, no hope, no love. I don't care what you say, your loneliness must torture you."

"Well, I don't feel lonely now." I didn't. I liked where I was, I liked lying next to her. She caressed my face, kissed me, and we drifted off to sleep.

Days passed. We were spending a lot of time together, but I tried to keep a set distance. She consistently tried to persuade me to get a job. Her pestering got so annoying that I eventually gave in and worked as a bus boy at a shithole joint. I hated it, but it was some sort of steady income. And I could afford to go out places with Veronica. I didn't seem to care where I was as long as I was with her.

She took me to galleries and introduced me to the world of fine arts. The rest of the time I spent alone with my guitar, admiring beautiful scenery. The only drug Veronica did was weed. She didn't even drink. So if I wanted to get fucked up, I'd have to do it on my own terms. But she inspired me, and I decided it was good for me to take a break from all the nonsense drugs I had been ingesting. And my mind felt clear, focused, and serene. I began to take pleasure in simplicity. It felt as if I was seeing the world through new eyes, experiencing it through new senses. Often I'd go to my little getaway, lose myself in my music, eyes closed, just listening as the mountains would whisper to me their hidden secrets.

I was on my way to Veronica's. It was a Tuesday, our usual meeting day, and I couldn't wait to see her to show her some of the artwork I had created the night before. I knocked a few times, but there was no answer. I tried the knob. The door opened and I cautiously entered. The place was empty. All the furniture was there, but all the stuff that made it Veronica's was gone. On her bare bed there was a hat she knitted that I always coveted. Next to it, a note with my name printed on it. It read:

Xavier,

Sorry to just leave like this, but I've never been one for goodbyes. I'm grateful to have met you and for our time together. When I look at you, beneath all the tragedy, I see a beautiful, talented person. Don't blockade yourself from emotion to lead a numb existence. Don't limit yourself, because if you wanted to, you could fly.

I believe in you,
V

Belief in me. The words filled me, attempting to fill the hole she had just dug within my heart. Another one lost. But how could she go without even a warning, without saying goodbye? It was no secret that she had planned on eventually leaving, but I guess part of me had hoped otherwise. Hope. If there was a devil, hope was his tool. I grew angry at myself for expecting anything else. I always preached that if one does not expect anything, one cannot be let down, but didn't follow my own motto. And once again I faced disappointment and heartache. But no, I wouldn't let myself become some pathetic lovesick fool. I had been careless and foolish, and I was paying for my mistake.

With Veronica gone, I decided it was my turn to leave as well. Trying to live that peaceful, "in touch" serene life obviously didn't work for my benefit. I was still abandoned. It was time to switch up the slow pace and spice things up. The very next morning I made my way to the train station. Next stop, Las Vegas.

Vegas was exactly how I had expected it to be. A city full of lights, greed, drugs, and lust. Definitely an interesting place, not too far off from the entrance to hell. There was really only one main strip, but there was enough on that strip to keep the darkest of creatures entertained. I assured myself that as long as I didn't let it consume me, I was safe to stay a while. I knew if I lost control, I'd be doomed. But I believed I would be able to handle it. However, I was aware of my Achilles heel: my sexual appetite. Knowing I wouldn't be able to keep that under control, I figured I would just have to make sure I was always stocked with Trojans. So many girls would travel there with the intentions of going completely wild, losing all inhibitions, doing things they would never dare to at home, without tarnishing their reputations. The grade school teacher was pounding shots and doing lines in the bathroom. The modest girl next door was dancing on the bar, lifting up her skirt and making out with her female friends. There, the ladies were on the prowl just as much as the men were. But exposed to such surroundings, my weaknesses began to stretch way beyond sex.

My second day there I was feeling weary after staying up all night having had nowhere to stay and very little funds to eat. I was plagued with thoughts of Veronica, and was growing annoyed at myself for dwelling on someone who was most likely not doing the same. I came across an elderly woman dressed in dirty clothes, preaching loudly in the street where I was playing my guitar. I tried to ignore her, until she came up to me. "Lovely music, son."

"Thanks."

"Why don't you play me a song?"

"Sure, what do you wanna hear?"

"Anything." So I played and sang the first thing that came to my head, and she smiled ear to ear.

"Oh, you could melt an old woman's heart. I bet your parents are proud."

I laughed at that. "Care to make a wager on that?" I asked, getting into the Vegas spirit.

"Bad relations with the folks?"

"No relations with the folks."

"Oh dear, I'm sorry."

"Don't be. I'm not."

"Well, you know who is proud of you? God is." I chuckled and started strumming a tune. The notion of God made me think of my grandmother, and I hated thinking of that woman. Plus, I thought if I believed in God, that would mean I was acknowledging the existence of hell, and I had worked so hard at shaking that fear. So, focusing on my guitar, I tried to block the woman out as to prevent such annoying thoughts. She continued, "God dwells within every person."

I paused my strumming. "Well he must've skipped over me."

"Nonsense. He's with you right now. He's everywhere. We are all his children, except he has granted us a frightening freedom that we take for granted." I rolled my eyes and focused back on my guitar. "Don't you believe in God, son?"

"Truth is, lady, I never really cared to think about it. I don't think there's a god in the sense of some great supreme being watching over us, loving us. That's bullshit."

"Well, what do you believe?" I shrugged and shook my head. She pushed on, "Everyone believes in something."

"Religion is just a crutch. Makes people feel life's worth living." I sounded like my mother, and cringed at such a thought.

"But regardless of religion, there has to be something you believe in, some reason behind existence. By denying yourself that, you are taking the easy way out through apathy. Search within yourself; you'll figure it out, what makes sense to you, what gives you peace. The key to reality lies within the human person. You hold all the riddles to the universe, if you just open your eyes wide enough to see. And get out of this city before it's too late." And with that she walked off and continued to preach.

I had grown so resentful of religion. I remembered everything I had read, everything my grandmother had sworn was true, but it never made sense to me, which made me resent it even more. But I never took the time to examine what it was that I did believe in. I thought of Dani. Everything she taught me always made sense to me. She used to say that we are all part of something greater; this something is everywhere, all around us, and we just have to do our best to live in harmony with it and the rest of the world. She said there is good and evil in everything and we must learn to balance them out. After my interaction with that woman, I began to question whether or not I was able to maintain that balance. I really didn't think of myself as evil. I never went out of my way to deliberately hurt anyone, I just reacted to things that happened to me. But I never went out of my way to help anyone, either. I just took care of myself. I asked myself whether or not that made me a "bad" person. I knew some really horrible creatures that did get off on and go out of their way to cause other people pain. But I began to wonder if doing absolutely nothing at all for anyone was just as bad.

My mind became overloaded as these questions circled about. Asking questions that one cannot find the answers to, that's where religion always stepped in. People need certain questions answered in order to continue on with their miserable lives. But Dani always said there was no definite right or wrong. That's what I had tried to explain to Avry in the institution. Certain things make sense to certain people, and the goal is just trying to find what makes sense to everyone as an individual. I eventually stopped caring enough to figure out what in fact that was for me. Who was I to know the answers to the universe's secrets? If the people around me didn't seem to think me worthy of anything, why would a god?

It was another day. Some news was spreading about how they found a guy that morning who had hanged himself in one of the casino's hotel bathrooms. I guess he had wagered a little more then he could handle. In that city, staying away from gambling seemed more difficult. It was everywhere I turned. There were so many places to choose from, and I was sure there was somewhere that would let me gamble despite my age. But I was fully aware I couldn't afford to lose even a dime. Especially considering there sometimes wasn't even a dime to lose.

The next afternoon, while running on pure caffeine and No Doze after drinking all night, I heard a voice while munching on a muffin. "Whoa, killer! Can it really be?" I knew that voice. I looked over to find a familiar crooked smile. There, to my absolute astonishment, stood Avry. Pleasantly shocked, I jumped up and we hugged each other tightly.

"What the fuck are you doing here?" I asked.

"Me? I've been here for about a year. When did you get here?"

"I just got here a few days ago."

"Damn, look at you," he said, looking at my piercings.

"Yeah, I took your advice. There used to be another one here," pointing to the tiny hole by my lip, "but I had, uh, an accident." I showed him my first tattoo and he immediately recognized it and smiled, then examined the rest of them.

"Invincible, huh?" he said with a smirk.

"That's me." He looked pretty much the same, except now with a bleached blonde Mohawk, way longer then it had been, and a nose ring.

"I can't believe this! Where have you been staying?"

"Around."

"Fuck that, you're staying with me. This is fate! It has to be!" He put his arm around me and began to tell me his story. As soon as he got out of the institution, he split like he had planned. He went to LA and squatted there for a bit, but hated it. He got into a fight with the wrong person and left to Vegas. He was working as a bartender and shared a small apartment with some metal head he had met. Then I summed up my adventures.

"None of this asking for change shit," he told me, "it's not worth it. I can probably hook you up with a bar-back job at the bar I work at. My manager loves me. She won't care that you're under 21; she's mad cool. I'm sure my roommate wouldn't mind you crashing on the couch if you were to throw in some money. No friend of mine will be sleeping in the streets. He'll probably be pleased; we could use the extra cash."

Sounded good to me. He took me back to his place. The whole way over there we couldn't shut up, just exchanging humorous tales. Veronica had already become forgotten memory.

"Welcome to mi casa." It was small, cluttered and messy, but no worse than the places I had been staying. At least it had electricity and running water. There was a packed bong waiting on the splintering wooden coffee table. The bong was about three feet high, dark blue, and in desperate need of a cleaning. He cleared the mess of clothing and magazines off the tattered brown leather couch and we took a seat. I peered around the room. The walls were covered in movie posters, including *Pulp Fiction*, *Reservoir Dogs*, and *Bully*. Noticing me examining the room, Avry said, "We have pretty different tastes in music, so we can only put band posters up in our rooms. Except The Damned right there." He passed me the bong and a silver zippo with an angry skull's face on it. "So I've noticed you must hold my advice in great value," he said, referring to my body décor and guitar.

"Yeah, I guess so."

"Well then, my boy, you are a wise one. So, play something. Show me what you got, fool." After we smoked, I picked up the guitar. I was nervous. After all, he was the person who had inspired me to play, and I wanted to impress him.

Afraid he wouldn't dig the kind of music I made up, I asked, "What would you like to hear?"

"Shit, something you wrote, man. You have written your own music, haven't you?"

"But of course. Okay..." I sighed, closed my eyes, let the weed dissipate, and began to play a mellow piece to fit the mood. I didn't open my eyes until I finished. His expression was the greatest compliment.

"Damn, you sure learned quickly."

"I had a good teacher. An old boss of mine."

"Great teachers help to mold, but the talent comes from within. See, I knew you had it in you. And you never told me you could sing."

I hadn't even been aware that I was singing. I was over exhausted and nearly delirious and I supposed it just came naturally.

"I didn't even know myself till I got the guitar."

"I've sang in a couple of bands, but my voice sucks. Luckily you don't need a pretty voice to belt out punk. But that voice of yours, very unique." He packed another bowl, inhaled it, then grabbed his bass. We smoked and jammed for over an hour. Our music seemed to flow together perfectly. We finally stopped upon the return of his roommate. He was a big burly dude, with shoulder length straggly brown hair that desperately needed a cut, and a scruffy mustache and beard. He was wearing a faded pair of black jeans, an old Megadeath tee, heavy black boots, and a silver ring on each finger. He nodded at me and headed toward his room. Avry stopped him and broke down the situation. He looked at me with a stiff expression, then back at Avry, and said in a deep husky voice, "Talk to me when he's got a job." Fair enough.

"We should go to the bar tonight and take care of business," Avry suggested, and I nodded in agreement. "C'mon, X, I'm starving, let's get some grub." He got to his feet, but I remained on the couch. "You getting up?" I smiled. "What?"

"It's just really good to see you, Av."

"Yeah, ditto." Those crooked teeth gleamed. "Now, to your feet, killer!"

"Um, Av, you mind if I crash for a couple of hours before we go to the bar? If I attempt to get up, I think I'll just fall over."

He laughed, "Yeah, yeah, ya dumb fuck." He grabbed me a pillow and I passed out immediately.

The bar was totally my kind of scene. A little dive hidden from tourists, with cheap beer and a loud crowd. The manager was a busty, tattooed, raven-haired biker chick in her thirties. It didn't take much convincing for me to get a job. "I told you it was in the bag," Avry whispered. "She loves me." I had a different perception on her welcoming of my employment by the way she was examining me up and down.

Avry had the night off, so we took a seat at the bar and two cold beers were slammed down in front of us. He grabbed his frosty glass and lifted it in the air. "Nothing quite like free beer."

"I thought you didn't drink. It made you crazy."

"Ah, those days are in the past." I looked at him unbelievingly. "As long as I watch my intake, I'm fine. I know my limit. When I get a happy buzz, I quit. Ask Geane here," he said referring to the middle-aged, tired bartender, who nodded. I lifted my beer and we clanked glasses. "To renewed friendship!"

"Here, here," I yelled and chugged my beer. "So Av, know any fine girlies you can introduce me to?" My hormones were ready to rumble.

He chuckled, "This town is full of 'em. They are like friggin' cockroaches here."

"So I've noticed." That entire strip was full of half-naked women, overflowing with silicone.

"Shit, I haven't gotten laid in so long. It's pathetic. All these fine women roaming wild, and I can't get one into the sack. So how's your track record going?"

"It's definitely going." I chuckled.

"How many chicks have you banged?"

"Shit, um, I dunno, don't really keep count. Over twenty."

"Yeah, right."

"Seriously."

"What?! Holy shit! And you were a virgin when I met you! How do you do it? You must have some killer freakin' game."

"I guess so. I'm just very forward, let them know how bad I want them. That seems to get 'em, as long as you're not sleazy about it. I don't know why people always say girls want a guy more when he doesn't show interest. That hasn't been the case with me."

"That's because you're good looking."

I shrugged. "And I've just been in situations where there are a lotta horny girls around."

"Oh, please."

"Honestly. Maybe I just exude sexual energy, cuz girls seem to come to me. At least that's what I've been told."

"Teach me your ways, oh Master of the Cooch. I need me some ass!"

I put my arm around him, "I promise, my dear boy, with good ol' Geane here is my witness, I'll get you laid." Geane smirked and rolled his eyes as he wiped down a glass.

"Woohoo! Cheers to that!" We clanked glasses again and continued to drink.

Living and working with Avry was awesome. Perfectly enough, his roommate dealt weed, so we stayed high while at home, and were drunk while at work...well, at least I was. Me and Avry made quite a tag team. We were living a constant party, and we were loving it. That city was always alive. There was always something new and exciting occurring, so I never felt settled in. I believed that when things became too routine, that's when life actually fell apart. And the drugs, they were just so steadily available. Avry dabbled here and there, but basically stuck to weed. But not me. A night that involved a smorgasbord of drugs was always a night to remember. We'd end up in some crazy place, with some new and crazy people who we'd probably never see again, forgetting where it was we had just come from. And free drugs were always so much sweeter. Somehow, I did manage to keep somewhat of a hold on the concept of moderation.

Aside from the constant and heavy inflow of vacationers, most of the "locals" were not actually born and raised in Vegas, just migrated there for one reason or another. Most of these people would go from job to job, apartment to apartment and think nothing of it. You could meet someone and suddenly they'd be gone and every connection you had to them was severed. That made it difficult to trust people. But then again, I never really did. But I had Avry, and I trusted him with my life. To hell with everyone else. They only served as a backdrop to our adventures.

Mostly locals hung out at the bar we worked at, with the occasional straggler tourist. Avry knew who the local big wigs were in the drug scene, and made sure to hit them off whenever they came into the bar.

There were always benefits to being on their good side. Avry would point them out to me so that I could get well acquainted. But I could usually tell who they were from simply observing them. The way they presented themselves, the way they interacted with other people. Some didn't wanna be bothered with the likes of me, but usually I was able to finagle my way into their circles. I'd entertain them with my music, and they would pester me to showcase my talent for their friends. But they mostly liked me because I made them money, rounding up customers for them but always being careful of who I sent. If I got them a new steady costumer or a big sale, they'd hit me off with some freebies. So in turn, drug running became my second job.

It wasn't long until I added some more ink to my body. I had become friendly with a local tattoo artist who was amazing, and his costs reflected his talents. But I was hooking him up with drugs, so he hit me off with a very cheap price for a tattoo. A very tremendous tattoo. It was a tribal which I designed, covering a large portion of my upper arm, traveling up my shoulder, spreading onto the top of my chest and back, all the way up to the side of my neck. I started to stretch a part of it by my rib cage, but the nerve collection there made it unbearable, so I cut it off. The finished product was absolutely amazing. It took a lot of painful sessions, but it was well worth it. Using his gun, I also tattooed thorns around my wrists, and a gargoyle on my thigh, which even impressed the veteran tattooist. Deciding some more jewelry was in order to highlight my new skin art, I had Avry pierce both of my nipples. It was only right that he had me do the same to him. He screamed like a bitch as I jabbed the needle through his areola.

One day while sitting on the couch waiting for Avry to get out of the shower, I pulled out my picture of Dani, and just examined it. I had made sure I had taken it with me everywhere I went, always keeping it hidden. It and my guitar were my only prized possessions. For the first time in a long time, it did not hurt to look at it. Looking at it actually made me happy. I wasn't alone anymore. I began to think that maybe it was her who led me to Avry. Maybe she was out there somewhere, still watching out for me. As I heard the bathroom door open, I quickly put it somewhere safe.

I fulfilled my promise to Avry in no time. Me and Av were pulling an all-nighter at this banging bar. I noticed this cute little Asian girl staring at me from across the room with a great big cheese on her face. She was waifish and petite, wearing practically nothing. She was twirling her long shiny black hair as she smiled at me, so I took it as a cue to head on over to her. A few drinks later, and we were making out in the corner. Suddenly we were interrupted by a girl who looked exactly like her. I thought the alcohol had me seeing double. As I rubbed my eyes, she laughed, "This is my twin sister," and they both started giggling.

"Wow...twins, huh?" They nodded simultaneously. That little light bulb in my head was shining bright. "Hey, I got an idea. Why don't me and my friend over there," I pointed to Avry, who was sitting at the bar bullshitting with the male bartender, "go back to your hotel? We can pick up a bottle of something, and well, do you girls party?" I said pointing to my nose.

"You mean coke?" I nodded. "We never did it before." They looked at each other and giggled, "but we're down to try it."

"Alright, let's go catch a cab. Yo, Av!" He turned and saw me pointing to the two adorable identical girls and he ran right over. We hunted down some coke, which was never a difficult task, and headed to the hotel.

Avry smoked weed as the rest of us inhaled the white powder. The girls were giggling and whispering to each other. You could tell they had never done the drug before. "Wow, this stuff is great!" one of the girls commented, and they giggled some more. I was so fucked up, and they looked exactly alike, I couldn't tell which one was the girl I had been making out with earlier. I didn't care. As I sat at the edge of one of the twin beds, I grabbed one of the girls, pulled her between my legs, and shoved my tongue down her throat.

As we made out, I kicked Avry in the leg, noticing that he was still sitting there, feeling awkward. He did not get the hint, so I peeled the girl away from my mouth. “Hey, sweetheart, why don’t you show my friend how to have fun? He’s a little on the shy side.” She giggled then jumped on top of him. Within a few minutes we were all butt-naked, fucking like rabbits. We were interrupted by a bang on the door. The girls jumped up synchronously and frantically began searching for their clothes.

“Who’s that?” I asked apprehensively.

“Shhh. Don’t say a word, that’s our father,” one of them whispered. “One second, Daddy!” Me and Avry looked at each other, eyes full of fright.

“What’s all that commotion in there?!”

“The TV, Daddy.” They turned to us. “Quick, get in the bathroom.”

As they shoved us into the bathroom, I whispered, “Uh...how old are you girls?”

They looked at each other and giggled. “Promise not to get mad?” We both raised our eyebrows. “Fourteen.” And with that they threw our clothes in and slammed the door.

As we got dressed, Avry muttered in near hysterics, “Fourteen! Freakin’ fourteen! Dude, I can go to jail! How the fuck did they get in the bar anyway?”

I heard the father’s voice. “Shhh...” I put my hand over his mouth. The noise ceased. A few minutes later they opened the door.

“He’s gone. Sorry about that, his and our mom’s room is down the hall. He just wanted to make sure we were back here.” Looking at them at the moment, they looked their age, and I was beside myself for not being able to have noticed. Eighteen was not too far around the corner for me, and fourteen just seemed way too young. Most of the girls I usually would score with were older than me. Me and Avry peered at each other and nodded.

“We think we should go.” I said as I headed to the door.

“But why? He’s gone.”

“I like my freedom.” Avry commented as he searched under the beds to make sure we wouldn’t leave any incriminating evidence. The twins pouted as we walked out the door.

Suddenly, an older male's voice echoed from down the hall, "Hey, I knew it! You two! What are you doing in my little girls' room?" An angry father, who was abnormally large for an Asian man, came charging at us from down the hall. "I'm gonna call the cops! Do you know how old they are?!" We started booking, running as fast as our legs could take us. Avry must've forgotten to buckle up his pants, because as we turned the hallway corner, they fell to his ankles and he almost fell on his face. I cracked up as he feverishly tried to pull them up. We jumped in the elevator, catching eye contact with the furious man. I laughed out loud and Avry stuck out his tongue and gave him the finger as we watched him through the closing doors. Once we were on our way down, we fell to our knees in hysterical laughter.

Alcohol had become one of our major food groups. It seemed that Avry had truly taught himself how to control his rage when he drank. If he slipped and drank more than he should've, we'd go back to the apartment and smoke till he passed out. Being away from his family life seemed to have put his demon into submission. But one night, after way too many pitchers of beer and numerous tequila shots, the demon was unleashed and I was finally introduced to it.

It had been a long and annoying night, having been rejected from several bars for lacking the proper ID. Finally we found one that didn't ask and began to drink heavily. Avry was sitting on a stool, his head in his hands. "Av, you alright?" There was no response. "Wanna go home?" No response. I figured best to leave him be, though keeping an eye on him as I flirted with a busty blonde showgirl. He finally lifted up his head to ask for another beer. A husky redneck entered the bar with some fellow redneck friends. As they passed by Avry, the husky one chuckled at the sight of him, then looked at his friends. I knew what was coming.

"Something funny, killer?" Avry slurred.

"You talking to me, boy?"

"Who else would I be talking to? Your fat ass is blocking my view of the rest of the bar."

"You better watch that mouth of yours, you little freak of nature," the redneck shouted right in his face. Then there was a crash, followed by a lot of blood. Avry had broken a beer bottle over the man's head. One of the guy's friends swung and knocked Avry in the face. I pushed the blonde aside and dashed across the bar and decked that guy straight in the chin. Fists came flying from every angle. I couldn't make out how many people were fighting, but it had transformed into a full-blown bar brawl.

I had one guy laid up on the bar when I saw another lunge at me through the corner of my eye. I dodged him, noticing he had a knife in his hand. He went to attack again. I ducked and he missed. But the third time was a charm and he sliced me on the side of my face by my ear. I didn't feel the pain, but I did feel the rage it caused. I grabbed the arm with the knife and we started to wrestle. The guy I had on the bar had gotten up and managed to get me into a chokehold from behind. I thought I was fucked for sure until the dude with the knife fell to his knees after being slammed in the back of the head with a chair, via Avry. I kicked him in the face as he fell forward, collapsing to the floor with what I was sure was a broken nose. Avry decked the guy who had hold of me, causing him to loosen his grip. I elbowed him in the chest then punched him in the jaw.

"You're fucking cut!" Avry screamed. I touched my face, and blood covered my hand.

"You stupid fuck!" I screamed as I kicked the bastard again. He was still on the ground and wasn't even attempting to get up. I took a quick look around the bar. All hell had broken loose. Avry, fully aware that he was responsible for that whole mess, grabbed me and led me out the door. We had to get through a bunch of brawling drunks to do so. A few more hits and swings, and we were out, and made a run for it. As we heard sirens, we ducked down an alleyway.

"That fat bastard got me good with a bottle," he said as he showed me a bunch of glass cuts on the back of his neck. "Put some pressure on that cut," he ordered, pointing to the slice. I pressed a clean spot on my shirt against my face. The shirt was covered in blood as well, but not all mine. "Shit, I haven't been in a brawl like that for ages; it felt fucking good. I needed that," he said with a smirk. He looked down and realized he had fucked up his hand as well. It was swollen to twice its normal size and was turning all sorts of colors. The sirens were gone, and there wasn't a doubt that they had reached the bar. We decided it was safe to head home.

I cleaned my face off revealing a small slice starting by my ear slanting down, measuring about an inch. Not too deep, but a definite scar. I claimed it a battle wound, and didn't mind the addition. Avry submerged his hand in ice. Our roommate came home and took one look at us. "What the hell happened to you guys?"

"Xavier was mouthing off, so I had to put him in his place." I threw my bloody shirt at his face.

"You guys have problems," and with that headed to his room.

Avry called out to him, "Hey, can we have some weed, you know, to dull the pain?" No answer. "C'mon, man, we're wounded!" A few seconds later he threw out a dime.

"You know," Avry paused as he inhaled a bong full of smoke, "I think I need to do that at least once a month. It doesn't have to be a royal rumble like that, but I do need to fight."

"Make love, not war, Av."

"Keeping all that anger inside me isn't healthy."

"But once you let yourself go, you won't be able to control it, and you'll end up getting badly hurt, in jail, or fucking dead. You're right, keeping it locked inside isn't healthy, but it's better than unleashing it to the world. The key is to conquer and destroy it." The weed was making me feel philosophical.

"Easier said then done, my friend. And you're one to talk. I saw you. You're a fuckin' animal."

"Who, me?" We broke out in laughter.

Avry was blabbing the fight story all over work the next night. The manager called me aside. "You poor thing," she said as she caressed my cheek by my wound. She was always very flirty with me, but she was like that to just about all the male employees. Always batting her eyes, flaunting her cleavage, with the occasional ass smacking. She had invited me to her apartment once after work, "to listen to this killer CD" of her friend's band, but I declined. Not that I wasn't attracted to her, but I thought sleeping with a woman who had power over me was dangerous. But that day, "Hey why don't you come to my place tonight? I'll let you cut outta work early. I'm having a few friends over, and a shitload of blow." Free drugs, I couldn't decline.

I left with her early, trying to slip by Avry. I didn't want him to know what I was doing because she had asked me to keep it quiet. Plus, he had recently sworn off coke and asked me to do the same, complaining that I was doing it way too often. I never agreed, but I said I'd try to space my blow sessions out more. It wasn't that he didn't like coke, but rather the problem being he liked it too much. It scared him. He was petrified of being addicted to anything. We came across a lot of addicts, to all sorts of drugs. We always wondered how they could let themselves fall so far as to be overrun by a substance. "You never expect it could happen to you, till it's too late," one crack head had once told us.

"Fuck that, it'll never happen to me," I replied. "My mind's too strong."

I rode to her place on the back of her Harley. There were a couple of other bikes parked in front. Noticing my hesitation, "Don't worry, honey, bikers don't bite. Not unless you want us to," she said with a wink. There were three guys and a girl waiting in front of her door. Two of the guys were huge and fully decked out in leather, one with a shaved head, the other slightly smaller with a red bandana on. The third guy was a skinny longhair, and the chick was an over-bleached blonde who looked as if she hadn't eaten for weeks. They were all about the same age as my boss, but time wasn't on their side.

"Who's this little boy?" commented the woman. I would've made a snide remark back, if I didn't feel the eyes of those intimidating men searing my flesh.

"Don't worry, he's cool."

"Damn, you're really going for them young these days," the longhair said, and they all chuckled.

As we entered the house, the blonde stepped back. "Cute ass though."

Then my boss grabbed it. "I know." I was trying to figure out what I had gotten myself into. As soon as we were situated, the biggest guy threw out an eight ball on the mirror laid out on the cluttered table. My boss threw out a few grams, and the blonde did the same. "An appetizer," the longhair remarked, and they all chuckled. Then we began.

Hours, many beers, and a shitload of coke later, we were still going strong. The others kept on with sarcastic remarks about my age, but coke is confidence in powder form, so I didn't hesitate to snap back. That actually made them respect me.

The girls snuck off to gossip in the other room. "Hey, no secrets, ladies!" the guy with the bandana shouted.

"Yeah, what are you two squawking about?" the longhair shouted.

"About how I'm gonna be shoving my fist up that skinny ass of yours later!" my boss shouted, followed by some laughter.

The biggest guy remarked to the rest of us guys in the room, "She's one insane bitch, ain't she?"

The bandana guy replied, "Especially in the bedroom." They all laughed and nodded. He looked at me, "Don't you think so, boy?"

"I wouldn't know."

"Shit, well then you're in for it tonight," the biggest guy huffed.

"Nah."

He laughed, "Why you think she brought you here?" I realized the truth behind that, but tried to laugh it off.

"Ooo-wee, she's gonna break you, boy."

I found that amusing and returned with another, "Nah." I tried to get my mind off the topic of sex, because once you get a hard-on with coke, you stay hard. The girls re-entered the room. I went to the fridge to snatch another beer and take a breather.

I suddenly felt hands wrap around my waist, accompanied with a female voice, "Pity she found you first." And with that she slid her hand downward and grabbed my dick. I turned around and the blonde let go and smiled. She stared at me with those worn-out eyes as she walked out of the kitchen. I was fucked: my dick was hard and there was no getting it down. The bulge was ridiculously obvious with the pants I had on. I tried to tuck it away and wobbled back to the couch.

After the sun had risen, and the coke was gone, everyone started to clear out. The one with the bandana lifted up the blonde. "I'm taking you home with me. Check you guys later." They chuckled as he carried her out the door. About a half hour later, the others started to leave as well, and the longhaired guy offered me a ride, being the only one with a car.

My boss answered, "He's staying here." She turned to me with a smirk on her face. I knew leaving would be a smarter idea, but I wasn't thinking with that head. As soon as the door closed, things went crazy. She went into her room, telling me to wait ten minutes. When she called me in, there she stood, in a black lace teddy, garter belt, and thigh-high spiked vinyl boots. I stood back, admiring the view for a bit. She definitely kept herself in good shape. She grabbed me by my shirt and flung me onto the bed. She then straddled me, ripped off my clothes and rode me like a power drill. We pounded away in every position throughout the entire length of the morning, until we finally collapsed. I had never experienced sex like that; pure, nasty, non-stop fucking. But I kept up the whole way. "Damn boy, I'm impressed," she remarked, puffing on a cigarette. She offered me one but I declined. "You do blow, but you don't smoke?"

"Never understood the point. Can't get you high."

She ran her claw-like nails down my body, pressing hard enough to leave behind red-skinned trails. "How do you feel about S&M?"

"Never really tried it, but always wanted to."

"Oh sweetie," she said, pressing her nails in harder, "we're gonna have fun."

Over the next weeks I was introduced to the incredible world of sadomasochism. Ropes, chains, gags, whips, bondage. She liked being the dominant one, which was my role of choice. I didn't like feeling dominated—powerless—but the whole experience was quite interesting, enjoyable, and addicting. I became aware of the true potential of autoerotic asphyxiation, which seemed to heighten orgasms by tenfold. She requested that I keep "us" a secret, due to the age and work status. I respected her wish. But I didn't like lying to Avry. I would tell him I was going to see a chick, which was the truth. I just tried to dodge the inevitable question: if she had any single friends. But he started to pick up on the suggestive gestures between me and her at work. He finally confronted me with his suspicions. He was still shocked when I told him. "You mother fucker. Just be careful, you're playing with fire. That woman is crazy."

She started to want to see me more and more. Whenever we didn't see each other at work, she'd be calling the house looking for me. Things kept getting more intense sexually. I started to feel as if she was trying to break me down, totally dominate me in ways that went beyond the bedroom. Something about being tied up naked, spread eagle, blindfolded, ball-gagged, choke chained, nipple clamped, and whipped by a woman screaming, "Who do you belong to?" just didn't feel right. Whenever I tried to reverse the role, she would just create some distraction, then come back and switch it on me.

She also started to get quite obsessive. Nights I wouldn't spend with her led to interrogations. Sometimes I'd even hear a bike repeatedly driving passed my apartment. Since she was trying to keep us undercover, she had to control her obsessing. But she didn't do a good job. If any girls at work tried to talk to me, she'd immediately have fifty things for me to do to keep me occupied. She started getting extremely bossy, and would scold me like a child in front of everyone. She was definitely becoming a major thorn in my side. The grand ol' party was being tainted. So I started to distance myself from her as best I could.

One day she called me up. "I need you to come over." I was stoned and not in the mood.

"No, not tonight."

"What? I'm not asking you, I'm telling you."

"Good for you, and I'm telling you no." She flipped out and went into a hysterical fit on the other end of the line. I knew it was time for "us" to end and I wanted to do it in person. She kept babbling as I stated firmly, "Shut up for a minute." Her not listening, I yelled out, "I'll be there in twenty minutes, we gotta straighten this bullshit out!" And with that, I hung up. I knew in her head she thought she had won. That made my skin crawl. The notion that anyone could possibly fathom the idea that they had complete control over me made me sick to my stomach, especially when it was coming from a crazy, power-hungry bitch of a boss.

When I got there, the door was left open for me. I entered to find her decked out in all leather holding a cat-o-nine tails. "You've been a bad boy," and she went to grab me. I pushed her away. "Oh, you wanna play a *big* boy?" she attempted to grab me again, but I pushed her arms hard and she backed up.

"We need to talk."

"Why waste time?" and she went for me again.

"Stop it, I'm not fucking playing." She ceased her advances. "Listen, I've had a lot of fun with you, but I'm not really sure what you're wanting from me here."

"I want you to be a good little boy toy and get on your knees."

"Boy toy? You must be out of your damn mind." She picked up on the anger.

"What's going on here? Why don't you wanna play?"

"I'm not gonna be your little lap dog who's gonna respond to your every beck and call. I don't work like that."

"Okay, shit. Relax, I thought you liked it like that."

"I've had fun, but this is over."

Not comprehending, "Shhhhh, don't speak."

"I don't think you're understanding me here. This here, you and me, has expired."

"What?!"

"Shit, let me figure out a way you'll understand. This thing between us has run its course and now its over. There will be no more sex games and no more of you and your controlling bullshit."

"How dare *you*?!" Her eyes filled fire and her voice with fury. "You're still wet behind the ears! Who the fuck do you think you are?"

"You need to calm down."

She slammed her fist against the wall, actually cracking it. "You don't tell me to calm down."

"But..."

"Don't interrupt me." She smashed a vase on the ground. That was more drama than I cared to deal with. I started to head towards the door. The bitch leapt towards me and grabbed my dyed black hair. I spun around and grabbed her wrists and pinned her to the wall. Somehow having her pinned, out of breath, with her heaving breasts pressing against me, damn hormones kicked in. I shoved my tongue down her throat and she wrapped her legs around me. We tumbled to the floor when the phone started to ring. We first tried to ignore it and carry on, but the bastard on the other end was persistent. It created too much of an annoyance, so she went off, bitching and moaning, and answered it.

Her attitude instigated an argument with whoever was on the other end, giving me time to reflect on the situation. I put my shirt on and zipped up my pants. She called from across the room, "Wait, wait!" I proceeded out the door. As I starting to walk down the block, she came out screaming, "Get back here! Don't you fucking hear me?" I did not respond. "If you keep walking you can't ever come back." More reason for me to keep going. "And don't think you're gonna ever step foot in that bar again, you hear me? You or your friend." I cringed. I didn't really care that I was fired, but I felt like a dick for getting Avry fired. He had warned me. I wasn't sure how he would react. He had to work that night, so I wandered around the lit streets for a while hoping to get home when he was sleeping. The plan failed.

His stare burned as I walked in. "That's some fucked up shit," were the first words that came outta his mouth.

"Yeah, I know."

"The bitch had the nerve to call up and have me sent home." I sat next to him and stared at the floor. He took a hit from the bong and said, as he exhaled, "Oh well, I can get another bartending gig easily. I am pissed, though. But hey, in all honesty, if I was given the opportunity to fuck her, I would've."

Wandering around all that time, I had sorted out a plan. "Let's just get the fuck outta this city."

"What?"

"For real. Let's just go. Maybe to New Orleans."

"What have you been smoking?"

"You didn't plan on settling here, did you? I'm sick of this place. If we stay here I'm gonna just end up ODing on coke or catching herpes. Let's just split tomorrow."

"Shit, you're nuts." He paused and pondered over the idea. "New Orleans, huh? Does sound good." I nodded. "Explore some other places along the way?" I nodded again. "What about Dave?" referring to our roommate. "We're just gonna fuck him with the rent?" I shrugged. "Wouldn't you feel guilty?"

"No, would you?"

"No, but I feel like I should."

I still had never really felt true guilt. I was aware of what I did and didn't see anything wrong with my choices. A "whatever happens, happens" mentality. At that specific point in time I felt I wasn't responsible to take care of the well-being of others. The way I saw it, the idea of responsibility to society came from the leaders, the ones on top, who preached to everyone to work as one as they sat back and watched their pawns and feasted on our riches. Fuck them. And fuck Dave. "It was his decision to let us live here. The true nature of free will is to accept that there are vast possibilities." Those damn Christian readings had somehow secretly implanted themselves permanently in my memory.

"You truly are fucked, but in your own twisted way it makes sense." After a few minutes of silent thinking, "Alright, we'll go in the morning." I told him to organize all the shit he could sell and shit he wanted to take. I also pocketed the weed. It was gonna be a long trip. But some drinks, smoke, music, good conversation, and various females to explore; the trip would be well worth it.

five

"CHAOS DEMANDS TO BE RECOGNIZED AND EXPERIENCED BEFORE LETTING ITSELF BE CONVERTED INTO A NEW ORDER."

Herman Heese

We were all packed and ready to go. Ready to get the hell out of Las Vegas. We each had a bag stuffed with belongings, and our beloved instruments. Av had to leave his amp behind, and was pretty bummed about that, though he got some cash for it. But I promised him I'd help him get a new one once we got settled. It was about time I got a new electric guitar as well. It was gonna be our first time traveling together, and we didn't know what to expect. Since we had found each other again, our lives had been overrun with sweet chaos, and we couldn't expect any less. Before we headed to the train station we had to make one stop. Avry wouldn't tell me what it was for, except that it was of the utmost importance. He led me to the spot where we first ran into each other.

"What are we doing here?" I questioned.

"Sit."

"Where?"

"On the ground, dick." So I sat down Indian style on the concrete sidewalk, and he did the same. He went into his army green duffle bad and pulled out his knife. The light reflected magnificently off of the five-inch blade, which curved to one side with two points slightly separated.

The handle was covered with scuffed black paint, with a picture of a half naked woman that looked like she stepped right out of a Greek epic. He huddled close to me to hide his actions, but no one seemed to care or even acknowledge our presence. "Give me your hand."

"What?!"

"Fine, I'll go first." He proceeded to slice the palm of his hand, fairly deep. "His face cringed, but he remained silent as he watched the blood deluge to the surface. "Now you." I stuck out my palm. Using his unharmed hand, he swiftly and sharply slid the blade through my flesh. I jerked back from the pain. He stuck out his bloodied palm, which was now almost covered in the crimson liquid. I grabbed his hand, placing my open wound onto his. We squeezed each other's tight. "Here we make a pact: to promise to stick by each other, always. To always know we can count on each other, through whatever curve-balls life throws at us. X, you're my best friend, my brother, my only family. *No matter what*, we always got each other. Forever."

"Forever," I vowed, and we squeezed tighter, both silently watching the blood make its way from our flesh onto the concrete.

As we entered the train station, we both had our hands wrapped in cheap tourist tank tops, and the slight blood stains were peeking through the white cotton. "So where to first, X?"

I looked at the map of the U.S. we had just purchased. "Well, Chicago is sort of along the way to New Orleans. Remember that little raver chick I met that was from out of town? I think her name was Madeline. With the short hair and funky glasses."

"Yeah, yeah I remember. Wasn't she like an heiress to some fortune?"

"I think so. Her dad left her a house and a shit load of money. She lives in Chicago and told me to look her up if I ever was in town. I know I got her number scribbled down in one of these damn books." The girl was cute but androgynous looking. She was in Vegas for her cousin's bachelorette party and we met at a bar. She wanted me to find her some K, so I did, and she kept giving me some for free all night. We hooked up in a drug-induced blur, and she seemed to really take a liking to me.

We hung out the rest of the time she was there, partying like crazy. She wasn't bad to hang with, and seemed to have a shit load of dough. I figured a contact in Chicago couldn't hurt. I found the number and gave her a call. She sounded ecstatic about the news. "Well, Chicago it is. I said as I hung up the phone.

No trains went directly there, so we had to catch a bus to Salt Lake City and transfer there to catch one to Chicago. We had popped some valerian root to help make the trip more bearable. The trip to Salt Lake City was not so bad, but from there to Chicago was around 32 hours. That ride seemed endless. In the beginning we were all fueled by anticipation, but soon cabin fever began to take its place.

We were about two hours from our destination and Avry was passed out and was drooling all over himself. I just sat there, people watching, wondering the destinations of everyone around me. I kept envisioning my own version of everyone's life story, and how the rest of it was going to play out. It was easier to envision anyone else's future than my own. But I liked it that way. Kept the element of surprise. As long as I had my brother by my side I didn't care where I ended up, or what happened to me. Eventually I drifted off to sleep.

I opened my eyes to find myself in the center of an empty train. The lights were flickering on and off, and the train was at a stand still. I could hear the pounding in my heart as I slowly stood up. I looked all around me, overwhelmed with disconcertion and fright. I started to walk down the aisle, checking the other cars. Not a soul in sight. I called out Avry's name but my cries made not a sound. I turned to look behind me, and I was greeted by that old shriveled face: my grandmother. She was wearing a long black cloak shadowing her face, but still revealing her eyes, which were as black as night.

As terror pulsated through my body, she opened her mouth as to let out a scream, but not a sound was heard. But behind her a fierce fire rose, and the glass windows busted inward, shattering glass all over us. I jumped and ducked from the impact, but she just stood there, silently screaming. I started running the other way, but with each step, a window around me busted in, launching shards of shattered glass all over my body. I used my arms to shield my eyes, and ran all the way to the last car, where there was a large door. I opened it and jumped out to find myself inside an endlessly dark tunnel, with the only sound being my heartbeat echoing at a mega volume.

I started walking, not knowing or seeing where I was going, sliding one hand along the slimy walls in an attempt to have some sort of direction. Suddenly, there appeared to be a faint light flickering at the end of the tunnel. I kept walking, trying to reach it, but the more I walked the farther it seemed to be. It grew colder and colder, and my body started to shiver and my teeth chatter. My heart grew weary and my legs grew tired, until I could walk no more. I collapsed to my knees, bereft of all hope of ever escaping the darkness. I buried my head in my hands and sobbed, and the breath escaping me left little clouds circling in the freezing air.

As the sorrow drained me of all remaining energy, I felt a warm hand touch my shoulder. I looked at the hand, but quickly grew fearful when I saw an old woman's wrinkled fingers. But just then the light grew brighter, and I looked up to see that the hand belonged to another woman. She was dressed in a white cloak, and I could not make out her face, but felt a certain comfort and familiarity from it. As the light and the warmth grew more intense, I soon recognized her. It was the old woman who was preaching to me in the street. She was smiling, and reached out her other hand to help me to my feet. I became blinded by the ever-growing light, and as I climbed to my feet...

"X, wake up!" I opened my eyes to find Avry standing in the aisle shaking me. "We're here." The train was still cluttered with travelers. I rubbed my eyes in an attempt to shake my previous visions, and began to gather my belongings. "Dude, what were you dreaming about? You were tossing around moaning."

"Oh...I...I can't remember."

"The bleeding stopped," Avry said as he showed me his bare palm with a blood encrusted line across the center. I took off the shirt from my hand and tossed it on the seat.

"You're just gonna leave it there?" he asked, and I shrugged.

As we stepped into the station, Madeline was there waiting for us with two of her friends. One was female, the other male, and all three were dressed in the same rave style: huge wide-leg pants that were all torn at the bottom, and tee-shirts with cartoons on them. Their wrists and necks were decorated with homemade, colorful plastic jewelry. Madeline's hair was shorter than it had been, now bleached blonde. She had a labret piercing and wore thick black pointed frames. The other girl was homely looking, but somewhat cute. Her pink streaked hair was fried from years of dying, and was pulled back messily in a ponytail. She had pink plastic plugs in her ear and a tiny pink stone in her nose. The guy was some kind of Hispanic, a few inches over six feet, super skinny, with messy curly brown hair. Judging from his feminine mannerism and appearance, I could tell he was gay. Madeline approached with a warm and welcoming hug, and I attempted to return it. After all, she was going to let us crash at her house.

"I'm so glad you're here! I didn't think I'd ever see you again." I smiled an insincere smile, but she bought it. I felt a bit awkward. She had obviously felt a lot stronger toward me than I toward her. Avry picked up on it and made a face. "This is Michelle, and Chris. Guys, *this* is Xavier," she said my name as if they had been waiting to meet me for ages. I introduced Avry, because she forgot to do so. "So how long you guys in town for?"

"Not really sure yet," I answered.

As we started walking to her car, Avry whispered, "Yo, what did you do to this chick? She's like in love with you."

"I know. Shit, I didn't even sleep with her." We piled in her big blue van. The outside was covered in multicolored stickers and the interior was covered with all types of furry and colorful decorations.

"It's like rave central in here, huh," Avry remarked, picking up a big Care Bears stuffed doll that was belted in to one of the back seats. They all laughed.

"You guys have never been to a rave, huh?"

"Nope."

"Well, you'll have to check out one while you're in town. They are a blast. Good music, good people. Oh, and I always have some kick ass party favors." Free drugs. I was sold.

We went straight to her house. She lived in the North Side, not too far from the Chicago River. As we pulled up to her house, me and Avry were greatly impressed. "You live here alone?" I questioned in amazement.

"Nope, these two live with me. It's too big of a house to be in all by myself. And my brother stays here when he's not at school. Listen, we thought you guys would probably be beat from the ride, so we figured we'd stay in tonight and just have some people over."

"Sounds good to me," Avry said, and I could tell he was already plotting on Michelle by the exchanging of glances and smiles.

The inside of the house was even more impressive. The floors were marble, and the white of the walls seemed to sparkle, as two beautiful classic paintings nearly six feet tall hung by the entrance. The living room was to the right, with furnishing that looked like it belonged in a medieval castle. Everything looked way too perfect to even touch, like it was just a display in a museum. And the entire place was spotless. I figured she must have had a maid come in, because there was no way a party girl such as herself would be motivated enough to keep that place so clean. The second floor was visible from the entrance, with a golden-hued banister being the only means of separation. As I stared up at the huge sparkling crystal chandelier hanging above my head, I asked "What did your father do?"

"He made boxes."

"What?"

She giggled, "He owned a company that made boxes for corporations that manufacture designer brands, like perfume and stuff. He started out with one machine in his garage, and turned it into an empire."

"So do you own the company now?"

"Most of it."

"What do you have to do?"

She smiled, "Basically, not a damn thing." Singed from a slight case of envy, I gave a half smile.

As we caught notice of naked stone cherub spitting water out from his mouth by the bottom of the winding staircase, Avry whispered, "You need to marry this broad."

She led us up to the guest room, which was bigger and better than any bedroom I had ever had for my own: cherry red wood furniture in perfect condition, books of various genres filling the cherry red shelves, a 32-inch television in the corner, and a wall covered with mirrors. "I hope this is okay," she remarked, and we chuckled. As we noticed a poster shrine to some young and attractive male celeb we didn't recognize, she stated, "Michelle usually stays in here, but she's gonna crash with Chris."

"She could stay in here," Avry remarked with a smile as he put down his stuff. She smirked at his comment. "Where's the bathroom?" he asked. "I desperately need a shower. My ass smells rank." She led us down the hallway and opened a door to the baby blue bathroom with gorgeous ceramic tiles covering the walls. As me and Avry ran our fingers along the walls admiring the texture, she opened the huge shower doors, revealing the four spouts in which the water shot out from.

"Wanna tour of the rest of the place?" she asked me, and I nodded. She showed me Chris' room, which was completely covered with sports paraphernalia, as well as swimsuit models. Completely thrown off by the extreme heterosexual male ambiance, she quickly cleared up my confusion. "This is my brother's room. Chris just uses it when he's not around. Otherwise he crashes in my room or the basement. My brother would flip if he found out. He's a complete homophobe. He'd probably be afraid that he'd be poisoned by gay residue. You don't have a problem with gays, do you?"

I laughed, "Not at all."

"Good, cause I swing both ways," she said with a wink. She led me to her father's room. It had an Asian motif, but very simple, almost peaceful. The bed was king-sized and very low to the floor. "Daddy loved Japan. All these knick-knacks he either bought there himself, or had 'em shipped. And that's Charlie," she said, pointing to a bonsai tree on the dresser by the window. "Daddy loved that tree so much. I come in here to water him and occasionally use this bathroom, but generally I don't like coming in here."

"What happened to your mother?"

"They split up when I was really young. She was just a gold-digger. They signed a pre-nup, and when she realized she wasn't going to get any money out of Daddy, she soon faded out of me and my brother's lives. It used to bother me, but I've worked it out in therapy. Dr. Shultz says sometimes you gotta just let go of things you cannot change."

"You see a shrink?"

"Oh, yeah. Dr. Shultz is my godsend." We walked down in the other direction of the hallway. "Here's my room." It too was tremendous. It was colored purple and mauve, and the bed was elevated higher than the rest of the room, with two steps leading up to it. Shear fabric hung from the ceiling encircling the bed, which was covered with stuffed animals. "I collect dolls from around the world," she said, referring to the shelves filled with beautifully handcrafted porcelain dolls of different ethnicities. One could've gotten the impression that a young girl still lived in that room, but definitely a young girl who had a very rich daddy. "You know, you could probably crash in here with me," she said, looking at me with dream-like eyes.

"That would be fine," I replied, as she bit her lip. She wanted desperately to kiss me, and she seemed like a girl who always got what she wanted. We started kissing, and as I my hand began to find its way up her shirt, we were interrupted.

"Ahem," Chris was standing at the door with his arms crossed. "Sorry to interrupt, I know you got a lot of catching up to do, but I just wanted to know what was going on for dinner. I'm starved."

"Let's order some Chinese."

"I can't find the number," he replied. Madeline rolled her eyes as she left the room to go fetch the number. As we walked out of the room, Chris flashed me disapproving eyes. I tried to ignore it and followed them down the curvy, carpeted staircase. But as I reached the top step, a still-dripping Avry bellowed from down the hall. I slipped away from the others. He stood in the guest bedroom's doorway, wearing nothing but a gold embroidered towel. "X, this place is outrageous. Can you believe this? And that Michelle girl keeps smiling at me. Yo, we gotta stay here as long as she'll let us."

"Xavier, what do you guys wanna eat?" Madeline's voice echoed from down below. The acoustics in that place were amazing.

"You, get dressed." And I scurried downstairs.

After some feasting and chatting in the L-shaped kitchen covered in stainless steel, we made our way down to the basement. "This is where everybody hangs out," Michelle said to Avry with a smile. And it was obvious. It was the only room in the house that was unkempt, with CD's, magazines, video games, and a huge variety of toys, some high tech, some simple, scattered about. The television was almost as big as the wall, and the stereo did not seem inferior at all. There was surround sound high up on the walls, along with two tremendous speakers in the corners of the room. There were three different types of video game systems to choose from, and an endless collection of games. The DVD and CD collection was of equal proportion, almost filling an entire wall of shelving. The walls themselves were covered in tripped out posters, red Christmas lights hung along where the ceiling met the walls, and glow in the dark stars flooded the ceiling. In the center of the room hung a gigantic disco ball. "This room is awesome to trip out in," Michelle commented, still seeming to be speaking to only Avry. There was a huge sectional black leather couch, a massive pile of fluffy multicolored pillows forming some sort of seating area, as well as several bright beanbag chairs.

"Pick a seat," Madeline requested. Avry made a flying leap onto the pillows. Michelle accompanied him, and he jokingly began to smother

her with a pillow. They seemed so comfortable with each other. But then again, that was how Madeline was when I had met her. I plopped on the couch, and Chris sat not too far from me. "There's a stocked fridge over there if you're thirsty," Madeline pointed out. The doorbell rang, and she quickly scurried upstairs before getting a chance to sit down.

As she left the room, Chris shifted his eyes to me. He didn't say a word, just flashed me a dirty look. I couldn't figure out his problem, but didn't wanna make a scene due to circumstances. I tried to ignore it as I began to rummage through her movie collection, and Avry and Michelle continued to play like children on the floor. Madeline soon returned with two guys and a girl. Two of them carted that same rave style, while one guy was dressed all in black, still with huge wide leg pants on and plastic jewelry, but with a gothic twist. He was covered in piercings and a tattoo peeked out from beneath his sleeve. Finally someone who wasn't overly bright and looking like a walking cartoon character. She introduced everyone and they all picked a spot to sit. My guess was that they were all a bunch of rich kids who had too much money and time on their hands. I felt out of place, but tried not to think about it. Madeline went inside her Care Bears book bag and pulled out a Ziplock bag full of tiny white pills. She proceeded to walk around the room and feed one to everyone. When she got to Avry, "What is this?" he asked as he examined the pill.

"Ecstasy. You guys never tried it, right? I think I remember you saying that."

He turned to me. "Hey X, this is the stuff that makes everyone look like invalids, right?" I nodded. He looked at Madeline. "You know, we always made fun of the people on this shit. Their eyes rolling to the back of their heads, chewing their lips, rubbing their legs. Like friggin' retards." The whole room gave him a nasty look for his comment.

Michelle pinched him, "C'mon, try it. It makes *everything* feel really good. And things that already feel good, feel even better." She gave him an insinuating smile.

"Fuck it," and with that he popped the pill into his mouth. He suddenly let out an angry yelp, "Ugh, this shit tastes fucking disgusting!"

"Yeah, that's why you're supposed to swallow it, not chew it."

"Ick! Why didn't you tell me that?! Holy Shit!" He grabbed a nearby soda, which belonged to Chris, and chugged it. Chris mumbled something to himself and rolled his eyes. When Avry tried to give it back, Chris told him to keep it, with a disgusted look on his face. His behavior was starting to piss me off.

"Well, it will hit you quicker now that you chewed it," Madeline stated. She then walked up to me and stuck out her hand with the pill sitting in the middle of her palm. "For you." I grabbed it and popped it my mouth, and she handed me a bottle of water to wash it down. "Everyone, set your clocks." And, completely in synch, all her friends looked at their chunky kiddie watches and clicked a button. "These are strong, it should only take a half hour, most forty five minutes." She looked at me and Avry. "Make sure you drink plenty of water, you don't wanna dehydrate. There's plenty in the fridge."

We all sat, flipping through the gazillion stations, tapping our fingers and waiting impatiently. I watched the giant clock with oversized digits that hung above the TV, counting each minute. Precisely 38 minutes later I felt a sudden tingly rush begin to sweep through my body. My sight started growing fuzzy and my head began to lean back. "Oh shit," Avry called from beneath the pillow masses, "I think mine's kicking in!" Everyone agreed. After a few minutes of tingly sensations, a feeling of nausea followed. I grabbed my stomach.

"Yo, Av," I called. He seemed so far away, "How are you feeling?"

"My stomach is hurting."

"Mine too." Madeline, who had been conversing with the others, sat next to me and put her hand on my leg. It felt like it weighed a ton. I tried to focus my eyes on her, "I think I'm gonna throw up," I warned. She smiled and put a little bin in front of me.

"Go ahead, you'll feel better." I leaned forward and water just poured from my mouth. Afterwards, I felt fifty pounds lighter. The fog grew thicker and the tingly sensation grew stronger. My body felt good.

I had somehow made my way to the floor. The lights were off, and the Christmas lights, stars, and black light posters were glowing in the background. My hands felt the need to fidget, so I was playing with some little doo-dad she had lying around. I was not very aware of anything or anyone around me, and really only cared about the colorful toy in my hand. Madeline saw my jaw was clenching and stuck something in my mouth. "Here, chew on this." I didn't know what it was, but it did the trick. I looked up at her with a great big smile and dopey eyes. "Do you want a massage?" she asked with the same wide smile and dopey eyes. Nothing sounded better.

Soon we were all sitting on the floor in a circle, everyone giving or getting a massage. It felt like the best massage I had ever received in my entire life. She made my body shake with pleasure, as my head rolled around in circles trying desperately to escape my neck. "Yo, X, you like it?' I tried to balance my head and find the source of the voice. When I noticed Avry looking at me, with Michelle's hands working their way all over his back, arms, and neck, I smiled and nodded. I watched around the room at everyone being so touchy-feely with each other, doing everything possible to make sure everyone was happy. "Do you need a pillow?" "Are you thirsty?" "Want some candy?" Everyone just seemed so in tune with each other. I felt in tune with Madeline, as her soft hands worked their way to my chest, under my shirt. The feel of her skin was so soothing and warm, I never wanted her to take her hands away. But to my displeasure, she stopped.

"I need some water!" she jumped up and ran to the fridge, and got sidetracked along the way by the other girl. I filled in her place, rubbing my hands up and down my own thighs. Just then the graver kid sat down next to me with a great big smile on his face.

"So, how are you feeling?" I gave him a thumbs up because words were too difficult. "So, I hear that you two, like, ran away from home or something." He seemed a bit on the feminine side.

"Yeah, something like that."

"Wow, that's so courageous." His eyes were barely open and through the fog it looked as if he were an Asian with three eyes. He kept talking and I just kept nodding, finding myself lost in the hard thumping beats blasting from the stereo, I looked up and it seemed as if the stars were pulsating to the beat. It was so beautiful. I was pulled from my peaceful gaze. "So I hear you got some kick ass tatts," the kid asked, still smiling. Without a word I took off my shirt. "Wow," he said as I gleamed with pride. "That's beautiful." He suddenly put his hand on my shoulder. "Well, I'm glad you're here." I looked at his hand, and was actually pleased it was there. Any touch felt wonderful.

"Me too," I responded, and at that moment I truly was. His hand was now massaging my inner thigh, and I didn't mind one bit. It didn't turn me on, just felt so good. It started moving up higher and higher, and I just fell backward, still shirtless, letting him continue. Right before it reached my groin, Madeline suddenly reappeared hovering above me. "Madeline!" I felt so unexplainably happy to see her, that I hugged her waist, reciting her name. I totally forgot about the kid's wandering hand, and he must've moved it upon her arrival. She squatted down and stuck out her tongue, revealing a tiny white pill resting on it. "Another one?" She nodded. I shrugged and sucked it off her tongue and chugged some water. I was so thirsty, I couldn't stop. And the water just tasted unbelievably good. So crisp, so refreshing. Then the graver kid popped back up in front of me holding a big shiny red box.

"Legos!" He shouted with such enthusiasm. He opened it and Madeline and the other guy friend began to jostle through it, collecting personal piles. Madeline grabbed a bunch and plopped them in front of me. "C'mon, it's fun." So, as I desperately tried to keep my head from wobbling, I started snapping pieces together constructing a shape. At that moment, Legos brought such an intense joy. I got lost in what I was doing and forgot anyone else existed. Soon I looked up and saw no one else was playing with them. Madeline and the other girl were bouncing up and down, dancing around the room to some crazy repetitive beat,

Avry and Michelle were playing with some kind of ball constructed of small plastic pieces that could expand to ten times its normal size, and Chris and the other guys were lost in conversation. I began rubbing my own legs again because it just felt so damn good. I stared back up at those beautiful stars. Madeline, sweaty and tired from dancing, walked up to me and stuck her hand out, "C'mon, dance with us. I love this song."

I shook my head. "I don't dance." I pulled her down. I wanted her near me and she was just so far away, so I told her so. She looked over at Avry. "Looks like those two are hitting it off." I nodded and smiled, but didn't care. I just wanted to touch her. She sat in front of me with her back turned toward me.

"Do me!" she requested, so I started rubbing my hands down her back. It felt like my hands were sinking into her skin. It felt almost as good as actually receiving the massage. The other pill began to creep up on me, and everything intensified by tenfold. Soon, without me even realizing, my hands had made their way beneath her shirt from the bottom, and I was rubbing her B-cupped chest. They then made their way down her flat but squishy stomach, to her groin on top of her pants, and back up again. I had her shirt pulled up in the back so that I was pressing my bare chest against her bare back, rubbing my face against her neck and cheek. Her skin just felt so amazing. The soft squeaks she was making sounded like music. I wrapped my legs around her and pulled her closer, softly kissing and licking her neck. I couldn't get her close enough. My hand wiggled into her pants. She was so moist, it felt heavenly, my fingers just splashing through her juices. If I could I would've put my entire body inside that warm sweet moisture. I didn't even realize it, but as I fingered her, I began humping her back. Suddenly my trance was broken by Chris' piercing voice, "Oh god! Get a friggin' room you two!"

She giggled. "Good idea." She pulled away from me and I whimpered like a baby. It felt so cold without her body close to mine. "I'll be right back." I pouted as she ran off, falling backward onto my back, staring up at the stars.

Finally, in what seemed like ages, she returned. She started to pull me to my feet. "C'mon."

"Where are we going?"

"Just follow me." As I staggered to my feet, I felt such a rush that I almost fell over. The room was spinning like a carousel ride. She walked up to Michelle and whispered something in her ear, and she got up and followed her toward the stairs. I walked over to Avry, whose face looked mangled, but happy.

"You going upstairs too?" He sounded like a lost child. I nodded and helped him to his feet, and we both almost toppled over. We wobbled our way to the staircase.

"Damn, X, where have you been? It feels like I haven't seen you all night."

I put my arm around him and we helped each other hold our balance. "I know! I've missed you." And right then I felt like I truly had. He grabbed my arm and looked at me.

"You know, I love you, man."

"I love you too."

"You are not allowed to leave my sight for the rest of the night. Deal?"

"Deal." We sounded like two little boys.

"Where are we going?"

"I have no idea." We clumsily followed the girls, who were hugging and almost skipping up the stairs, all the way to the second floor, and into her father's bedroom.

"Don't touch anything," Madeline whispered as if someone would hear us. We tiptoed through the room into the master bathroom. As we stepped inside, I felt like I was entering a palace. The beautiful cream-colored marble tiles and gold-plated plumbing shined with sheer excellence. I had to physically touch the wall tiles to make sure they weren't an illusion.

"I feel like I'm in Egypt," Avry commented, and we all agreed. In the center was a tremendous Jacuzzi big enough for all of us. It was already filled with steaming, bubbling water. The girls giggled and began to strip. Me and Avry followed their lead. I was still shirtless, but found myself having a bit of difficulty getting my pants off. The entire room was pulsating and my body felt so tingly. Madeline ran over and helped me. As she unbuckled my navy blue Dickies, I became fixated on her bare breasts. Like an innocent child, I started pinching and pulling at them, completely amused by their consistency and texture. She playfully shoved my hands away and stripped off my pants. In all the commotion, I had forgotten why I was getting naked. "Get in the tub, silly." And she led me in, where Michelle and Avry had already made themselves comfortable. As the hot water made contact with my skin, I felt like I was gonna implode. I settled in and felt weightless.

"This is amazing," I muttered and they all agreed. I had totally forgotten about the naked women around me. I laid my head back and let my hands and arms float to the surface.

"You know what's amazing?" Madeline said. "That you guys are here! I can't believe it."

"I know," said Avry. "This was the best decision."

"Definitely," Michelle remarked with a doofy smile.

Madeline grabbed my arm and I lifted my head. "I didn't think I'd ever see you again, Xavier. I hoped I would, but doubted it."

"Yeah, dude, she wouldn't stop talking about you when she got home. Till the day you called, your name kept being mentioned."

"Aww," I said like a lovesick puppy. "I thought of you too." I hadn't, but at that moment I really believed I had.

"Now you're here. It's like a dream come true."

"Totally" Avry said, squeezing Michelle, eyes rolling viciously. "God, everything just feels so right. You...me...here. I don't want to stop touching you," he said as he ran his hands across Michelle's naked body.

"You know what would feel really good?" remarked Michelle. "Kissing you!" And she and Avry passionately tongued each other as we looked on smiling.

Madeline looked happily at her friend, "You guys are so cute together!"

"Aww thank you, honey," Michelle said with a smile and stuck her hand towards her friend. Madeline pulled her close and then they suddenly began kissing. That caught me and Avry off guard, and suddenly hormones kicked in.

"Wow," said Avry, "I'm in a Jacuzzi in a mansion with two naked chicks making out. Pretty sweet." The girls were sensually hugging each other.

"Wanna see us do more?" Madeline asked. We simultaneously nodded.

"You guys first," Michelle ordered.

"What?!" Avry exclaimed. "I'm no fag."

"I'm not asking you to fuck him, just a kiss."

"No way," I chuckled.

"C'mon. What's the difference? You're best friends. C'mon." They both put on pouty faces. Madeline went to lick Michelle's chest but stopped, "Not until you guys kiss."

Avry looked at me. "Dude, I've never seen two girls go at it live. I don't care if you don't."

"Uh...Okay." It seemed like a normal thing to do at that moment. I was so fucked up, so I figured it would feel good. And I just felt so connected to him, like we could do anything. So I leaned towards him, clenched my eyes shut, and we kissed. It was sloppy and wet, and slightly awkward, but still had a pleasurable sensation. I jokingly pinched his nipple and he jumped back and we both started laughing.

"See, that wasn't so bad," Madeline remarked. She turned to her friend, gave her a big grin, and they viciously went at it, licking and fondling each other's entire bodies. My insides felt as hot as the steamy water. Soon Madeline had Michelle leaning up over the edge of the tub. Avry was kissing her as Madeline was licking and kissing her clit. I had always been more a hands on kinda guy, so I jumped in. I started squeezing Michelle's exposed chest, and licking her next to where Madeline's mouth was. As she moaned in pleasure, Madeline quickly pushed me away from the excited girl, and straddled me, with her tongue down my throat. As water began splashing everywhere, she stopped and whispered in my ear, "Wanna go to my bedroom?" And I nodded, too stuck to speak.

We stumbled to her room, butt-naked, dripping water on the carpet all along the way. We tumbled, laughing hysterically, into her bed. It felt like it was made of feathers. We started kissing, but I kept zoning in and out, and she had to repeatedly call my name out to make sure I was paying attention. Everything was just so foggy. She went down on me, and her mouth felt warm and wet like the inside of a squishy fruit, and I found myself laughing at my own metaphor. It was feeling fantastic, but I just couldn't get hard.

"I'm sorry," I apologized. "I don't know what's wrong."

"Oh, it's normal for guys when they are on E. These pills are strong."

"There's no way I'm gonna be able to have sex." Feeling a bit useless, I decided to pleasure her to make up for it. My pride was at stake, after all. So I kissed my way down her stomach and between her legs. She was soaking wet, but though I knew it would've felt amazing, I wasn't thinking of sex. I had to focus and keep myself from simply playing with the strange oozing orifice. So I kissed and licked, trying my damnedest not to drift off. She wriggled and moaned with delight, which enabled me to remember what it was I was doing. Finally she came, gripping onto my hair. The tugging felt like a massage and I just pressed my face against her groin. When I removed it, it was wet and sticky, and I loved it. I crawled up into her arms, and she smiled with satisfaction.

"That was so amazing," she whispered as she stroked the back of my neck. My ego was fed, because the task at hand was quite difficult considering my mind was floating in and out of consciousness. We lied there and she kept stroking my skin. "I can't believe you're here. I'm not gonna want you to ever leave." Her words felt as good as her touch. At that very moment, I never wanted to leave. "Do you believe in fate?" I nodded. "Us meeting, I think it was fate."

"Definitely," I said, feeling lost in the moment. I was so comfortable, it was ridiculous. She kept whispering sweet nothings; how she felt an insane connection to me, of how she wanted to know everything about me, etc... And I listened, enjoying every minute of it, agreeing whenever I felt it necessary. She insisted I go get my guitar, so I ran across the hall, still butt-naked, and grabbed it. Playing was difficult, but the music was like an orgasm in sound. I was too fucked up to sing, so I just strummed along, her eyes watching me in dreamy wonder. When I could no longer use my fingers properly, I put the instrument down and curled up next to her. "You're mine, Xavier, at least while you're here. Who knows, maybe you'll stay."

"I'm all yours, baby. I'm not going anywhere." I truly meant it while I was saying it. Eventually the fog overpowered me, and slumber, as well as her arms, held me captive.

I woke up with a pounding headache. At first I forgot where I was, and who the girl was laying next to me. Recollection soon came back as my energy faded away. I felt like complete shit. Everything hurt. Even my brain hurt. I climbed out of bed and let my legs hang over the side as I gripped my temples. I felt like I was decaying inside. Slowly the night began to come back to me. As I looked at Madeline still sleeping, all the wonderful things I felt toward her the prior night no longer existed. I couldn't believe how much I had wanted her near me, because at that new day I wanted to be as far away from her as possible.

I made my way out of the room and into the bathroom. As I sat on the bowl, pants up, head still between my hands, I remembered kissing Avry. My insides cringed at the awkward thought. It had felt so right then. Everything had felt so right. That fucking drug. It completely screwed with my head, inventing its own thoughts and feelings, and using my words to speak them. I probably would've told my grandmother that I loved and missed her if I'd had the opportunity. I wanted to throw up. Partially because my body was feeling nauseous, partially because I was disgusted with myself for falling completely under the drug's spell.

I remembered how retarded everyone looked, and figured I must've looked the same. I realized I was gonna have to deal with Madeline, who could have really meant what she had said, thinking I had too. I just wanted to run as far away as I could, but my body was having enough difficulty standing. There was a knock on the bathroom door. "One minute!" I shouted.

"That you, X?" It was Avry. I opened the door and pulled him in. "What are you doing in here?"

"Hiding."

"I feel like absolute shit. My entire body aches. Even my insides hurt."

"Me too."

"I'm really digging this chick. She seems to think I'm the sexiest thing she's ever seen. There's no accounting for taste. We tried to fuck but Mr. Winky wasn't cooperating fully, so it wasn't all that. But I did bust a nut, and it felt fucking awesome."

"I couldn't even do that. That second pill killed me."

"Shit, you took another one? Damn. Well, you looked like you were really feeling Madeline. You were all over her, and not just, like, in a sexual way. I've never seen you like that with a chick."

"It was the fucking pills."

"So you don't like her?"

"She's all right, but I dunno. I said some crazy shit to her. I was wrapped up in the moment. I didn't mean any of it. I feel weird being here now."

"So you wanna leave?" I did. I wanted to run from my stupidity. "Please, just give it a little longer. I never clicked with a girl like this."

"It was the drugs, Av."

"Nah, she was digging me before we took them." He was right. I had never seen a girl been so drawn to Avry before. It must've really felt good for him, so I agreed to give it some time and see what happened. I really believed the reason he was actually liking her so much was really due to the fact that she was feeling him. She wasn't that hot at all. She did seem kind of cool, though. I guess beggars can't be choosers.

"Ok, but no more E. At least for me."

"Maybe at the rave."

"And be like that in front of a whole bunch of strangers? God knows what I'll do. I kissed your dumb ass last night, for fuck's sake."

"Holy shit! I forgot about that." We both stood silent for a minute as the memory filled his head. "Yo...uh...let's just pretend that never happened." I agreed and we shook on it.

I walked back to the room because my body desperately needed more sleep. I climbed into the bed and Madeline wrapped around me. I didn't even want her touching me, but it felt as if I had no choice. I slowly inched away from her until I was mostly free, and I struggled back asleep.

For the next weeks, we hardly went out, only occasionally to a bar or a club, but she usually had the party come to us. I guess that was the benefit of having a place like that to yourself. I smoked a shit load of weed to keep me calm, and tried not to ever get too drunk because I was afraid I'd flip out on Madeline. She was all over me, constantly. Always hugging, kissing me, holding my hand. It made me wanna vomit.

I would've loved to explore the actual city of Chicago with Avry, but Michelle was attached to his hip, and where there was Michelle, there was Madeline. I actually liked Michelle's company more than Madeline's, but it could've just been because it wasn't me that she was all over. And Chris was never far behind. I felt like some demented version of the Partridge family. The sex was pretty good, but she just became so annoying afterward, wanting to cuddle and caress. Being touched in such a way by someone who I didn't want to be touching me, it made my skin crawl. I took my frustration out in the bedroom, with the sex getting rougher and rougher.

She would do anything I asked her, so I found myself asking her to do odd and degrading things to amuse myself. I'd use sheets to asphyxiate her, but she seemed to like it. Or at least pretended to. She had never tried anal, so I made her do it raw, and had her suck my dick afterwards. Things like that. She never questioned a request. Maybe it was exciting to her, or maybe she just wanted so badly to please me that she was willing to do anything to do so. The thought of it being the latter turned me off. Part of me knew it was wrong, but I just felt so resentful towards her, as it she was forcing me to stay there.

But I could have left whenever I wanted to. It was just that Avry had never looked so happy. He and Michelle were really experiencing what Madeline thought me and her were. And in actuality it was a perfect set up: two best friends dating two best friends. I just felt so fake, but I knew he'd do it for me. And it was kinda cool staying in such a luxurious place, and having absolutely everything paid for. As those notorious Chicago winds picked up a seasonal chill, she even took me shopping to get warmer clothes. She was my sugar momma. The idea of it was nice, but the reality sucked.

One plus was that she and all her friends loved listening to me and Av jam and sing, and at those moments I felt content there. It was those frequent occurrences which kept me sane. I didn't like playing for just her though, even though she always wanted me to, because I could feel her emotion towards me growing, like a tangible energy, trying to consume me. It wasn't that she was a terrible girl, it was just that she seemed too into me, trying to be whatever she thought would make me happy. Like a robot. But she seemed to be like that with everyone. She had so many friends, and was generous to all of them. She wanted to be everything to everyone. They all showed the greatest enthusiasm towards her in her presence. But I wondered if they'd be so enthusiastic if you took away the fancy house and constant drug supply. If there was nothing more to her than her herself, would anyone care then?

She would ramble on, telling me everything about her past, and I had to make believe I cared. She had a tendency to over-dramatize everything, like it was going to impress me. She wanted so badly to relate to me, so she made her life out to be this terrible tragedy, which often reminded me of Jack. I'm sure her life had its difficulties and pangs, but I couldn't understand people who longed for pity. My shit was fucked, but I never expected, nor wanted, anyone to feel bad for me. So I refused to share myself with her. I gave her little pieces of my life here and there, but she kept wanting more. It wasn't that I didn't trust her, or felt she would judge me. I just didn't *want* her to know. I did not want her pity. I did not want her thinking she understood me. She never would.

One morning, while I was by myself in the kitchen crunching on cereal, Chris walked in. He grabbed a bowl and slammed the cabinet shut loudly. He then slammed the bowl on the table, and proceeded to show his aggravation through his demeanor. I could feel his angry eyes watching my every movement. I finally couldn't take it anymore. "What's your problem, bro?" I asked, annoyed.

"Oh, whatever do you mean?" he said sarcastically, in his diva-like voice.

"I seem to get the impression that you don't like me," returning the sarcasm.

"Well, I guess you're not as dumb as you look." I clenched my fists. I wanted to belt him right in that snide mug of his.

Instead, I took a deep breath. "What the fuck did I do to you?"

"I think you're using my friend. A poor little homeless punk hit the big time with Madeline. You and your friend are taking advantage of her, and I don't like it one bit."

It took every ounce of self-control for me not to hit him. I didn't wanna be there in the first place. We were just fine without her and her money. He continued, "I see you roll your eyes when she hugs you. Poor girl, she's oblivious, but I'm not."

"Oh yeah, and what exactly are you doing here? Do you even have a job?" I barked.

"I'm in between bartending jobs," he said snidely. I laughed out loud. He got more angry as he went on, "For your information, I have my own money from my own family. I've known Maddy, like, forever. She was so crushed when her father died and begged me to move in. I don't need her house or her money. But you on the other hand, you don't have a pot to piss in. Where the fuck would you be if Maddy wasn't letting you stay here?"

"Me and Av were doing just fine."

"Then why did you come here? Stupid girl, always just lets everyone walk all over her. She's too generous for her own good. Why don't you do her a favor and just leave?"

"From my perspective, it seems like me staying here is doing her the favor."

"Oh, what, you think she needs *you*? Puh-lease. She can have her pick. I think she's just fascinated by you, God knows why. I guess you're just so opposite from her. She's always been obsessed with trash. Wanting to fix it up and make something beautiful out of it. But you, you're really not worth the effort."

"You're just a stupid fucking pillow-biter," I said ignorantly as I threw my bowl in the sink.

"You sly master of words!"

"Fuck you!" I yelled as I walked out of the room.

"You wish," he yelled back, needing to get the last word in. I charged upstairs, fuming. Who was *he* to judge my worth? He didn't know me from a hole in the wall. His opinion meant nothing to me. But still, somehow, his words caused me to realize that I had felt better about myself while living in a rundown abandoned building with a bunch of runaways, even while sleeping on a park bench, than I did there.

I peeked in Madeline's room to find her still asleep. I crept inside and plopped on the floor by the door, lost in thought. In reality, how *could* she care so much about me when she didn't really even know me? All she knew was what I chose to show her, and that wasn't much. We never really conversed, at least from my perspective. She just spoke and I tried to listen, answering with concise responses when necessary. All that was left was the physical. Could someone be so attracted to someone physically that their mind simply transforms it into something more? I had found women beautiful, but left it simply at that. What forces someone to take it further, what causes them to believe it is anything more than raw lust? As I searched deeper, I began to think that Chris was right, that I in fact was just her project. I probably wasn't worthy of such devotion.

Me and Madeline were lying together in her bed watching TV. My focus was on the movie on the screen, but hers was on me. "Xavier?" I wanted to ignore her, but I knew it would be impossible.

"Yes?"

"You can stay here as long as you want. I really don't mind. I know Michelle doesn't mind." I thanked her and continued to stare at the moving pictures on the screen. "Xavier?" I sighed. I knew there was no way out of the conversation. I looked at her, as she said in a soft, emotional voice, "I think I'm falling in love with you." My heart missed a beat. "I know it sounds crazy, but I can't help it. I hope you'll be able to let me in one day. I would never hurt you. I don't know, but in my heart, I feel like you could be 'the one.' I don't expect you to say it back, I just wanted to let you know." My hard exterior softened. There was so much sincerity in her eyes. I knew she truly meant it. There weren't many people in the world who felt like that for me and in my heart I knew I should not take that for granted. I desperately wanted to feel it back. I wanted to look at her with those same eyes she was giving me, with that same intense energy, and tell her that I loved her. But I couldn't. I just didn't. I kissed her forehead and pulled her close.

Time passed and she fell asleep, but I just lay there staring at the ceiling. I couldn't understand how one person could feel so strongly for someone and the feelings just not be reciprocated. How could someone feel like I was 'the one,' the person they were meant to be with, and I not feel anything similar for them whatsoever? Was it me? The strongest I had ever felt for a girl in that way was for Veronica. My heart had let her go a long time ago, and though it hurt at first, it wasn't much of a struggle. So in my mind, if I could let it go so easily, it couldn't have been love.

But here was this girl who felt this insane connection to me, but in fact it was just all in her head. People mold reality to fit their perception of what it should be. But then again, maybe she really was falling in love with me. Who was I to say anything on a subject I knew nothing about? In the past I had never longed to know and feel romantic love. But lying in her arms, seeing her look at me in such a way, I desperately longed to understand. Maybe it was I who could never understand her. Either way, feeding my utter selfishness, her words felt good.

We were getting ready to go to a rave. A couple raves had passed and she had been begging me to go, and I had fought it, but finally caved. I was getting annoyed of her pestering me about it. Her favorite DJ was scheduled to be spinning at this one in particular, so she was even more annoying about it.

I didn't wanna go. My nerves were on edge and part of me just wanted to get on a train and flee, with no warning, just leave. But I knew such a suggestion would never fly with Avry. The girls were busy applying all their glitter and beaded jewelry, filling their little backpacks with candy and E toys. I had on a pair of ripped jeans, a studded belt, and a faded black tee with a white DARE logo.

"You know what it's gonna be like, Av? A buncha colorful bouncy boys and girls doing their little raver bop throwing sparkles on everyone. Everyone overwhelmed with fake love and happiness, feeling themselves up and everyone else around them. And fuck, can you really stand that music? It all sounds the same, like a power drill driving through your skull. Madeline is always trying to play some "sick" tracks for me, but I can't tell the damn difference."

"It does get pretty annoying."

"I'm not going," I snorted.

"Why?"

"Cuz I don't want to."

"I don't really want to either. But I promised Michelle I'd check it out. C'mon dude, don't leave me hanging. It's a new experience."

"You guys ready?" Madeline's voice called from downstairs. Avry questioned me with his eyes, and I rolled mine.

"Yeah," I called back.

I was quiet the entire ride there. I felt like I was trapped in a tiny white room with four walls closing in on me. I had left home so that I wouldn't have to answer to anyone, let alone some girl. But I felt like I owed her something. Not because of what she was doing for me financially, but because she cared so much about me. And I hated her for it. Funny, I was deprived of love growing up, and now that there was someone who felt that way for me, I wanted to just throw her away. But I couldn't leave, not without Avry.

When we walked in the venue, the initial appearance was just as I expected. The flashing lights were making circles in the huge open area. The beat was hard and fast and nauseating. Excited that they had gotten by security with their drugs, the others scurried to the bathroom to pop their pills. I wanted nothing to do with that drug. Neither did Avry, which offered me some sense of relief. But I really didn't wanna be around a buncha E-tards. Me and Avry made our way to the bar. It seemed like no one was drinking alcohol, but that didn't stop us. We bought beers with the fake ID's Madeline had conjured up for us, and chugged them down fast. He decided he wanted to go find Michelle. I stayed put, and kept drinking.

A girl wearing sparkly nylon wings scurried by, offering me lollypops. I gracefully declined. Everyone was so happy to be there, like they were experiencing some great salvation. I just kept drinking. Madeline came over and started dragging me around, introducing me to faceless people. I smiled and nodded and immediately forgot their existence. "I'm gonna dance," she said, and I made my way back to the bar. I drank some more, watching her. She was a good dancer, totally letting the music take her over. She looked so beautiful right then. So free. I couldn't understand. Why didn't I want her? I couldn't figure it out. But I just knew I couldn't make myself. I looked at her and I felt angry. How could I be angry at someone for loving me?

I decided to look for Avry, but when I found him he was busy making out with Michelle. I looked at them and became envious. I wanted to feel what they were feeling. Two people sharing the same energy, melting into one another. The only thing I could relate to that was lust. That I knew. But there had to be something more. Something I just didn't get. I grabbed another drink and went into the upstairs room, which was playing a type of music called jungle. I could tolerate that music more because it wasn't so repetitive. And the dancing was way more creative. I was impressed as I watched people pop and slide all over the floor. Some were even break-dancing, something I had always found fascinating. And the style of dress was not so far off from mine.

There was one girl, she was dark skinned, either Hispanic, black, or mixed, with long dirty blonde dreads, baggy jeans with her boxers peaking out, a tiny black tank top, flat and tight pierced belly, and tusks in her septum. She moved so fluidly to the music, each body part having its own motion, as her head swayed about, her eyes closed tight. It was like she actually was the music in tangible form. It was so erotic, I started to get hard. I leaned against the wall, sipping my beer, and just watched her every curve flow with the rhythm. Lust. That I knew. The song changed and she opened her eyes, breaking that musical bond. She stuck out her tongue in exhaustion and started to walk towards the wall to the bench beside me. We made eye contact, her eyes being a beautiful honey brown, as she sat down to catch her breath. I just kept drinking.

"This DJ is tearing it up! What's his name?" It took me a moment to realize she was talking to me. I looked down at her, her flawless skin covered in a layer of well-earned sweat.

"I'm not sure."

"Oh, okay. I'll find out later."

"You're an amazing dancer."

"Huh?" The music was blasting, so I repeated myself. Fully aware of her talent, she gave a cocky smile. "Thank you! This music, it's like a drug to me. It takes me over. Do you dance?"

"Nope."

"Then what are you doing here?"

"This is actually my first rave."

"Yeah, what do you think?"

"I like this room," I said with a flirtatious smile. Picking up on my insinuation, she blushed.

"God, it's so loud over here. Follow me." She led me down the hall to an open lounge area, where all the walls were covered with beautiful graffiti burners too complex to read.

"Sorry, it's just impossible to hear anyone in there." She plopped down on this big red couch that barely had any springs left. I sat next to her, sinking in. The room was filled with kids on E, K, and whatever else, massaging each other, blowing bubbles, and using glowsticks to trip each other out. "A bunch E-tards, huh?" she commented.

I laughed, "Yeah. Everyone just looks so ridiculous on that drug."

"Yeah I know. Shea," she stuck out her hand. "My name's Shea, by the way."

"Xavier." We started bullshitting and forty-five minutes later we were making out. No one around seemed to notice. It felt good to touch a girl other than Madeline, to smell the scent of an unfamiliar female. To wonder what she tasted like. She wouldn't let me put my hands down her pants, but I kept persisting. I just wanted to taste her. Just as I was about to fulfill my conquest, I felt cold water sting the back of my head, splashing onto the girl. We leaped up from the cold shock to find Chris standing there, arms on his hips with this angry, yet satisfied look on his face, and Madeline running in the other direction.

"I knew you were a worthless piece of shit," Chris barked snidely and walked away. I just froze. His words invoked visions of my grandmother's face, mocking me.

"Your girlfriend, I presume?" the annoyed girl remarked as she tried to shake off the water.

"No."

"Well, whoever she is, she seems pretty pissed. You should probably go after her."

"Yeah." So I got up and went to find her. I caught a glimpse of her running toward the exit. I called her name, and she stopped in her tracks. I didn't know what to say to her. I didn't wanna say anything. I wanted to just leave. But I knew that was the pussy way out. I stood behind her in silence, picking my brain for something worthwhile to say.

"How could you?" she whimpered, without even looking at me. "How could you lie in my bed and hold me just last night, then make out with someone tonight, at a place *I* took you?! I even bought you the damn ticket!" I still could think of nothing. I knew the truth would not help the situation. "So have you been using me? Is that it? You just needed a place to stay?" Still no response. "I've done everything I could to make you happy. God, I'm an idiot. How could I think you'd ever love me? Am I not pretty enough?" More silence. "Dammit, say something!" She finally turned and looked at me.

"Uh...something?" I half smiled, but she didn't find it amusing. "I...I don't know what to say. I didn't mean to hurt you. It just happened."

"That's it? That's your excuse?" That was the truth. I wasn't thinking about her when I was fooling around with that other girl. I guess that was the problem.

"I never meant to lead you on. I never wanted a relationship. I just wanted to check out Chicago."

"So it was never about seeing me. Then why didn't you tell me that?"

"I thought I had made it clear." I really did. I told her we were coming to Chicago. I never said we were coming to visit her. I never said I expected anything more. She just offered and I accepted. It's crazy how two people could look at the same situation and see it in two completely different lights.

"Well, you have to pack up your shit and get out of my house. C'mon, we're leaving. The others will find a way home."

"I'm not going without Avry." So we went to find him.

"What's wrong?" Michelle asked worryingly.

"Xavier has made it pretty clear he doesn't feel for me the way I feel for him. We're gonna get outta here," she was choking back tears. I just stood there, emotionless.

"We'll go with you," Michelle said, flashing me a dirty look.

We sat in silence the whole way back to her house. I felt a tremendous sense of relief. No more pretending. I figured it was time to move on. I figured Avry would want to stay, and as much as that thought hurt, I knew I had to go. Avry followed me to the guest room as I began to pack my clothes. "Where you going?"

"To New Orleans." I was so caught up in the moment. He started gathering his belongings too. "What are you doing?"

"Going with you."

"What about Michelle?"

He shrugged. "You planned on just bouncing without me? What the hell is wrong with you? Forever, remember?" I smiled. The unanticipated response brought such a warm comfort. "There will be other girls," he said, trying to convince himself. "It just felt good, you know, having someone look at me like that."

Madeline entered the room. She handed me two hundred and fifty dollars. Overwhelmingly thrown back, "What's this for?"

"I know you have no money. I wouldn't be able to sleep knowing you were roaming the streets without a penny to your name," she said, teary eyed. That made me feel terrible. After what I had just done to the girl, she still cared.

We all sat in the car ride in silence. Michelle was with Avry in the back, and they sat quietly holding each other, and I could see tears running down Michelle's cheeks though the rear view mirror. Avry caressed her hair, kissing it softly, trying desperately to keep composure. I glanced over at Madeline. Tears were running down her face as well, but she kept wiping them in an unsuccessful attempt to hide them. Finally the silence was broken, "You know Chicago is a big place. You don't have to leave the city just because you aren't staying with me." I could hear the pain in her voice, tinged with regret. She didn't want me to go. Despite everything, she still didn't want to let me go. Deep inside she must've been hoping that I wanted to stay. That maybe she could still convince me to love her. Fucking hope. I didn't know what to say. I didn't want to hurt her any more, but I just wanted to get as far away from her as possible. "I... just wanna get out of here." Not the right words. Madeline choked back her tears, took a deep breath, and said not another word.

six

"TEMPTATION USUALLY COMES IN THROUGH A DOOR THAT HAS DELIBERATELY BEEN LEFT OPEN."

Arnold Glasow

We sat half asleep at the train station, waiting for the next train out, which was heading to Tennessee, and figured we'd get a connect toward New Orleans there. I just wanted to go. When Avry hugged Michelle goodbye, I could have sworn he was going to cry. She was hysterical, begging him to stay. Despite his nonchalant attitude, I knew he didn't wanna leave her. I knew he was just doing it for me. But I can't say I wasn't happy with his decision. As he laid with his head back, eyes half-way closed, I turned to him and said, "Thank you for coming with me. I'm just so used to people...walking out. I've just kind of come to expect it. But you...you stayed. You don't know what it means to me."

"Don't worry about it, man. Seriously." But I couldn't help it. After what Chris had said to me in the kitchen and at the rave...his words stripped me of the sense of confidence I had achieved. I had once again proven my family right. But by Avry coming, it meant that I must've been worth something for him to wanna stick around. I felt like I should've felt guilty for hurting Madeline, but I didn't. It wasn't my fault that I didn't share her feelings. Why should I have felt guilty for something I had no control over? Maybe I went about it the wrong way, but the end result would have been the same. If no matter what you do, someone is gonna get hurt, is it that important to how you do it? Would it have hurt her any less if I just said, "Hey, Madeline, I really don't wanna be with you." In my mind I figured that would've hurt her more. At least the way it ended she could just walk away thinking I was an asshole and be glad she was rid of me. And what I was doing to her was far worse than me kissing some other girl. I was allowing her to believe in something that never existed. A lie. At least now she could see it for what it really was. See me for what I really was. Maybe she was having better luck at that, because I really didn't have a fucking clue.

"You know, all that kiddy candy raver shit was a bit much. Sometimes I felt like I was a pedophile." He was still trying to convince himself.

After some silence, "Hey Av, are you in love with Michelle? In all honesty?"

"Nah...well, I don't know. Maybe. But it doesn't matter."

My insides sank. "You don't ha..."

"Shut up, I already made my decision. Like I said, there will be other girls." He sounded so convincing, but I could see through his mask.

"Av, what makes a person fall in love? I mean, is it a conscious decision? Does a person get to choose?" I wanted to understand.

"No way. If that was the case then there would be no broken hearts."

"Is your heart breaking?"

He looked at me with an intense glare in his eyes, "If I tell you no, will it make you feel better?" I lowered my head in shame. "Look, X, I'm not gonna resent you if that's what you're worried about. I did consciously choose to come with you. I'll be fine, dude. I've been through worse. Besides, I know you would've done the same for me."

Either Avry was a great actor, or he had an amazing ability to repress. We were joking and laughing on the train as if it had never happened. Sometimes I'd see him wander off somewhere in his head, but when he saw I noticed, he'd pull himself right back. But, despite his efforts to hide it from me, I noticed him caressing the blue and yellow beaded bracelet wrapped around his wrist.

When we hit Knoxville, Tennessee, we decided to get out and hit up a bar. We wanted to get back into tag-team mode. I needed to snap him out of his hidden funk. We wandered into to a redneck bar not far from the station. Bad decision. They took one look at us in there and wouldn't cease their stares. The bartender wouldn't serve us, so we got pissed, leading to a violent outburst. Bottles and fists flying. I could've sworn Avry knocked one guy's eye out of its socket. But soon we were surrounded. We stuck by each other's side and just charged like raging bulls, making our way through. And once we were on the run, there was no catching us. Avry too was blessed with quick feet. The whole experience was a much-needed rush. When we finally stopped running, we felt exhilarated, and through the aching, we couldn't stop laughing.

After that, we decided that we wouldn't get off the train until we reached our destination of the Big Easy. The anticipation of arriving in that notorious city grew with each passing hour, especially after talking to several travelers who told us their drunken tales of Mardi Gras. After much day-dreaming and jamming with other musical nomads in nearly empty train cars, I realized that my purpose in this world was to create as much as possible, in every way, shape and form, my predominant medium being music. My ability to create was all the proof I needed that I was worth something. This was heightened by the fact that anyone who was in the car listening to me play would come up to me, young or old, letting me know that I had "incredible talent," never seeming annoyed by the melodic noise I was creating. And I never got tired of hearing it. Whether I would make money from it was not significant. Ideally it was an appealing notion, but it wasn't my motivation. The sting of Chris's words began to melt away.

When we finally arrived in New Orleans, a whole new world opened up, and it was love at first sight. Virgin eyes to the city were unable to see the evils it held.

There were so many others like us: new arrivals. All planning on just a temporary visit, not knowing they would never leave. I remember meeting an old man there a few days after our arrival, who said, "Be careful boys, if this city wants you, it'll keep you." I brushed him off as just another crazy old loon.

Avry landed a bartending gig, and I found a job at coffee shop. I didn't mind it because I got to eat for free. They had these little sugar-coated pastries called beignets that became one of my major food groups. We found a small two-bedroom, roach-infested apartment right outside the French Quarter. No matter how hard we tried, we couldn't get rid of the little soldiers. At least they weren't the size of the tremendous fuckers that dwelled in the Quarter. It didn't really bother me. I finally had a room that I could really make my own.

I didn't have much money for fancy decorations, so I just stuck to basics, like posters, my artwork, and the artwork of some of the incredibly talented starving artists who filled the streets of that city. There was one painting I stumbled across of a man playing a saxophone, with a night scene of the city behind him. The music he was creating was symbolized by colors and shapes. There were many paintings I saw with similar scenes, but there was just something about that one in particular. It was so vivid, you could actually feel the music, through which you could understand the man's pain. It reminded me of myself when I was playing the guitar. And to think, I only paid ten bucks for it. Right beneath where it hung on my wall, I finally took out Dani's picture and set it out for display. There was no need to keep her hidden anymore.

I learned that I was more of a slave to my desires than I had ever expected I would be. The alcohol was everywhere, and so cheap. For a dollar you got what looked like a bucket of beer. They had this drink there called a Hurricane. Liquid poison. And they were definitely not stingy with quantity. They even had *drive-through* daiquiri shops. That city could turn the pope into an alcoholic. We were amazed at how you were allowed to drink in the streets. People ventured around the French Quarter blatantly fucked up and nobody gave a fuck.

In the beginning, we'd hang around the bars on the infamous Bourbon Street. That was where Avry's job was. But that was also where all the ignorant drunken tourists were. Despite the fact that it was nowhere near Mardi Gras, horny out-of-staters would walk around with beads, screaming at every girl they saw to show them their tits.

Many complied, and that was always fun to watch, unless it was a fat sloppy redneck. Sometimes the guys would even whip out their shit for some horny ladies. But the constant odor of puke, the rude rednecks, and puddles of slushy grime became too much, and we found that the bars on Decatur were more our kind of scene. They were mostly filled with locals, and freaks of all kinds.

Sometimes we'd just drink and wander the Quarter, or sit and jam out in Jackson Square Park, next to all the tarot readers, artists, and street performers. I'd strum along as some crazy guy on a unicycle would juggle bowling pins in front of a fascinated audience. A gypsy would be telling an amazed visitor all her future's secrets from the lines on her palm. On the corner, a man painted completely silver would pose perfectly still as a confused passerby would examine him, wondering if he was actually real. On the other corner, several children would stick bottle caps to their shoes and tap away, capturing the hearts of older women. The punks would scream out for change for beer, cursing anyone who would not exhibit generosity. The wannabe vampires would creep by, with their dental acrylic fangs, some actually implanted into their gums, living out the daily lives as if they were truly part of some Ann Rice saga. And in the middle of it all were me and Avry, watching, absorbing, joining in whenever it seemed appropriate. It was more than we could have ever expected, and we couldn't tell whether we should've been proud to be a part of it, or be running for our lives.

With the alcohol came the drugs. Soon I made the right acquaintances, and learned that liquid acid was flowing like water. I did it several times. Avry was terrified of that drug, and I didn't wanna do it around anyone else, so I did it alone, and had a blast. The Quarter became like a giant playground. Everyone there seemed out of their minds, so no one could even notice that I really was. Colors leaking from the sky, every movement being followed by a smudged prisma-colored trail. It made me feel like I was losing my mind. One time I spent what felt like hours chasing the moon thinking it was a giant fire in the sky. I'd get lost in these weird circles of thoughts that were going nowhere but seemed so important at the time. I thought I was having great epiphanies but when I came to I realized they made absolutely no sense. So I decided that was enough of acid, it wasn't for me. Ecstasy was everywhere as well, but I refused to go near that drug again. So I kept searching for a better high. I loved GHB when I tried it, but kids started to OD on it left and right, so it became hard to find. So my search continued.

After only a month there, Avry told me I was starting to slip, starting to lose control. "You can't let the drugs control you. It's all good as long as you are the one in control."

"I am," which we both knew was a lie, but I was good at denial. Drugs, alcohol, and sex were my masters, and I was a good slave, enjoying the ride, in exactly the right place.

There were strip clubs on just about every damn corner of the inner part of the Quarter. Some were little shitholes with strung-out chicks trying to support their habits, some with more classy, superbly-fine, silicone-filled women. I just viewed such places as wallet-draining teases. But Avry seemed to love them.

He became addicted to this one place in particular. He would go in right before work, and for what he thought was a decent price, one of the girls would take him to the back and suck him off, pretending that she thought he was the hottest thing she had ever seen. I couldn't understand paying for sex, but then again, I never had a problem getting any. He was always pestering me to go with him, and finally I agreed. There was this one brunette in particular that he had been raving about. She wasn't the type of girl to go to the back, so that made him want her even more. After an hour there, she sat next to me and started flirting, as all strippers do. They are all such amazing actresses. But then she offered me a free lap dance, which turned into three. She slipped me her number right before the last song ended.

When I told Avry, instead of resenting me like most would, he patted me on the back and said, "Good job, killer," with a sincere grin. Sometimes he amazed me. No matter what, he never resented me. I got him fired from a job he loved in Vegas, but he never resented me. We'd walk into a bar and every girl he would point out would end up flirting with me, but still, he never resented me. It was because of me that he had to leave the one girl who ever really cared about him, yet still, he never resented me. He never took that bracelet off, and occasionally I'd catch him caressing the smooth beads, day-dreaming of what could have been. He never mentioned a word of such thoughts to me, so as to make sure that I would not feel badly about it, and I pretended that it went unnoticed. And he never resented me for it. As soon as we stepped outside of the club, I threw that number out.

It was a rainy September night, after a kick ass party in the warehouse district. I was coming down off of speed when me and Av headed over to this guy's place with about five other people. Meeting people to party with was never a problem in that city. We sat around a nearly crumbling coffee table and hit some nitrous. I was flying, completely content with my current state of existence. Then she came in, and rearranged everything.

Five foot nine, thin as a rail, bright fire engine red hair that was shaved on the sides but hung down to her ears from the top, pale skin, patches of light brown freckles on her cheeks, blue eyes accentuated by the dark circles around them, large poutey lips (blow job lips as me and Av would call them), tattoos, several piercings – a medusa, two hoops in one nostril, and a lip ring on the opposite side. She had not a drop of makeup on, and not a drop was needed. She was wearing a homemade skirt held together by safety pins, black construction boots with different-colored laces, black and white striped knee high socks sticking out beyond the boots, and a tiny white tank top with no bra. I was immediately hooked.

She was with another girl, as skinny as she was, and they both came in and sat down on the floor by the TV. The two of them chatted and giggled amongst themselves for a while. I watched her every move. Her smile contained crooked teeth that gave the illusion of natural fangs. "The red head?" Avry whispered in my ear, noticing my fixated stare. I nodded. He passed me the blunt. I took my hits then called to her.

"Hey, wanna hit this?"

She turned and smiled. "Yeah, no doubt." She retrieved the phillie with her bony fingers, brushing against mine in the process. Her nails were short and bitten, with traces of black polish. I tried my hardest not to get excited as she brought it to her mouth, wrapped her sexy full lips around the tip, and sucked in a full load of smoke, slowly releasing it into the air. But once she repeated this process, my attempts failed.

"What's your name?" I asked.

"Delia. This is Ginger," and she pointed to her dark-haired emaciated friend, who waved.

"I'm Xavier, this is Avry."

"Cool." She took an extra hit before passing it to her friend. "I haven't seen you around here before." Her voice was coarse and scratchy, though very high pitched, reminding me of the sound of ice cubes crackling against a splash of warm water. Sexy as hell.

"Me and Av moved to New Orleans just recently."

"Cool." She turned back around and faced her friend.

I pursued on. "Are you from here?"

Her attention quickly shifted back to me. "Been here for three years, moved here from Cincinnati, but I'm originally from Detroit." Another wanderer. We started to swap travel stories. She slid over by my chair and we got stuck in conversation for hours. People came and went, and the sun shone bright, but we wouldn't have noticed. I studied her face like a mystery. When she laughed, she would squeak and her eyes would squint up. She would chew the inside of her lip when she was trying to remember something. All the smalls thing I took notice of.

Apparently she had been on her own since she was twelve. She had this rough, don't-take-nobody's-shit persona, but with a sweet charm that was incredibly alluring. Her almost curve-less body still had an extremely sensual appeal. It was almost difficult for me to look her straight in those clear baby blues, which was an unusual occurrence for me. The first place I always looked at a person was in their eyes; they reveal so much about a person. So many people's were empty, holding no new discoveries. But hers ran so deep, I was afraid of getting completely submerged in them.

We got into the topic of tattoos and shared our own with each other. She had a lady bug on her neck right beneath her ear, a vine with purple flower buds wrapping around her ankle down to her toes, and Celtic tribal across her lower belly beneath her pierced belly button, and a black red nautical star on the inner part of each of her forearms. I told her I was dabbling with the idea of getting a tattoo gun. "Cool, maybe someday you could hook me up with one."

"No doubt," I automatically replied.

"Okay, but you better go and get good first. I'll fuck your ass up if you fuck up on me. Seriously," she said, followed by a sweet giggle and devilish smile.

The room was empty except for the host who was busy playing video games, me, Delia, Avry, and Ginger, who Av was trying to get on. Somehow, a while back, the conversation had switched to drugs, when, "So, do you wanna get high?" Ginger proposed. Delia giggled.

"I am high," Avry remarked.

"I'm not talking about weed." The girl replied as Delia giggled some more.

"What you got?" I asked.

"I don't know if they'll be down for it," Delia said grinning, eyes focused on mine.

"I'm down for anything," matching her stare.

"Dope," the chick responded.

"Well you said you weren't talking weed, so dope as in heroin?" Avry questioned with an arrogant tone.

"Yup."

"Hell no! Fuck that." He sounded offended for being offered.

"How about you, green eyes?" Delia held that same smile. I peered over at Avry, who was monitoring my every move.

"Nah, no thanks." I wanted to say yes. Every bone in my body wanted to say yes. I had never tried heroin, but I had always secretly desired to.

I was aware of its evil. I had met my fair share of junkies. I saw how it completely destroyed a person. If the devil was real, he existed in powder form. But it still drew me in with its seductive temptation. At that moment I knew the devil was standing right before me, whether in the little baggie or in the flesh of a blue-eyed girl.

Realizing the hesitation behind my declination, Delia remarked, "You don't have to shoot it, you know, you could just sniff it." Those eyes.

"That's some shit," Avry mumbled under his breath, but loud enough for everyone to hear. "You girls must be pros at this, huh?"

"No, it's not like that," Ginger replied.

"Just an occasional party favor," Delia added. Avry chuckled and mumbled some other crap while shaking his head. "Let's go to the bathroom," Delia beckoned and the girl followed. Delia's skirt slid up as she stood up, revealing little white cotton panties with cherries on them. Suddenly I was ripped away from my lovely fixation.

"Bullshit, those bitches are junkies. I bet you the wind could blow them over."

"I don't know. But that one has really caught my attention."

"That bitch is bad news, X. I'm telling you, it's written all over her." He could tell his words made no difference. "It's on you, bro. But don't say I didn't warn you. She's a fucking junkie. Just don't go in there without battle gear. But, shit, man, if you fuck her you'll break her in half. You like that look?"

"It's sexy on her."

"Whatever you say." She finally returned, eyes more sunken, smile wider, movements slower.

"Bye guys," her friend called out. Avry gave a nod.

"Bye," I responded. Delia smiled at me and waved, and with that, she was gone. I wanted to go after her, but I didn't have a clue what I would say. I just stared at the door.

"Fuck them." Avry interjected.

The next couple of weeks I managed to save up for a tattoo gun. I knew a guy selling one cheap, with a shit load of packed needles and ink. Avry was the first person I tattooed. Around his wrist, I drew this tribal of his choice. It was nearly flawless. "Do you like this city?" he asked as the needle traced the stencil along his wrist.

"Definitely. I like it a lot here. I definitely wanna hang here for a while."

"Really?" He was surprised. "I don't know, man. There's something not right about this place." He was right. New Orleans had a strange power about it. There was more beyond the fierceness of its temptations. The air there, it seemed to be saturated with the miseries of those lost, who wandered the streets reminiscing of what it was they once searched for. It would follow you wherever you went, lurking in the shadows. You could either get absorbed in it, or run from it. Avry knew which way I was heading, but I convinced my subconscious otherwise. "I don't know how long I'll be able to stay here."

"Well, I'm out when you're out. But could we please stay at least a month more?"

"A month, I think I can manage."

I tattooed myself next; a spider on my foot. It came out looking so realistic that it was scary. Me and Avry showed my work off, telling people about other fictional characters that I graced with tattoos as well. Word spread, and people started to request tats. They were paying shit, but it was still a cash flow.

One night, coming home from work with two busty strippers and this other dude, I saw her, Delia, in Jackson Square Park. Her hair was all shaved down to peach fuzz, except for two long chunky pieces in the front, similar to the Chelsea style. She had on tight red plaid bondage cutoffs, and a halter top showing her flat pale inked stomach. Once again, no bra. "Hey you," she said with a smile.

"Hey!" I stopped as the others kept walking. They eventually stopped and waited impatiently.

"Fancy seeing you 'round here," she said playfully. She had a bit of dark make up smudged around those eyes, making them even more striking.

"Yeah, I'm coming from work."

"Oh, well I won't keep you," she looked back at the people waiting for me, turned back to me and winked. I smiled. The other guy called out to me, as the stripper I had picked tapped her foot. "Better get going, handsome," she whispered. I smiled, and began to walk toward them, turning around to catch another glimpse of her, she doing the same. Suddenly, "Hey Xavier!" She remembered my name. "There's a show Saturday night upstairs at the Palace. Band called Brainwashed. Some friends of mine. Come check it out." It was phrased more as a demand than an invite.

"Yeah, I'll be there," I immediately answered, not aware of my pathetic desperation.

I was buzzed even off such a short interaction. That girl was seeping with sensuality. It wasn't just her looks, though she was absolutely beautiful. It was the way she carried herself: how she moved, the way she talked. She had this confident, flirtatious aura about her. When I returned to the others, my buzz was shattered. The girl I was with looked pissed. "Is that your Tuesday girl?" she asked sarcastically.

"Oh, stop that shit." I smacked her ass, and we continued to walk.

"What band?" Avry asked with intentions of coming with me.

"Brainwashed," I didn't want him to come because I didn't want him to see the actual reason I was going.

"I think I heard of them. What do they sound like?"

"I don't know."

"Are they any good?"

"Don't know."

"Then why you so anxious to see them?" So I told him my reasoning. "Oh, I see. Play with fire, my man, and you will get burned."

"Her friend will probably be there."

"Not my style." Then to my surprise, "I think I'll just stay home tonight." I was glad. I didn't want him there, watching my every move.

"Okay, I'll catch up with you later."

The place was pretty packed. A few familiar faces, but none the one I wanted to see. Compelled by the music, I started dancing in the pit, the healthiest release of aggression. Several songs later, sweaty and out of breath, I stepped out.

"Hey." I was startled by a poking in the side. Delia was standing behind me. "You like the music?" Those front pieces were bleached blonde with pink tips, and the peach fuzz on her head was pink as well.

"Yeah, they're fucking awesome."

"The singer is my ex." She turned and focused her attention toward the stage, smiling at him. I could tell her little comment and gesture was made to see my reaction. That girl was a catalyst, which drew me in even more. She then jumped in the pit and started dancing. Her little skirt went up and down, and her loose, barely-there breasts bounced. I wanted her badly, right then and there. I went to the bar to regain my composure.

Two bourbon and cokes later, "Taking a break?" she asked, glistening with sweat.

"Thirsty." She smiled and walked away. I saw what she was doing. She was gonna pop up by me now and again to see if I'd follow, or just for the pleasure of teasing. She went around to several groups of people, mingling for but a minute, then moving on. But she kept shifting her eyes to me, even when she was in the middle of a conversation. I knew how to work such a female; I was no amateur to the game myself.

I started to mingle as well. Conversations erupted, flirtation occurred. I would wait a while to see if she noticed, and sure enough she did. Aware of each other's methods, we acknowledged each other's glances rather than pretending they went unnoticed. At the last song of the last band, she swerved up to me, "So whatcha doing after the show?"

"That depends," then I downed my drink.

"On what?"

"On what there is to do."

"A bunch of us are gonna go hit up this bar on Royal."

"Sounds like a plan."

"Meet you outside in a few." And so I did.

There were about eight of us altogether, and we all began to walk to the bar. Me and Delia lagged behind, caught up in conversation. "So how was the other night, Don Juan?" She gave a little sarcastic grin.

"Not bad."

"Oh yeah? Which one was yours?"

"The brunette."

"Good taste."

"Yeah, but that was then."

"And what's now?"

"I'm not exactly sure, still working it out." We eventually hit the bar. It was a tiny place and full of people. We could hardly hear each other.

After a couple of drinks and vocally strenuous, though entertaining, conversation, "Wanna go someplace quieter?" she asked.

"Where did you have in mind?"

"My place."

We took a cab over to her apartment, which was located in a really shitty part of town. It was a tiny one-bedroom apartment, messier than me and Avry's. She shared it with another girl and guy, but she said hadn't seen them for days. There was no TV, just a tiny boom box of a radio, and she threw on a hardcore CD. "So I take it you've been fantasizing about me," she commented as she began to roll a joint.

"What brought you to that conclusion?"

She started licking the paper. "I can see it in your eyes, the way you look at me. Like the sight of me has triggered some twisted fucked-up fantasy and it keeps replaying in your mind."

"A little sure of yourself, aren't you?" She laughed at my comment. "So you can see all that in my eyes?"

"Yup," she said confidently as she slid her leg close to mine. She lit the joint and blew smoke right in my face. We chatted as we sucked the joint down to a roach. There was never a moment of uncomfortable silence. After some good conversation, sacrcastic jibes, and a whole lot of laughter, she said with a smile, "So you ready to get really high?"

When she came out of her bedroom, she was carrying a little black box. She emptied its contents on the rug where she sat: three hypodermic needles still in their packages, a lighter, a bottle cap, a tourniquet, a little bottle with a dropper lid containing water, a few bags of, according to her, top grade heroin. She started to mix up her concoction. "You are a pro at this," I commented.

She smiled. "No way. Seriously, it's not a habit. It's just a coincidence that both times I've hung with you were the right occasions." I doubted that, but I tried not to let it plague my mind. She lit the lighter under the liquid in the bottle cap, then pulled it into a fresh needle. "Stick out your arm."

"What happened to sniffing it?" My nerves started to kick in. The questions of "what if I did too much", and "what if I liked it too much," entered my mind.

"You could do that, but you're totally getting gypped." There was a moment of silence. "Look, this is a new rig, never been used, so you don't have to worry about that." I stuck out my arm. She placed the needle in her mouth as she tied the tourniquet around my arm. Our eyes were focused on one another's, and a smirk remained on her face. As she pulled it tighter, with the whole scenario of what was going on, and those hypnotic eyes of hers, I began to get extremely turned on.

As my vein elevated with an appetite, she plunged the needle into it, then released the dragon. A warm rush spread throughout my entire body, like a cozy blanket covering me from reality. I fell back. I watched through the fog as she proceeded to shoot herself up. It was the most erotic sight. She then fell next to me. This gave new meaning to the phrase "comfortably numb." Everything felt as if it were the way it should be, her body laying next to me. She put her hand in mine. I turned and submerged myself into her stare. Face to face, so close, it felt as if our energies were flowing into one another's. And it wasn't only the drug. It was her.

She smiled, and then we kissed. No kiss had ever tasted so sweet. It started off slow and sensual, then went sort of violent, like we were trying to choke each other with our tongues. I was enjoying the sexual aspect of it all, but in no way jonesing for sex itself. It didn't feel possible to get hard. I felt good enough anyway. Then an epidemic of itching spread throughout my entire body. I had to halt the kiss and attack the enemy. She laughed, "The itching is a bitch at first, but it gets bearable the more you do it."

Sunlight woke me up. I was lying on her living room floor, shirtless. There were two guys and a girl going about their business, stepping over me. The light burned my eyes as I sat up. They all acknowledged my presence with either a "hey" or a nod. Delia exited the bathroom, newly showered, her pink, nearly bald head shining in the light from beads of lingering shower water. "Hey you," she said when she noticed I was awake.

Suddenly I became overwhelmed with an uncontrollable urge to vomit. I dashed for the bathroom, just making it to the toilet. "Not again," she giggled. As I hovered over the toilet, the night slowly came back to memory. I was basically in and out of consciousness the entire night. I didn't remember what we talked about, but I did remember a lot of laughing, rolling around, and of course that amazing warmth. We didn't have sex, I was sure of that. We did lie and caress each other's bodies for a while. Hence the missing shirt. And I remembered several trips to the toilet to puke.

As the morning nausea began to cease, a strong sense of a foreign feeling spread through me. At first I thought it was the remains of the heroin, but than I realized what it really was: happiness. Just the recollection of the night spent with her, and, of course, my new favorite drug, brought me what I believed to be happiness. And it wasn't like the E. It felt real even when the drug was gone. I should've known right then and there that I was doomed.

I pushed myself to my feet and left the bathroom. There was a round of introductions. Apparently they were all her friends, who had decided ten a.m. was a good time for such a social call. I spent the rest of the day with her. All of us ventured back to the Quarter. Me and Delia kept getting caught up in our own private conversations, once again. When we started to talk, the rest of the world seemed to melt away. “Hey, listen,” I said, “What we did last night, I can’t be doing that a lot.” I still had some sense in me.

“Yeah, I know, of course not.” She had such conviction in her voice.

“Cool, as long as that’s understood.”

“I told you, it’s not a habit or anything.”

We started to spend a lot of time together. My head had become completely full of her. No other female had ever had such an effect on me. When I wasn’t with her, I wanted to be. I would drive Avry crazy with, “Delia this,” and “Delia that.” Everything reminded me of her. I loved that she was so unpredictable, and I always anticipated what she was gonna say or do next.

I wanted to know everything about her. And I wanted her to know everything about me. I felt as if she could truly understand me. I knew that was a lot for both of us, but I was sure it would happen in due time. I could just freestyle songs endlessly for her, both instrumentally and vocally, only stopping when my fingers cramped. She completely consumed me; an unquenchable thirst.

The first time inside of her, it felt as if I was being welcomed home. Her bare skin pressed against mine felt so right. I wanted to know her body, inside and out. When she wrapped herself around me, I fell into her. She told me that she liked to be dominated so I pinned her down so hard she had bruises on her wrists. She begged for me to choke her, and as I did, we came simultaneously. The ultimate relief. I had had my share of women, but no woman ever felt like that. And then I said it. As we lay next to each other, sweaty, satisfied, lost in each other’s eyes, I said, “I finally understand.”

“Understand what?” she asked, puzzled.

“Love. I finally get it.” If I could have, I would have had our bodies melt into one.

“Are you, sir, trying to tell me that you are in love with me?” She had a smile from ear to ear.

"Yes, ma'am."

"Say it. I wanna hear you say it."

"I love you."

"Say it again, but this time I want you to say my name."

"I love you, Delia."

She rolled onto her back and stared at the ceiling, closed her eyes and replied, "Aww, thanks." I saw her holding back a grin. I pinched her, hard. She giggled and rolled back to face me. "I love you too, Xavier. You belong to me."

"Oh, is that so?"

"Yup. And fortunately for you, there's no way out of this deal. So, now that we're all lovey dovey, get your ass up and make me a love song." Without hesitation, I complied.

Delia and Avry didn't mesh at all. He thought she was no good for me. But that aside, he said he just didn't like her as a person. She picked up on his negative vibes, and would say that he was just jealous of our relationship. "He probably wants you," she'd say, which I knew was bullshit. I wanted them to get along so badly. I couldn't understand how two people I cared so much for couldn't like each other. But whenever all three of us would hang, there would be this constant tension hovering around. I tried to hook him up with her friends, but he wanted nothing to do with them. I just couldn't get it. But it didn't matter. Nothing could pull me away from her. I wanted her more then I had ever wanted anything in my life.

seven

"We cannot in advance insure ourselves against the weakness or the malice of our free will."
Christian Encyclopedia

We'd just shoot up occasionally in the beginning. Always something going on that she labeled as a "special occasion." At first, I didn't notice her constant trips to the bathroom, pinned pupils, utter mellowness. But soon I began to pick up on it all, as well as noticing that her tracks never seemed to heal. When I would notice, I would want to be there with her, so sure I could control it. Finally it was at my request. "Let's get high," and so it began.

It started off as a trip to Utopia. Me and her, it was like some dark love story in the movies. Two twisted, fucked-up souls that connected on some intoxicating wavelength that no one else could reach. It finally felt like home. The dope accentuated the whole experience. A complete release from the dreary world around us. Not a worry in the world. She always kept my attention, which was a difficult feat. Most people bored me, but not her. She always kept me guessing. And she was always changing her look; new haircut, new color. She made most of her clothing, acquiring most of the basis of her designs from thrift shops, or just stealing some from laundromats. Sometimes she'd use materials like curtains or sheets. We'd spend hours constructing outfits. Together we could shoplift anything. We'd rack up so much at arts and crafts stores. Our only hurdle with stealing was our appearance. If we could tell someone was on to us, we'd either drop what we had, or make a mad dash, never to return.

Together we seemed to make every night an adventure. One night, after shooting up at her place, we decided that it would be a good idea to go creep through the cemetery. She was raving about how awesome they were, the graves being all above ground since the city was built below sea level. We snuck into the St. Louis Cemetery, giggling like children. She showed me the resting places of voodoo practitioners, pointing out the x's etched into their gravestones. "Hey, you ever do it in the cemetery?" she whispered. I shook my head with a smile. She grabbed my hands and led me to a flat, low grave, surrounded by higher ones that blockaded all sight of it. She pulled down her underwear and propped herself up on the half crumbling stone. She stared in my eyes, the moonlight reflecting in hers like a sparkling river, begging me to take a swim. I removed my pants, keeping her stare as I climbed up inside of her. The gargoyles watched in envy at us make love, as a corpse continued to decay beneath us. As we were getting ready to leave the cemetery, Delia noticed the entrance to one of the mausoleums crumbling apart. "Psst!" she called to me. "Wanna sneak inside?"

"I don't think we should."

"C'mon, this guy's been dead for over fifty years. I wanna see what he looks like." She broke inside as quietly as she could, and I followed her in. It smelled rank, like intense rotten mildew, and I couldn't help but gag. She seemed not to be affected by the stench. "Whoa!" she whispered. On top of a stone bench laid the remains of what used to be a man. There was no flesh, only bones, with tethered pieces of matted clothing. Her eyes widened as she looked on in awe. I stood by the door, feeling uneasy. "You gotta come here and look at this." As I walked over, my stomach turned. I had never seen anything like it before. I don't know if it was the stench, the sight, or the dope, but I was forced to puke. "Oh god," she laughed. Wiping my mouth, I took a closer look. It was unbelievable to think that those remains were once part of a walking, breathing man. She started to touch the bones.

"What are you doing?"

"Shhh. I wanna take a souvenir."

"Are you nuts? Don't you dare."

She didn't listen. She reached for the skull and pulled it from the rest of the body. It detached with just a little yank and a low crack, dust flying everywhere.

"Delia! Put that back," I muttered through coughs.

"Too late." She held it up to her face, closely examining it. "You're coming home with me, mister," and then she shoved it into her purple knapsack. Feeling the incredible urge to flee, I grabbed her arm to pull her out. As we exited the mausoleum, she pulled back to read the name of the deceased. "William, William Badeaux," she said aloud.

"C'mon." I dragged her along and we swiftly escaped the crime scene. When we got back to her place, she made a spot for that damn skull on one of her shelves.

When I told Avry of our adventure, he gave me the most disgusted of looks. "That's messing with some wrong shit. I don't know what's wrong with that girl of yours. That mother fucker is gonna haunt you."

She loved that thing, always calling it by name. She'd greet it whenever she entered the room, and said her farewells as she exited. I fucking hated it. In her twisted mind, she thought it was jealousy, but that wasn't it at all. Avry's words stuck. And I just didn't feel right having some strange dead man's skull looking at me, watching me get high, watching me fuck my girl. When we were in that room, with that thing there, I felt as if we were not alone. Like some unseen force was hovering over us. Always watching us. She told me I was just being paranoid, but I had the feeling she felt it too. I knew she did. Only difference was, she liked it.

She herself was a talented artist, but her specialty was constructing things out of so-called junk. She would collect things from garage sales, people's and store's garbage, or just steal a little something that caught her eye, whether it be from a person or an establishment. She'd stick something here, glue something there, and somehow found a way to make it beautiful. It was actually quite amazing. I jokingly nicknamed her the Trash Master.

When I got confident enough, I inked a large, intricate pair of angel wings on her back. It was my best work yet. She was so appreciative and proud, and went out and got a whole wardrobe of backless shirts to show them off. Staring at my artwork on her back as we fucked doggystyle was such a rush. And then, one dope-filled night, we heated the tip of a blade and seared each other's initials in the flesh of our inner thighs. To us, at that moment, we were conducting the most romantic symphony. We were binding ourselves together for eternity, forever to be a part of one another. We swore we'd never regret it.

Me and Avry were drifting farther and farther apart. "Can't you see what you're doing to yourself, what you're becoming? Ever since we got here, you've been losing yourself. And ever since you've met her..."

I didn't know what he was talking about. I was flying. So inspired, creating so much music and art. I felt as if she completed me, as if she could truly see me, and I her. She too had been alone the majority of her life. She spent most of her childhood in a trailer in Detroit. No father; he split before she was born. Her mother made the rounds, always dating scum. She never paid much attention to Delia, unless she was doing something wrong. So Delia started getting into as much trouble as possible, just so she could get the attention she so yearned for. But eventually her mom started to ignore all her behavior. And her mother was so open about her sex life and exposed Delia to sex at a really young age. Delia would often walk in the trailer and find her mother getting it on with some stranger, right on the couch. And her mother could have cared less; she just kept on going, screaming at her daughter to scram.

People ended up labeling Delia based on her mother's actions, automatically figuring "like mother like daughter." Since Delia was being labeled as such, without even having had sex yet, she thought to herself, "fuck it." She lost her virginity at twelve, and admitted she had been promiscuous, but I didn't care. Shit, look at my sexual history. But one day some guy she had been messing with called her to come over for a "party." Turned out the only ones at that party were him and four of his friends. They attacked her, and she was too weak to stop them. When she told her mother, the woman just told her to keep her mouth shut and not cause any drama.

That was when she left. Robbed her mom blind and hopped on a bus. She moved around a lot, spending a lot of time in the Midwest. She said she did what she could to get by, having started to strip at the age of fifteen. She told me one story about when she was working in some club in Ohio. They pretended they didn't know she was underage, but they knew damn well. One day a hideously fat and dirty excuse of cop came in as a customer and took a fancy to her, he too knowing full well that she was a young one. He wanted to take her to the back and have his way with her, but she refused. Turned out the club was paying off the cops because they were running a drug ring, and as long as the money came in, the corrupt cops didn't care. So as not to ruin their set up, her boss dragged Delia to the back and the power-hungry cop started to rape her. She managed to get a hold of his gun, and shot him in the leg mid-thrust. Still pointing the gun, she grabbed her shit and ran out, threatening to shoot anyone who got in her way. She fled to the nearest bus terminal, ditching the gun in the process. That was one of a billion stories.

Like me, she had whole lot of acquaintances and party buddies, but not many people she would call friends. Actually, she had no one she would call a true friend. Not one since she was nine, when her only real friend was killed by a drunk driver. She had no one who ever really cared about her, gave a shit if she lived or died. But I did. She knew it. And she didn't want to lose that.

One day, while she was at the store, I just couldn't take it anymore. I sat at the edge of the bed, doped out, glaring into those empty eye sockets. I could have sworn he was laughing at me. I went into the kitchen and grabbed the rusted frying pan, and smashed that bastard into skull bits, put the fragments in a plastic bag, and threw him in a garbage bin outside. It felt great. When she got back, she immediately asked, "Where's William?"

"He started acting up, so he had to go." She wouldn't speak to me for the rest of the day. I spent the next few days working with a local street artist, creating a stone skull as a replacement. I made a little plaque and wrote "William II." She smiled when I gave it to her and I hoped all was forgiven. But she still held some bitterness, and knowing that drove me crazy. I asked if there was any way for her to truly forgive me, and she decided that I should get a tattoo of a decaying skull on the side of my thigh, in memory of William. So I complied, wanting desperately to please her.

No one ever thinks it will get them. You start off using sparingly. Then it's a few times a week. Soon you find yourself using just about everyday. Then, one morning you wake up and feel like complete and utter shit. Upset stomach, cold sweats, unnecessary panic. You figure, "Shit, this sucks. I should just get high, you know, to take away the pain." Then everything is perfect. Never been better. Then everyday, same story. Soon you can't get through a day without it. Can't function until the dope-thirsty veins are quenched. It's the first thing you think about when you wake up, the last thing on your mind before you go to sleep. But as long as you constantly have it when you need it, you're okay.

For a while, that's how things were. We were both making money, managing to work while being high. I was still working at the same coffee shop, and she was working as a shot girl at a bar on Bourbon Street. We'd give ourselves just enough to make it through our shift without getting too fucked. It seemed like a package deal. I was maintaining pretty well, but I noticed she had started to slip. She had been living like that for a while. Too long. If only I wasn't too high to see my future in her eyes, maybe I would've been able to save myself.

She was working, and I was hanging around with some guys in Jackson Square. One turned to me and asked, "So what's up with you and Delia?"

"Why?"

"Just wondering, I've heard some stories about her."

"Like what?" He was drunk and willing to talk without inhibitions.

"Just that she is into some evil shit."

"What kind of evil shit?"

"I don't fucking know, that's just what I heard. Maybe Satanism or some shit." I tried to laugh off his remarks. But I was infected with curiosity about how such rumors came about.

The next time I saw her, "I heard some shit about you."

She was braiding the front of her blue streaked hair. "Like what?"

"That you're into some evil shit."

She cracked up. "Oh yeah, and who said that?"

"People."

"Oh, I see. Well, people are idiots."

"Well, where did they get that idea from?"

She sighed, stopped braiding, and turned to me. "When I first got here I hooked up with these guys that were all into Satanism. You know anything about that?"

"Not really."

"Well, summed up, it's basically the worshipping of the self. You are your own god, everything that happens to you is in your own hands."

"Makes sense."

"Yeah, but these guys were all about it. It was a complete religion for them, and I'm not one for religion, so I cut them off. I guess that's what 'people' were talking about."

"Are you into black magic and shit?"

"I've dabbled, but I'm not into it anymore. I found a more direct way of doing the same type of thing. Think of it more as the ability to manipulate. If you can break into people's minds, you can get them to bend to your will." I smiled. "You would totally get off on it. We should play." Things took a very dark turn at that point.

After watching Natural Born Killers way too many times, we decided to try a similar threesome. We found a girl at a local goth club who said she'd be down for some games with us. I had threesomes before, but none of the girls ever mattered. I asked Delia if she was sure she would be able to handle it, and she assured me she was. We went back to Delia's place. We tied the naked girl up, and she watched as me and Delia went at it. Then Delia went over to the girl and began to touch her, putting on a show. The girl was gagged. The exhibition was getting me so excited, I thought I would burst. Delia called me over as she removed the gag from the girl's mouth. I stuck my dick down the chick's throat as Delia licked, nibbled on, and fondled the girl. But our eyes were locked on each other the whole time.

There was a brief moment when I took a look at the girl, bound and nude, sucking me off. Then my eyes shifted back to the beautiful creature wrapped around her. It was an incredible sight. But something seemed wrong, throwing the whole spectacle off. The girl was enjoying herself. She wanted it. She liked being tied up and degraded. That made it all wrong. She wasn't supposed to want it. She wasn't supposed to get off on it; only we were. Noticing this, I no longer wanted to keep up with the charade. I busted a load in the girl's face, and got dressed. Delia noticed the sudden change in attitude.

"What's wrong?" she questioned as the girl looked on, confused, yet satisfied from the face-full of cum.

"Nothing." I didn't wanna explain.

"I know something is, so just spit it out. You weren't enjoying this? I thought you would. What is it, does it bother you seeing me touch her?"

"No, not at all."

"Then what?" I kept trying to avoid answering, but she pressed on.

The girl repeatedly called out in the background, "Hey! Hello? Could you guys untie me?"

"Wait a fucking minute!" Delia screamed at her.

"Excuse me?" the girl said, copping an attitude.

"Listen bitch, I'm having a conversation with my boyfriend, here. If you don't shut the hell up for minute, I'll put this gag back in your mouth and throw you in the Mississippi."

"Fuck you!" the girl snapped.

"What did you say, you stupid bitch?" Delia went over and grabbed the helpless girl by the hair. "Don't you understand English?" As she pulled harder on her hair, the girl's eyes clenched in pain. An erection started to return. Delia released her hair as she flung her back. The girl's eyes filled with water, but she held back on the tears. The stench of her fear was turning me on like crazy. I threw Delia against the wall and we began to engage in an extremely violent fucking round. We fell to the floor by the girl, who could do nothing but watch. She started to mutter something. We paused, looked at each other, and acknowledged the same idea. Delia reached over and gagged the girl again. We both wanted to do certain things, but each of us wasn't sure how far the other wanted to go. I wasn't really sure how far I wanted to go. So we left it alone and continued on with each other. Once we were done, we untied the chick and we all left. The girl was completely silent as we parted. We never caught her name.

Delia's power of manipulation was strong, and she taught me well. Together, it seemed like we could make anyone do anything. The easiest targets for our games were the younger kids who'd hang around the Quarter. Some would wanna experiment with dope, so we'd help them, with the condition that they owed us one. Others just wanted to hang out with us, infatuated with me or Delia, or just wanted to be down with the older Quarter kids. They became useful on so many levels. Young impressionable minds, so easily swayed. First we'd give them a test; get them drunk, stoned, then convince them that some innocent passerby was trying to start with them. We'd make sure to pick someone around the same age who looked like they wouldn't just shrug off some punk kid getting in their face. Then one of us would say something along the lines of, "You're gonna take that shit? You can't let people disrespect you like that." Instigation. Persuade them to go kick some ass.

If they went to fight them, and the person backed off, or especially if our protégé won, we'd make them feel like gods, and I'd hook them up with a free tattoo. If they got in a fight and started to lose, we'd get their backs, as if we really cared for their well-being. Whether they lost or won wasn't the point. What mattered was whether or not we could convince them to try. After that we had them. They were "in" or so they thought. I was the big brother they always wanted, and Delia was the girl that they would masturbate to. We started to realize how little the limits were of what we could get them to do for us. We figured, why dirty our hands if we could get someone else to do the work? Vandalism, destruction, robbery – profits split with us of course. We made them feel like they were super villains. And they ate it up like starving strays. Some were latch key kids with families who neglected them. Some had just run away from home, had nothing and no one. We became the family they longed for. Lonely kids in a lonely world, desperate to feel wanted. A feeling I had seemed to have had forgotten.

"You know," she said as she stroked my hair, the sweet taste of H flowing through our veins, "no one will ever care for you like I do." I believed her words. "No one in this world gives a fuck about anyone else but themselves. Some just fake it better than others. They spend their lives wrapped up in trying to be an exemplary person, top of the ladder in civilized society, pretending they give a fuck about their fellow man, when in fact what they really wanna do to their fellow man is spit in his face, rip him off, and fuck his wife. Everyone wears a mask. But you see, we're different. We're beyond that, that's why we're superior. I looked my whole life for someone like me, and I've found you." She kissed my forehead. "There's no one else out there who can understand. They can't see you. But I can." I ate it up, forgetting about the one person who had once enabled me to see myself.

Me and Avry hardly saw each other any more. I was a different person, according to him. "I knew you were apathetic towards most things, but I didn't know you were born heartless as well," was his response when he heard one of our kids boasting about how he had helped us rob a drunken tourist couple.

"He's going around, shouting it all over town?" I was infuriated at the thought.

"Look at you, you don't even see nothing wrong with it. The boy's like, fourteen. What the hell happened to you? You're too occupied with your smack and that she-devil to give a fuck about anything else."

"You're just jealous."

"Jealous? Of what?"

"Of my relationship with Delia. Of what we have."

He became filled with anger. "Of your drug-induced romance with Rosemary's Baby? Yeah, right. I pity you, actually, for being so fucking blind. For having such wretched taste in women."

It was my turn to get angry. "How dare you talk about Delia like that? You know nothing about her, or us. You could never get a girl near her level."

"Fingers crossed." The expansion of my anger was visible. He looked at me and said, "What, you wanna hit me?" I wanted to. "Go ahead, Xavier," oddly using my full name, "hit me." But hearing him say those words, I knew it wasn't what I really wanted to do. I went to put on my shoes and get out of there, when he interjected, "I'm leaving here in a week." I paused and looked at him. "Don't look so surprised. That supposed month has been long passed. The only reason I was staying here was for you, and I never fucking see you anymore. I'm going to New York." He had made arrangements to leave without even discussing it with me. "You're welcomed to come with me, but I'm not going anywhere with that bitch." My anger resumed. I put my shoes on and walked out without a word, slamming the door behind me.

A week came and went in which I only saw Avry in passing in and out of the apartment. And, just like that, he was gone. So much left unsaid. I didn't want it to be like that, but our pride prevented us from caving. And there was no way I would leave Delia. I remembered a conversation we had, a few weeks prior to his departure, over a shitload of whiskey. "I miss you, man," he slurred.

"I miss you, too. We never hang out anymore."

"It's just I don't like seeing you all strung out."

"I'm not strung out."

"Whatever, man, that's not what it looks like from this angle."

"C'mon, dude, I don't want another lecture. Let's just chill. I'm finally happy, you know."

"Are you?"

"Yeah, man, I am."

"I wish I could say that's all that matters. Everything fades when the smoke clears. All that you're left with is yourself and the truth."

"Well at least I know I'll always have you."

As that memory plagued my brain, I walked into his bedroom and looked solemnly around the room. Empty. His posters were left half torn off the wall, as if he had done it in a fit of rage. I looked on the bed and noticed a cloth lying right in the middle of it. I picked it up to examine it closer. It was a white tank top with a blood stain in the center. The shirt he had used to soak up the blood from our pact. He had kept it this entire time. I looked at the scar on my palm. "So much for forever." I threw the shirt back on the bed and slammed the door. I choked back a tear as I filled the needle, and soon forever faded away.

eight

"AND WHEN THE LIGHT OF FAITH IS WITHDRAWN, THERE INEVITABLY FOLLOWS A DARKENING OF THE MIND, REGARDING EVEN THE VERY MOTIVES OF CREDIBILITY WHICH BEFORE SEEMED SO CONVINCING."

Christian Encyclopedia

I packed up my shit and moved into Delia's place. So many people were always flowing in and out of there, crashing there. I didn't even know who half of them were. They just came, got high, nodded out, woke up and left. Sometimes there'd be the occasional straggler who wouldn't go away for days until we threw them out.

The place was a complete wreck, but we were too lazy to ever clean it. The garbage cans were overflowing, with blood-stained tissues spilling out onto the floor. Butts formed mountains in already full ashtrays, which was quite a feat considering neither me nor Delia smoked cigarettes. Dirty clothes were thrown all over every room, often completely hiding the stained carpet. Crumbs and food remains were scattered everywhere, counters were stained from neglected spills, rotted food sprouted new forms of fungus in the fridge, and takeout bags were everywhere, filled with week-old leftovers. The bathroom was the worst, with the toilet, sink, and shower tub stained with scum and grime, resembling that of a sewer. One time, the toilet stopped working for a few days, so we just used plastic bags and threw them out the window. A few days after the toilet was fixed, a vicious odor started overwhelming the entire apartment, and we couldn't figure out where it was coming from. Finally we discovered the source: we had forgotten to toss a feces-filled bag out, and it was just hiding under some trash. Through all this, the filth never really bothered us. We were too high to care.

Delia had managed to turn whatever feelings I had toward Avry's departure into anger. "Good riddance," she'd say. "You don't need him, anyway. He was just trying to hold you back." And I believed her. What he was holding me back from, I didn't know. "Friends are worthless, and you of all people should know that. They are good for amusement at times, but they won't be there for you when you need them. They don't really care about you. You have me, and that's all you'll ever need." And I believed her. "Anyone you trust will just use your trust against you. Trust is a weakness. Do you want to be weak?" And I shook my head. "Then always remember that, and you'll get by just fine. But *you* can trust *me*, of course. I'm different. I'll never do anything to hurt you." And I believed her.

As I was entering the apartment after copping, I walked in to find a much panicked Delia pacing back and forth, grabbing her multicolored hair. She was mumbling to herself, biting her lip, not even noticing my entrance. "Delia," I called out in an attempt to grab her attention. She did not respond. I looked toward the floor and saw what the commotion was all about. There laid a girl, sprawled out, face down on the carpet, her tangled brown hair hiding all evidence of her face. In shock, I dropped the book bag I was gripping. Delia was still pacing and I grabbed her by the arm. Startled, she stared up at me, eyes widened.

"Oh god, oh god," she muttered, and gripped back onto her hair. I knelt down and lifted the girl's head by her knotty hair. Her face was pale; her eyes pulled open, with bloody drool dripping from her colorless lips. I dropped the head in fright.

"Fuck, X, what are we gonna do?"

I fell back onto my ass and hugged my knees, my heart racing. "What happened?"

"What the fuck do you think? She... she was high when she got here. I started shooting up, and she did some more. She just kept going. Then she just started convulsing and this fucking foaming spit came pouring out of her mouth. Oh fuck, oh fuck!" Delia's entire body was trembling. I had never seen her so terrified. I stood up to embrace her and she fell into my arms. Though I myself was terrified, it actually felt good to see her like that. It showed me that she was not impenetrable. But moreover, her weakness gave me strength, as it made me feel like she needed me. I stroked her hair as she gripped my shirt like a frightened child. "What are we gonna do?" she asked, voice shaking. "We can't call the cops; they'll lock our asses up in a second."

"Calm down, baby, just relax," the words serving as a comfort tool for myself. I couldn't go to jail. No cage. I started sweating and I had that dropping feeling in my stomach, much like the feeling one gets from a plummeting drop on a rollercoaster. Suddenly she pulled away and started shaking her head and hands like a dog trying to dry itself off. She then started smacking herself in the head, as she verbally scolded herself to get a grip and think. She froze for a moment, turned to me, eyes possessed. "We just gotta get rid of the body! Nobody knows her. She ran away. I think she's from Alabama or some shit. Anyone who does know her around here will just figure she split." The words sounded like music to my ears. No one would know; no one would miss her. Fuck, I didn't even know who she was. Delia ran to the kitchen and returned with a machete. "Where the fuck did you get that?" I asked as she walked back in the room looking like a predator from a horror movie. She ignored my words, as she hovered over the girl and raised her arms, grunting like a wild beast. "Delia!" I yelled and grabbed her arms from the back, mid-flight. She yelled out in fury as I forcefully secured her arms and tore the rusted blade from her grip. "What the fuck is wrong with you? Are you crazy?" Her eyes were like a blank screen, bulging from her emaciated face. I shook her by the shoulders in an attempt to break her rage-filled trance. "Delia!"

"It'll be easy to get rid of her in pieces."

"You can't just chop a girl up in our living room."

"You're right," she said, breathing heavily. "It'll make too much of a mess. Maybe if I get some drop cloths, or..."

Her actions intensified the situation, making me feel as if I had just committed murder. My adrenaline was pumping, almost to the point of excitement, but that feeling was greatly tainted with fear. "No, there's no need for that. If she does get found, it will look like fucking murder. We'll just dump the body, in one piece. This way if the cops do find her, they probably wouldn't even investigate. Just another dead junkie runaway." I said the words, oblivious to the fact that they could easily be applied to me. As if that girl was inferior to me.

Delia leaned her head against the wall with her arms lowered to her side, rolling her forehead back and forth against the stucco. She took a deep breath and then stood completely up. "You're right, you're right." She grinned, and let out a light chuckle, "Sorry, I'm just freaking out." She laughed harder. "It's not like it's the first time this has happened to me. It's just the first time it happened in my apartment." She combed her greasy hair back with sweaty hands, and took another deep breath. "Okay, okay. She's a small girl. We'll just get a large trash bag, and call up one of the kids. A couple of them used to live out by the swamp. They'll know where to take her."

I caressed her face. "That's my girl." She smiled at me, wrapped her arms around me and stared into my eyes.

"Everything will be fine," she said before she sucked my bottom lip, reclaiming her empowered persona.

We called one of our boys and he immediately rushed over. Tim was his name, and he was about seventeen years old. The girl was very petite, so we curled her in a ball and put her in a commercial-sized trash bag and double bagged it. I just wanted her gone. I wanted it all over with. Delia was tense and barking orders at me. I carried the bag to the car in as a nonchalant manner as I could. It was pouring outside, and as I nearly slipped on the wet pavement, Delia smacked me in the back of my head. "What the fuck was that for?" I snorted.

"Fucking be careful," she whispered angrily. I rolled my eyes and continued to the car. Nobody noticed; nobody cared. We were just the freak eccentric druggies who lived on the block. Tim had an old SUV that he had borrowed from someone in family and we popped the back door and placed her in the back end of the truck. As we went to get in the car, we noticed a young boy no older than thirteen in the front passenger seat. "Who the hell is this?" Delia asked angrily.

"It's my cousin," Tim answered.

"Why the fuck is he here?" I asked, my nerves starting to resurface as the rainwater poured down my face. There was no need for any more witnesses.

"Don't worry, guys, he's cool."

"Yeah, I'm cool," the boy interjected in a squeaky voice.

"Whatever, let's just get the fuck outta here, I'm drenched," I ordered. "You, kid, in the back." The boy climbed over the seat next to Delia as I got in the front. "You better not take us anywhere where we will be seen," I said as I stripped off my drenched shirt.

"Don't worry, I have just the place. It's like two hours away."

"Whatever, man, just drive." I turned up the radio, blaring the recording of Tim's untalented punk band. I didn't want talk. I just wanted to get there.

"Here," Tim said as he reached beneath his seat and pulled out a bottle of Jack Daniels. I immediately twisted off the cap and took a hearty swig.

"None for you," I replied. "We can't risk getting pulled over." I passed it to Delia, who took a giant gulp and passed it to the boy. He took a small swig and made a face of disgust. "C'mon, kid, if you wanna hang with the big wigs, you gotta play like them," Delia remarked. Trying not to diminish any chance of being cool, he then took a giant swig, after which his entire body cringed, followed by a hacking fit.

The drinking continued. Delia was wearing a white tank top, and as usual, no bra. Her shirt was drenched and her nipples were shining through. As I watched the two from the rear view mirror, I caught the boy staring at her chest, almost drooling. I lowered the music. "Watch your eyes, boy," I said with an attitude, being wound up as tight as a virgin asshole. He nervously switched his stare to outside of the car window. A few minutes later, his fixation resumed. I could've sworn he started touching himself, but it was probably my paranoia of the entire situation. I turned around and looked him dead in the face. "So you like what you see?"

"Huh, I, I don't..."

"Save it. I saw you staring. That's okay. They're a nice set of tits."

"Relax X, he's just a kid," Delia commented, as his cousin just laughed.

"I am relaxed; I was just stating a fact."

The many swigs of the booze were kicking in hardcore. I reached over and pinched her nipple and she playfully smacked my hand away. The solemn mood lightened up, with the alcohol almost releasing the reality of the dead body in the back. After some mindless chit chat, Tim asked, "So who's the girl?"

Angry at the fact that I was snapped back into reality, I smacked him on the backside of his head yelling, "What the fuck did I tell you on the phone? No fucking questions!"

"Wait a minute," the boy said. "There really is a dead girl in that bag?" Delia couldn't help but chuckle.

"Are you for real?" I asked angrily. "Do you think we're taking this ride for our health?"

"Shit, Tim, I thought you were messing with me."

"No you little dipshit," Tim scolded.

"You're not gonna freak out on us now?" Delia asked in a low raspy voice, leaning in close to his face.

"No, no. I'm fine." He quickly turned and looked at the bag, then turned back around. He repeated that action several times.

"Shit, little man, do you wanna take a peak?" Delia asked, clearly affected by the booze.

"Fuck yeah." The two climbed onto their knees facing the back.

"No fucking way, sit the fuck down," I screamed.

"Aw, c'mon X. Let him see."

"Everybody, sit down!" Tim yelped

"You shut up and drive," I barked.

"C'mon X. there's not a single person on this road, and it's so damn rainy and dark, no one could see in. And I bet he's never even seen a naked chick before," she said with a devious smile.

"She's naked?" The boy asked, filled with frightful anticipation.

"No, she's not naked." I answered

"But she can be," Delia interjected.

"Don't you even..." But Delia just told me to shut the fuck up as the two turned back around to the body. She pulled the girl out.

"Stop!" I called out as Tim whimpered. But it didn't matter. She was on a roll.

"Holy fucking shit," the boy muttered in awe. Delia reached back around into her bag and pulled out her switch blade. She proceeded to cut open the girl's shirt and bra.

"What the fuck are they doing back there?" Tim asked, horrified. He was the only one with half sense in the car, considering he was the only one sober.

"Nothing; drive," I said as I buried my head in my hands, knowing where things were heading.

The boy was quivering from disgust, but could not remove his eyes. Delia was smiling. "Go ahead," she said, "touch her." I put up the music up and continued to drink. Since the boy was too frozen to move, she grabbed his hand and placed on the dead girl's breast. He began to rub her, but soon pulled away, eyes still stuck. Delia laughed above the music. "Hey," she whispered, "are you a virgin?" The boy silently nodded. She put her hand on his face and turned it so he was staring right into her eyes, their noses almost touching. "I bet you'd love to lose your virginity, wouldn't you?" she asked seductively as she bit her lip. Now stuck on Delia, he nodded. She put her hand on his thigh. "Well, now's your chance."

"Um, um, I...I don't know," he terrifyingly stuttered. She then grabbed his hand and put it up her shirt, right beneath her breast, whispering, "C'mon, I promise you a kiss." I saw what she was doing, but still kept trying to ignore it.

Now the boy was excited, and the mix of his young male hormones were causing a total lack of judgment. Not to mention the fact that he had swigged a shit load of whiskey, probably never even having had tasted hard liquor in his life. "Okay," he whispered back, not wanting to remove his hand from beneath her shirt. She pulled it out herself, and began to push him toward the back.

Tim lowered the radio. "What the hell are you doing, Joey?"

"I'm gonna lose my virginity." I turned and looked at Delia, who flashed me a grimace.

"You're gonna fuck a dead girl?" Tim yelped.

"Why not?" Delia asked. "She won't know the difference."

"You're a sick bitch," I said to her.

"And you love it."

The boy hovered over the body. "I don't think I can do this," he murmured.

"Oh yes you can," Delia said as she reached over and pulled down the girl's pants. The boy was still frozen, just staring. "Shit," Delia said as she examined the girl's body. "She's probably dry as fuck. Hey, Tim, you gotta lubricated condom?"

Tim, who was now amused at this point, threw back his wallet. As I glared at him, he remarked, "Fuck, if he has the balls to do that, then let him." I shrugged. I was obliterated by that point. Nothing was real.

Delia pulled out a blue-wrapped condom and handed it to the boy. He unbuttoned his pants and hovered over her. "Guys, I really don't know if I can do this."

"Do you know the mechanics of it?" Delia asked sarcastically. He just nodded. She turned back to me. "Aww, he has stage fright." She leaned forward and wrapped her arms around me. "Let's help him out, baby."

"No way, this is all you." I replied, taking yet another swig

"You guys are all fucking nuts," Tim remarked, but seemed to be enthralled by the whole fiasco.

"C'mon," she begged me like a little girl. She started kissing my neck and rubbing my chest in a way only she knew how. I closed my eyes, and let myself zone out as she made her way down to my pants. She nibbled on my ear as she whispered, "C'mon baby, I need you inside of me right now." I opened my eyes to find her staring straight through mine. She kissed me passionately, one hand still down my pants, the other pulling me to the back seat. Without releasing our lip lock, I climbed over the seat to the back. She violently pushed me down, and pulled her off her pants and proceeded to straddle me, kissing my neck and chest the entire time.

She was dripping wet as I slid inside her, and at that moment I was completely oblivious to the young boy hovering helplessly over the naked stiff directly behind me. She was moving her body in a rough up-and-down, circular motion, causing me to penetrate so deep inside her that I thought I was gonna break something in there. I pulled off her shirt and nibbled on her nipples, not caring one bit about the spectators. The entire time she was fucking me like an animal, she was staring the boy in the eyes.

By this point, the boy was ready to go. He put on the condom and proceeded to shove himself inside the lifeless body. As he did this, Delia moaned in both physical and mental pleasure. Through her groans, I could hear the boy moaning as he began to penetrate. Noticing that reality was settling back in for me, Delia just fucked me harder. Soon all the living people in the car were screaming in pleasure as the car was swerving all over the road. I yelled to Delia that I was about to cum, and she quickly jumped out and wrapped her mouth around my shaft to swallow. As soon as I let off that amazing relief, Delia tumbled into my lap, chuckling. I realized we were stopped on the side of the road. "Why are we stopped?" I asked as I tried to catch my breath.

“Shit, I didn’t wanna crash,” Tim commented. He had obviously been jerking off in the front. Delia started laughing as she looked toward the back. I turned to see what was so amusing, and found a shocked half-naked boy, leaning against the side of the back, knees to his chest, just staring at the violated body. I couldn’t tell if he was happily in shock or scared shitless. Delia just kept laughing. I pushed her off and climbed back in the front. “You, start driving,” I ordered, trying to get the situation back in order. “Delia, put your shirt back on. And you in the back, put her away and climb back to your seat.” Tim was laughing as he started back down the road.

“What’s so funny?” I asked.

“That was fucking sick!” he said, sounding absolutely delighted.

Delia helped the boy shove the girl back in the bag, and then he climbed back over, stupefied. She put her arm around him and kissed him softly on the lips. “You are the coolest kid in the world,” she said, rubbing his hair. He cracked a slight smile. She pulled his head to rest upon her bosom, and all his regrets seemed to have melted away.

When we got to the site, the rain had subsided. Tim cradled the bag in his arms, as Delia walked with her arm around the boy’s shoulder, and I lagged behind with the bottle of Jack in one hand and a shovel in the other. Tim was right; the place was perfect: nothing but open empty swamp. Delia decided to wait with the boy as me and Tim trudged through the messy, muddy slop. We found a good spot and threw the bag down, and proceeded to cover it up with surrounding mud and branches. A tremendous sense of relief mixed in with the intoxication. It was over.

Now completely filthy, we hurried back to the car, where Tim had stashed towels and thermoses full with water to wash off the mud. As we were about to climb into the car, the prior events began to sink in, along with the extreme amount of alcohol. I suddenly began to projectile vomit as everyone chuckled. I wiped off my mouth, put my hand on Delia’s shoulder as I asked, “By the way, what was her name? I just want to know in case I start hearing people look for her.”

Delia looked at me without a care in the world, and responded, "Hell if I remember." She shrugged me off, climbed in the back seat and slammed the door.

The entire ride home, Delia and the boy joked playfully in the back, Tim downed whatever was left of the Jack, and I just stared out the window, trying not to vomit, watching the blurry world pass me by.

nine

"PERSONS MANIFESTLY GO THROUGH MORE PAIN AND SELF-DENIAL TO GRATIFY A VICIOUS PASSION THAN WOULD HAVE BEEN NECESSARY TO THE CONQUEST OF IT."

Bishop Joseph Butler

I remember every millisecond of that night so clearly. It was the second night of Mardi Gras. The city really wasn't that far off of how it always was, just with a billion more drunken people. We were at a small bar on Decatur. It was pretty packed with both locals and tourists. By the bar there was an attractive, voluptuous blonde, definitely not a local. She was sporting beads around her neck and consuming more alcohol than she could obviously handle. She was acting flirty with the girls she was with, as to put on a show for any guy watching. When I walked past her on my way to the bathroom she grabbed my arm and said, "Hey sexy," and started giggling. I wasn't sure if she was doing it as a joke; I didn't seem like the guy she would normally go for. Then I noticed she was sporting a tank top with some cheesy pop, wanna-be metal band's logo on it, so I guess she figured she could have something in common with me. I smirked and brushed her hand off. She made a little squeak, showing her dismay. As I took a piss, I couldn't get the idea outta my head.

I told Delia what had happened. "She couldn't handle us," she remarked.

"I know," I said with a smile that contained no ulterior intentions. She grimaced and went to the bar. I thought she was just going to get another free drink from the bartender we knew. But then I noticed her go up to the girl and whisper something in her ear. They both looked at me, and the blonde smiled and waved. I waved back. She came over to me, but Delia stayed at the bar, not looking back. I was a bit confused. The girl was flaunting her large chest in my face, giggling, flirting. I looked over at Delia. She saw the girl's behavior, and smiled and winked. I figured that was my signal to proceed. So I accepted her flirting and returned it. The blonde was basically on my lap at that point, whispering things in my ear as she brushed her lips against my skin. She was from a college in Texas, and on vacation. She had a strong southern accent, which fit the profile perfectly. I put my hands on her hips, moving them along with all her motions.

"How you kids doing?" Delia returned with a beer for each of us.

"Great," the blonde said, and started giggling.

"I knew you two would hit it off," Delia said with great sarcastic exaggeration, then threw me another wink. That last beer hit the girl hard and we knew that any more and she'd be puking her guts out. She could barely stand, so she leaned on me, her face so close to mine. Her friends came over to us.

"Is she okay?" one asked. I wrapped my arms around her.

"Yeah, don't worry. I got her." They didn't look satisfied.

They tapped her on the shoulder. "Hey we're going to Bourbon Street." Delia and I looked at each other.

"Okay, see ya," she answered, much to me and Delia's pleasure.

"You're not coming?"

"No." She was still leaning all her weight on me. "I'll just see you at the hotel later." They looked at each other in discontent, but still went on their way, leaving their drunken friend in our mercy.

"I'm sooo drunk," she giggled.

"I know," I said as I stroked her fine, golden hair. As her breasts pressed against me, I grabbed the back of her head and started kissing her neck, making my way to her mouth. She went along willingly. I put my other hand under the table and down Delia's pants. The girl sat on top of me, not noticing my hand on Delia, or her hand on me. "Hey, let's get out of here," I whispered, nibbling on her earlobe.

"And go where?"

"My place."

"I don't know..."

"C'mon, I got some coke there." I felt it was obvious that she was the type of chick who would get off on that. We headed to the door. Delia followed.

"She's coming?"

"Yeah, she's my roommate." The girl was stumbling all over the place, eyes rolling all around her head. I held her up as Delia walked behind us, laughing. We took a complete roundabout way to our apartment.

When we got there, the girl stumbled to the couch. "Dang, this place is a mess." She looked a bit disgusted, but was too drunk to really care. We were finally away from the watching eyes of the outside world, and the mood shifted. The blonde turned to me and asked, "So where's your room?"

Delia pointed. "That's our room."

"Our?" After a few seconds of pondering, "Wait, are ya'll a couple, of like swingers, or something?" We just smiled. "I appreciate the offer and everything," it was difficult for her to form whole sentences, "but I don't swing that way."

"That's not what it looked like at the bar," Delia said as she sat next to the girl, making her obviously uncomfortable.

"I was playing around with my friends at the bar. I'm strictly dickly," and laughed at her own remark. "It was just all in good fun. But I'm not into this three-way business, so I guess I'll just be going." She tried to stumble to the door, but was unsuccessful and tripped along the way. I helped her up. She laughed, "I'm fine, I'm fine. If ya'll could just explain to me how to get back..."

Delia blocked the door. "We're just kidding, silly. We're not a couple, we just wanted to see your reaction." A look of total confusion came over the girl's face. I pulled her close in an attempt to comfort her.

Obliviously drunk, she went along, and we began kissing. Delia went and put on some music, then went to the bedroom and grabbed our handcuffs. She waved them so I could see them. As we kissed, I grabbed the girl's wrists and pinned them behind her back. Delia swiftly came and locked the handcuffs on.

"Hey!" the girl shouted.

"Shhhh," Delia asserted as she used one of her knee high socks and wrapped it around the girl's face, gagging her. She pulled her blonde hair and whispered something in her ear that I couldn't hear, and the girl's eyes became engulfed in horror, as Delia licked the side of her face. "Where should we put her?"

She dragged the terrified girl into the cluttered bedroom. Tears were falling from her face. At first her fear threw me. I was hard, but at the same time everything was feeling a bit too intense, almost causing me to back out. Delia knew how to calm my nerves. After she bound the girl up with rope that we used for bondage games, she whipped out some dope. We did only a little, as to not affect our ability to perform. But just enough so that the world around us wasn't real. It was whatever we made it to be.

"Shall we undress her?" Delia questioned me.

"I want you to do it." So she went into the kitchen and came back with the largest knife she could find. The girl's panic-induced breathing got heavier at the sight of the blade. The tears just kept pouring. My blood rushed. Delia cut open the girl's shirt. She ran the blade over her heaving chest, pressing ever so slightly enough to leave tiny scrapes that would heal in a few days time. Then she cut her bra, releasing her DD-cupped breasts. The girl was wearing tight blue jeans, and Delia rubbed the blade against them, pressing it flat along her crotch. She unzipped the jeans and pulled them down.

The girl struggled, until Delia slapped her across the face. Then she put the blade to the girl's throat. My dick was throbbing, yet I flinched at the sight of the slap. Delia untied the legs so she could slip the pants off. The girl was overwhelmed with terror, but no longer tried to resist.

Delia laid the girl on her back, then began to undress herself, revealing the beautiful collection of skin art on her pale flesh. She caressed the girl with one hand, as she ran the blade across her with the other. Then she began to lick the girl's body, turned to me, then licked the blade and asked, "Are you just gonna stand there and watch, or are you gonna come play?" I remained still for a moment. I was enjoying the sight from my safe objective position. I knew once I joined in, everything would change. But it was much too tempting to resist.

I removed my clothes and went over by the girls. The blonde layed there, almost hyperventilating, clenching her eyes shut. Her sobs could be heard through the gag. I caressed her body; it was beautiful. As I touched her, I began to lose myself. I grabbed her skin, tightly squeezing her breasts, then nipples, feeling her body twitch from the pain. I started to bite her nipples as Delia nibbled on her clit hard enough to make her squirm. I wanted to be inside this helpless creature, I wanted to have her completely under my power. I pushed an understanding Delia away from the girl's pussy. Delia was loving the sight of me allowing myself to get totally absorbed by the situation. When the girl realized what was about to happen, she attempted an escape, but got absolutely nowhere.

Her struggles got me into it even more. "I like it when they fight back." Delia giggled at my comment. I was running on pure adrenaline. As I entered her, it was almost as if I lost total control of my entire being. Like someone else was in control of what I was doing, saying. But there wasn't anyone else in control of me. Everything I was doing was by my own will.

Since I had her hips pinned, Delia pinned her torso, holding the knife up to her neck. The girl whimpered and stopped fighting. "They always give up so easily," Delia said, right before she went to hand me the knife. My heart pounded as I took it from her grasp. I ran the blade along the now motionless girl's stomach, as I pushed myself deeper inside her. She was a bit wet. Weird how the body reacts instinctively against the mind. I was convinced her body wanted me inside of her.

Delia sat on the girl's face and rubbed her clit all over it. The girl thrashed her head around in an attempt to breathe, making Delia moan. On account of Delia's moans, the girl's cries, the powerful piece of metal in my hand, and the dope running through my system, I felt like a god.

I was fucking the girl so hard and deep, I could feel her clenching her pussy walls in pain. Either the pain or the fear caused her to dry up, and my dick began to tear her insides. I watched the blade against her skin. I envisioned it digging into her flesh, splitting it open like a fresh fruit, spilling her bloody ambrosia over her pink skin. I wondered if it would taste just as sweet as it would look. I pictured Delia sharing with me in a taste, and as the humanity spilled out of her, me and my girl would grab each other's blood-drenched bodies and make violent love. Then it came.

Somehow I managed to catch myself, and I pulled out and came all over the girl's chest. I had never experienced an orgasm like that. It took me a moment to realize my fantasy had been just that. I fell over, dropping the knife. Delia laughed at the sight, and curled up next to me. "How you feeling?" I then laughed and pulled her closer, losing myself for a moment in her smell, forgetting about the naked body bound next to me.

"So what should we do with her now?" She picked the knife back up. The girl couldn't control her crying. We sat her up and tried to calm her down so as to shut her up. The cries got louder and louder, even from behind the gag. Her sobs were banging against my ear drums, giving me a headache.

I tried to shush her. "Stop crying," each cry a reminder of what we had just done. Finally I couldn't take it anymore, and I smacked her, yelling, "SHUT UP!" She did. Her eyes were still running, bulging from her head, all puffy and red from crying. Mascara stained her cheeks. She looked like a child who had just witnessed her parents gruesomely murdered. I put my head in my hands and knelt down next to her.

Delia wasn't finished. She wanted more. She wanted all of the girl, not just her dignity and self-respect. She ran the blade along the girl's bare, sore crotch. She was about to stick the blade inside the petrified girl until, "Delia, no!" I grabbed her hand that was gripping the knife. "That's enough." She rolled her eyes, but ceased her actions.

How we were going to get rid of the girl was an issue we didn't tackle beforehand. Delia was about to shove a couple of her Vicodin down the girl's throat. "Wait," I stopped her, "she drank a lot, that might kill her."

"We need to keep her calm." Having lost all energy, the girl seemed basically lifeless as Delia held her up by the shoulder.

"I think she's calm," I remarked. Delia used a wet cloth to wipe the girl down. She put the girl's pants on her, but her shirt was ruined. I went to the payphone and called one of our kids. "Hey, I need a favor." He came over, no questions asked, with his car. Delia wrapped one of her jackets around the girl. She had her hotel key in her purse. On the ride there, Delia had the girl in her lap, and did a convincing piece of acting, instilling fear into the girl so that she wouldn't go to the cops.

When we were a few blocks from the hotel, I had him pull over. Delia threw an oversized hoodie on and walked her to the room. Just another couple of drunk tourists stumbling in after a wild night on the town. When she got to the room, she unlocked the door, pulled her jacket off the girl, and pushed her in. She quickly scurried down the hall, hearing a large thump coming from her room.

The next day was when I realized things would never be the same. I had done something so awful, and enjoyed it. But I didn't want to ever do it again. As much as I tried to convince myself otherwise, as perfect a job as I did disguising it to her and myself, I felt guilty for what I had done to that girl. I finally understood the guilt, and I didn't like it one bit. Delia, on the other hand, developed a taste for it. She wanted to make it a frequent occurrence. But she was aware of my position. Either way, me and Delia had shared something that would bind us together for the rest of our lives, whether that's what I wanted or not.

ten

"WE CAST AWAY PRICELESS TIME IN DREAMS, BORN OF THE IMAGINATION, FED UPON ILLUSION, AND PUT TO DEATH BY REALITY."

Judy Garland

I sold my tattoo gun. Money was getting tight. The guy I sold it to gave me a good offer and said I could rent it from him whenever I wanted to. At first I did, but that soon stopped. The money had a more important purpose. Dope. Though my habit was utterly apparent, I still lived in denial, still convinced myself I had control. I swore I could stop if I wanted to. I lied to myself through the feverish sweats, violent nausea and diarrhea, aches and pains, and fierce need. Need. It was no longer a choice, it was a necessity. An essential part of survival. The one I tended to first. For when I didn't, I was overpowered by its fury. Both the solution and the problem.

Delia was fired from her job, but I somehow managed to hold on to mine for a while. Until the boss caught me shooting up in the bathroom. Then we were both unemployed, penniless, and strung out. We didn't want to start turning on each other in frustration, so we kept working out methods of obtaining money. We'd go to tourist traps, pick out the drunkest chick. The best were the ones who would leave their purses unattended. Some had to be distracted while Delia robbed them. She was good, could even pickpocket wallets. She had a lot of practice in her day. But even with that, it wasn't enough.

We managed to convince these two kids to hold up couple of grocery stores. We got them a gun, some crackhead sold it to us for cheap, and looked out, and they just had to do the rest. We made out pretty sweet. But soon we were making the news and we knew it was time to cool off, at least for a while. So we had them switch their targets to individual people. We'd spread our targets out throughout the city. Catch someone drunk, or just walking alone, stick a gun in their face and take everything we could, down to their shoes. Mostly those kids did it for us, having slowly become strung out themselves. But I had to do it myself a few times because me and Delia were fiending and just didn't wanna share. But I never held onto the gun; I'd just borrow it from them. I was nearly 21 and if I got caught, I'd be in a shitload of trouble, so it was best not to keep any evidence. But still, it wasn't enough. We rummaged through all our belongings, selling and pawning anything we could get even a few bucks for. "How about this?" Delia asked when she stumbled across the frame containing Dani's picture.

"Yeah, we could probably get something for it." So she took out the picture, tossing it among the other trash that was spawning in that apartment. But still, it wasn't enough. It was *never* enough.

One desperate day, "Why don't you pawn that?" she asked, pointing to my guitar.

"No way, that's my baby. I've had that guitar forever."

"So then it's old, and you can get rid of it, get a new one or something."

"It's old but in good condition, new strings. Scratches yes, but no cracks."

"Oh, c'mon. We can get a fair bit for it. If you want we could get it back when we get some money."

"No, I love that instrument more than anything." She looked offended. She turned away, folding her arms.

"You hardly play it anymore anyway." She was right. Too much of my energy had been focused elsewhere. Whenever I would try I was always way too fucked up to function.

The day went on, and the pain became unbearable. By the end of the day there were two junkies nodded out on the floor, accompanied by a couple of empty bags of dope, and no guitar.

Not being able to play music was like being stuck in my grandmother's house again. I felt so empty, so worthless. As each day passed, my desire to play grew and grew. I had never wanted to play so badly in my life. I had been neglecting it for so long, but when the ability was taken away, the desire regrew stronger. "Stop worrying about that," she'd say.

"I'm never getting it back." She knew it was the truth; but she couldn't have cared less.

Me and this other kid were on our way to a dealer's house, while Delia was god-knows-where. She was pulling the disappearing too often lately. But she always came back with dope for me, so I didn't complain. But that day I couldn't wait.

It was the type of chill out dealer, who wanted everyone to stay for a bit and get high there. But he was also the kind of guy everyone hated to be around. Most feared him. He liked to push the weak around, flaunt the power he obtained from his status. He had a whole entourage of fellow assholes that followed him around. I never put up with his shit, and he hated me for that. The feeling was mutual. But when you need to score and the options are limited, you take what you could get.

The second we stepped inside the house, he gave me that good old over- exaggerated welcome, smacking me on the back. I pulled away. "Oh, relax, kid." He made my skin crawl. We went into the living room, where one other guy was sitting. I just wanted to get my dope and leave, but of course, it wouldn't be so simple. We sat on the couch. He brought out the dope, collected our money, and insisted we shoot up there.

The dealer turned to me and said, "So how's that pretty little piece of ass of yours?"

"What the fuck did you just say?"

"That girly of yours, how is she?" He said with a grimace. I tried to brush off his presence and zone out to the background music. He laughed at my attempt and continued on. "I saw her the other day," he regained my attention, "around my boy Andy's way." I gave him an interrogating glare. "Wearing one of those little skirts of hers. Poor thing, she was so sick, so desperate for a fix. But don't worry, Andy took real good care of her."

I gained full control of my high. I had just done a little bit, enough for a fix, but not enough so to cause my guard to be let down. In case he'd say something stupid, like that, I'd be ready. I got to my feet and walked in front of where he was seated. His boy stood up, but that didn't phase me. He laughed and said, "Hey, hey, no need to get all worked up, take a seat."

"I don't wanna hear another word out of your mouth about my girl."

He laughed on, "Hey, don't get mad at me. It's not my fault your girl's a junkie whore." I swung down on him and clocked him in the face, then in turn got clocked in the head myself by his boy, and stumbled onto the couch. The kid I was with tried to make a run towards the door, but the dealer's friend stopped him and they started fighting. As the dizziness faded, I stood back up and went at the dealer again. He pushed forward into my torso, and I fell to the ground with him on top of me. I was continuously beating him in the head and chest, causing him to loosen his grip. I rolled on top of him, still hitting him, and then started banging his head on the ground. I felt a foot slam me in the side, but it didn't stop me. Then another caused me to fall over and off the barely conscious dealer.

As another kick headed my way, aimed at my face, I noticed a shiny piece of metal tucked in the dealer's waist; a handgun. Everything was moving so fast, I never gave him an opportunity to reach for it. I instinctively grabbed it and pulled it out and cocked it back. The guy froze, and stood angrily, but motionless, with fear in his eyes. I climbed onto my feet. I looked over at the other kid who was kneeling on the ground in pain, covered in blood. In the standing guy's hand was the source, a blood-stained butterfly knife. The sight of the blood and the feel of power in my hands completely overwhelmed me. My heart was pounding.

For a moment all sound faded out into silence. And then "BANG." Without even realizing it, I fired a shot, straight at the man's heart. He fell to the floor. I turned to the dealer, who was crawling on the floor, moaning in agonizing pain. Without hesitation, I fired another one, aimed at his head. I lowered the gun and looked at what I had done. For a brief moment I became entranced. When I snapped out of it, I instinctively ran their pockets for a fat wad of cash, and scooped up all the dope I could quickly find. Then I ran.

"Pack your shit," were the first words I said when I got home, to find Delia vegged out, staring at the wall.

"What's going on?"

"We gotta get out of here as soon as possible," I said as I wiped off the gun which I had forgotten to toss.

"Why?" She looked shocked as she saw the weapon.

"I just killed two people."

"Shit," she actually said with a grin. She excitedly jumped to her feet and helped me pack up some clothes. "Who?" I gave her a quick rundown. "Holy mother fucking shit!" she screamed with delight when she saw the goodies I managed to snatch. "Was the other kid still alive?"

"I don't know."

"Why did you keep the gun?"

"I don't know."

"Where are we going?"

"I don't know."

We ended up heading to Florida. Delia knew some people that lived out in Hollywood there that she claimed that they would let us stay with them. During the whole train ride I wanted to ask her about what the dealer had said. But I never dared. If it wasn't true, she'd get incredibly offended and angry. If it was true, she would never have admitted it, and still act greatly offended and angry. I figured it would be best kept quiet, with part of me not even wanting to know the truth. Before we left Delia quickly set out to find one of our kids who had been itching for a gun and sold it to him. She wanted to take it, but I didn't want to walk around with that heat. Not after I had experienced its power. It was too dangerous.

As we sat on the train I turned to her and apologized. "I'm sorry you had to leave New Orleans. I know you really liked it there."

"It's cool, it was time for a change in scenery. And how could I possibly be mad when you came bearing such gifts?"

"So who are these cats you know in Florida?"

"These two guys, Peter and Jonathan. I met them the first year I was in New Orleans; they came for Mardi Gras. They ended up coming back the next year for it, then visited two other times after that. I always let them crash at my place. Peter, that boy can drink. And I never even knew there was a Hollywood in Florida until I met them. I wonder how far it is from Miami. I've never been there but always wanted to check it out." She was rambling on but I had stopped paying attention. My mind was fixated.

"I don't remember meeting them."

"You didn't."

With the dealer's words still torturing my thoughts, "Did you fuck them?" She gave me a deeply offended look, clicking her tongue and turning to face the window. "Simple yes or no answer will suffice."

She turned back towards me, with that same look. "Fuck you."

"No, that wasn't one of the options. Yes or no?" I had just gone through too much defending her honor. I didn't believe my question to be inappropriate.

"No, okay? Shit, first you come home, make me pack my shit and leave on account of your stupidity," when just a minute before she had totally approved of my actions, "I figure out a safe place for us to crash, and you start interrogating me about it. Don't be such an asshole."

I was brushing off her words, still swept up in the idea of her fucking someone else. "So if I asked these guys if they fucked you, they'd both say no? Because if you did, it would be better if you just told me now."

"Are you fucking kidding me? What did I just say? Would you rather we'd sleep in the streets?" Silence followed. I stopped asking her questions about it, but my mind couldn't stop its torture.

We called the guys once we arrived in Hollywood. The guys seemed shocked at our arrival, but came right away to get us. Peter was a short skinny kid, with long frizzy hair, glasses, and bad skin. Jonathan looked almost exactly like him, except with short red hair and freckles. They had told her to look them up if she was ever in the neighborhood, but hadn't expected her to ever be. Nevertheless, they seemed quite pleased at the sight of her. Delia gave them the rundown on our situation, of course fabricating the reasons we had to leave, and they agreed to let us stay there for a bit.

I didn't care for them from the start, but I knew they were of use to us, so I bit my tongue. They weren't bad guys, but I couldn't help but dislike them. I would watch Delia with them, her and her usual overly friendly manner, that any red-blooded male would eat up. But I didn't say a word about it, to them or her. They hooked us up with excellent dope. They seemed like classic cases of bored rich boys gone rebellious. They weren't that rich, but managed pretty well, their lives and their habits. I think Mommy and Daddy paid for their apartment to get their druggie asses out of the house and off of the streets, so as to not make Mommy and Daddy look bad.

I kept to myself. The weather there was awesome, I didn't even mind the humidity. New Orleans, after all was a sauna in the summer. But I didn't care for the city much. Half of Hollywood was very hick with mullets aplenty, the other half was Hispanic. There were bars along the beach, which was cool, but I just wasn't in the mode to go out and meet anyone. I'd spend a lot of time just wandering the beach alone. There was so much going on in my head, I didn't wanna deal with any of it. I thought about Avry, how I wished he was there with me. How I'd probably never see him again. I thought about the poor girl we violated and the nightmares she must've been having. I thought about the dead junkie, wondering if anyone was missing her. I thought about what had happened in that dealer's house. I felt no remorse for taking their lives whatsoever. That notion bothered me, being that murder is supposed to be the greatest act of human atrocity, and I had done it twice without blinking an eye. I thought about the possibility of getting caught, which freaked me out more than anything, but didn't really believe it would happen. I thought about my guitar, about how much I longed to play music. As much as I despised dwelling on such thoughts, I would have rather thought of them than the other tormenting image: the idea of anyone sticking their dick inside of Delia.

I wanted to learn where to score for myself. I didn't like depending on anyone for that. After almost two weeks there, I decided to score myself. But I was desperate and sloppy, and sure enough, I saw those flashing cherries come flying around the corner. I started running as fast as I could, with nowhere to go. For the first time ever, my trusty feet didn't save me. The cops fled their car and came charging after me. Suddenly I felt large hands grab my waist, and tackle me to the floor. The cop shoved his knee into my back and pressed my face into the cement. "You think you could get away, boy?" he said with a heavy Floridian drawl. Soon the other caught up and they chuckled at their catch as the officer pulled the cuffs as tight as he could.

I stared out the window, my face, hands, arms, and knees stinging from the dirt-filled scrapes. The cuffs were so tight that they were cutting off all circulation to my hands. "Hey, you think you could loosen these things? I can't feel my hands."

"Shut the hell up, boy. That'll teach your junkie ass to run from the police." And they both chuckled. I stared back out the window. A cage. But I wasn't scared of that. I was more afraid of the dope thirst that was already beginning to burn within me.

There was only one other person in the small cell, and he was busy pacing back and forth in anger, mumbling to himself in frustration. I sat in the corner and stared at the filthy floor. It felt as if the holding pen was getting smaller and smaller. I started to sweat heavily. After about fifteen minutes, one of the cops called to me and took me to the precinct bathroom.

"We don't want you freaking out and getting sick on us." So he let me inhale some of the dope they had found on me. I couldn't believe it. I desperately wanted to do the whole bag, but he just let me have a taste to keep me under control.

After several hours of staring at the floor, they transferred me to central booking where I remained until morning. I stood in front of the judge, emotionless. Sentence: twenty-eight days in rehab and six months probation.

Detoxing exists in a class of pain all itself. Besides the physical trauma of nonstop vicious and sweaty vomiting and diarrhea, there is this constant fear. You can't sleep, so it's there all day and all night. Feeling scared to death, knowing there's one thing that could make you all better, put an end to all your suffering, and you can't have it. Hiding under the blankets, trying to escape the hallucinations of my grandmother's melting face, two dead men come back for retaliation, a little boy fucking a corpse, and a battered Texan girl holding her intestines in her hands. You grip the sheets, screaming to anyone and everyone to please save you. For fuck's sake, why won't anybody save you?! After the initial detox, you can actually function like a human being. But that panic is ever-lingering.

Staring at the ceiling, lying in that bed, I felt like I was back in the institution all over again. But this time, there would be no Avry to save me. When I was able to get a hold of myself, I climbed out of my sweat-drenched sheets and took a shower for the first time in what felt like an eternity. The reality of where I was slowly began to sink in. I was stuck in there, surrounded by strangers, while Delia was out there, with those guys. Getting high. I had spoken to her from a payphone in central booking, and she had been there to watch me get carted off to rehab, with this pathetic look on her face, high out of her mind. God, how I wanted to be high outta my mind. Just a little taste.

I wandered out into the hall. I was cold and shivering, hugging myself. All the faces looked like twisted Picasso paintings. I didn't wanna be there. Anywhere but there. But I knew it was better than jail.

As I walked down the hallway I passed one guy leaning against the wall, and he completely freaked me out. He was skinnier than Delia, with his skin looking like it was trying to escape his bones. He had red, dry, cracking patches all over his face, and as he stared at me with his bug eyes looking as if they were about to burst out of his head. I had to take a moment to contemplate if he was actually human. The nausea began to bubble again in my stomach, and I ran back to the room to puke.

As I hovered over the toilet, I wondered if I looked to others how that guy looked to me. I stood up and stared in the mirror. The black circles under my eyes were forming their own continents. I was paler than ever, my skin having an almost blue tint. I lifted my shirt and stared at my protruding rib cage. I was skinnier than I had ever been, looking like one of those starving children from those fundraising commercials. Somebody, please feed this emaciated child before he withers away into nonexistence. I ran my fingers across my tattoo. I guess I wasn't as invincible as I had thought I was.

The center was full of variety, with alcoholics, coke heads, crack heads, speed addicts, pill poppers, and fellow junkies. The junkies would make fun of the crack heads, saying that they were the lowest of the low, selling their soul for a ten minute high. The crack heads would make fun of the junkies, saying they were the lowest of the low, sticking dirty needles in our arms, etc., etc. I found it all ridiculous. We were all in the same boat, slaves to a substance that we believed to be the light of our existence, when it in fact was darkness we were drowning ourselves in.

We'd have to sit in circles and share our experiences and feelings, much like in the institution. My first circle, the counselor was a thin, hunched over, blonde man with tiny circle glasses who was a recovered coke addict. As we sat in a circle discussing how life is about choices, blah blah, all I could think about was getting high. Just one hit, and I would be fine. His voice shot through me like a thousand tiny needles. All of their voices were just aggravating noise. I started sweating. Just one hit. I wanted to just get to my feet and run, just as fast as I could, forever. They made us complete a form, asking us to list what we held as most important in our lives. All I could think to write was Delia.

I hardly slept that night. I was in a room alone, which was one plus. I just stared at the ceiling, thinking of nothing but getting high and Delia. I had spoken to her earlier that day. I wasn't allowed to see her just yet. I didn't think I wanted to. Not while in there. I didn't want her seeing me all caged up like that, and she said she understood, promising me she'd be right there waiting for me, counting the days. She even cried. I never heard her really cry before. Like a true heartfelt cry of sadness. She said that the thought of not having me around for that long made her wanna kill herself, but knowing I'd be returning to her arms made it all worth it. A bit on the dramatic side, but hey, that was Delia.

For me, being separated from her for that long was a scary thought. I missed her touch, her smell, her taste. But I couldn't shake what that mother fucking dealer had said to me. I figured it had to be true, how else would he have remembered her? I started to wonder how she always managed to score; what kind of schemes she was running. She always (at least as far as I knew) would share with me, and I just never questioned the how's. The idea of her whoring herself out for dope was too much for me to handle. So I tried not to think about it. I knew she'd be out there the second I got out. But what she would be doing in the meantime was what was driving me mad.

The next day we had a speaker come talk to us. I sat in the back huddled in a corner, trying desperately not to make eye contact with any of the creatures around me. I was disgusted by all of them. I couldn't be like them. Not me. They were all sickly-looking, desperate, pathetic losers. But not me. Suddenly the speaker arrived and stepped in front of us. I took a quick peek. He couldn't have been much older than me. My focus shifted back to the floor, as I prepared myself for more useless blabber. But, as he began to speak, it was if he was a fisherman and his words were a line pulling me in. He spoke of how his mother had left him with his grandparents, who wanted nothing to do with him. He ran away and lived like a bum, bouncing from place to place, fucking anything with a pussy that came his way. He had started getting high at the age of twelve, first weed and alcohol, then coke and crystal, until finally he was introduced to dope. "It was like a sweet savior," he said, still staring at the floor. But it just was never enough. He watched everyone around him evaporate from the drug. His best friend overdosed and died right in front of him, but he still didn't stop. He got arrested and sent to rehab. But as soon as he stepped foot outside, he went and copped. He robbed, he beat, he got robbed and beat. He pimped out his girlfriend and prostituted himself for a few dollars or a quick fix. But it never was enough. Finally he found himself lying in an alleyway, butt naked, ass bleeding, in a pool of his own vomit staring into a starless sky, wondering, "How the fuck did I get *here*? This can't be all I'm worth." And it hit him. Either he was going to have to change or he was going to die. And that's when it hit me. I decided I was going to fight it.

Days passed, each one being an obstacle in itself. I started to take the sessions on full force, and they were actually helping. But just when I thought I was well on my way to recovery, a craving would kick in like no other, and it was back to square one. One day at a time, as they always said. But there was just way too much time in there for thinking. And no matter what thoughts came into my head, it all wound up back at her.

I started to wonder, for the first time, which had a heavier weight, the positive influence Delia made on my life, or the negative. I couldn't imagine life without her. But I remembered that once I couldn't imagine life without Avry. Nothing negative ever resulted from our friendship. And I had just thrown him away, like he was nothing, for her. But I knew that when I touched her, smelled her skin, everything made sense. But even that was starting to fade. I'd lie next to her and wonder if I was the only one she was lying like that with. I knew she loved me. She was just so lost, so broken. "That bitch is pure evil," Avry had once said when we first got together. She was evil, and I fell in love with her for it.

They encouraged us to interact with others and build bonds. But I found that extremely difficult. It had been so long since I had interacted with people on a sober level, I couldn't remember how. So mostly I just listened. But this one girl, Cheryl, wouldn't let up. She would consistently sit by me, spark meaningless chitchat. When I'd speak in discussions, which I actually found to be therapeutic, she would stare at me, eyes opened wide, absorbing every word. I pretended I didn't notice. She was an attractive girl, with straight light brown hair and oval brown eyes. One morning she sat next to me as I pretended to watch TV.

"I'm leaving in a week," she said with a smile.

"Oh, uh, congratulations, I guess," I responded, tripping over my words.

"Yeah, thanks, I guess. But I don't wanna leave."

"What? Why wouldn't you wanna leave?"

"You've never been in a place like here before, if I remember correctly."

"Nope."

"Everything seems so easy when you're safe inside these walls. But once you're out there, everything changes."

"Well, gotta just take it one day at a time," was all I could think to say.

"Yeah, I know. But this is my third time in here. I hate leaving here." I turned and looked her in the eyes. She was a lot more attractive than I had allowed myself to perceive her as. She was young, younger than me, and had this lost look of a child on her face. "I used to model, you know."

"Yeah?"

"Yeah. I was from a small town in northern Florida, and was always popular. The boys loved me. Everyone told me I should be a model. So I went to Orlando, and ended up scoring a modeling contract. I moved out there on my own. But I just didn't seem to fit in with the other models. There were just so beautiful, so skinny. They kept telling me I needed to lose weight if I was gonna make it big. There was so much pressure to always look perfect. Always being judged by your appearance. Always had to wear certain clothes, walk a certain way. I was used to being a tree-climbing tomboy, but now I had to make sure I had the right designer's bag with matching strappy shoes, or else I'd be a laughing stock.

"Sounds ridiculous."

"Well, maybe, but at the time it was everything. A lot of the girls used to sniff coke to curb their appetite, but I have a bad heart so I was afraid to. This one model, she was so beautiful. She never sniffed, but stayed so skinny. She never let the pressure get to her. I looked up to her so much. I wanted to be her. So calm and together, so graceful. So beautiful. So desired. Then one day she wanted me to come to one of her parties. I was so excited, I was early. So she invited me up to her room. She took out a needle and she showed me her secret. She shot up between her toes to hide any evidence. No one knew." I was listening closely now.

"So I started. And, god, was it great. All the pressure would slide right off me. My nerves were totally at ease. And I was skinnier than ever, the other girls were actually jealous of me. But I just kept doing more and more. And I became a mess. They said I was in violation of my contract and sent me home. My parents were horrified when they saw me. I felt like such a disappointment. The whole town had faith in me, they really believed that I was gonna be the next Cyndi Crawford. But I just turned out to be a loser junkie. They sent me here. But as soon as I got out, it wasn't long until I was shooting up again. And so the cycle continues. But I don't wanna anymore. I really don't. But it's just so hard. God, listen to me, I am babbling."

Her eyes were beginning to tear, and I wanted to wipe them. Wipe away her sadness, her fear. Tell her it was all gonna be okay. But instead I just turned my head toward the floor and said, "I'm sorry."

"It's not your fault."

"I know. I just don't know what to say."

"Just tell me I'm gonna be strong this time."

I looked her in the eyes. They told me of her fear, her weakness. I knew she would not make it through a week. "You're gonna be just fine." She smiled as a tear rolled down her cheek.

The next day they had us do an activity where one person would stand in the center of a circle and symbolize everyone's drug of choice. Then a person would be picked to stand up and confront the "addiction." They tried to make sure that whoever was in the middle shared the same addiction as the person picked to confront them. Things got pretty intense. People started screaming and cursing at the top of their lungs, and often the "addiction" would break down in tears, or both of them would. I didn't want to go but they made it seem as if I had no choice. Cheryl was chosen to symbolize my addiction. At first, with everyone's eyes on me, I could think of nothing to say. But the counselor egged me on. "C'mon, think of everything heroin took from you," he said. "Now think of her as heroin. She's the reason why you're here. Think of everything you lost because of her. Start by naming that."

I began to speak at a low tone, looking at Cheryl's feet as she stared me in the face. "Well, I had to move away to a place where I know no one, and got stuck in a cage and thrown in here. My guitar, I lost my guitar. No, I sold my guitar, for you," my tone slowly began to rise. "I miss my music, and the stupid dope I copped wasn't even that good. Now it's gone and I can't get it back. I lost...Avry. He's gone. Some best friend. Just walked away. He promised me forever, and then he just left. Just fucking left!" I started yelling.

"Once upon a time all I wanted was to sit and jam out with my best friend. Now I can do neither. All I can do now is worry about how I'm gonna score, who I'm gonna rob." I started yelling louder, going off on random tangents, talking about the rape, about the murders, but in a way that could not really make sense to anyone. I screamed out, "We did that to her and fucking loved every minute of it. Sick fucks! What the hell is wrong with me? But no one will understand." I was looking straight in Cheryl's face now, but I wasn't seeing her. I wasn't seeing anything.

"I did that to them because of you, it's all for you! And he was probably telling the truth. It was probably for nothing!" Somehow, my subject had switched and it was as if I was screaming at Delia. "You stupid bitch, you're probably fucking them right now! They're probably running a train on your whore ass as I'm rotting away in here! And you're probably loving it! It gets you high, doesn't it? That's all that matters, isn't it? Fuck, you have all of me, and you just give yourself to anyone who will get you high! You stupid slut bitch!!"

Suddenly I felt hands grab my shoulders and shake me. "Xavier!" a male voice shouted. I was snapped back into reality to find myself directly in front of a trembling Cheryl, face drenched in tears. I stepped back and leaned over, grabbing my knees, trying to catch my breath. I was in shock by what had just come out of my mouth. I wanted to take it all back, just pretend I never said it. Not that Delia would ever know, but I wanted to take it back for myself. Wash all such thoughts away. I didn't mean it. I couldn't have. She wouldn't do that to me. Not her. Not to me.

Days passed, and the urges subsided more and more. I was very active in all forms of therapy, and interacting with the others, exchanging horror stories, goofing around, cracking jokes. These were all people who could understand, because they knew exactly what it was like. They asked us to complete that same activity of labeling what we valued, to see if anything had changed in our perception of what was important. This time, instead of placing Delia first, I put my music. I made a promise to myself to get another guitar as soon as possible when I got out.

The realization that I had given it up all for dope helped me a great deal with my battle. I resented it, knowing that it was the cause for me giving up my true passions. For losing Avry. I started to think of it as the cause of all my problems. All me and Delia's problems. I wondered what would happen between me and her without it. If we would exist without it, if it was what held us together. I decided that we were more than that, whether the other reasons be just as unhealthy or not, there were other reasons. We were the darkness that swelled in one another, all we saw when we closed our eyes. We didn't need dope, it was holding us back from our true potential, as individuals and as one. Or so I believed. I swore I was ready to kick.

When I told Delia that I wanted to kick, her first reaction was to laugh. But when I remained in silence on the other end, "Oh, you're serious." Then some more silence. She finally said she was proud of me and that she'd support me one-hundred percent. It felt good to hear her say that, and I wanted desperately to believe her, though in my heart, I knew better.

My 28 days were finally up. At first the time was crawling, but the last week and a half flew by. I was afraid. I finally understood what Cheryl meant. The notion of kicking was all fine and dandy when the option wasn't around. But I would soon face the real test. But I was ready, at least I thought I was. I was strong. I could do it. And with Delia on my side, I could beat anything. Delia said she was going to be picking me up. I wasn't exactly sure how I felt about seeing her. Terrifyingly excited would be the best description. She was there waiting for me, behind the wheel of Peter's car. Her hair had all grown out to right under her ear and she had it slicked completely back. It was dyed platinum blond and black, giving it the illusion of a skunk's tail. She leapt out, ran to me, and jumped into my arms, wrapping her legs around my waist. The smell of her skin came back to me as if I had never been separated from it. We kissed passionately. "C'mon, let's get you outta here," she said with a welcoming smile.

We got into the car. "I see they are letting you drive their car now?"

"Yup. Cool, huh?" It was too early to deal with such thoughts. During the car ride home, she rambled on about all the crazy events that had recently gone down in her life, all the "awesome" people she had met, blah, blah, blah. The guys had let her stay with them the entire time, and supposedly were cool with my return.

I still wasn't familiar with the city and its neighborhoods, especially from a car's view, but I knew we were off course when we ended up in this secluded little side street. "We'll have no privacy in the apartment," and with that she started kissing me. Then she climbed over to my side, straddled me, wearing no underwear. It had been so long. I hadn't even really thought about sex in there. There had been two times when I had gotten lost in sexual fantasies, always with her as the other main character, and I ended up having to jerk off in the bathroom. But considering the fact that I had once been so obsessed with it, the absence of sex was not devastating. But being inside her right then, it just felt so good, so needed.

I came quick, but hard. She climbed back to the driver's side. We stared at each other with great big smiles, and I caressed her face. I got lost in those hypnotic eyes. I was happy to see her. We were gonna make it through this. That happy little bubble was quickly burst as she, with that devilish smile, went into her book bag and whipped out two bags of "ridiculous shit." So much for one-hundred percent.

"I thought I told you... you said you'd back me on this...you promised."

"Yeah, I will, if that's what you want. I just thought it would be rude if I didn't offer," and she proceeded to cook up.

"Delia," my heart was racing, my blood boiling.

"Look, I said I would support you, I didn't say that I was gonna kick too." I stared as the needle swallowed up the venom, salivating, like a starving wolf. At first I tried to tell myself that she just didn't understand how difficult it was for me to watch, having never even tried to quit herself. But I couldn't convince myself of such a lie; she knew exactly how difficult it was for me. That was why she did it. As it flowed through her system, she laid against the seat, eyes rolling back. "Like I said, ridiculous shit." And with that, my first attempt to kick was brought to a swift end.

Old habits die hard. In my case, mine was alive and kicking. I had to see a probation officer once a week. Delia had managed to find some straight edge kid who would let us use his piss for a price. He'd piss in a vial, and I'd hide it in my ball sack. The officer never watched me pee, and violá, clean piss. I just had to shoot up in places I could hide. Luckily, I was assigned a P.O. who couldn't have cared less. She was a tremendously overweight black woman who was always too preoccupied with one thing or another to notice my obvious appearance as a junkie. As long as my tests came out clean.

My immediate relapse had triggered a deep depression in me. Weeks passed, and the depression grew deeper and deeper. Delia hated seeing me like that. She bitched that I wasn't being myself, that I was withdrawing myself from everybody, including her. I even started watching a lot of TV, since there was absolutely nothing of interest for me to do. I'd get high and stare at the screen as it sucked out what little thoughts I had left. One day she came to me and plopped a wad of money in my lap, "For a guitar. Maybe then you'll act alive."

"Where did you get this from?"

"Does it matter?" It didn't.

I bought a used black Hernandez acoustic. And I played on. Shot dope. Played some more. Shot some more dope. During this whole time, Delia faded in and out of the picture. Those extraordinary moments that were induced by her presence lessened more with each passing day. Two guys were letting me live in their apartment, no questions asked, as long as I cleaned up after myself and didn't eat all their food. So I'd sit in their home, get high and strum on my guitar, while they would go out and party with my girlfriend all over town. I never complained. Besides the times I'd go out collecting change, I would just stay in, getting lost in my music, flying high through a world in which nothing existed but me and each fluid chord. A world in which nothing mattered, and I had not a single fucking care in the world, not even a single fucking thought.

One late night when the troops arrived home, I was sitting on the floor, holding my guitar, fucked out of my brain. Delia was just as fucked. She came and sat down next to me, with a huge smile across her face. She rambled on about her night's events, as she stroked my hair. "Hey you wanna hear a song I just wrote?" I said with a smile. I hadn't shared a song with Delia in a while so she looked pleased. She came and sat next to me as I started to play and sing:

I look in the mirror, see the face that I despise,
I try to turn away, but from myself I cannot hide

Then I realize, this is my fate I can't escape it
I have no choice but to give in and embrace it

Do you fear all that you cannot see? I fear all that lies within me.

So I lie in this casket I have created
By the truth, all my fantasies have been invaded
All masks torn off, I no longer can disguise
When you cannot feel, how do you know that you're alive?

"That's all I have so far."

She looked at me in disapproval. "Fuck X, that was really depressing." She got up and went to the kitchen. "I'm gonna make myself something to eat then go to bed." They didn't care when she ate all their food. She gave me one last look as she left the room, one that almost seemed full of pity. Then, through the dope haze, I saw it. I looked into those eyes and saw unending blackness. I saw her. Only it was me. Maybe it was just put on by the music I had just written. But it was as if I was looking into a mirror, and what I saw was an image of all the things I despised in myself.

I finally asked the question I knew the answer to. We were sitting in front of the television when I said to Peter, "Did you and Delia ever fuck?" Jonathan cracked up. Soon Peter couldn't help but join in.

Through his laughter, "You're buggin' bro," more laughter from both, "Nah, nah." It confirmed my suspicions; she was fucking *both* of them.

More time slipped by. I would rub my fingers back and forth over the scar, over her initials, wanting to just rip off the entire chunk of flesh.

"How could you say something like that?" She was screaming over my guitar as I remained in silence. "Hello! Anyone home?" She was obviously not pleased with my question to the boys once she heard of it. I kept on playing. She started crying, "Baby, please, where are you? I miss you." I kept on playing. Her mood suddenly took a turn, and as she walked out, "Fuck you, Xavier." I kept on playing.

One day I was feeling quite sick, and not from lack of dope. My throat was killing me, my body ached, and I had a slight fever. An intense depression decided to join the party. Delia was getting ready to go clubbing, all expenses paid for by her two friends. "Hey do you think you could possibly just stay here with me tonight?" I never asked her to stay home with me. She did what she pleased. But I knew if I was left alone I'd flip out, I could feel it coming. I just wanted to kick back with her, get high, and pretend life was okay.

"But, babe, Sir Mouse is spinning at the club tonight. Some insane tekstep." Suddenly she was a fan of techno-type music. That's what all her new party pals all liked. "You should come, it's gonna kick ass." She wrapped her lanky arms around my narrow waist. "C'mon, come out with me. We'll have so much fun, I promise."

"Nah, I feel like complete shit. Please, just kick back with me tonight. We'll have some dinner, watch a movie or some shit. Please? I really need you to do this."

She kissed my forehead. "Oh, sweetie, I'm sorry, I just can't. I promised everyone I'd be there." She grabbed her bag, and gave me another kiss, this one on the cheek. "Feel better, babe, I'll see you later if you're up." And with that she left. But I wasn't alone. My dope was there, ever faithful. There to wash it all away.

I started having nightmares every night. Some about Avry, some about Delia, some about that girl we destroyed. This one recurring dream with Delia really scared the hell outta me. They began with her trying to eat my flesh, but I would always manage to escape. Then soon the dreams morphed into me actually eating her flesh. They would get more intense every time. I'd tear her apart, bit by bit while she screamed in agony. The more she screamed, the more I ate.

Then one night I had a beautiful dream, a beautiful escape. A dream of another world, a world in which I was at peace. One of those dreams that are so vivid, yet cannot be explained in words. But then I woke up, and in a few seconds, the haze faded, and I realized it was only a dream. The real world had shown its ugly face, and my heart clenched. I would wish for such a dream every night following, another escape, one that didn't have to be injected intravenously. Sometimes in dreams we dilute the reality to which we are forsaken.

I was dragged along to some junkie bitch's house, surrounded by a bunch of uninteresting people. Delia ended up running off, conducting "business." One girl kept giving me dope, so I stayed a while. As the room cleared up a bit, the girl who lived there rolled over by me and started kissing my neck and rubbing my leg. I let her. She started to unzip my pants. I had never cheated on Delia. But at that moment I didn't care about that, or anything for that matter. No matter what she tried, I couldn't get hard. I just pushed her off of me and she tumbled to the floor. I looked over at her and became ashamed. I couldn't even fuck anymore, something I used to be able to always rely on. I was hardly fucking Delia. I was constantly haunted by visions of her fucking tweedle dumb and tweedle dumber. And whoever else she might've been banging behind my back. So with sex barely in the picture, all I had to assure myself that my heart was still beating, besides dope of course, was my music.

When you hit such a level in your life, everything just starts to flow in its own dark, cold manner. You are cut off from all other forms of life except the ones you could get something out of. There are different classes of those type of people. The ones who give to you because they love you and are in denial of what you are, such as rich parents of "accomplished" kids, ignorant girl or boyfriends. A type I unfortunately knew little about. Then there are the ones you use up. They catch on to your intentions and you have to move on. Finally, there are the ones completely aware of what you want from them, comply, and expect the same in return. Those were the type I mostly associated with. Friendship was something I only saw on TV. Love was a dangling memory.

It was the worst fight we had ever had. The place was empty except for us. She initiated it, being furious at my distance. She couldn't understand where I was coming from. She had mastered her role, temporarily convincing herself in the process. It all started when she tried to come on to me. Stripping, parading around me. It had become so hard to look at her, especially in those black hole eyes, so I just stared at the wall behind her. "Hello!" she yelled, and I wearily shifted my eyes on hers. "Why won't you look at me?"

"I am looking at you."

She grabbed her clothes. "What's your fucking problem? You mope around here and never wanna do anything. I don't know what you're so upset about, you got the setup here; a place to stay, don't have to work, don't have to worry about how you're gonna get high. Your probation is up in a month. Shit, you got it made. And for fuck's sake, why don't you ever wanna touch me anymore?"

"What are you complaining about? You got the whole city taking care of that." I had held that in for so long, letting it out was like taking the greatest shit of my life.

"What?" still wrapped in her own lies. I just shouted it all out, everything I knew was going on, acknowledging the fact that I was aware why we were able to always be supplied with dope. Those assholes were such ugly bastards, they would do anything to ensure a constant fuck from what was once a stunning girl.

"I take care of us," she cried out. "You know I love you, I gotta take care of us." I knew in her head she believed that that was what she was doing. I knew that because I knew how she worked, how every cell functioned. But I couldn't accept that, and I started to scream, and she cried harder. Suddenly I burst into laughter, and I just couldn't stop. More tears. She threatened suicide, and I laughed some more. She finally ran out of the room. And it ended with that, never to speak of it again.

One day I was once again dragged out from my self-imposed confinement to take a trip to Miami. The boys were picking up a bunch of primo stuff from a connect they had recently acquired from there. Delia was psyched about checking out Miami, and somehow coerced me into tagging along. As the guys did their thing, me and Delia lounged out on the beach, only slightly high off some whack shit, waiting for them to return with the real goodies.

I watched the waves crash against the shore in silence, as Delia people-watched, admiring the perfect physiques. I hadn't seen the sun in so long, I felt as if I was being cooked alive. Parched, I got up to grab a drink. As I got to the shaded boardwalk, I removed my dark sunglasses, exposing myself to the world around me: half-naked, tanned beauties rollerblading by, shirtless chiseled men with their frosted tips and designer frames, families with fanny packs and "Miami Beach" T-shirts licking ice cream cones. I felt completely out of place. But then again, those days, every time I left that house I felt out of place.

But it was different that day. I felt like some hideous creature that just emerged from the tar pits. I hadn't showered in a couple of days, I didn't bother to comb my hair, my clothes were ratty and torn, my lips were chapped, and I wasn't high enough not to care. Plus my paleness seemed to glow like a floodlight in the sun. I wanted to just run and bury my head in the sand.

Suddenly I caught notice of one girl up a ways. She was walking with a boy, smiling and laughing, her long brown hair blowing in the wind. I stopped in my tracks. Veronica. I didn't really believe it. "It couldn't be," I thought. But as she got closer I realized it truly was her. She looked even more amazing than I had remembered. Just as she caught notice of me, I quickly turned my attention to a boardwalk hat rack, pretending to not have noticed her. But I just couldn't help but take another glimpse. Her head was turned and she looked at me with these disappointed eyes, as if she recognized me but was hoping she was wrong. I threw my shades back on, and quickly turned around.

"Xavier?" she called out. I pretended not to hear. "Xavier, is that you?" she called louder, but I just kept walking. I desperately wished that she thought she was wrong. That the person she once "believed in" could not be the same rotting excuse of a person she just saw. Because he wasn't.

When I returned to where Delia was, she trying to seek shelter in the shade, her pale skin having turned a light shade of pink. I walked right passed her, toward the water. I removed my shoes, and walked right to the shoreline, letting the water hit my feet, feeling the sand squish between my toes. It felt amazing, new and real. I stared out into the endless sea. I thought of Lake Tahoe and my time with Veronica. It seemed like eons ago. The peace I thought I once felt there, I began to think it was all just a dream. I couldn't even fathom such a feeling. It couldn't have been real. I started picturing myself just diving in the water and swimming as far as the eyes could see. Just letting the sea take me away with its drift. I could almost hear it calling my name. "Xavier!" Delia barked. "Damn, I've been calling you, couldn't you hear me?"

"Sorry. I was thinking."

"You walked right by me. What's wrong with you? You look like you've just seen a ghost."

"I did."

"What? What are you talking about?"

"Nothing, it's just hot out here."

"Your pants are getting soaked," she chuckled. I looked down and saw my pants drenched up to my knee. I hadn't even noticed. "C'mon, space cadet, the guys will be back any minute." So I followed.

My probation was finally over. Delia arranged a party in the house to celebrate. A whole bunch of people that I cared nothing about. She even hired two strippers. I tried to pretend to be excited, but even that was hard. So I just got really fucking high. I sat there, trying to hold on to semi-consciousness as they proceeded to make out and rub their naked bodies all over me. Eventually the struggle became too difficult, and I just nodded off as everyone enjoyed the festivities around me.

One rainy afternoon, I had just copped and got to the apartment, ready to grab my guitar. It wasn't there. I sat in silence, waiting.

The door flung open, and there she was, with a smile on her face. "I just scored some primo shit." I remained in silence. She sat down and started to cook up.

"You sold it, didn't you?"

"Huh? What are you taking about, babe?" focused on the bottle cap.

"Don't play dumb, bitch."

"Hey!"

"You fucking knew, you fucking knew, you stupid whore." I was erupting with rage.

"You need to calm down."

I took a few breaths, calming a bit, and continued on, "Just fucking admit it."

"Admit what?" she seemed frightened; she could sense what was growing inside me.

Fed up, "ADMIT IT!" as my fist broke through the wall.

"Okay," she screamed. "But you told me you were gonna be needing some. I was broke and the guys are gonna be gone all day."

"I got my own!"

"Yeah, I noticed. But how was I to know? I'm usually the one hooking your ass up."

"Bullshit."

"It's true! Besides, all you do is just fiddle with that damn thing all fucking day. It's not normal."

"Shut up, just shut up! This isn't about that. You took the one thing that mattered to me."

"I thought I was that!"

"Once upon a time, but then you decided to be Queen Slut of the Underworld. A strung-out junkie whore, that's what you are. How can you fucking stand yourself?"

Her eyes told of the pain she felt from my words, but she fought on, "Well maybe if you'd fuck me once in a while I wouldn't have to search elsewhere else for dick." She was trying to return the pain. It felt as if a drill was digging into my temples. I grabbed my head. That just added fuel to her fire. "And you know what else? I didn't sell your guitar, I fucking smashed it!"

And that was it. I whaled her right in the head. She fell immediately to the floor, blood running from some orifice on her face. I picked up a picture frame and smashed it over her. After that, I blacked out. I came to hovering over a bloody, boney, pale-skinned, terrified, little girl. I just stared at her, for how long, I don't know. I knew that when I first hit her, I felt a rush. A reminder of what it felt like to be in control. But after, when I was looking at her, that didn't matter. I was looking at a girl I once loved more that anything, a girl that just a few moments ago, I enjoyed pounding the hell out of. She looked up at me, and in her eyes I saw nothing, absolutely nothing at all.

I quickly packed up my shit and took the dope she had just copped. I also did a run-through of the place, taking anything of value that they hadn't gotten to first. On my way out I called Peter's cell phone. "Hey you should come home quick. Delia needs to go to the hospital. She's not ODing, just got hurt." And I hung up. As I was about to step out of the apartment, I stopped. I wanted to look back. She was still on the floor, crying. She didn't say a word. The only sound was her loud, heart wrenching sobs, as she choked on her tears. And I knew she wasn't crying from physical pain, or from fear, or from the fact that I had just hit her. She was crying because she knew it was over. I no longer belonged to her, nor she to me. Everything we had was gone; it had died a long time ago. And we were the ones that killed it. She knew when I walked out that door I would never return; not to that apartment, not to her. What was done could never be undone. I walked out the door, and didn't look back. Next stop, New York City.

eleven

"WHEN WE WALK TO THE EDGE OF ALL LIGHT WE HAVE AND TAKE THE STEP INTO THE DARKNESS OF THE UNKNOWN, WE BELIEVE ONE OF TWO THINGS WILL HAPPEN. THERE WILL BE SOMETHING SOLID FOR US TO STAND ON OR WE WILL BE TAUGHT TO FLY."

Patrick Overton

It was about a thirty-six hour bus trip to New York, during which I hardly moved from my seat unless it was to go shoot up in the bathroom. I stared out the window as the world passed by. I tried to figure out what exactly it was that I had become. I wondered what it was supposed to feel like to be alive, to live in the same reality as the rest of the world. What reasons there were to get up and face each new day. Then a feeling of hatred dissipated through my body. Pure, raw, hatred. For her. I thought about how good it felt to hit her. How much I wanted to keep going till there wasn't a breath left in her. Funny how close love and hate really are. Two insatiable desires. Both overwhelm you with passion. Both cause you to act irrationally. Both blind you. Same shit, just on opposite sides of the spectrum. And I don't think it is possible to ever really, and utterly, hate someone without ever having loved them first.

I thought about how I had killed two people, and how I didn't care. I asked myself if I was lacking something that most people had, something that linked me to the human that supposedly existed inside me. I wondered if I lacked a conscious, because the only thing I ever heard it say was, "Watch your ass."

New York was tremendous and in constant motion. Each borough was its own separate universe. I was drawn to Manhattan instantly. I especially liked the East Village. It was a place where everyone who seemed to create their own realities came together. Similar to New Orleans, without that constant morbid feeling. Certain parts of Manhattan were way too pretentious for my taste. I felt like I was pollution there. Spending most of my time in the Village, I quickly found a hook-up. It was easy. Various spots there were like junkie central. Tompkins Square Park, for one. At 8am that place was crawling with jonesing creatures in search of their antidote. As much as I didn't want any part in such activities, I needed to.

I wanted to kick but I knew it wasn't going to be that easy. And I didn't wanna make those first days in a new city, especially one as big as New York, any more difficult by excluding dope from the picture. But I knew I *needed* to, and believed I was ready. I desperately wanted to get clean. I tried not to get too well-acquainted with any of the junkies, for I knew I would just be leading myself into a trap. But I didn't know how to associate with any other type of person. I had been around them so much for too long. I tried to just keep to myself at first. But I could hardly bear myself either, which is the worst, because the one person that we are always stuck with is ourselves.

I couldn't afford to send myself back to rehab. I thought about trying methadone, since it was possible to get on the streets. But using a drug to stop using another drug really didn't make sense to me. If I was gonna be using, it was gonna be dope. But I had to stop, somehow. I felt myself decaying. I was a homeless addict all alone. I had no other choice. I wanted to find Avry, but I couldn't let him see me like that. I missed my music more than anything. It felt like millennia had passed since I had created anything besides a dope mix. I felt like such a cliché. Just another one of society's rejects; a pathetic result of a painful childhood who decided to take revenge on the world by rejecting it, and was failing miserably.

The thought of any human physical contact made me ill. But I did miss it, what it once felt like. The feel of another's skin. I missed how it felt to just lie in bed next to someone I loved. But it was all an illusion, the whole fucking time. It left me with absolutely nothing, not even a shred of who I was before, which I was starting to believe was never much to begin with. But I knew there was a point before her in which things seemed to make sense, in which I was content. At least that's what I thought when looking back. I had made more than my share of mistakes and bad decisions, but I was always able to pick myself up from them. And I had Avry. I blamed everything on her; it seemed so natural to do so. My blood would boil as visions of her face would pop into my head. The only thing I could do to calm myself was to envision my fists smashing into her face.

Through word of mouth I heard about these people; for an affordable price they would lock you in a room, and keep you in there until you detoxed. They sometimes would even help you get a job. They considered themselves missionaries, and they *were* in a sense. Supposedly, one of them lost his sister to dope and felt like he owed it to the world since he could not succeed in saving his sister. Whatever the cause behind, it didn't matter. It seemed like a good first step. The place was out in Brooklyn.

After what seemed like a never-ending subway ride, I arrived at my stop. Coney Island. I went to take a quick look at the famous amusement park, trying to stall the inevitable torture. The old wooden rides, that creepy smiling face at the entrance way; it looked like a scene right out of an old horror movie, making the whole experience even creepier. It was a gloomy day and a gloomy area, and I felt as if I was walking with a grey cloud hovering over my head.

After some circling around, I eventually found the place. It was in an old red brick building, and the bell was labeled as "The Pollacks." I rang it. I was told to ring it three times in a row, so I did. No answer. I rang three times again. "Yes?" a woman's voice crackled through the intercom.

"I'm looking for...salvation." That was what my informant told me to say. That phrase in itself made the whole experience even more disturbing. The door buzzed and I pushed it open, having to use all my strength. As I climbed up the piss-drenched steps, my heart started pounding. Non-artistic graffiti was scribbled all along the walls, including the words "SALVATION." I started wondering what I had in fact gotten myself into. My informant was just some bum junkie; maybe he was setting me up. Not that I had much to steal. Maybe they were sick serial killers who were gonna skin me and wear my flesh as amusement.

My heart pounded harder, and I thought that it might rip out right from my chest and start rolling down the steps. It wasn't too late to turn back. That's what I told myself as I reached the third floor. 3H. Though a little voice kept telling me to run, something else was pulling me to knock on the door. It opened, and two brown eyes peered from behind a chained door. "Hi...um...uh," I felt like I was gonna puke, "the salvation thing." He unchained the door and let me in. The apartment was a lot bigger and neater than I expected. There was a round table in the middle of the room covered by a cheap, flowered plastic tablecloth. Around it sat three people: a forty-something-year-old woman dressed in a long flowing skirt and colorful head wrap, a man about the same age in worn out jeans and a black T-shirt, and another younger woman wearing what looked like pajamas. The man who answered the door was tall and built, with gelled blonde hair, dressed in a white wife-beater and tight faded blue jeans.

"So, you come for help?" the standing man said with a heavy Russian accent. I nodded, still not sure what to make of the situation. I noticed a small boy hiding under the table, hugging the older woman's leg. She stroked his hair and said something soothingly to him in Russian. "Well, you come to right place," the man continued. "How you hear of Missionary?"

"From someone I met by St. Mark's Place. I think his name was Harry."

"Harry? What he look like?" I described him. "Ah, yes, Harry. I know who you talking about. We help him, get him job, but he just go off and shoot up again. You can't save 'em all, can you?" I shook my head. "What is your name?"

"Xavier."

"Come, Xavier, sit, sit. No need to be afraid. We here to help you. My name is Ignatz." He put his arm around me and led me to an empty chair at the table. The little boy fled from beneath the table and hid behind the older woman's chair. The man went into another room to fetch a folding chair. The others stared at me in silence. The older woman smiled warmly, baring yellow teeth, and put her hand on my shoulder. I couldn't help but cringe.

The man returned and unfolded the chair, and sat facing me. "Xavier, so you want to stop poisoning yourself with heroin?" I nodded. "You come to right place. We take care of you. We put you in room, and you cannot leave until detox done. You break anything, you pay for. Afterward we give you list of NA meetings, you choose if you want to go. The rest is up to you. You have job?" I shook my head. "Maybe we help with that. You give us a little out of paycheck in beginning, till all paid up. We don't ask much, just shows us you serious. People on drugs only spend money on drugs. And you have money now?" I nodded. "Good. We have our own methadone clinic. You want methadone?"

"I don't know. I don't really see the point in that stuff."

"Yes, I know idea is silly, but it helps a lot of people. I don't know. It's up to you. We monitor, but you have to pay every time you pick up. You understand everything?" I nodded. "Do you have any questions?"

"Yes. Why?"

"Why what?"

"Why do you do this? Just curious. Why would you wanna help someone like me?"

"You want to know?" I nodded. "Ten years ago, my sister, she come to me, she ask me for help. She say she take drugs, shoot in body. She want to stop but don't know how. I didn't know what to tell her. I tell her to just stop if she wants to. One week later I find sister dead from overdose. Lying half naked on bathroom floor with needle still sticking out of arm. I loved my sister very much. My father died in Russia when we very young. Mother take us here in hope of American dream. I failed as the man of family. I cannot shake guilt. My wife here," he signaled toward the older woman, "Vera. We meet in support group. She lost best friend to heroin. Magda and Sasha," pointing to the others, "same story. I need to find a way to make up for my neglect. We have other jobs, but this, this is something we do to help. But we not rich, we need money to help. I have little boy now," he said, pointing to the terrified child. "Answer question?" I nodded, still not really sure why he would want to help me. "Now you know about me, so I must know about you. Tell me, about yourself."

"Uh, what do you want to know?"

"Everything that led you to this point. From far as you remember up to you knocking on this door."

I paused. I took a deep breath, opened my mouth and gave the quickest rendition of my life's tale, stuttering along the way. Words just started flowing out of my mouth, as if I was in therapy. I didn't know them from a hole in the wall, but I found it easy to talk. Maybe because I felt like that by sharing my story I would be shedding my past. I told them about my grandmother, my uncle, Dani, I even told them about my aunt's boyfriend. I told them about Vegas, about Avry, about Delia and what we did to the ignorant kids. I only left out the tale of the Texan girl, the corpse we hid, and the dealer, in fear they would deny me help. Then I told them how I wanted to find my best friend, but I couldn't let him see me in the condition I was in. How I needed to create again in order to feel like I wasn't a complete waste of oxygen. How I just wanted to remember what it was like to actually feel anything other than being high and angry. I finally really wanted it, and that was why I was able to tell them.

"Life is hard. But no reason to throw it away for drug. You musician and artist. I artist too. Must make art and music, not waste talent on getting high. Too young to waste life. I help you. You speak to me with sincerity in eyes. When do you want to begin?"

"Uh...now." They looked at each other and said something in Russian. "Is that okay?" I questioned.

"Yes, yes. We just have to take boy to grandmother's. You have money?" I handed it to him and he counted it: thirty bucks. "Is this blood money?" I shook my head. I had stolen it, but no blood was shed. Some drunken asshole cursed me out for no reason, and I later found him passed out cold on a bench. Times were rough. "We find you job, you help us, okay?" I nodded. He led me to the back room, as his wife went and fetched clean sheets. The room was basically empty and the window was boarded up. There was a connecting bathroom, with no mirror. His wife scurried into the room and made the bed quickly. When she finished, Ignatz asked, "When was last time you shoot up?"

"A couple of hours before I got here."

"Okay. If you hungry, shout out for food, we slide in," he pointed down at the door to what looked like a tiny sliding pet door. "But I doubt you get hungry." He stuck out his hand and I shook it. "Good luck. I check back when screaming and crying stops." And with that he walked out, and I heard a bolt slide as well as another lock click. Then my stomach sank.

It was worse this time; something I thought couldn't be possible. The panic crept up on me like a sly fox hunting its prey. Heart thumping. DO-DOOM, DO-DOOM. It was echoing throughout the room like a speeding train was in those four walls and I was tied helplessly to the tracks. Hours upon hours passed, and I just screamed and screamed, pleading for help, crying out like a torture victim. I felt like a torture victim. My skin was peeling from my flesh and crawling all over the exposed bone. I flung myself against the walls, begging them to let me out. I banged repeatedly on the door. "Get me the fuck out of here!" Why weren't they opening the fucking door? I often could not even make it to the toilet to vomit, but didn't bother to clean anything up. I stepped in the watery slop, slid through it, but it didn't matter. Covered in my own excretions, I just kept screaming.

The ceiling was crumbling on top of me. I could see the paint chipping, and soon the entire thing began cracking. Chunks fell to the floor, as dusty pieces landed on my head. "Help, get me out, I'm gonna get crushed to death!" But no one seemed to care that the goddamn place was falling to pieces. I pressed my palms against my temples, as if I was trying to crush my skull. I just needed to make the pain stop. "Oh god, make it stop!" I shook my head violently as if I would be able to wake myself up from the horrible nightmare. Yanking at my hair in frustration, I managed to rip some of it out. I stared at the loose strands in my hands, and for a few moments thought my entire head was shedding and I was soon going to be completely bald. A bald shriveled-up junkie with asbestos poisoning.

As more time passed, the panic slowly subsided, but the pain: the pain would not stop. I was so cold but I couldn't stop sweating. My clammy skin was covered in a dirty sheen. My body shook violently, as my screams turned to whimpers. I hugged the pillows, saturating them with desperate tears. "Please," I muttered, not even sure what it was I was begging for.

I heard a woman's voice on the other side of the door, singing softly in Russian. I followed her soothing voice, searching for any type of comfort. I crawled off the bed onto the floor, through the vomit, and leaned the side of my sweaty face against the door. She had to be directly on the other side, sitting on the floor as well. Her voice was beautiful, and though I could not understand her words, they offered some peace. Maybe she would help me. "Please," I whimpered at almost a whisper, placing my hand against the door. "Please help me. Let me out. I just need a little bit. Just to make the pain stop." The tears poured out like waterfalls, as my pleas grew louder. She just started singing louder. And I cried harder. "Please!" My face was swollen from the crying and it felt like my eyes were bulging so far out of my head that they may just fall out, but I couldn't stop the tears. "Please!" She kept singing, and finally I cried myself to sleep.

I woke up and found myself curled up in a ball beside the door. The worst was over. At least the physical worst. I was covered in sweat, vomit and piss, and was nauseated by my own foul stench. At least I had managed to make it to the toilet to shit. I pulled myself to my feet and stumbled to the bathroom, stepping over my puddles of filth. I grabbed the rough toilet paper and wiped them up. I then tore off my saturated clothes and went into the shower, where I must have remained for at least an hour, just letting the steaming hot water burn my flesh. When I finally stepped out into the steam-filled bathroom and began to dry myself off, I heard a knock on the door.

"Xavier?" Ignatz called from the other side.

I paused before I answered. "I'm okay, Ignatz." I heard the locks unlatch, and he entered as I stood wrapped in a towel.

"How you feel?" He tried not to wince too much at the sight of the room and its smell.

"Like hell."

"You were in here a long time." I couldn't tell how long I had been in there since I could not see the sun from the room. It felt like an eternity. I didn't want to know. "You hungry?" I shook my head. "You must eat something. Please. I give you buttered roll. Put clothes on, come."

"My clothes are filthy."

"Of course they are." He smiled and shouted something in Russian. His wife came back with a pair of loose-fitting grey sweatpants and a white T-shirt. I got dressed and met them in the kitchen.

"You know, you scare my wife in there."

"I'm sorry," I said as I tried to force down over-chewed pieces of the roll.

"She worry. She... does not matter. You okay now, no?"

"I wouldn't say that, but I'm not writhing in pain." I chugged down a glass of water hoping for some assistance with the chalky bread. I stared quietly at the table.

"Okay. Well," he put on a pair of cheap black-framed glasses and pulled out a piece of paper and began to read, "You must go to meetings.

Meet other people like you. They help you. Good environment. There are some good ones all over city. Where you live?"

"Uh...I...um..."

He looked up at me over his glasses. "You no have home?" I shook my head. He looked at his wife and spoke in Russian. "Well, first things first. I make call. I know people who rent room in Bronx. I know from work. But you must give rent or make me look bad, and I get angry. I nice guy, Xavier, but not so nice if you make me angry. Understand?" I nodded, feeling physically intimidated for the first time since I was a child. I was in no condition to defend myself against that man. I weighed as much as one of his legs.

"So, you need job. Can you be bus boy?" I nodded. "I made call, you go meet with my friend tomorrow for training. He has restaurant in Manhattan. He know about Missionary, he lose brother to drugs. But you cannot let me down. You late, don't show up, act rude, you lose job, and no more help. Understand?" I nodded. "You can stay here tonight, if you clean up mess, help my wife clean rest of house. Is okay?" I nodded.

As I felt my stomach clench in a knot, "What about methadone?"

"You want?" I nodded. Funny how people change their minds once situations are rearranged. He got up, took a key from his pocket and went into the other room. He came back with a tiny prescription bottle. "This one for free. Try to preserve. We slowly bring down milligrams, till you no need anymore. If I feel you abusing this, I cut you off completely. I am not drug dealer. I know this helps though. I go in room, have things to do. You go scrub floor, clean up smell." I tried to stand on my weak, shaky legs, but was unsuccessful.

"You weak, eat more. Give strength." I took another bite and suddenly gained strength as I leapt to my legs to go puke in the bathroom.

I was washing the dishes and Vera was drying them, humming softly. I looked over at her, and she smiled. "You have a beautiful voice," I said. She did. So soothing, like the sound of frosty waves crashing against the sand.

"Thank you," she graciously replied, blushing.

"Is that a Russian song?"

"No, from Broadway play they show on TV. I love plays, but we no get to go to Broadway. Ignatz took me once. Oh, it was wonderful. But sometimes they show on TV."

"I never saw a play."

"No? Oh, you must. New York good place to see one. So many. Beautiful music, beautiful dancing. So much fun. When I little girl in Russia, I play piano and sing. I loved it, and was good. I dance too. Think maybe one day I come to America and sing and dance in famous Broadway show. But when get here, need money, so need job. I speak no English, so hard to get job. I sat in hospital for twenty hours until they gave me job. They so surprised, and felt bad, so they gave me job. Taking blood. And I worked eighty hours a week. No time for dancing. But always time for singing." She smiled and continued her work.

I looked back at her, this time really looking at her. Her face wore the pain of a lifetime, yet still had a sweet softness to it. Something I was not used to seeing in anyone. I was so used to being around bitter people. And even as she spoke of lost dreams, she seemed not to have one ounce of bitterness in her. I continued washing. The situation was finally hitting me. These people, these amazing people. I couldn't understand why they were helping *me*. Who were they? How did I end up there? Was I just lucky? I doubted that.

Just as I began to question this, my eyes caught notice of something through the window. A blue jay. I had never seen one before. It perched on the windowsill, and I could have sworn it was looking right at me. The window was slightly open and I could hear it chirping a song. It could have sworn it was singing in the same melody as Vera. I felt something sweep over me that I had never felt before. Was something out there looking out for me? There had to be. Something I couldn't explain. But why did it care about me? A warm rush dissipated through my body, in much the same way dope did. But this was different. This was real.

I paused to catch my breath. I looked up just in time to watch the bird flutter away. Something was different inside me. I felt a feeling I had so long forgotten. I felt... hope. I was there for a reason. It was not just plain luck. Something led me there. Why, I could not explain. And at that moment the "why" didn't matter. I looked back at Vera, and it was almost as if I could see her aura. This light shining all around her. And it was beautiful. I paid attention to the melody she was creating, and began to hum along. She paused and looked at me with warm welcoming eyes. She returned to humming, and we began to harmonize as we emptied the sink.

Later that night, Ignatz fed me some soup and gave me a book to read about living sober. He had to leave for work, so the other guy I had met when I first arrived, Sasha, came over to keep an eye over the house while I was there. As Sasha ate his dinner, Vera called me to take a seat in the living room. "Come, come, sit." She had a videotape in her hand. She smiled as she put in the tape. It was a film version of the play "Chorus Line." "This good play, nice music. You like." She patted me on the shoulder and sat down with eyes full of awe. I watched with her, as she sang along to every song. I enjoyed the pleasure she received in watching the play more than the play itself. She was like a child at a petting zoo. It's funny how such a simple thing could bring a person so much joy. I wondered if I had ever felt such a humble pleasure.

Afterward, I tried to read myself to sleep, in a constant struggle to fight off thoughts of getting high. *I* didn't want to get high, but that tiny demon living inside me did, and he kept whispering to me. "Just a taste," he said. "Tell them you need some fresh air. Go by the park, get just a taste." It wouldn't shut up. But I stayed focused on the words on the page, even if they weren't registering completely. I finally drifted off, but not before hearing someone slide the bolt on the bedroom door shut.

The next day I hopped on a train to Manhattan to a tiny Russian restaurant on the West Side, accompanied by that same book and a newfound hope. I had only taken a small bag of stuff with me from Florida, which included a little bit of clothing and one of my sketchbooks that I had managed to salvage. All of my clothes hadn't been washed in god-knows how long, so I kept on the fresh clothes Vera had given me. I got a little lost on the way, not being familiar with the subway system, and was fifteen minutes late. I was supposed to be meeting a man named Nathan.

"You are late!" he scolded as I walked through the door. His accent was lighter than Ignatz's and the others'.

"I'm sorry, I'm still new in Manhattan. I don't know my way around."

"Ignatz told me. I'll excuse you this time. But *only* this time. So you want to work?"

"Yes."

"Ever been a bus boy?"

"Yes."

"You come in every day you scheduled?"

"Yes."

"You stay clean?"

"Yes."

"You say anything but yes?"

"Yes." He chuckled. He showed me around introduced me, and gave me a quick rundown of my duties.

"Listen, Brooklyn is a far trip. I live there. I see Ignatz often. I get methadone for you. I deduct a little bit from your paycheck first weeks for Ignatz. Only a little. I don't trust junkies, you know. But Ignatz's wife says she has a good feeling about you. And he has faith that you'll stay clean. And I trust Ignatz and Vera. So therefore, I will trust you." Trust me? Someone he didn't know from a hole in the wall. I was so mistrustful of others, the idea sounded preposterous to me. But I liked hearing it.

After I was done there, I headed toward the Bronx, to an address Ignatz scribbled on a piece of paper. There was a room for rent there. It wasn't the place he originally thought to send me. He did not know the people directly, so I was on my own. I couldn't believe how much he had done for me. I was trying to figure out a way to repay him. I felt like I owed him. I had never felt like that before. When I had asked him how I could do so, all he said was, "Stay clean, that payment enough." Fair enough.

The address was located in a ghetto area in the Morris Park section of the Bronx. As I walked through the streets reading the house numbers, I felt all eyes on me. It seemed to be a predominately Hispanic neighborhood, and there I was, a skinny, tattooed, pierced white boy in a completely foreign land. I thought there would be no way the people would rent to me. When I knocked on the door, a middle-aged, extremely short Puerto Rican woman answered the door. She was a bit taken aback by my appearance, but after I stated my business, she let me in. The house was cluttered, and two young boys rushed by me, yelling at each other in English. She screamed at them in Spanish, and apologized to me. The house seemed to be filled with tiny square carpets that were placed next to one another, forming the illusion that it was one giant multicolored carpet. The only clue that gave it away was that when you stepped on each section, it would slide apart from the rest. As I entered the living room, I noticed a big crucifix hanging over the couch. I literally jumped back when I saw it.

"Something wrong?" she asked. I shook my head. I reminded myself that I wasn't a boy and these people were not my grandmother. It was just a damn piece of wood and it could not hurt me. It could *not* hurt me. Her husband was only slightly taller than she was, with a heavy Puerto Rican accent that was almost impossible to understand. Noticing my difficulty, she spoke for him. They seemed pretty desperate for money so they agreed to rent it out to me. It was a tiny room, with white walls and an antique dresser. There was a tiny TV, but she said they only got a few stations. Not that it would matter to me.

While living there, I kept out of their way, and they kept out of mine. In the beginning, some people in the neighborhood would try to fuck with me, me being one of the few white people there, and just about the only freak. I tried to stay away from any physical confrontation, and I was successful. Eventually they got used to me and left me alone. I went to work, came home, and read. I acquired a newfound love for reading. I read history, biographies, fiction, basically anything I could get my hands on. I felt like I was filling my mind with knowledge it was desperately starving for. A new kind of escape; one that was not causing my deterioration.

When I was at work, I did my job, and didn't really talk to the other employees. They were mostly Russian, except for the few Mexicans, and both groups were usually engaging in conversations in their own languages. It was busy, relative to its size, and the shift I worked was the busiest of all. I picked up another sketchbook and began to draw again. It had been so long since I had drawn anything, and at first I was frustrated with my work. But I fought through it, knowing it was one of the few things I had to focus on to keep my mind away from getting high. I drew myself a picture of Dani, from how I remembered her, to make up for the picture that I threw away. I hung it up on my wall, and when things seemed hard, I'd look to the picture and talk to her, asking her for strength. And I could have sworn that when I asked for it, it was given. Maybe it was all in my head, maybe it wasn't.

Through Ignatz's and Nathan's supervision, I was being weaned off the methadone, slowly, very slowly. But despite all the things going right for me, I had internal wars going on inside of me. I was fighting my demons, and they were powerful mother fuckers.

Everyday, right before I'd get into the shower, I'd see it in the mirror, laughing right in my face. Her initials, DB, right there, inscribed in my flesh, taunting me each passing day. Reminding me exactly why I needed to keep fighting.

I went to several NA meetings throughout Manhattan and the Bronx, but just couldn't get into the spirit of it all. The people were very welcoming and understanding, but in my eyes it seemed as they had traded one addiction for another: meetings. I guess being addicted to meetings was a lot better than being addicted to dope, but it just didn't feel right for me. The only way to make NA work the way it worked for them was to make it my life. And I just couldn't do that. I wasn't ready to try and connect to anyone. And I didn't want to constantly wallow in my problems. And honestly, the constant talk of dope actually made it harder for me. So I decided to only go to a meeting when I felt like I was gonna cave. Instead of copping, I would just go hit a meeting and remind myself why I didn't want to do it. My life wasn't exciting and adventurous. It wasn't daring and full of mystery. But I was living. And I was the one in control.

I knew I wasn't ready to drink alcohol again, figuring it would just impair my judgment and lead to me getting high. I figured I eventually would be able to. Just not yet. But I did keep smoking weed. I wasn't high on a constant basis, just when I had some off time and wanted to create. According to NA, I wasn't clean, but weed was in no way controlling my life or serving as anything else but an anxiety repressor, so I saw nothing wrong with the occasional joint. No blunts, no binges, just a joint here and there. I decided I had to choose what the best way was for me to live, and I was feeling secure in my decisions. At least that's what I convinced myself.

It was time to start looking for Avry. I wanted to show him how I had changed. I wanted to get on my knees and beg him to forgive me. I wanted to let him know that I realized he was right and I was wrong, and I would spend the rest of my life making it up to him. I missed him in such a deep way that it was painful. It might have just been because I was lonely and I knew the connection between us was possible and previously established. Or maybe I felt I needed him, to be truly whole again. To remind me of the person I used to be. To remind me how to enjoy things, how to speak freely, how to be confident, how to be someone that people wanted around. Whatever it was, I needed him.

I started to scope out shows, looking for him, figuring that he would've assimilated into the New York punk scene. So I started going to any show I heard about, and could afford. I enjoyed seeing music live, feeling the sounds vibrate through my bones. But usually I'd just lean against the wall by the stage, listening, absorbing, watching the people in the pit. I couldn't jump in there. And I was having problems meeting people. I just couldn't talk to anyone. I'd just examine all the people engaged in the art of conversation. I especially couldn't talk to females at all. I'd freeze up. If one would strike up a conversation with me, I couldn't respond, regardless if they were attractive or not. I didn't want to put the effort in. They'd walk away, rolling their eyes, clicking their tongues. Even one of the Russian girls at work, who was attractively tall and voluptuous, had made a few attempts to hit on me, but I gave her the cold shoulder. Not trying to be an asshole, I just didn't wanna bother. I wasn't even horny. My first priority, right next to finding Avry, was getting another guitar.

One morning I just couldn't take the sight of it anymore. I had a terrible dream. I was in the woods, digging and digging. Delia was standing behind me with her arms crossed, watching, smiling. Finally when the hole was deep enough, she pushed me in. I screamed for her to let me up but she just leaned over, chuckled and waved. I tried to claw my way out, but I was getting nowhere. Dirt came falling over my head as someone began to fill up the hole. I screamed and pleaded, but slowly the dirt consumed me until I woke up drenched in sweat. I went to the bathroom to shower and clean myself up, and there it was, like usual, laughing at me. Her initials branded into my thigh.

I shoved a towel into my mouth, took the blade off my razor and attacked the scar. Cutting over scar tissue elevated the pain factor, and I bit onto the towel in agony as I tore through the wounded skin. But I welcomed the pain. I watched as the sharp metal sliced through pink tissue like crimson butter. I completely mutilated it and I was covered in blood. I cleaned myself up, then cleaned up the spillage all over the bathroom. I didn't want one of the others in the house to have a heart attack thinking I was a serial killer, and throw me out. All cleaned off, it looked like just another ugly scar, a permanent mocking reminder of what I used to be.

I finally saved enough for a new acoustic guitar. It was like being reunited with a long lost love. It took a bit of adjusting to get back into the flow of it. But soon it all came back. I had catching up to do, for all that time wasted. Those days spent high in Florida, there were moments in which I became the music. It was like we understood each other and worked as one. It wasn't the same without the dope, but fulfilling nonetheless. It would divert my mind from the ever-lingering thought of heroin. One of the boys who lived in the house would sit by the door and listen to me play, with his ear pressed against the door. I knew he was there, but he would still play it off like he wasn't, scurrying away if I opened the door. I didn't mind him listening, I rather enjoyed the audience.

I would go play in Washington Square Park. Smoke a joint, play and sing. Sometimes the Rastafarians would ask me to play reggae, and throw me a bag of weed if they were happy with my performance. It was funny; they'd often sell stragglers fake weed, but would give away the real shit. The park was always filled with people. There were a lot of others like me there, referring to the public music playing and public stonedness. Some people would go there to hang, to read, to walk their dogs, or just sit and people-watch.

Among all the musicians, I usually caught the attention of the groups of people nearby just hanging out. They'd compliment me and make requests. Even ask me to come hang out with them. Music has a strange power over people. But I usually graciously declined. I even made some money playing. But I didn't do it for the money, though, I just enjoyed it. The positive feedback was pay enough.

On one sunny day in the park, I was sitting playing my guitar, when a fairy fluttered by. She was 5'2", petite, chin-length cropped bleached hair, huge bluish green eyes that had a burst of yellow around the pupil, just like a cat's. Her eyes were so big they took up most of her face. She had a tiny nose, little pink lips. Her face's proportions resembled that of a Japanese anime character. She was dressed in a knee length white vintage dress, and was scribbling in a sketchbook by where I was playing. It didn't seem as if she even noticed me. But when she got up, she approached me. "You have an incredibly beautiful voice." She had a slight accent, I figured it for either Australian or English. I wanted to say something, but I didn't. I just couldn't speak. I somehow managed a smile. She smiled back, reached into her little fuzzy black purse and pulled out two dollars, dropping them into my guitar case. She kept her smile as she walked away. I had never felt so cheap in my life.

She started going to the park quite often. Or it might've been me going more. She was always scribbling in her book. Sometimes she'd sit on the other side of the park, far from me. I was never sure whether or not she noticed me. Sometimes she'd sit by me, always dropping in a dollar or two when she left. When she was near me, I knew she was listening to me play, no matter what she pretended to have her attention on. It would sometimes feel as if I were just there playing for her. And I knew she could feel it.

I finally spoke. "You know, you don't have to keep giving me money," as she dropped some bills in.

She smiled. "But isn't that the reason you're out here?"

"For you to give me money?"

She giggled, "I meant to make money."

"Oh, well, no, well yeah, I guess, sort of..." I fumbled over my words.

"I tried to teach myself the guitar, but it didn't work out. Now it just sits in my closet unused."

"Well...um.. it's easy."

"For you maybe."

"Well, uh, yea I guess." I kept stuttering

"Well, See ya!" She said with a smile and began to walk off.

"Yeah, see ya," but she was already too far to hear. I looked down and noticed it wasn't a dollar that she had dropped in. It was a piece of folded paper. I reached in, took it out, and opened it. It was a drawing of me holding my guitar, and it was fucking incredible. On the bottom, in some fancy script, it read: Angelika 555-0828. I couldn't call.

After that, it was a while before she showed up at the park. As if she was waiting for me to call. She started coming less often, always sitting on the other side. I wanted to talk to her, but it felt impossible. Partly because I had lost my ability to socialize, and partly because she just had this amazing presence, so strong that it was intimidating. She would still look over at me and flash a sincere smile, sometimes wave. I would respond with similar actions, then quickly shift focus back to my guitar.

I was at a show at CBGB's and had met this big punk dude who had his head half-shaved, the other half spiked out, nearly a foot long. "Yeah, I know who Avry is." His words stunned me. "Long black mohawk, fucked up teeth, words "fuck you" tattooed on his hands.

"Yeah, that would be him."

"Shit, it's fucked what happened to him."

"What are you talking about?"

"You don't know?"

"Know what?" My heart was clenching.

"Fuck man, he tried to blow his brains out a little over a month ago."

His words wouldn't register. "What did you just say?"

"Dude tried to kill himself. Got himself all laid up like a vegetable."

"What? We must be talking about someone different."

"Doubt it, not many Avry's who look like that. And you said he was originally from Cali, right?" I nodded. "Sorry man, but it's gotta be the same guy. He would always be at my gigs. Cool dude. He just lost it after his old lady threw him out."

Everything was spinning. Blood racing. Over a female? "He's still alive?"

"Yeah, as far as I know. But just by a machine."

I was filled with questions. "How did he do it?"

"What do you mean how?"

"Like how did he shoot himself? How did he place the gun?"

The guy flashed me a look of disgust. He had just told me my friend had shot himself, and I wanted to know the dynamics. "Fuck man, I don't know. To his head." A moment of silence followed.

"Where is he?"

"Don't know. Some hospital in Manhattan I think. If he's even still alive."

I cringed at the thought. "Who was the girl?"

"I don't know. Never met her. I don't think she hung around the scene." The band onstage finished sound check and started to play. The guy left to watch as I sat silently, alone at the bar. I remained there, motionless, until the place was cleared and I was told to leave.

twelve

"THE LOST ENJOY FOREVER THE HORRIBLE FREEDOM THEY HAVE DEMANDED."

C.S. Lewis

That was too much to handle. I didn't know how to react. Everything was supposed to work out once I was clean. Wasn't that the point? That wasn't something I had ever dreamt would be a reality. My emotions didn't know which way to go. Hatred came along, at him for giving up, over a girl. That angered me so much because it was too close to home.

I couldn't take it. I fell off. I gave in, lost control. Relapsed. Got high. And higher. And higher. I didn't want to stop. Subconsciously striving for an OD. Giving up. Totally willing to give myself, body and soul, to the beast.

I don't remember getting there, but somehow I ended up in Washington Square Park, lying on the ground, world fading. And I wasn't scared. Instead I lied there with a smile on my face. I was ready for anything. Then I saw two beautiful bright lights shining above me. I was lifted by a couple of sets of hands. Then I blacked out.

I woke up shivering on a futon in an apartment decorated with various shades of red. The waft of incense flooded the room, filling my nostrils. I sat up and rubbed my eyes. I felt like complete shit. "Hey." I was startled by a soft soothing voice. It was Angelika. She was wearing sparkling pajama pants and a matching tiny T-shirt, and that unforgettable smile. "Drink this." She handed me a steaming cup. I smelled it and winced.

"What is it?"

"Just drink it, it'll make you feel better." I shifted my gaze back and forth between her and the cup. "Why would I go through all this trouble if I was just gonna poison you?"

"Fair enough." I took a sip. It wasn't too bad. I quickly downed the rest.

"We weren't sure how serious you were. You didn't seem to be dying, just on the nod hardcore. So I thought it best to just take you home and let you rest instead of sticking you in the hospital. Luckily, it looks like I made the right decision."

"What if it was the wrong one?"

"Then I'd have a dead boy lying on my futon. But I have always trusted my instincts." A moment of silence. "Relapse?"

"Excuse me?" I said.

"Well, you never seemed high when I saw you, so I'm figuring it was a relapse."

Defenses naturally went up. I just turned my head and looked out the window, which was framed by a set of velvet red curtains.

"I knew you were a junkie, I just knew."

"I'm not a junkie. I've been clean for a while."

"Ah ha! See? I knew it, it was a relapse." She smiled. "Hey, I'm sorry."

"How did I get here?"

"Some friends and I were hanging out by the park, and we saw you laying there. You're such an amazing musician, I couldn't let you end it right there like that." My defenses went down. "So what caused the relapse?" I hesitated responding, so she pressed on. "Hey, what do you have to lose by telling me?" So I told her how my only true friend had put a gun to his head and I felt like it was my fault. That maybe if I had been there he wouldn't have done it.

"He just wasn't the type of person who would do that. Not over a girl. I need to talk to this girl."

"What are you implying?" Foul play. I didn't wanna say it, but she understood. "You're just hurting. It's natural to wanna blame somebody. It's nobody's fault, and definitely not yours."

"But if I had been there..."

"Things probably would've ended up the same way. People do fucked up things when they're in love, irrational things. Things they may never do otherwise. Love is twisted like that." That sounded true enough. Right at home for me. But at the same time, for the first time, I asked myself if I was just trying to blame Delia for my own dissension. I sat silent.

"So do you usually go out and pick up junkies and bring them back to your place?"

"No, just the pretty ones." That smile." So once I get you outta my hair, are you gonna go get high?"

"No." And I meant it. The urge to give in went away. I don't know if it was the positive energy flowing out of that beautiful girl, or the mission I had created for myself: find this so-called girlfriend and see what led to Avry blowing his brains out. Find out if he, in fact, was still alive. I *had* to find him. That obsession combined with her energy made the words, "I'm done," ever so real. She seemed to believe me.

"You're welcome to stay awhile." I felt like shit. I didn't think I could move.

"I'm afraid I won't be great company."

"Oh, hush now. I'll whip you up some food, throw on a movie and we can just veg out. If you wanna talk about what happened, feel free. If not, it's okay."

"Um...okay."

She made me a delicious omelet, complete with bacon, but I could only eat half. As I tried to force the meal down, I analyzed her every word and move. She was bubbly and talkative. There was just something about her that I couldn't put my finger on that made her so unlike anyone I had ever met. "What kind of accent is that?"

"You can hear it? Most people can't tell."

"Most people are idiots." She giggled. She had the cutest laugh.

"I'm from a little country town in Australia called Wagga Wagga."

I couldn't help but laugh. "Is that really the name?"

"She threw a napkin at me. "Yes, it's an Aboriginal name."

"How did you end up here?"

"My dad brought me. He was an engineer, wanted to work in New York. My mom died when I was young so it was just me and him. But he died too."

"Oh, I'm sorry."

"It's okay, I am alright with it now."

"You miss them?"

"Well, I don't really remember my mom. She died from cancer right after I was born. She had another baby from another guy, and she found out that she had skin cancer when he was five. She had surgery and it was supposed to be gone. Then she found out she was pregnant from my father. They had just been married. That same week, she found out the cancer was back. The doctors told her that if she had me, the cancer would spread and have to go untreated, but I'd be safe. She decided to just start the treatments after she gave birth. She refused to get rid of me. Everything seemed to be okay until two days after she had me. She died that day, and my dad and grandmother took care of me.

"All I have is one picture of her, and a whole lot of stories. She was an amazing woman. Real stubborn type. Farm girl. Since she was real young, her mom would give her whiskey before bed, so that when she grew up she'd know how to handle her liquor. I stayed in contact with my brother and that grandmother, until she passed away, her husband having been long dead. Then I hardly ever saw my brother. But my dad took good care of me."

"So what do you do, Miss Angelika? You seem to be doing pretty alright for yourself."

"I waitress at this really nice French restaurant in Midtown. But that is just to pay the bills. I just started school for my Bachelors degree in Graphic Design at Parsons."

"You're a graphic designer?"

"Well, that's the goal. I love art and was always really good on computers. My dad taught me a lot. I love my classes, and I am doing really well."

A creative, strong, successful woman wasting her time with me. It just didn't make sense. "Why the hell is a woman like you helping out a guy like me, seriously?"

She showed me her arms. Scars of tracks. Old, but still visible. "Because I understand." I was pretty shocked, but at least now it made sense. "So, how about you? Where's your family?"

"I don't have a family."

"Everybody has a family."

I didn't want to tell her my personal business, but I figured I owed her something for what she did. "My parents were drug addicts, left me with my psycho grandmother. She pretended to raise me until she dumped me on my aunt, who let me do whatever I pleased until shit happened and I split when I was seventeen." An easy rendition. "I wasn't close to any of them so I don't consider them family. The only person who shared my blood line that I cared about died in a car crash when I was young." She looked at me with pity and it made me cringe. I didn't want her fucking pity.

"Do you ever think about your parents?" I shook my head. "You don't ever feel upset, like they just gave up on you?" So many questions.

"Nope. My father seemed like a bastard, I didn't wanna know him. All I really remember about him is how uncomfortable I felt when he was around, so I liked it better when he wasn't."

"What about your mom?"

"There was a point when I did resent her for... for..."

"Abandoning you?"

"Yeah, I guess. But it was more then that. It was as if she was trying to punish me. Otherwise she wouldn't have left me with that family."

"But they were your family, too."

"But she knew how they were, more than anyone. Everything she hated them for putting her through, she had to know they were gonna do to me. And she still left me there. Why would you want your child to suffer the same fate? I don't understand why people even bother having kids nowadays. Why would you wanna bring a life into this fucked up world anyway? It's like condemning them."

"So what you're upset about isn't the fact that she left you, it's the fact that she left you there?"

"I don't know." She just kept going. Like a damn shrink. But I just kept answering like a damn patient.

"Would you rather she have had taken you with her?"

"Shit, that probably would've been worse. Probably would've left me alone starving for days in a rats' nest while she went off to get high."

"I know it's kinda hard to really know, but looking back, what would you have rather she'd done, taken you, or left you?"

"Jesus, don't you ever quit? I would have rather she had fucking stayed, try to clean her ass up, and take care of her kid. Isn't that what a parent is supposed to do?" She nodded, slightly intimated by my raised voice. I took it down a notch. "I would have rather her to not have found it so easy to just throw me away."

"Addiction is a crazy thing."

"Hmph." I hadn't really thought of it from that perspective. I had always known my mother was an addict, but it never clicked. Drugs were the one connection I had left to my mother. I should've understood her actions more than anyone. But that didn't rectify them. It didn't make the fact of the matter any less painful. It didn't justify anything. Not for me, not for her. Drugs couldn't be used as a crutch. It didn't work that way. I began to wonder if she ever thought about me. If she ever thought about finding me. If she ever cried at night about me. If she regretted walking out. If her actions haunted her every moment of her life. I hoped they did.

"So what exactly brought you to dope?"

"A girl."

"See? Like I said, love can make you do crazy things."

"Hmph, love."

"It was love, wasn't it?"

"At some point it was. I remember it like an old dream, like one of those dreams that completely blow your mind, so you save 'em in your memory and every so often think back about it, dwelling for a moment on the fact that it was just a dream."

"Sounds like it was beautiful. Tragic, but beautiful."

"From this perspective it's hideous. I see it for what it really was and it disgusts me. I wasted too much of my life, lost years, lost a friend." I fought to hold my composure as I thought of Avry "Have you ever been in love?"

"Puppy love, infatuation. At the moment I was wrapped up in it, but nothing really serious. No one I miss. I think that if you truly ever love someone, and then they are not in your life anymore, whatever the cause, a piece of you goes with them. But then again, I've never truly loved someone, so who am I to assume such things?"

I sat in silence for a few minutes. The whole situation had become way too intense. I finally spoke, "Look, this Q & A is a ball of laughs, but enough already."

"Okay, I'm sorry. It's just when you find someone half dead in a park with a needle in their hand, you might wonder what actually led them to that point."

"It takes a lot more than neglectful parents and an evil bitch of a girlfriend."

Some more silence. "Well, listen. If you ever need someone...if you ever feel like you're gonna fall off, you can give me a call." Poor girl. She truly wanted to help me. But she couldn't. Just another female in search of something broken to fix, fascinated by things she couldn't understand.

"Look, Angelika, right?" She nodded. "I see what you are trying to do. But I'm not the kind of guy you seem to think I am."

"How do you know what I think?" Her big bright beautiful eyes looked at me with sincere intensity. Maybe she could have been a positive influence on my life. Maybe she could have been the one to show me what it was like to live in the light. Show me all the beautiful things in the world that Delia swore were just illusions. Remind me that the darkness I had grown so accustomed to was not the only way. Part of me wanted to take her hand, kiss her passionately and wash all the pain away. But it couldn't happen that way. Maybe in another time, maybe in another life. I put my hand against her flawlessly smooth cheek.

"I see what you are trying to do, and don't think I don't appreciate it. But you can't save me." She looked at me, but remained silent. "What you did for me last night, that was... I couldn't be more thankful. But I can't give you whatever it is you are looking for. I'm sorry." Her eyes saddened, but she said not a word. Somehow she knew we were understanding each other. "Maybe someday...someday I'll take you out for dinner, tell you some tall tales of adventure. But for now, my beautiful fairy, I must bid you adieu."

I needed answers. Maybe he was awake. Maybe he was getting better. I would call every hospital in NYC until I found him. "But, fuck, what was his last name?" I screamed out in frustration. Holy shit, I realized that I didn't know my best friend's last name. He had to have told me, I just couldn't remember. Fucking drugs. Or maybe he never told me. I wondered if I had ever even told him mine. It never really mattered. Our last names were our only connection to a life we were trying so desperately to escape. I'd find him, somehow. We had found each other before, we could do it again.

I spent the following days going from hospital to hospital, asking for him by first name. The smaller places actually tried to look him up. But the receptionists in the bigger ones looked at me like I was crazy. How could I not know his last name? One night after a long day at work, I got to my room and tried to pick up my guitar, but I couldn't play. I was mentally exhausted. I dropped the guitar on my bed and fell to my knees on the floor. "Please!" I screamed aloud, probably waking someone in that house. "Please! If there is a god, a goddess, whatever the hell you are, please help me! Please help me find him." It was the only time

I ever called out to a higher being like that. Ever. I was so desperate; I needed a fucking *pair* of crutches.

I decided I would go to every show I heard about and look for the guy who had told me about Avry. I needed to find that ex-girlfriend. She was my only ticket to finding Avry, to finding out what happened. I was so stressed out by this mission that I felt that I could crack at any minute, and it was the last thing I wanted to do. If he was awake, he needed to see that I was no longer the mess he fled from. For someone who went a large chunk of his life without being afflicted with guilt, I was now submerged in it.

"Look, sir," she said with an arrogant attitude, "I can't help you if you don't have a last name. It's a big hospital." Mount Sinai was a huge hospital.

"But Avry isn't a common name. Maybe you could just skim..."

"That will take me forever, and I'm very busy." She turned to help the person standing behind me.

"Dammit!" I slammed my fists on the counter and her body jerked in fright. "Couldn't you just try!? Avry was my best fucking friend and I need to see if he's okay! What the fuck is wrong with you people!" Her eyes widened and she grabbed the phone to call security. "Forget it, I'll go." I was ready to give up. I thought I'd never find him. As I was walking toward the revolving door, "Excuse me!" a female voice shouted out. I turned to see a stunning 30-something year-old hazel-eyed woman with long red hair, dressed in a nurse's uniform. I looked behind me, unsure who it was she was calling to. It couldn't have been me. "I couldn't help but overhear you at the desk." She was talking to me. She had to be. I looked her straight in those sparkling eyes. My heart sank. She looked like..."Did you say that you were looking for someone named Avry?" I nodded without a word. "One of my patients is named Avry Ramery. Is that the one?"

"I...I don't..." I was having trouble speaking. Everything seemed foggy.

"Gunshot wound to the head?" I nodded. Avry Ramery. I shook my head trying to make sure I wasn't hallucinating.

"You know he... he's in a coma." I nodded. My heart skipped a beat. He was still alive. "He's in room 314. I'm going up that way. Let's get you signed in, and you can follow me. I'm heading in that direction." She turned and started to walk. At first I stood motionless, watching as her perfectly proportioned hips swished back and forth, her long bright hair bouncing not far behind. Was I a child again? Had all this time in between been one long dream? "Are you coming?" the nurse called. It wasn't a dream, it was all real. And that wasn't Dani. But she looked so much...I silently followed.

When we got in the elevator, I couldn't stop staring at her. She looked to the ground, blushing, and I realized I was totally gawking. "Do you know what happened to him?" she asked, sounding genuinely concerned.

"Not really." Still staring. "I haven't seen him in so long. I heard he... he did it to himself. Is that what the doctors think?"

"Yeah, self-inflicted. There was an investigation, but that was the conclusion." We passed the second floor. I must have been making her incredibly uncomfortable. She started rubbing her wedding ring, as if to show me that she was not available. But I wasn't looking at her with hormones in mind, despite her immense attractiveness. The resemblance was so strong, that I just wanted to embrace her. I wanted her to wrap her arms around me and tell me everything was going to be okay. "His face is all bandaged up. It might be hard to recognize him."

"I'll recognize him." A bell sounded, letting us know we reached our destination.

As we walked through the white doors, "I have to warn you," she said as she led me down the long narrow hall, "they don't think he's going to wake up. I don't know how long they are going to keep him on the machines." Her eyes were lowered in the corners, showing her difficulty of telling me such news. She stopped in front of a door. 314. She put her hand gently on my shoulder. "This is it." I didn't want her to move her hand for all eternity. I placed mine on top of it. She was a bit startled but didn't flinch. Her skin felt so soft. I didn't want her to go. But she wasn't Dani. She couldn't be.

"Thank you," I said, and she smiled warmly as she pulled away. I turned to the doorway. My mind was spinning. I entered the room and the sound of all those machines echoed through my head. There he was, dressed in a white hospital gown with small blue nonsense designs, wrapped up in a white sheet. Tubes were coming out of him from every angle. And just about his entire face was wrapped in white bandages. But I could still tell it was him. Long, greasy, uneven, black hair flowed down his shoulders onto the bed. I took a deep breath and walked closer. The half of his face that was exposed was so swollen, it looked as if it was filled with water. But I saw the corner of that crooked smile. Avry Ramery.

My throat swelled up and I felt as if I couldn't breathe. I wouldn't let myself cry. I walked up beside him. "Hey Av," I forced out. "It's me, X." Maybe he could hear me. I grabbed his hand with FUCK inscribed on it. "Jesus, Av, what did you do to yourself?" I stood there in silence for a few minutes. It was physically painful to see him like that. I could have sworn my face was throbbing in the exact same spot. I held up his hand and looked at his palm, then looked at my own. The same scar. Despite what he had thought, I never let mine heal.

"I fucked up, Av. We were supposed to be forever, and I let you go. But you walked away. I did some fucked up things." I felt salty liquid start to accumulate in the corner of my eye. I tried my hardest to hold onto it, not to let it go. "Avry, I need you to wake up, man, You have to wake up!" The tear started to make its way down my cheek. I couldn't take it. I let go of his hand and ran out. I made it out into the hallway and just puked all over the linoleum as patients and nurses looked on in disgust. Then I ran to the elevator. I had to get the hell out of there. It was just too much.

I didn't want to be alone. Seeing Avry like that, and that nurse. My mind was overwhelmed. I wanted to go get high. Make it all go away. So I called Angelika.

She sounded happy to hear my voice, though a bit worried by my tone. Why she let herself worry about me, I couldn't understand. Why all these strangers gave two shits about me was a complete mystery. But I didn't want to try to decipher it, just wanted to accept it for what it was before it was gone, like everything else. She told me to come over.

We sat in silence for a while. I didn't mind. I just needed someone there. I became overwhelmed with all these different emotions at once, hitting me from every angle, and I didn't know how to deflect them. So I just let them take control. Then something strange happened, something that hadn't happened since I was in the institution. I started to cry, and I couldn't stop. Just as I felt I was about to collapse, she pulled me near her. I fell into her embrace and cried for what felt like ages.

Finally, when I could shed no more tears, the crying ceased. But I felt a million times better. I'd needed that for so long. It was a release. But I did not want to move. She ran her fingers through my hair and rocked me back and forth. I finally removed my face from her tear-drenched shirt. I was too ashamed to look her in the eyes. She grabbed my chin and lifted my head until our eyes met. "You have nothing to be embarrassed about," she said earnestly, picking up on my uneasiness. "Everyone needs to cry. How do you feel?"

"Better."

"You hungry?" I nodded. She walked in the kitchen and started to fix me up a sandwich.

"I am really sorry." I couldn't completely shake the embarrassment.

"Don't be. Do you like turkey?"

I nodded. "If he doesn't make it... he'll never know how much he meant to me."

She put the last piece of bread on top and handed it me, grabbing a bag of chips for herself. "I know what it feels like to lose someone when things have been left on bad terms. You always wonder if they had any idea how much you cared. But it's something you can't change. You'll make yourself mad wishing you could. And besides, you have to be optimistic. He might make it through, you know."

No, he *had* to make it through. "Is that what happened with you and your father?"

"Yeah," she replied with a full mouth.

"Tell me about him, if it's not too uncomfortable for you." I needed to get my mind off of Avry. I needed to hear someone else's pain so that I wouldn't be so wrapped up in my own. And besides, I liked hearing her speak.

She finished crunching and swallowed. "What do you want to know?"

"Anything, everything."

"Okay." She crunched through a few more chips at full speed and then took a deep breath. "Well, when I was six, my dad copped the urge to go back to school. So we moved to Melbourne so he could attend a university and study engineering. At first, I hated it. I was a country girl. The city was intimidating. And I missed my grandmother. But my dad seemed to love it. He was doing really well and getting praised for it. I was young, but I still understood what it meant to him. I've always had the motherly instinct. He was happy with where he was and with what he was doing, so I didn't want to change that. He got a good job."

Then when I was eleven, he decided we had to move to New York. He had the fever for success. He'd received much recognition in Melbourne, and felt like he had accomplished all he wanted to there and needed to move on. He actually believed that when we arrived here, everything would fall into place. Of course, it didn't. He didn't realize how much we'd lose with the exchange. And he didn't realize how expensive Manhattan was going to be. And how competitive it is. But he was determined to live in the Big Apple. Manhattan was the place to conquer in his eyes, not even realizing it was everything that he despised."

He couldn't find a job. We were living in this shithole in Washington Heights. I was the only white kid at school. I had no friends. I was this little pale, country-grown Aussie chick. I stuck out like a sore thumb. I mostly kept to myself. I tried really hard to adjust to everything. But I despised the entire city. I cried every night, but I went to school every day with a smile for my dad. He knew it was fake, but it still helped him to sleep at night. What kept him up was the fact that he despised it as well."

She searched in the bag for chip residue, and then licked her fingertips. "He didn't know how to live in the ghetto. He wasn't working as an engineer, rather a mail clerk for some Manhattan company. He couldn't assimilate into the New York mentality at all. He never complained to me, but I could tell, though he was oblivious of my knowledge. But I knew that man inside and out. I could read him like a book. And so I knew it made him feel better thinking that I thought he was happy and everything was going fine."

"The power of denial."

She gave an agreeing nod, and continued, "So my dad finally meets this guy, Pito. He hadn't met anyone he really clicked with, so when he found Pito, he was thrilled. They started going to bars. Pito's wife watched after me, with her two other kids, Alex and Gina. I got along with Alex, but Gina was a bit bratty. Anyways, these excursions started happening more and more often. My dad was starting to act strange. Really hyper at times, really moody at others. We were drifting. I started to hang out a lot with Alex. I had nowhere else to be. He was sixteen, really tall, tan-skinned Dominican. I ended up losing my virginity to him. Hurt like a mother fucker," she giggled. She had the cutest laugh.

"My dad was never around. And when he was, he'd act so weird. I missed our talks, our jokes. We used to be so close. Then, boom, we didn't even know each other. I started searching through his room in search of some clues behind his behavior. I found an eight-ball of coke, and I knew exactly what it was. Up to that point, all I had ever done was alcohol and smoke two cigarettes. I didn't like drugs, what they were. He was the one who had always taught me of their evils.

I sat in the roach infested kitchen, the bag of coke on the table, waiting. At 2am he arrived home, drunk as fuck, flying. I looked at him with tears in my eyes. He looked at me, then at the bag, and just burst out crying. He fell to his knees, then went into the fetal position crying out about how sorry he was. I was bawling. I went over and knelt by him." She paused briefly, the emotion of the recollection getting to her.

"He grabbed and hugged me, and we cried. Eventually we got to our feet. He repeated how sorry he was to have failed me and promised to stop. A week later he went out with Pito, and accidentally left a bag on his nightstand. Stupid prick, just leaving it there. I found it. I left it out on the kitchen table and went out with Alex. When I got home, the coke was spilled all over the kitchen table... and my father was hanging, dead, in the bathroom. He couldn't handle how he had fallen in my eyes. I sat against the wall and stared at his dead body for what must've been hours. Then I finally called 911. I just stared in silence as they took his body away. I was all alone. I got stuck in a group home with a bunch of fucked up kids with their own dreadful dramas."

She was on a roll, spilling her life story. I didn't mind listening. I was amazed. I saw none of her pain and trauma in her eyes. They seemed to hold on to none of it. I admired her for that, and envied her. "At first I was terrified," she continued, "But I wouldn't be the weakling. My mother was a strong woman, so I knew I had it in me. I grew a set of balls the size of Texas. I had to, there was no other choice. It was a really intimidating place for me, but I was a strong girl and realized I had to adapt quickly. I became obsessed with partying. Started experimenting with drugs, anything and everything, except coke. Not even once. Then one day I stumbled upon heroin..." A short silence. "Well, that's enough about me. Now your turn."

"My turn? What do you want to know?"

"Anything, everything," she said with a smirk. I suddenly grew tense. I was so ashamed of who I was, how could I let this wonderful girl see that person? Then I looked into those big bright eyes. She had just seen me cry; only Avry had before her. Suddenly my shame melted away and I felt this intense closeness to this beautiful girl. If it had been Delia, she would be mocking me, yelling at me to man up. But not Angelika. She was something so different than anything I had ever known. So I began to tell her my life. Not in full detail, but enough. When we got to Delia, she began to question, poke and pry. So I told her more than I wanted to, but it just flowed out of my mouth. I didn't tell her my darkest secrets. I didn't want her to be afraid of me. I needed her.

When I finished, "Thank you for sharing yourself with me."

"So are you completely disgusted?"

She giggled solemnly. "No. Everyone makes mistakes. You may have made, uh, a *lot* of them. But this is your chance. Not many people get second chances. Consider yourself blessed. You have the chance to make right of everything."

"How?" I was looking at her as if she were some unearthly creature sent to save me. But she wasn't. She was only human.

"I can't answer that. Only you can."

"I just wonder where I would be now if I never fucking met her. If I had just listened to Avry."

"How quick we are to point the finger."

"What?" My defenses went up a bit.

"Did she hold a gun to your head and make you shoot up? Did she make you do all the things you did to get more dope?" I wanted to answer yes, it felt like she did, but she didn't. I did it on my own free will.

"The sooner we accept the responsibility of the mistakes we made, the sooner we can let them go. You want Avry to wake up so he can forgive you, but first you have to forgive yourself."

thirteen

"And in man as well as in angels, He has placed the power of choice (for angels are rational beings), so that those who had yielded obedience might justly possess what is good, given indeed by God, but preserved by themselves..."
Irenaeus of Gaul

It was so hard going back there, but I had to. I owed him way more than that. I sat in the hospital by his side, staring at the window. "You know Av," I couldn't help but speak to him. Maybe he could hear me. "I did some really fucked up things once you left. Things that haunt me. Things that would've even made you cringe."

I looked at him. I swore he could hear me. I started to tell him. About the girl we raped, how that kid fucked a corpse before we threw her into the swamps to be forgotten, how I shot two guys dead. Those were things I never spoke of out loud. Things I swore I'd never tell another living soul. But he deserved to know. I wanted him to know what I had become. That he was right. He deserved that satisfaction.

But I didn't think he'd be happy to have been proven right. So many people get off on knowing that what they foresaw to happen had become concrete reality. Even if the outcome was negative, they were still right. Self satisfaction. So what if your friend got injured, lost everything they had, etc? They should've listened to you in the first place. That ever faithful, "I told you so!" But I didn't think Av was like that. But he should've been. I would've rather him awake and smug than asleep and silent. Speaking those words aloud seemed to yank a giant weight off my shoulders.

"Those two guys. I don't feel remorse for that. I feel like I should, but I don't. Does that make me a terrible person, Av? That's what drives me crazy about it. How can I feel remorse for hurting two people I didn't even know? But that girl. What we did to her. It tortures me. Well, honestly, at first, sometimes when I'd think about it, I'd get off on it. I'd remember that fear in her eyes, and it would feel like a high, just remembering the power I had. But after things started crumbling, and the surface of everything was being peeled away, my outlook on it started to change. What were once erotic dreams transformed into nightmares.

"The remembrance of that same fear which once served as the ultimate aphrodisiac became a vile poison, reminding me of the monster I had become. My first reaction was to hate the girl, like it was her fault I was feeling that way. Then I started to recognize her as a person that I had scarred forever. I now have something in common with all those people I have despised throughout my life who have caused permanent damage to me. And that idea sickens me.

"When I brought it up to Delia once, she of course found a way to make it sound appealing. 'Just think,' she said, 'we have the power to completely change someone's outlook on life. She'll remember us until the day she dies.' Then, to make herself not appear so utterly evil, she'd twist things in some demented way, say shit like, 'We taught her a valuable lesson. She should've been more careful whom she trusted with her body. She should've known better than to go home with some strangers. What did she expect? At least now she knows better.' Like we were helping her by showing her exactly what people are capable of."

"You know, Av, I wanna blame Delia. For everything. For my drug use, for you leaving. For all those things I did. But it wasn't her fault. I know that now. She constantly fed me these fucked ideologies about the way the world worked. But it was my decision to listen and accept them. Her word was like scripture to me at one point. It was fucked, I would never doubt anything that she said, as if she had this secret knowledge that no one else had. I was looking for guidance, someone to hold my hand and show me the way. And she was there and told me what I wanted to hear, which I then confused for the truth. She gave confirmation to my anger and disgust, so I therefore thought it valid.

But it was all bullshit. I just thought I found someone who was like me. But it wasn't all of me, just the things I kept hidden inside, things best kept hidden. She made me feel like I was supposed to let all that out. And for the first time I was feeling something, and it was intense. I didn't care where it was coming from, I just didn't want it to stop. But I didn't have to look so far. You were there the whole time. Someone like me. Someone who could really understand. And I turned my back on you. I'm so sorry, Avry. I'll be right here. Everyday until you open you eyes."

I had suddenly been promoted to waiter at my job after one of the guys quit unexpectedly on one of the busiest nights. They launched me on the job without any real training, but I had been paying enough attention and it wasn't a brain twister of a job. I was hoping that maybe I could afford to get a place of my own. But I wanted to wait. In case he woke up; we could get a place together. It had only been a week since I had found him, but it felt like an eternity. I figured he was bound to wake up soon. He had to.

Angelika and I were spending a lot of time together. I had a friend again. It felt good, but I wanted more of her. But I held back on that. I didn't want to push another person away. I had brought my guitar to her place that night upon her request. It was such a welcoming change having someone pushing me to be creative. "So what are you going to play me?"

"What do you want to hear?"

"Something you wrote." Flashback to Avry in our first apartment. I shook my head to shake the memory, and just began to strum away my newest creation:

Hard to take a step back, and just look at what we've become
The remains of two lost souls, whose lives have become completely strung
All once seemed so clear, but then we chased the dragon into the sun
Now all shattered and torn, what's done can never be undone

Your eyes, they once held me, now they scare me, yes they frighten me away
All you are now is the poison that has caused your self decay

How will you cope, my fallen angel, now that you know I cannot stay
How do you live, my fallen angel, all I've become is what's driven me away
How do you do it, my fallen angel, get up and face yourself each day

Once I looked at you and what I saw was an image of myself
That's what angers me the most, capability, my demon inside has a life all itself
Now I can see what lies ahead, and to fall to such a fate I refuse
I pity those as broken as you, those who have missed their chance to choose

Those eyes, they once held me, now they scare me, yes they frighten me away
The beast, it still haunts me, the one that stole your soul away

How will you cope, my fallen angel, now that you know I cannot stay
How do you live, my fallen angel, all I've become is what's driven me away
How do you do it, my fallen angel, bear witness to your own decay

No more artificial remedies, no more artificial kicks, no more artificial love, no more artificial bliss

I once knew you, my fallen angel, thought I'd always wanna stay
I once could feel you, my fallen angel, funny how things just fade away
I once loved you, my fallen angel, now I despise you more each day

She soaked it in, remaining silent for a minute. She seemed a bit upset at the content. But then she smiled. "That was powerful."

"Thanks," I said, blushing. She ran her fingers along my face to show her appreciation. Her skin was so soft.

"Are you ever gonna let go of that anger toward her?"

"I doubt it."

"To hold onto such anger is to limit yourself. And to hate someone is just wasted energy. You could be placing that energy toward something positive. Trust me, if you were to let go of that anger and hatred, you'd feel like a thousand pound weight had been lifted off your shoulders."

"And how do I do that?"

"Well, for starters, you have to forgive her."

I laughed. "Yeah, right." It was getting late and my eyes were getting heavy. I wanted to spend the night there, with her. But I did not dare invite myself, and she did not even suggest it. "Who was this girl?" I thought aloud as I sat in the corner of the subway car. She definitely was not the type of girl to spend hanging around society's rejects. It was really hard to believe she ever was a junkie. I almost pushed the idea clear out of my head, placing her on an ever-ascending pedestal. Regardless of her past, the person she had become was beautiful in every sense of the word. So I couldn't help but keep wondering why the hell was she wasting her time with me. I jerked off three times thinking of her before I finally fell asleep.

"If you could relive any day of your life, what would it be?" I pondered over her question as we swayed on the swings.

"I guess, the day I found Avry again." I grew uncomfortable and she sensed it, so she quickly came up with a new question.

"If you could be doing anything in the world right now, what would it be?"

Seeing what it feels like to be inside you, was my true response, but instead I said, "Lying on a beach on some tropical island, pina colada in one hand, joint in the other, and you lying next to me, wearing a cute little bikini and a smile." She blushed.

"Sounds good to me."

"I have a question for you. But I'm afraid it will turn things on too serious a mode."

"Okay, give me a second to prepare myself." She playfully closed her eyes, counted to three, took a deep breath and said, "Okay, I'm ready now."

"What brought about, oh, I don't know, your awakening, per say? What was the final trigger that made you kick?"

Her playfulness faded. "I just lost everything. My life, myself. I used to always swear that I was so in touch with myself, I prided myself on it. But then I lost that. And it just grew so cold."

"I hear ya. But there was no one thing in particular that happened that made you say, 'Okay, this is it?'" I could tell she didn't like the direction of the conversation, and started getting all edgy. I knew she didn't want to keep talking about such matters, yet I pushed on anyway, for reasons unknown. I knew I had skeletons that would probably make her squirm, so maybe I was just trying to see if she was hiding any, so I wouldn't worry so much about my own.

"Hey, let's get off this serious business, I'm in too good of a mood for that." She leapt off her swing and ran up behind mine and started pushing me, rambling off diversion chitchat as the swing gained height. "Hey, do you know how to spider swing?"

"Huh?" She then ran to the front of my swing, grabbing the chains to stop the movement.

"Spider swing." She jumped on my lap, her face to mine, one leg on each side. She started pumping her legs, causing the swing to move. I was a bit in shock.

"Pump your legs, silly." And so I did, and we started swinging pretty high. I miraculously maintained control over down below, trying not to stare too hard into those tremendous eyes piercing right into mine. Suddenly, when we had gotten pretty high, she did a flip off, landing pretty much perfectly. "Ta da!"

I was very impressed. "Shit, I'd definitely break my neck if I tried that."

"I've had a couple of close calls myself." I skidded to a stop. She wiped off the dust that splattered on her shins. "Well, I gotta get to class."

"Yeah, I'm gonna head over to the hospital. Hey, before we part ways, one more question." I had to twist deeper. I just couldn't let it go. Looking for a way to word it just right, to find whatever answer it was that I was looking for, "What, whether it be an event or, anything at all, what do you regret most in your life?"

A melancholy expression invaded her face. "That's for another day. See ya." She turned and walked off, and all I could do was watch.

"You know, Av, knowledge. That's what sets us apart from the animals. And consciousness. You know, in some ways, consciousness weakens us, lowering natural instincts. It breaks up our wholeness and divides us within ourselves. On one side there is desire, and the other, morality. I had been a slave to my desires for too long. I often wondered what life would have been like if I had just been a little stronger. Maybe if I was a little more moral. Or maybe even a little more whole.

"But you gotta ask, what is a life without being able to bask in the pleasure of your desires? There is a reason you desire them. What if I was able to maintain a productive life and still be getting high? Would it be alright then? What if I never hurt anyone but still slept around? Who's to say that my desires are unreachable? But I guess the proof is in the pudding, ain't it? I didn't turn out to be a success story...I guess I have no choice but to accept that I fucked up. That world wasn't for me, Av. Sure it was exciting, sensual. But the consequences weren't worth it. Eventually the reality was going to show its ugly face. I lost control. But what if..."

I was suddenly interrupted. "Excuse me," a female voice said from the doorway. "I didn't know anyone was here. I'll come back." In front of me stood a stunning female with brown crescent-shaped eyes, pin straight dark brown hair with baby doll bangs, and an olive complexion. She was wearing tight black pants and a tight tiny shirt that exposed her tight, pierced belly. I had been strumming my guitar as I was jabbering on.

"Are you here to see Avry?" I asked, hoping she didn't hear my psycho babble.

"Yes. Are you a friend of his?"

"Yeah." She was so sexy it was almost unnerving. "Are you?"

She nodded. "I've never seen you around. Where do you know him from?"

"From California."

"You came all the way here to see him?"

"I live here now." I walked up to this stunning creature and stuck out my hand. "I'm Xavier."

She shook it. "Bridgette. Xavier? I remember him mentioning that name."

"Oh yeah? What did he say about me?"

"That you were his best friend when he was younger. Told me a buncha stories. But I'm pretty sure he said you were dead." That hurt, badly. As if a dozen knives were being repeatedly jabbed into my back. I had become dead to him. But I guess I deserved that.

"We parted on very bad terms. I came here to fix things."

"Oh, I see," she said with a grimace. Then it dawned on me. This was the girl. The one he put a gun to his head for. As I made this realization, I yanked my hand away and took a step back. Avry had always wanted to know what it felt like to know the touch of a beautiful woman. I guess he sure as hell finally found out. "How's he doing?" She asked.

My demeanor changed as hatred for this female rose. "Well, he's in a fucking coma."

She flashed an offended look. "No shit," returning the attitude.

"It's you."

"What's me?"

"You're the girlfriend he did this over."

"Go fuck yourself," and she turned and walked out. Chills ran down my spine and I decided I couldn't let the opportunity slip away. "Wait!" I shouted as I scurried after her. She turned around and put her hand on her hip.

"What?"

"I wanna talk to you about what happened."

"Why should I give you the time?" I wanted to punch her straight in that beautiful face.

I took a deep breath. "Because I traveled all the way from the bottom of the country to come find my best friend, and found him laying half dead in a hospital bed and the only fucking clue I have to why is you."

"It's not my fucking fault."

"Prove it."

"I don't have to prove shit to you." She started walking away.

"Then do it for him. You owe him that."

She froze. "What do you want from me?" she asked, facing the other direction.

"I just wanna talk." Some silence.

"Fine. Let's go to the cafeteria and grab a coffee."

We took the elevator in silence down to the cafeteria, and took a seat at the nearest empty table. There were people everywhere, each with their own tragic story, I was sure. But they all just faded into a non-existent background as I stared at her lips, waiting for her to speak. As she licked her lips, trying to collect her nerves, I looked up and stared her dead in those seductive eyes. They told me she was a conniving, manipulative cunt that must've been one hell of a lay. "What is it you want to know?" She couldn't look me back in mine. Shame, I figured.

"Everything. Start from how you met."

"You're not gonna blame me, are you? I didn't cause this. He was fucked up way before me."

"Then why did he do it as soon as you threw him out?"

"I never said he could live there in the first place. I'm not his fucking guardian!"

"Relax, and explain."

She fiddled with her fingers, staring at the floor as she told her story. "We met at the bar I was working at. He was friends with one of my friends. We started hanging out, then hooking up. He started calling a lot, not understanding the fact that I wanted to keep things casual. So I started to back off. Then he shows up at my door one day with a bag of stuff, saying he got thrown out of where he was staying and asked if he could stay a couple of days. He had no place to go, how could I say no?" She took a deep breath, still staring at the floor. "Days passed, then weeks. He was still there."

"Were you fucking?"

"God, aren't you crude?"

"I don't have time for pleasantries. I just want the facts." She clicked her tongue. "Well, were you?"

"Okay, okay. Don't rush me. It's a little hard for me to talk about." Another deep breath. "We did a couple days into it. But I knew it would lead to trouble, so I said I had a boyfriend. I didn't. I was seeing other people, but nothing serious." She batted her eyes. I wasn't sure if it was just how she was, but every motion of hers seemed flirtatious. I was pretty sure it was natural, because other actions of hers displayed her uneasiness with the topic.

"He got upset, but tried to play it off like it didn't faze him. I said I would never bring this so-called boyfriend to the house while he was there, of course thinking it would only be a few days." She looked up at me. Her eyes were the perfect definition of bedroom eyes. "As time went by, he kept assuring me that his plans were gonna follow through any minute and he was gonna be out. I didn't have the heart to ask him to leave. Then one drunken night when we were alone, we slept together again. I was so drunk, I didn't know what I was doing." She took another deep breath. "The next morning he was all over me, and I felt like a complete bitch if I just pulled away. So I did it again. A pity fuck. I know it's messed up, but I fuckin' did it."

Her tone got louder, as if she was defending herself against my assumed judgments of her. "I got dressed and went to work. After that, I tried to avoid him, always running in and out of the apartment, saying I had some place to be. I didn't mean...I just didn't know how else to react to the situation. He finally persuaded me into telling him exactly what was going on. So I told him the truth; that I didn't wanna be with him in that way. And he flipped. He didn't understand how one day I wanted him, and then didn't the next. I didn't have the heart to tell him it was because of the alcohol.

"When I just kept telling him I couldn't explain the reasons, he took it the wrong way. Kept interpreting it in a way that ended with me really wanting him in his mind. So I had to tell him." Her eyes grew watery and I clenched my fists. "He just stood there, silent. I asked if he was okay, but he didn't answer. He got up and walked to the door. I called his name but he didn't answer. He came back the next day and tried to pretend everything was okay, but he wasn't doing a good job.

"Days kept passing and he didn't even seem to be looking for somewhere else to go. Things had become so uncomfortable. He'd stare at me from across the room. Just stare. Then his eyes followed me if I got up and moved. He was acting crazy. Every time I'd leave the house, he'd ask me twenty questions about where I was going, what I was doing. And when I got home he'd interrogate me; I felt like a fucking prisoner in my own home. I didn't know what he was capable of." A tear ran down her face. "No disrespect, but that boy had problems. If you were as close to him as you claim you were, you know that."

She paused briefly, wiped her face, and fiddled with her hair. "I finally asked him to leave. I had a guy friend of mine waiting in my room, just in case my telling him to leave didn't go well. Avry started crying, begging me to let him stay, to give 'us' a chance." She started to choke on her words and more tears came. "He just kept going on about how much he cared about me. I hugged him in an attempt to calm him down; he was hysterical." I could never picture Avry crying over a girl. He must've fallen for her hard. The image almost made me ill.

"So we hugged and he started to calm down. Then he squeezed tighter," a big sigh, "and started touching and rubbing me, and wouldn't stop. I told him to, but he wouldn't listen. He kept repeating that he loved me and kept forcing himself on me till I screamed. When my friend heard me screaming he came out. He slugged Avry in the face. He lost his balance and nearly fell. They started scrapping, but that first punch must've gotten him good, because he could hardly focus."

The image of someone hitting Avry angered me so much. I had always been there to defend him. Why wasn't I there? "You just stood there watching?"

"I started screaming and they finally stopped," she yelled out from behind tears. "I asked my friend to go wait inside the room by the door, so he did. Me and Avry just stared at each other. He was bloody and full of tears. I told him to wait a sec while I went and packed up his stuff, dropped it at his feet, went into my bedroom and closed the door. That was the last time I ever saw him...awake." With the exception of her sniffles, we sat in silence for a bit, both of us just staring at the ground. She went into her little black purse, pulled out a tissue and wiped her eyes and nose.

I broke the silence. "Where was he found?"

"On the top of some roof downtown. Some kids went up there and found him. I think they said it was like ten minutes after it happened."

"Where did he get the gun from?"

"I dunno, he always carried it around."

"Avry carried a gun?"

"Yeah. He was getting into all sorts of trouble when I met him. He felt like he needed the protection."

From himself. "What kind of trouble?"

"I don't know. He wouldn't talk about it. I think he owed the wrong people a lot of money. I really don't know. I didn't want to know. Look, I'm not a bad person. I did care about him. I would have never expected him...I didn't want...Fuck, I don't know. Shit, I still have nightmares about it. All the time. People who knew both of us, they look at me like it was me who tried to kill him. But it wasn't my fault. I couldn't help it if I didn't like him in that way. I couldn't just make myself."

More silence. I thought about Madeline. Funny how your actions come back to slap you in the face. I briefly thought about what would have happened if Av had stayed with Michelle. He probably never would have had to be put through the shit he went through. He could have been happy. But he gave up that chance, for me. I felt as if it was me that had put that gun to his head. When she noticed me zoning out in my own thoughts, she grabbed my hand and looked me in the eyes. I had never came across a female with such sexual energy, it was insane. Part of me wanted to beat the shit out of her, the other half wanted fuck the living daylights out of her.

"Listen, I have to go," she said, wiping away the remainder of her tears. "I just wanted to stop by and see how he was doing. You said you live here, in New York, right?" I nodded, not sure where this was going. She went into her bag and pulled out a pen and another tissue. "Take my number. Keep me updated on how he's doing. If he wakes up, I don't think he'd want to see me. Maybe you can tell me some Avry stories. I'd love to hear about him from someone who knew him well." She scribbled it down and handed it to me. She stood up and put her hand on my shoulder. "It was nice meeting you."

And with that, she walked away. Was she hitting on me, or did she sincerely wanna hear about Avry? I stared at the tissue. Should I call? I thought to myself. Whether or not it was her fault, Avry had tried to kill himself over *her*. Why did she give me her number? It would've been disgusting of me to betray him as he lay fighting for his life. Beyond disgusting.

Then I started thinking about everything that had happened the past few days. That Dani look-alike appearing, leading me to him. Was all of this happening for a reason? I could get Bridgette back for him. Make her feel the pain he felt. Would he have wanted me to get her back for him? Then I remembered that blue jay, the one that showed up at the missionary. The way I felt when I saw it. It surely wasn't a sign for revenge to come. It couldn't have been. It felt too pure for that. As she walked out the door, I threw her number to the floor.

I went back to Avry's room and just stared out the window into the bustling city that never ceased. I began to think of Delia. I began to question why it was that I was so angry at her. Did she ever force the needle into my arm? No. She never forced me to do anything. She just manipulated me through her words. But I was too weak to see past them then. And what I did to those kids, to that girl, that was my own manipulation. Who was I to say I was any better than her?

I hated her so much for betraying me, for fucking everyone else. But I saw nothing wrong with me sticking a gun to someone's face and stripping them down to their boxers, and stealing everything, including their dignity. I was so angry at myself for everything I had done, everything I had lost, including precious time, and I didn't wanna live with being angry at myself. I couldn't bear that extra baggage.

So instead I laid it all on her. She was not there to defend herself, so it was perfect. But it wasn't her fault. She was so broken, so used and abused. *She* was so weak. She saw something in me; something to reassure her that she wasn't alone. Why wouldn't she want to do anything possible to keep that? But then why did she consistently cheat on me? It was for the same reason I'd convince a preteen to go rob a corner store. Feed the beast. That was the easiest way for her. She was no longer a free person, just a slave. She did what it asked her to do, just as I did. But we chose to be its slave. We allowed it to pull our strings, instead of fighting it. She had lost all hope of anything better, just as I had once felt. But seeing it from the other side, everything just looked so different.

There was another way. Pain was just part of the struggle. But I couldn't understand why I always lost everyone I had ever given a shit about. Like life was playing some sick cruel joke on me. People often try and form connections between their miseries, as if they were all part of life's great plot against them, once again giving them something to put blame on. Maybe karma has something to do with it, maybe it is, in fact, life getting back at them. But sometimes shit just happens. I thought about people who are overall good people, who have done nothing hurtful to anyone, and still end up suffering, like being crippled or horribly deformed. I tried to figure out why people are dealt such cards. Maybe it was punishment from a previous life. Maybe they were being tested for some higher purpose in the next life. I didn't know where that left me.

I looked over at Avry's comatose body. I finally knew the "why." It had been eating away at me, inside the whole time, as I desperately longed to understand. But I didn't feel any better. It didn't make it any less painful. I spoke aloud to him. "You know what just I realized, Av? Love, in many ways, holds a lot of the same qualities as dope. When you're hooked, it's all that exists, what keeps you going. Your purpose, your excuse. The problem and the solution. It's what keeps you up at night, and gives you reason to get up the next day. The driving force behind all your actions. The escape from all other thoughts. Something that makes you wanna live; something that makes you wanna die. Once it has you, it consumes you, and you have no choice but to follow, no matter where it takes you."

fourteen

"SIN IS NOT CONFINED TO THE EVIL THINGS WE DO. IT IS THE EVIL WITHIN US, THE EVIL WHICH WE ARE."

Karl Barth

After being around Bridgette, I realized how much pent-up sexual frustration I had manifesting inside. I needed to get laid, that night. I knew Angelika wasn't going to fill that void, I wouldn't even dare try, so I had to look elsewhere. It had been a while since I had gone to a bar and randomly picked up a chick, and actually followed through with it, but the hormones were flaring and it came back to me like riding a bike. Within two hours I convinced a cute, pierced Asian girl to take me back to her place. Easy as cake. It had been so long since I had been inside a woman. As much as I wanted it, it didn't seem to put out the fire. I remembered how I used to be willing to fuck anyone at anytime. It didn't matter if I knew or cared about them. A nut was a nut. But a lot had changed since then. I craved something more. After I came, I lay in the dark, realizing that the one thing in the world that had once brought me the most pleasure had now become just as mundane as everything else.

I ended up passing out at the girl's house. When I woke up she was still sound asleep, and I wanted to get out of there ASAP. She had served her purpose. I called Ang from her phone.

"Hello?"

"Hey, it's me," I whispered.

"Isn't it kind of early?"

I looked at the clock, which read 8:30am. "Yeah, I guess it is. I was wondering if you'd wanna grab some breakfast."

"Where are you? Why are you whispering?"

"Um, this girl's house." Silence followed.

Finally, "Oh." More silence.

"You there?"

"Yeah, um, I'm actually too tired. Late night studying. Take a rain check?" I could sense a shift in her tone. Jealousy. I couldn't help but smile. After I hung up the phone I grabbed all my shit as quietly as possible and walked out the door. Suddenly, a strange feeling hit me. Guilt. Then I got pissed at myself for allowing any female to get to me. We weren't even fucking. But the point that weirded me out was that when it all came down to it, it really didn't matter. It would've been friggin' wonderful to actually do it, but spending time with her was enough, at least for the time being.

She offered companionship, which I needed more than anything. We did flirt, but nothing too extreme. Any time I even somewhat made physical flirtation, she'd immediately back off. But it was obvious that she wanted me. I was aware that females often got off on having a guy chase them, but she wasn't like that. She wasn't like other girls. She was different than anything I had ever seen. There was nothing artificial about her. And everyone could see it, everywhere we went. At her part-time job, she told me how she would get balloons and flowers from everyone for her birthday. The same scenario at the shelter she volunteered at. Even the junkies would pitch in. Every store we went to around her neighborhood, she'd be greeted by name, and she'd flash that smile and chat a bit. Even the bum on the corner, who would curse me out for not giving him change, would pick flowers from windowsills to give them to her when she passed by. Even on the rare occasions when she couldn't give him change, he was always happy to see her.

It was weird being around someone like that. I felt like a weed growing in the most beautiful of gardens. Sometimes it felt nauseating to be around her, because it made me uneasy with myself. I wasn't like her.

I would never be like her. I wanted her, I truly did. But I just couldn't. Not her. I felt too unworthy, too filthy, like I'd be poisoning her. But for some reason, Ang saw in me what Dani saw in me, something that I had believed to have died with her. Maybe I was willing to wait for Angelika in hopes that feeling would be resuscitated in me as well.

I was in the hospital the next morning the very second visiting hours began. I had a terrible feeling the prior night, and could barely sleep a wink. I sat in silence, listening to life support machines create non-patterned rhythms. It's funny how the most random memories surface at the most inappropriate times. As I stared blankly at Avry's motionless body, I remembered this one winter evening in New Orleans, when it was unusually cold. I was sitting on the stoop of some junkie's house, sipping a beer, relishing in the rare cool breeze. I spotted a young girl, no older than nine, walking up the block toward me. She was walking barefoot on the cracked and littered pavement, wearing nothing but a long white t-shirt. Her face was stained with tears as she tried to control her sobs. Her eyes were full of fear and anger and her arms were wrapped around her body.

As she walked hurriedly passed, still crying, I remember breaking out in uncontrollable laughter. As I sat by Av's hospital bed, I couldn't for the life of me recall what I found so damn funny. Had I become so utterly cold that the sight of a child suffering seemed delightfully amusing? As I looked at her, I didn't for one moment stop to consider what it was that she was fleeing from, why she was crying, or why she was half-naked on the coldest night of the year. I didn't care. And I couldn't stop fucking laughing. I was wondering if there was anyone watching me from afar, getting the same kick from me that I got from her. Maybe my life and pain was just somebody else's comedy reel. I was still waiting for the punch line.

As I sat lost in memories, a nurse walked in, her face hanging so low it appeared as if her skin would just drip off. I took one look and I knew. I knew the day would come. I was expecting it the entire time. But somehow prior knowledge didn't make it any less painful. "I'm sorry, but we just can't keep the life support running anymore. There doesn't seem to be any chance that he's going to wake up and..." blah, blah, blah. Her voice muffled into an indiscriminate drone. I felt my gut tighten.

"Maybe justa little longer. Maybe he just needs more time." I pleaded, trying my damnedest to hold on to any lingering hope.

"I am sorry, we can't...blah blah blah" and as her voice faded out every last ounce of remaining hope seeped out of my pores.

"Well, it's not like I have a fucking choice in the matter, so why the fuck are you acting like you're asking my permission?" The anger boiled in my gut. She gave me a sharp look, not appreciative of my language, though trying to be understanding of the matter. I didn't want her sympathy. I didn't want her candy coating. "Just pull the damn plug and let him fucking die. He's probably better off anyway."

Her eyes were full of unwanted sympathy. I wanted to just punch her face. "Would you like to say your goodbyes?"

I took a deep breath and clenched my fists, holding back my true desire. "Yeah, I guess, so."

"I'll give you a minute," she said as she walked out, as if she was doing me some great favor. I walked up to the bed. There he was, so close, yet a million light years away. I wondered if he had actually heard me at all those past weeks, or was it all just wasted? But then again, what wasn't wasted time? My entire life was about just finding different ways to waste time. I remembered this girl Sara from New Orleans once said to me, "All there really is in life to do is live, fuck, create, kill time." I couldn't have agreed more. I walked up to his bed and stared down at him.

"Well, Av, this is it. This is where we part ways for good. Isn't quite how I pictured our reunion, but hey, nothing ever is, is it? At least I get to say goodbye this time." I was a lot calmer than I had expected to be. Numb almost. I grabbed his hand, introducing our matching scars. "I love you, Avry. You are my best friend, my family, my heart. Forever. But our time here is over. And it is all because of me. Oh well, in the words of you, my brother, I never said I was anything special." And with that, I let him go. Forever.

I calmly made my out through the revolving doors into the blinding sunlight, and stood squinting as I stared blankly into the grey overcast sky, the surrounding buildings' skyline forming a sky-rise citadel. I don't think I ever really believed he was going to wake up. But that day at the missionary I had allowed myself to once again fall victim to that overrated emotion that I'd sworn off so long ago: hope. It always lets you down. It's like a self-torturing device. It builds you up, blurs reality, keeps you elevated, hovering right above the truth. Sure, it does push, give you meaning, but in the end the freefall into reality is so much more terrifying the higher hope takes you.

I should have known better. That was the way my life had always been. I guess I figured just because I got clean the whole world around me was going to morph into a proud parent. But nothing really changes. It's funny how something so life-altering, so meaningful to one person, could have such an insignificant role in the overall scheme of things. I thought about when I'd seen the blue jay. I grew disgusted at how pitiful I was to believe that feeling was real. Another damn illusion. In a world filled with illusions, how is anyone supposed to know what's real? Is there even such a thing?

I wanted to stick a needle so deep into my arm with my middle finger pointed way up to the sky. That would show them. Only problem was, there was no "them." There was only me. And I'd be the one getting fucked in the end. I knew that. Every inch of me knew that. But I also knew that once that H would hit my vein, I wouldn't give a flying fuck about "them," me or anything else. Wash it all away. But if I took even one taste, I knew it would be over. I didn't have much. There wouldn't be any reason for me to stop. Then I realized there was one reason. Her.

Angelika, I needed to see Angelika. I needed to know I wasn't completely alone. I wanted to hold her, inhale the scent of her flesh, taste her, remember what it once felt like to me to be inside a woman. Suddenly, whatever pain of loss I was feeling manifested into this intense desire. For her. I didn't know if it was a defense mechanism, all I knew was that

I *needed* her. I called her and told her I was coming over. I didn't ask. I told her. She was going to wash it all away.

"Oh, Xavier, I'm so sorry!" she wrapped her fragile arms around me and ran her perfectly-manicured fingers through my hair. I had never been so close to her, I didn't want her to ever let go. I squeezed her back, and I could tell it was unexpected, because she seemed to jerk from a bit of shock. But she didn't fight. I kept squeezing tighter, and she started to attempt to pull away. I didn't want to let go. I almost felt that if I let her go she would disappear. Everything I cared about always seemed to disappear. I finally let go and she took a step back, and I could sense she felt slightly uneasy, but was willing to let it go given the circumstances.

I looked at her, as if I was looking at her for the first time. She was so beautiful. Those huge bright eyes. They told the story of suffering, yet held this sweet innocence. Like the eyes of a child who did not yet realize that they were wrongly being abused. I just stared at her. She looked like an angel, my sweet fairy, so untainted, so pure. Her delicate features looked so fragile, like a porcelain doll. If only everything in the world could be so undefiled. At that moment I wanted her more than I ever wanted anything in my life. I walked toward her and she took a step back. "Are you okay, Xavier?"

"I love you, Angelika." I did. I loved her so much that I felt it like a boulder in the pit of my gut.

"Listen, you're just upset because you lost your friend. Don't start talking crazy."

"I'm not talking crazy. I love you. I do. Everything about you. Your heart, your soul, you are so different from all the other trash in this world. You are so pure."

"No, I'm not, Xavier. You are just seeing me the way you want to right now." I walked closer and she continued to back up.

"No, you're different. You can take me away from all this." I looked at her and it was almost as if she was glowing. She could save me. I was ready to let her save me. She could make it all go away.

"Sweetie, sit down, relax." I just kept waking toward her. I needed her to save me. She had to. She stumbled backward over her throw rug and landed with her back against the wall. I walked closer until I was directly in her face. So pure. I touched her flawless skin with the back of my hand. As she started trembling, her innocence glowed brighter.

"I'm not going to hurt you, Angelika. I love you." I leaned in and kissed her soft pink lips. She turned her face but had nowhere to go to pull away.

"I think you should go now, Xavier."

"No. I need to be here with you." I went to kiss her again, but she reflected my move and my lips landed on her rosy cherub cheek.

"You should leave."

"No!" I yelled. I couldn't leave. I couldn't understand how she couldn't see how much I needed her. She was staring behind me, anywhere but in my eyes, so I grabbed her face to make her eyes meet mine. She seemed so scared and I couldn't comprehend why. I wasn't going to hurt her. I needed her. I had to have her. It was meant to be. As I stared into those big beautiful eyes, a single tear formed in one of their corners and dripped down her cheek. I rubbed the wet remains with my thumb. "Don't cry, baby. I told you, I'm not going to hurt you. I love you. I would never tarnish your innocence."

"What is this delusion of yours that you think I am this innocent little girl? I'm not."

I put my hand on her lips. "Shhh..." I didn't want to ever hear her say those words.

"Please, Xavier, please don't do this," she said in a whimper. So softly, so sweet. I wasn't going to hurt her, I was going to show her that we belonged together. I went to kiss her but she tried to wiggle away, so I squeezed her face tighter and met her lips with mine. She tasted like raspberries. She started squirming all around so I pushed all my weight against her. If she would only give in I believed I could make her see. The soft kisses became hard ones as I felt the whole of her body against mine. I needed to be inside of her.

"I want to see you, all of you. Take your clothes off." Tears were rolling down her cheeks continuously, highlighting her innocent beauty.

"Don't do this. Please don't do this." I placed my finger over her lips.

"Shhhh. Let me take your clothes off." I went to lift up her shirt but she began to struggle. "Stop it. Be still." But she wouldn't listen. She started wriggling around like a crazy person and I smacked her to snap her out of it. The second my hand made contact with her fragile face, she froze. I didn't want to hurt her. She just needed to stop fighting it. She needed to just let me show her. "Lift up you arms."

She looked at me with teary sweet eyes. "No."

"Ang, lift up your arms."

"No!" she yelled. I didn't like the way her voice sounded in that tone. I didn't want there to be yelling. The sound of her shrill plea frustrated me and I yelled back, "Just lift up your fucking arms and stop making this difficult. Once you see, you'll understand!"

"See what? Why are you doing this?"

I was getting angry. I didn't want to be angry. This was supposed to be pure. I wondered why the fuck couldn't she just lift up her goddamn arms. I was getting angry at the fact that I was getting angry. I grabbed at her shirt and began to yank it off. "I don't know why you're being difficult." She pinned her arms against her side so I couldn't pull it up, so I just tore at it until it ripped apart. She screamed and as a natural reaction to the noise I smacked her again. "Stop acting like a maniac!" I yelled. I didn't want it this way. She just needed to be calm and let me love her.

I put my hand over her mouth. "Look, I don't want to hear you scream, okay? Just be quiet. You aren't alone, I am not alone. Things are going to be okay." I looked down at her. She had no bra on and the remains of her shirt hung off her arm, exposing her tiny, pale, perky breasts. I ran my fingers along her skin, as if I were outlining them. Her body was quivering, and I was convinced it was just from the intensity of situation. She needed me as badly as I needed her.

I ran my hand down her milky stomach to her crotch, which was shielded by faded blue jeans. I began to unbutton her pants and she started to struggle again, breaking my lustful trance. She grabbed my hands and tried to pull them off, but her tiny fingers were no match for mine. I tried to ignore her and continue unbuttoning them, but she kept prying at my hands, her nails scratching my skin. Suddenly I felt my ear ring and saw stars. She smacked me dead across the face. It was my natural reaction to smack back, with three times the intensity of her pitiful attempt. I didn't want to hit her.

"Why!?" I grabbed her face hard and pushed her against the wall, slamming the back of her head into it. She clenched her eyes from the impact. "Dammit, just stop fighting me. It will be so much easier if you just stop fighting it. If you keep this bullshit up, you're going to make me hurt you bad, and I don't wanna do that!"

"Then don't." She tried to cover herself up with her arms, but I grabbed her by the wrists. I couldn't understand why she'd want to hide such a beautiful sight. When I grabbed her wrists she started squirming again, so I squeezed tighter. The more I squeezed, the more she struggled, until I slammed her arms up against the wall, bashing the back of her hands against it several times, causing abrasions.

"I thought you didn't wanna hurt me!" she cried and more tears dripped. I looked downward at her bare chest, arms spread open, welcoming me, and my hormones began to rage. I leaned down and began to suck her pink nipple while keeping her arms pinned back.

Just as I began to lose myself, she once again broke my concentration. "STOP!" she screamed. Now I was getting really frustrated. I let go of one of her arms and punched the wall by her head full force, breaking through the stucco. My knuckles were cut and bleeding, but I couldn't feel the pain. Terror filled her eyes. I didn't want her to fear me. I wanted her to need me. I wanted her to love me. "Just let me do this. It's gonna happen, it has to. I promise you, you'll enjoy it. We're meant to be together. You'll see." I licked her cheeks where the tear residue glistened. They tasted salty sweet. Suddenly the fear left her eyes and her face went expressionless.

"So it really doesn't matter if I want this or not?" It didn't. I needed it. I physically needed it. So did she, she just didn't realize it yet. She didn't want to accept it. I unbuttoned her pants and she stood there, letting me, like a good girl. Her body was still shaking, but the tears ceased. She looked so beautiful. That angelic innocence.

I pulled the jeans to the floor, exposing lacy pink panties. I could smell her and the scent was intoxicating. I slowly began to pull them down, as an erection began to scratch against my pants. She didn't fight. She didn't move. She just stood there and allowed me to admire her like a perfect statuette. My heart was beating so hard I could feel it in my fingertips. Her light brown pubic hair was perfectly shaved into a tiny sliver, as if she had been waiting for me to see it. Inside of her was my freedom. My escape from everything; an end to all my pain. I took my clothes off, keeping my eyes fixated on her. Her expressionless face, like a drawing. I pressed my naked body against her and my dick felt like it was going to explode. I wanted her in the bed. I took her by the hand. "Come with me to the bedroom."

"I'll say this one more time. I don't want to do this, Xavier. If you love me like you say you do, you'll stop right now."

"Shhh."

"Xavier, I'm not gonna fight you. I can't win. I know that. But please don't make me do this." My dick was throbbing and I couldn't wait any longer. Sheer lust took control of me. I needed to be inside her. I picked her up like a baby and carried her to the bedroom. She laid her head against my shoulder and I felt more tears hit my skin. My sweet aching fairy. Together we would wash all the pain away. I laid her down on the bed. She looked up at me with those watery lights, her naked body glowing in the dark room. She was so petite, so fragile-looking, like a little lost girl. A little girl who hadn't yet been tarnished with the evil that saturates this world. With the pain that is life. It was so beautiful. "You look so angelic, I almost wanna cry."

"I'm no angel, Xavier."

Her words were ruining my fantasy. "Don't speak. Don't say a word." I started climbing onto the bed on my hands and knees. As I hovered over her, she whispered, "You are going to regret this, I promise you. It's not too late to stop."

"I said don't speak!" and I put my hand over her mouth. I ran my tongue along her chest cavity down her stomach toward her pussy. I could feel the heat radiating from it; she wanted me as badly as I wanted her. She needed me. I tasted her and she squirmed silently. It had the perfect amount of bitterness and I just buried my face there. If it was possible, I would have shoved my entire head inside her, let her consume me, let her drown me in her juices. She didn't fight, or really move at all. Just laid there. That was all I wanted her to do. Just lay there and let me show her.

I sat up and looked at that angelic face. So unsullied. I wanted to see how she looked in candlelight. "Do you have any candles?" She nodded and pointed toward her dresser, revealing two maroon scented candles with a set of matches between them. I climbed up and walked toward the dresser. As I struck the match, I felt a sharp hard blow to the back of my head, accompanied by a crashing sound. As ceramic pieces crumbled around me, my knees grew weak and I held onto the dresser to prevent myself from tumbling to the floor. My ears were ringing and my sight was blurry. I put my hand on the back of my neck and when I removed it, it was covered in blood.

I turned and saw her naked body fleeing the room through the fog she had created. "What the fuck did you do that for?" She wasn't so helpless after all. I pulled myself up to my feet and ignored the pounding in my skull. As I ran toward her, I grabbed her by her hair, pulling so hard she screamed as she lost her balance. I wrapped my hand around from the back of her to cover her mouth, and she bit into my flesh. As a reaction to the pain, I clocked her in the back of her shoulder and she immediately released her mouth.

She lost balance but I held her up by her hair. I wrapped my arm around her neck so that she couldn't move. I was running on pure lustful rage. It obviously was not going to be the way I wanted it to be, but either way I was going to have her. "Now you listen to me, you fucking bitch, I didn't want to hurt you but you fucked me so now I don't give a shit. You wanna play tough girl, I'll treat you like one. You're the one who is going to be regretting."

I spun her around so she was facing me, and her face was clenched up and filled with pain. My erection suddenly returned. That fear I wanted to disappear so badly was there again, but this time I welcomed it. I wanted it. Holding onto her hair and neck, I threw her harshly onto the floor, and she flew like a rag doll. She landed on her hip, using her hands to block her from hitting her head. I kneeled down, forcefully turning her face to the floor. I used one hand to push down on her back, and I knew with a little more pressure I could have snapped her spine. I pulled her hips up and spread her ass cheeks. My dick was so hard I could have broken through steel.

I began to shove myself inside of her ass. It was so tight, it almost felt as if it would be impossible to fit. She was clenching herself up, sobbing uncontrollably, and the more she cried the harder I pushed. It felt as if I was completely tearing through her, and I could almost hear things ripping apart inside. I was going to show her. When I was halfway in, she stopped clenching, realizing the harder she fought the more it would hurt. Her anal cavity was gripping so tightly onto my shaft it was painful, but pleasurably.

As soon as she relaxed, I shoved myself deeper and deeper, until my entire cock was inside her tiny virgin ass. I could have sworn I was digging into her intestines as the tip of my dick pressed against some soft inner lining. If it was possible I would have shoved myself so deep inside that it would come out of her mouth. She was mine now. Without lubrication, the traction burned and I could feel my skin chaffing into bloody patches. So I just fucked her harder, until the pain was numb.

Her soft intermittent sobs sounded like a music box playing in the background, reminding me of the one in my mother's room. Back when *I* was still innocent. No one could remain like that in a world like this.

I was showing Angelika that reality, stripping it away bit by bit with every lustful thrust. I pressed my body on top of hers, wrapping one arm around to squeeze on her breasts, the other on her neck to keep her still. I railed her harder and harder, and I could hear things popping as I got deeper into her gut. I squeezed her frail body and pressed my pelvis as hard as I could against her, her bony hips bruising mine. I could feel the cum building up, ready to explode inside her. I was going to fill her insides with all of myself.

I clenched my eyes shut, gripped tighter, pounded faster, until the cum slowly made its way to the head of my dick, and finally I shot out the orgasm of a lifetime. It seemed to last for several minutes, and my dick spasmed inside her torn-up ass. I felt tingles shoot down my toes and up through my fingertips, and my entire body went numb. I laid on her, frozen from the intense pleasure. She did not move, and I could have stayed inside of her forever. I finally caught my breath, propped myself up and pulled my dick out of her now lubricated, bloody hole.

She still lay there, face to the carpet, motionless. Suddenly, the haze that I had been existing in faded as I realized she still wasn't moving. My heart thumped through my chest. "Ang?" I whispered. A dry lump formed in my throat. "Angelika?" I turned her over, and her expressionless face stared at me, eyes frozen open. She wasn't blinking. I put my ear to her mouth. She wasn't breathing. "A-Angelika," I said, and I began to repeatedly smack her face. No response. I put my hand to her throat. There was no pulse. She was fucking dead. In the midst of everything, I must have been squeezing her neck too tightly. I didn't let her breathe. I fell back onto my naked ass and then I began to shake. "What have I done? What have I done?" Not only had I destroyed this beautiful, amazing girl's dignity, but I robbed her of life. I wanted her, and I took her. All of her.

And I had loved every second of it. Then it dawned on me. I had been wrong all along. The demons I had been trying to tame were not a separate part of me. They were not there from an outside source. They were *me*. I was the monster I had always feared. They had all been right all along: my grandmother, my aunt, Delia. I had spent my life running away from something I could never escape. It was inevitable that the darkness inside me would win. It was who I was. It was time to stop fighting it. Avry was gone, Dani was gone, now Ang. There was no one left to protect myself for. There was only me and my evils. The time had come to accept that.

I enjoyed feeding off of other's pain. I had been fed off of for so long, maybe the only way I could live in peace was to take back what others had stolen from me. There was not a drop of innocence left in me, maybe not even a drop of humanity. I was a fucking monster, worse then the beast I shot into my veins. Worse than anyone I had blamed for anything. And, at that moment, I accepted it. What else was there left to do? Destined to be alone, destined to live in pain. Destined to afflict my pain upon others. Maybe I was something special, because to be something so wretched was not such a common thing. It was all I had going for me. Nothing else. Just me and my music, the only companion I would ever need.

I stood up and got my clothes. I had to get the fuck out of there. My cum was all inside her; they wouldn't have a problem tracking me. It was time to leave New York, go somewhere, anywhere. It didn't really matter. Everywhere I went it was the same thing. I got dressed and walked back to Angelika, beautiful sweet Angelika. Even battered and lifeless, she still was glowing. I knelt beside her. I needed something to remind me of how I felt that very moment. It was the most pivotal moment of my life. In accepting the reality of who I was, I felt this intense peace. I was no longer searching for answers to nonexistent questions, trying to find imaginary exits. The struggle was over. With fear, with anguish, even with dope. There was nothing left to escape.

I went into the kitchen and grabbed a knife, went back and cut off a lock of her hair. I caressed her lovely face, skin still soft and warm. I kissed her colorless lips and tasted the remains of her humanity. I took whatever I could find of value in her house and left. I opened her window and stared up into the sun. I absorbed its vibrant rays, feeling like a new person. The world looked different now. As if I was seeing it for the first time. It was over now. She in fact did save me. Sweet Angelika. I knew she would.

Author Biography

Jessica Spinelli was born and raised in New York. After graduating with her bachelor's degree in journalism from St. John's University and spending five years in the publishing industry, she decided to switch gears by earning a master's degree in media studies from New School University.

Spinelli works as a television associate producer on shows for channels such as TLC, the Travel Channel, Discovery Channel, and National Geographic. Her creativity travels through many outlets, and she enjoys writing, directing, and producing music videos, as well as painting, fashion, and writing.

Spinelli currently lives in Connecticut with her boyfriend, son, and Boston terrier.

Made in the USA
San Bernardino, CA
09 June 2016